**What people are saying about *New York Times*
bestselling author**

JoAnn Ross

"Ross is in fine form…plenty of sex and secrets
to keep readers captivated."
—*Publishers Weekly*

"Ms. Ross takes her audience on a thrilling
roller-coaster ride that leaves them breathless."
—*Affaire de Coeur*

"[Ross delivers] a moving story
with marvelous characters."
—*Romantic Times*

Praise for bestselling author

ISABEL SHARPE

"Isabel Sharpe's wry writing style [is] a cross
between Elizabeth Bevarly and Jennifer Crusie."
—*Amazon Reviews*

"Isabel Sharpe is a name to watch
in the romance genre."
—*Painted Rock Reviews*

"Smart and spicy…"
—*Romantic Times*

New York Times bestselling author **JoAnn Ross** has written over seventy novels and has been published in twenty-six countries, including Russia, China, France and Turkey. Two of her titles have been excerpted in *Cosmopolitan* magazine, and her books have also been featured by Doubleday Book Club and the Literary Guild. JoAnn lives with her husband in Tennessee.

Isabel Sharpe sold her first book in 1998 and has gone on to publish nine more, all of which showcase her unique blend of contemporary romance and laugh-out-loud humor. Nowadays Isabel has firmly established herself as one of the most popular, witty and original writers around. Isabel lives in Wisconsin with her sons and is a member of Romance Writers of America and Wisconsin Romance Writers of America.

JoAnn Ross
Isabel Sharpe

WINDFALL

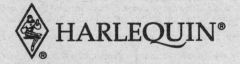

TORONTO • NEW YORK • LONDON
AMSTERDAM • PARIS • SYDNEY • HAMBURG
STOCKHOLM • ATHENS • TOKYO • MILAN • MADRID
PRAGUE • WARSAW • BUDAPEST • AUCKLAND

HARLEQUIN BOOKS 2-in-1 COLLECTION

Copyright © 2003 by Harlequin Books S.A.

ISBN 0-373-83584-1

The publisher acknowledges the copyright holders of the individual works as follows:

WITHOUT PRECEDENT
Copyright © 1986 by JoAnn Ross

WITHOUT A NET
Copyright © 2003 by Muna Shehadi Sill.

This edition published by arrangement with Harlequin Books S.A.

® and TM are trademarks of the publisher. Trademarks indicated with ® are registered in the United States Patent and Trademark Office, the Canadian Trade Marks Office and in other countries.

Visit us at www.eHarlequin.com

Printed in U.S.A.

CONTENTS

Dear Reader,

Writing has always been a very personal thing for me, and like many of my stories, *Without Precedent,* which was written as a Harlequin Temptation romance novel in 1985, mirrors my own life.

Like my heroine, Jessica O'Neal, I was a divorced, working single mom. Also, in those days when women still foolishly believed in the myth of Superwoman, I was struggling to bring home the bacon, fry it up in the pan and still muster up enough energy to play family cheerleader at my daughter's dance recital. (Okay, in my case it was my son and YBA basketball games, but you get the idea.) As for a sex life... Did I mention I was a single working mom?

By the time a man very much like Quinn Masterson (my ex-husband, actually, but that's another story) came storming into my life, I'd given up believing in happily-ever-afters, and while *Cosmo* was touting love as a dynamite complexion brightener, I'd come to the conclusion that it was very bad for a woman's independence.

Both my fictional hero and my real-life one set about proving to their skeptical women that marriage truly could be a union of equals, two people sharing a life based on mutual respect and love. It wasn't easy, but they eventually won us over and now Jessica and I are both living our own happy endings.

While I'm writing longer, more complex novels these days, Jessica and Quinn's love story—set in San Francisco, one of the world's most romantic cities—remains one of my personal favorites and I'm delighted Harlequin has chosen to reissue it.

Happy reading!

JoAnn Ross

WITHOUT PRECEDENT

JoAnn Ross

CHAPTER ONE

FORCING HERSELF TO IGNORE the thousands of hot needles pricking her legs, Jessica O'Neill reminded herself that pain was all in the mind. The fact that her thighs felt as if they were on fire was merely a temporary mental aberration. While Jessica had been repeating that axiom for the last four blocks, the words were beginning to ring false, even to her own ears.

Only a fool took up jogging on San Francisco's hilly streets, she considered, urging her weary body back to her Haight Ashbury town house. Or a masochist. Jessica decided she was probably a little of both. She dragged herself up the concrete steps and leaned against the bright blue siding, gasping for breath. Just then she heard the telephone ring. And ring. And ring.

"For Pete's sake," she muttered, flinging open the screen door, "you'd think someone could answer the damn phone."

Her rubbery legs proved scant support, and intent on reaching the telephone, Jessica failed to notice the matching set of Louis Vuitton luggage in the foyer. She tripped, sprawling ignominiously over the oak flooring. The strident demand of the telephone was unceasing, and giving up on walking for the moment, Jessica crawled the rest of the way into the front parlor of her Victorian home.

"Jill," she shouted upstairs to her eldest daughter, "turn down that music! Hello?" she got out, lying on her back, gasping like a grounded trout, her breath stirring her unruly auburn bangs. The room was suddenly bathed in a brilliant light as an eleven-year-old girl aimed a video camera at her.

"Knock it off," Jessica snapped, scowling into the camera lens.

There was a stunned silence on the other end of the phone. "Are you talking to me?" a hesitant female voice finally asked.

Jessica was still waving her hand at the whirring camera. "No, not at all.... Mallory Anne O'Neill, get out of here," she hissed at the aspiring cinematographer.

The caller's voice was a frantic combination of a screech and a sob. "You have to do something!"

Now what? Jessica sighed as she struggled to a sitting position. "Jill!" she shouted again, covering the mouthpiece with her palm before returning to her hysterical client. "Mrs. Thacker? What's the problem?"

"It's Keith!" the woman wailed.

Vowing never to handle divorce cases once her law career was established, Jessica closed her eyes, garnering strength to continue this conversation. "What's he done now?"

"I can't believe it! Mrs. O'Neill, I want that man arrested. Right now!"

"Mrs. Thacker," Jessica crooned in a calm, authoritative voice, "why don't you take a deep breath and start at the beginning?"

A sound like a steam engine came across the line as the woman obviously followed Jessica's advice. "It's my Mercedes," she said finally in a voice that cracked slightly, but was at least understandable.

"He had it stolen," Jessica guessed.

She was at her wit's end with the antics of Mr. and Mrs.

Thacker. Jessica empathized with her client—what discarded ex-wife wouldn't—but the term "civilized divorce" was obviously not in the Thackers' vocabulary.

"I only wish he had," Sylvia Thacker wailed, her voice high enough to shatter glass. "Then at least it would still be in one piece.... The bastard cut it in half. With a hacksaw!"

"A hacksaw?" Jessica arched an auburn brow. "Is that even possible?"

"He left the saw behind. Shall I call the police?"

"Let me handle it," Jessica suggested. "I'm certain if I contact your husband's attorney, we can settle this without pressing charges."

"I'd rather see the creep in jail," the woman muttered.

"I'm certain you would. But if we press charges for this act of vandalism, you may end up behind bars yourself. He could always countersue for your little display of temper last week."

The tears stopped abruptly as Jessica's client recovered her poise. "I thought you were supposed to be on my side, Mrs. O'Neill. Mr. Bennington assured me that you were quite capable of handling my divorce."

The threat was sheathed in silk, but Jessica recognized it for what it was. Mrs. Sylvia Thacker née Montgomery, came from one of San Francisco's oldest families. One suggestion to the head of Bennington, Marston, White and Lowell that the newest member of the firm was not treating a valued client with due respect and Jessica would be lucky to end up working in the public defender's office.

"Of course I'm on your side," she said quickly. "And if you're certain you'll be all right, I'll hang up now and contact your husband's attorney immediately."

"Tell him that if I catch that worm of an ex-husband on

my property, I'm going to shoot first and ask questions later,'' Sylvia Thacker warned.

''Please don't do that, Mrs. Thacker. I'm sure we can all come to an amicable settlement.''

''Terrific. Now I've got Pollyanna representing me,'' the woman muttered as she hung up the phone.

Jessica went onto her knees, riffling through her Roledex on the cluttered desk top. ''Marston…Martin…Masterson. Quinn Masterson, you'd better still be in your office,'' she mumbled, knowing it to be a long shot. It was past seven o'clock, and if the man's reputation was halfway warranted, he usually spent his evenings in far more pleasurable pursuits than working on legal briefs.

His answering service confirmed Jessica's suspicions. The woman agreed to try to get a message to Mr. Masterson, but her bored tone didn't give Jessica a great deal of confidence. She was debating what to do next when her eye caught an invitation she'd glanced at and dismissed several weeks ago. The San Francisco Committee for the Preservation of the Arts was having a fund raising ball at the Fairmont Hotel. The chairman of the ball was none other than Quinn Masterson. As Jessica read the date on the invitation, she decided her luck was looking up.

''Mrs. Thacker's having trouble with her husband again, right?'' The youthful voice cut through her musings.

In the midst of her client's problem, Jessica had forgotten all about the video camera still trained on her. ''Put that thing down,'' she instructed firmly. ''I'm getting sick and tired of living in a goldfish bowl.''

Blue eyes as wide and vivid as Jessica's held her mother's stern gaze with implacable purpose. ''It's my class project. Do you want me to fail?''

''I want you to find another project,'' Jessica snapped.

"Whatever happened to rock collections? Or Styrofoam models of the moon?"

"I'm doing a sociological study of a family in transition," Mallory O'Neill stated resolutely. "You'll love it."

"I doubt that, since I already hate it," Jessica countered, raising her voice to be heard over the throbbing beat of rock music. "Jill," she called, going in search of her eldest daughter. "I'm going out."

Jessica followed the sound to the upstairs bedroom shared by two of her three daughters where she found her thirteen-year-old lipsyncing to the latest Cyndi Lauper record.

"Hey!" Jill protested as Jessica lifted the needle. "I'm rehearsing for Mallory's movie!"

"That shows how much you know about cinema vérité," Mallory sniffed, still filming the confrontation. "It's true life, dummy. You're not supposed to rehearse. Boy, are some people dumb!"

"Mallory, if you don't put that camera down right now, you're going to have your first experience with censorship," Jessica warned. "And, Jill, from now on, when I'm conducting business at home, I'd prefer to forego the background music, okay?"

Her daughter shrugged, irritating Jessica unreasonably as she blew an enormous pink bubble through pursed lips.

"Sure, Mom," she agreed nonchalantly. "But I didn't hear the phone ring."

"I'm not surprised since the noise level in this room was somewhere between a jackhammer and the Concorde. Where's Sara?" she asked belatedly, realizing that she hadn't seen the youngest O'Neill daughter.

"Sara's out shopping with Gran."

"Gran?"

"Yeah. Gran says everything in our refrigerator is loaded with additives."

"I don't see where my additives are any of your grandmother's concern. Mallory, turn that camera off!"

"I don't want to miss your expression when you hear the news," Mallory argued.

"News? What news?"

"Gran's moving in with us," Jill answered her mother.

Jessica blinked, forgetting the whirring camera capturing her stunned reaction. "In here? In this house?"

Mallory bobbed her strawberry blond head in the affirmative. "Isn't that neat? She's bound to get me an A on my project. Just think, three generations of women living in the same house, all experiencing the slings and arrows of divorce."

"That's ridiculous," Jessica returned instantly. "Your grandmother has been married forty-six years. She'd never get a divorce."

"That's not what she said," Mallory put in. "Tell her, Jill."

"She says she's left Gramps," Jill confirmed.

Before Jessica could answer, the phone began to ring again. "That's going to be Mrs. Thacker," Jessica said with a sigh. "Jill, tell her I've gone to meet with Mr. Masterson." She spun around, fixing her middle daughter with a stern glare. "And turn that thing off!"

"All right," Mallory muttered, reluctantly lowering the camera. She spoke quietly in deference to Jill's conversation. "But I would have loved to show how adults make their kids lie for them."

"It was her," Jill acknowledged, hanging up the phone. "Are you really going out?"

"I've got to," Jessica said reluctantly, the idea not on her hit parade of things to do with a rare free evening. "But there's plenty of stuff in the freezer for you to heat up in the microwave for dinner. I shouldn't be long.''

''Are you going out like that?''

Jill's voice was laced with teenage scorn as she eyed Jessica's pink sweat suit. Jessica, in turn, fixed her daughter with a slow, appraising look, taking in the dark hair slicked back with styling gel, the neon orange sweatshirt, kelly green vinyl pants and suede boots.

''You're a fine one to talk, kiddo,'' she said. ''I figure if I can put up with the punk look, you can survive a mother who has more important priorities than looking like a fashion plate.'' Jessica grinned over her shoulder as she left the room. ''Tell your grandmother I won't be late. She's got some heavy explaining to do.''

''Radical!'' Mallory clapped her hands. ''I just know I'm going to get an A this year.''

''Off the record,'' Jessica warned, wagging her finger. ''I don't want this family's private lives dragged through your junior high school.''

''We've already had our lives dragged through the press,'' Mallory pointed out with deadly accuracy. ''This at least will be the truth.''

From the mouths of babes, Jessica considered as she took the bus to the Fairmont Hotel atop Nob Hill. She'd done her best to protect the girls when the news of her divorce had hit the papers, but, after all, Brian O'Neill had been in the public eye for some time, including his unsuccessful campaign for governor of California. When the word got out that he'd left his family for another woman, the spotlight had shifted to Jessica and her three daughters. Fortunately, a story about graft payments to certain members of the city council had drawn the attention away from them, allowing a fairly normal existence the past three years. Although it certainly wasn't the luxurious Marin County life they were used to, Jessica privately thought the changes had done them all good.

She smiled at the liveried doorman, ignoring his arched brow at her attire as she entered the elegant hotel. Looking neither right nor left, Jessica crossed the thick black-and-red lobby carpeting to the desk.

"May I help you?" The young man looked doubtful, but his polite, professional smile didn't waver.

"I'm looking for the Arts ball," Jessica explained.

"It's in the main ballroom, but—"

Jessica gave him a dazzling smile. "Thank you very much," she said, heading off in the direction he'd just indicated.

QUINN MASTERSON was bored stiff. He'd always hated these things and, at age forty, was beginning to lose patience with the pretence that he found them at all enjoyable. While he understood the need for charitable organizations, and the necessity of well-meaning individuals to direct them, he'd never gotten to the point that he felt comfortable. As he nodded at the clutch of women around him, hoping that he was answering with the proper phrases at the appropriate times, he wondered if they ever suspected he felt totally out of place in the luxurious ballroom, surrounded by all these glittering people.

Face it, Masterson, he told himself. *Deep down, you're still that Missouri farm boy struggling to learn the two-step.* His bored gaze circled the room, looking for someone, anyone, he could carry on an interesting conversation with.

His green eyes locked on the slender woman standing in the doorway. She certainly didn't belong here, he mused, eyeing her pink running suit, which stood out like a sore thumb amid the sequined and beaded gowns of the other women in the room. Her auburn hair had sprung free of the ribbon at the back of her neck, creating a brilliant halo around her head that he found far more enticing than the stiff, well-coiffed hairdos of the women surrounding him. Some distant memory tried to make itself known in his mind, but Quinn had no time to dwell on it now.

She was obviously arguing with the man taking tickets at the door, but while she appeared determined, Quinn had the impression that this was not a lady used to making a scene. What was she doing here? While no answer came immediately to mind, Quinn had every intention of finding out. She'd piqued his interest, and it had been a very long time since a woman had done that. His mind went into gear as he tried to come up with some way to escape this inane conversation before she got away.

"No, I don't have a ticket," Jessica told the guardian of the door for the third time. "I've no intention of attending the ball. I only want to speak with Mr. Masterson."

"I can't let you in without a ticket, ma'am," the elderly man stated firmly. "Those are the rules."

"Oh, for heaven's sake," Jessica huffed, her breath feathering her curly bangs. "This is ridiculous!" She watched as three more couples handed over their five-hundred-dollar tickets and achieved immediate access. Then an outrageous idea occurred to her.

"Excuse me," she stated sweetly, "but it is very important that I speak with Mr. Masterson."

"I've already explained—"

Jessica's blue eyes were absolutely guileless. "I know— the rules. But would it be breaking those rules if I asked you to take a message to Mr. Masterson for me?"

He rubbed his jaw. "I don't know."

"It's a very short message," she coaxed.

"I don't see where any harm would be done by that," he allowed.

"Thank you." Jessica rewarded him with her prettiest smile. Leaning forward, she placed her palm on his arm and lowered her voice slightly. "Would you please tell Mr. Masterson that Trixie is here with her cheerleader outfit and needs to know if he wants her to wait up in his room, as usual."

Jessica's expression was absolutely bland as she ignored the gasp of a couple who had just arrived. The ticket taker's face blossomed to a hue rivaling a lobster's, and his eyes widened as they took a jerky tour of her body, clad in the soft cotton jersey.

"Why don't I just get Mr. Masterson for you and let you deliver the message in person," he suggested.

Jessica nodded. "Thank you," she agreed sweetly.

Quinn had just about decided to forego social tenets and walk away from the quintet of babbling women when he was rescued by the doorman.

"Excuse me, Mr. Masterson, but there's someone here who insists on speaking with you."

Quinn's eyes cut to the doorway where the woman still waited. Her blue eyes were directed his way and for a long, timeless interval their gazes held, exchanging any number of messages, each one more personal than the previous. He couldn't believe his luck.

Jessica recognized the man instantly. Quinn Masterson's picture had appeared on the cover of innumerable magazines. He also showed up regularly in newspapers and on television. But none of those mediums had captured the essence of the man.

He was gorgeous, she admitted reluctantly. Thick, sun-gilt gold hair fell over a broad forehead. His eyes were bright green and seemed to light with something akin to recognition as he came toward her.

"You must be a genie," he stated immediately, his emerald eyes warming provocatively.

Jessica hadn't missed the gleam of appreciation in his gaze as he'd stared at her from across the room. While she knew she was no beauty, she still received her share of appreciative glances from men, even if Jill did consider her thirty-five-year-old mother "over the hill." Under normal situations, Jessica liked being found attractive. What had shaken her to her toes was the fact Quinn Masterson had stirred something long forgotten within her.

"A genie?" she asked blankly, ignoring his outstretched hand.

"There I was, wishing for you, when you popped up. Just like that." He snapped his fingers.

"Not exactly just like that," she countered, unreasonably irritated by his boyish smile. "I'm here to find out what you're going to do about your client sawing a brand-new Mercedes in half with a hacksaw."

Quinn arched a blond brow. "A hacksaw?"

"A hacksaw."

"I assume you're talking about Keith Thacker."

This was the woman Keith Thacker consistently described as an ill-tempered harridan? While Quinn had known Keith for years and knew of his wife's social status in the city, this was the first time he'd actually met Sylvia Thacker. Lord, he considered, staring down at her, while Keith could admittedly be accused of irrational behavior from time to time, letting this woman get away proved he was downright certifiable.

Jessica nodded, causing a few additional strands of unruly auburn hair to spring loose. "That's exactly who I'm talking about. You have to do something about your crazy client, Mr. Masterson. The man is literally driving me up a wall!"

Two red flags waved in her cheeks, revealing a barely restrained inner passion, and Quinn decided Keith was indeed crazy to leave this woman for that twenty-year-old art student. Although he usually attempted to convince his clients to try marriage counseling, Quinn knew he wasn't going to recommend that option this time. In fact, tomorrow morning he was going to call his old college buddy and inform him he couldn't handle the case. There would be a definite conflict of interest, since Quinn had every intention of winning Thacker's wife.

"Let's go somewhere quiet and talk about it," he suggested, cupping her elbow with his palm.

Jessica shook off his hand. "We can talk about it right here," she insisted. "Besides, aren't you needed in there?"

He waved off her concern. "Don't worry about it—they'll carry on without me just fine. Are you hungry? I know a little place in Chinatown that the tourists haven't discovered."

"Are you asking me to dinner?"

"Have you eaten?"

"No," Jessica admitted.

He grinned down at her. "Then I guess I am."

"I'm not dressed," she protested, suddenly feeling out of place in the glittering crowd. She'd been so angry when she'd come down here that the contrast in attire hadn't disturbed her. Now, seeing herself through Quinn Masterson's attractive green eyes, Jessica felt hopelessly disheveled.

"I think you look great," he argued. "I don't know many women with your hair color who'd dare to wear hot pink, but it sure works on you."

Instructing herself not to blush, Jessica dragged her mind back to business. "I'm here to discuss your client," she stated firmly, rocking back on the heels of her running shoes.

"And we will," he agreed, his palm pressed against her back as he urged her down the mirrored hallway. "Just as we'll discuss that little trick you pulled."

Jessica stopped in her tracks. "Trick?"

"Emptying the house while the poor guy was at work. That was playing dirty pool, Mrs. Thacker."

She stared up at him uncomprehendingly. "I'm not Mrs. Thacker."

Now Quinn was confused. "Then who are you?"

"Jessica O'Neill. Mrs. Thacker's attorney."

"I thought George Bennington was handling the divorce for her."

"He assigned it to me last week. Didn't you get my letter?"

"I've been out of town," he answered distractedly, as he attempted to remember exactly where he'd seen this woman before. "Jessica O'Neill," he mused aloud. "The name rings a bell."

"I'm not surprised," Jessica said dryly, waiting for the recognition to hit.

She didn't have to wait long. "You're Brian O'Neill's wife."

"Ex-wife," she corrected.

"Ex-wife," Quinn repeated, telling himself he shouldn't sound so damn happy about her marital status.

But he felt as if he'd been waiting for Jessica O'Neill all his life, and it was a distinct relief to discover she was available. Not that it would have mattered, of course. It only would have made things a bit messier if she'd had a husband out there somewhere.

"I suppose I should tell you I'm sorry," he said slowly.

Jessica merely shrugged in response.

"But I'm not going to," Quinn decided. "Because I've always had one firm rule in life."

"And that is?"

He reached out, tugging on a bright russet curl that kissed her cheek. "Never look a gift genie in the mouth."

It was only a few blocks from the Nob Hill hotel to the Chinatown restaurant and since the early spring night was unseasonably balmy, Quinn and Jessica decided to walk.

"What did you tell Ernie, anyway?" Quinn asked. "I've never seen the old guy's feathers as ruffled as they were when he came over with the good news that you'd come to the hotel tonight to see me."

Knowing that it wasn't going to do a lot for her professional image, Jessica nevertheless confessed, drawing a deep, appreciative laugh from Quinn, who proceeded to imitate the stuffy doorman perfectly. He continued to disprove the theory about lawyers being as dry as their documents by treating Jessica to a series of impersonations, spoofing some of the city's more illustrious individuals.

"You're terrible!" Jessica's blue eyes were gleaming with tears of laughter as Quinn portrayed an eccentric, left-wing councilman with uncanny accuracy.

"Hey," he complained with a grin. "I thought it was pretty good."

"It was," she admitted, forgetting for the time being that she had every reason to be furious with Quinn Masterson. His client's behavior had been unconscionable. "If you ever give up the law, you can always have a career in show business."

"A few clients like Keith Thacker and I'll consider it," he agreed. "A hacksaw?"

"That's what Sylvia claims." She gave him her sternest expression. "Now I suppose you're going to claim you had nothing to do with it."

The look had as little effect on Quinn as it did when she

used it on the girls. Instead of being intimidated, he appeared wounded by her words.

"Me?" Quinn flung a hand innocently against his chest. "Are you really accusing me of using such tactics?"

Jessica honestly had her doubts, but although she had just taken on the case a few days ago, the couple had been driving her crazy. She couldn't help taking some of that frustration out on Quinn.

"What if I am?"

"Then, Ms O'Neill, I'd be forced to point out that what we have here is a case of the pot calling the kettle black. I suppose you didn't have anything to do with your client absconding with every last thing in their house the day before she filed for divorce?"

Jessica rose to her full height in an attempt to look him straight in the eye. Just under five foot six, she'd always considered herself reasonably tall, but Quinn was at least two inches over six feet. That, plus the fact she was wearing running shoes, put him at a distinct physical advantage.

"Of course I didn't. Besides Sylvia didn't take everything. She left his clothes."

"Which she cut to shreds."

"Touché," Jessica murmured. "Whatever happened to civilized divorces, anyway? Those two are driving me up the wall."

"You're not alone," Quinn muttered. "Do you think that's possible?" he asked suddenly.

"What?"

"Civilized divorces. Do you really believe a man or woman can give up someone they love without a lot of anger?"

"I did."

He stopped, looking down at her with a thoughtful expression. "If that was actually the case, perhaps you didn't really love your husband," he suggested.

"That's ridiculous," Jessica snapped, drawing her arms about herself in an unconscious gesture of self-protection.

How had they gotten on the topic of her ill-fated marriage, anyway? She didn't like discussing it with anyone; she damn well wasn't going to discuss it with a man who'd been voted San Francisco's most eligible bachelor so many times that he'd been elevated to the Hall of Fame.

"Besides," she said tightly, "what do you know about marriage?"

"Not much," he remarked. "But after fifteen years of practicing law, I know a hell of a lot about divorce. And it's rare when the parties involved don't end up at each other's throat."

"I didn't have any choice," Jessica found herself admitting softly. "I had three daughters I wanted to protect from being hurt any more than they were. Speaking of which, I need to let them know I'm not going to be home for dinner."

"You can phone from the restaurant," he assured her, his hand lightly on her back once again. Jessica tried to ignore how right his touch felt, how much she was enjoying his company.

Just then she made the mistake of glancing in a darkened store window, and her heart sank at her reflection. She looked at least ten pounds heavier in the jogging suit and her hair was a wild, unruly cloud springing out in all directions from her head. She looked as if she'd just gone ten rounds with Larry Holmes and felt like groaning at the contrast between her disheveled appearance and the formally dressed man beside her.

"Look," she stated suddenly, "this is a bad idea. I'm sorry I went off the deep end about the Mercedes—I believe you didn't know anything about it. Why don't I call you at your office tomorrow and we can work out a fair settlement?''

''What's the matter?'' Quinn asked, his heart sinking as he viewed Jessica's determined expression. She was going to get away, after all. He vowed not to let that happen.

''I have to get home.''

''Are your daughters alone?''

Jessica had always been a lousy liar and knew better than to try now with a man renowned for his ability to read a jury. ''No,'' she admitted. ''My mother's with them.''

His grin practically split his tanned face. ''Terrific. Then you don't have anything to worry about.''

That's what you think, Jessica thought, trying to make sense of these errant feelings she'd been having since she and Quinn Masterson had exchanged that long look across the ballroom. It was too corny to be believed, but it was true. Something indefinable had passed between them, and Jessica was unwilling to pursue its cause.

''Jessie,'' he murmured, two long fingers cupping her chin to raise her eyes to his coaxing smile. ''You wouldn't really leave me to eat alone, would you?''

''You weren't alone back there,'' she argued, tossing her head in the direction of the Fairmont.

''I felt alone.''

''Oh.'' Jessica thought about that for a minute, understanding the feeling. She'd always felt like that on the campaign trail, even though she'd been continually surrounded by members of Brian's staff. ''How do you feel now?'' she asked softly.

Jessica was entranced by his broad, boyish grin. ''I feel terrific.'' Then his expression suddenly turned unnervingly sober. ''Please have dinner with me, Jessica. I can't remember when I've wanted anyone's company quite so much.''

If it was a line, Jessica considered, it was certainly working. She didn't think she could have turned Quinn Masterson down if her life depended on it.

"I have to get home early," she warned.

"Don't worry, Cinderella," he stated with a bold, satisfied smile. "I promise to get you home before you turn into a pumpkin."

CHAPTER TWO

JESSICA WAS SURPRISED as Quinn led her up a set of back stairs to a small, intimate restaurant over a store filled with tourist paraphernalia. She'd grown up in San Francisco, but had never run across the Empress Pavilion.

"Is this place new?" she asked as they settled into a high-backed, private booth.

"No. Bruce Tso took over the management about five years ago when his mother retired. She ran the place for fifteen years before that."

"I've never heard of it."

Quinn grinned. "Once you taste the food, you'll see why Bruce doesn't have to advertise. Actually, it's off the beaten track for the tourists and lacks the celebrity status a lot of the natives require." He seemed to be studying her, waiting for her reaction.

Jessica silently compared his attitude toward dining with that of her ex-husband's. Eating with Brian O'Neill had been an occasion to be in the public eye; he'd never select a quiet, out-of-the-way spot like this. Which was one of the reasons they seldom went out together in the later years of their marriage. She'd disliked having her meal constantly interrupted by other diners who shared Brian's compulsion for table-hopping.

"I like it," she murmured.

Quinn visibly relaxed. "I thought you might. How adventuresome are you feeling tonight?"

Did he have to even ask? Here she was, practically picking up a strange man, agreeing to share an intimate meal while dressed like Little Orphan Annie. For a woman known to plan every waking hour of her day, she was definitely throwing caution to the winds.

"What did you have in mind?" she asked in a low, throaty voice. Good Lord, Jessica considered, was she actually flirting?

Quinn decided that if he was perfectly honest with her, she'd probably think he was certifiably crazy. She didn't look like a woman who'd believe in love at first sight. He had a vague feeling Jessica O'Neill was extremely practical and down-to-earth, under ordinary circumstances. But this was no ordinary night.

"The house specialty is Szechwan, but some of it is admittedly a little spicy for American palates."

Jessica laughed delightedly. "Does the chef know how to cook *la chiso ch'ao chi?* It's my favorite."

Quinn was not surprised to discover that Jessica shared his enjoyment of the spicy chicken sautéed with peppers. Accustomed to acting on instinct, he had known at first glance Jessica was precisely the person he'd been seeking.

Quinn had set a master plan for his life back in college. After law school he'd sign on with a prestigious firm, concentrating his energies on becoming one of the best legal brains in the country. And though he had no intention of living like a Trappist monk, neither was he going to allow himself to get involved while learning his craft. He would become a senior partner by the time he was forty; then, and only then, would he turn his energies to creating a family.

Well, he'd turned forty last month, he was a senior partner as planned, and it was time to concentrate on finding a wife. Quinn was pleased but not overly surprised by the fact that Jessica had shown up exactly on schedule. He'd always been lucky.

"You're going to love it here," he promised.

Jessica's gaze swept the room, taking in the enchanting Oriental atmosphere before settling on Quinn's handsome face. "I already do," she said.

Jessica was vaguely aware that the dinner Quinn had ordered was superb, but if anyone had asked her what she was eating, she wouldn't have been able to answer. All her attention was focused on Quinn Masterson—even on the smallest of details. She observed the unruly lock of blond hair that seemed destined to fall over his forehead, noted the way little lines fanned out attractively from the corners of his green eyes when he smiled at her, which was often. His deep baritone voice, she decided, seemed to be coming from inside a velvet-lined drum. Everything about him fascinated her, and Jessica was amazed when the waiter took their empty plates, bringing them a fresh pot of hot tea.

Taking a sip of the fragrant brew, Jessica lifted her eyes and was unnerved to find Quinn staring at her intently.

"I keep trying to remember where we've met," he admitted.

"We haven't."

"Of course we have," he corrected amiably. "I never forget a face. Especially not one as lovely as yours. Just give me a minute and I'll come up with it."

"You're wasting your time," she said firmly. "Watch my lips, Quinn. We've never—I repeat, never—met. You're undoubtedly remembering me from the news coverage of the campaign."

"Nice," he murmured.

"What?"

"Watching your lips. I think that could easily become my second favorite thing to do."

He didn't have to mention his favorite pastime—the innuendo hung there like a living, breathing thing in the close confines of the booth. Just when she thought she was going to scream into the thick, swirling silence, Quinn tried a new tack.

"Have you lived here all your life?"

"Yes. Although I spent the last few years of my marriage in Mill Valley."

He appeared not to have heard the bitterness in her voice that came from all those years of playing the dutiful little suburban housewife for a man who had belatedly decided career women were more stimulating.

"That's not it," he mused aloud, more to himself than to her.

Jessica realized it was useless to argue with this man once he'd made up his mind about something. Oh well, she thought, he'd eventually have to realize they'd never met. Because if there was one thing Jessica knew with an iron-clad certainty, it was that this was not the type of man a woman could meet and forget.

Possessing an eidetic memory, Quinn knew he'd met Jessica O'Neill before. The idea was disconcerting, because this was not the type of woman a man could easily forget. Her hair was a gleaming sunlit auburn, laced with strands of dark gold. Her blue eyes, fringed with lush, dark lashes, were beautiful. His gaze moved down her slender nose and came to rest on voluptuously full lips.

"Jessica O'Neill…Maybe I'm going by the wrong name. Aren't you Judge Terrance MacLaughlin's daughter?"

"That's right. But I haven't been Jessica MacLaughlin for fifteen years," she protested.

Quinn's lips tightened into a firm line. Then he shook his head and gave her a devastatingly attractive grin.

"Don't worry about it, I'll get it eventually," he assured her. "Ready to go?"

While Jessica would have loved to stay until the studiously polite waiter threw her out, she suddenly realized she and Quinn were the only patrons left in the small restaurant. She agreed, smiling an apology to the patient staff clustered in a far corner of the room, obviously waiting to go home to their own families.

"Did you leave your car at the hotel?" Quinn asked as they exited the restaurant.

"I don't have a car."

He looked down at her with interest.

"It's expensive to keep a car in the city," she pointed out somewhat defensively. "Besides, San Francisco is an ideal walking city."

"I agree. But why do I feel that your decision to rely on public transportation goes a little deeper than locating an affordable parking garage?"

"That station wagon seemed to symbolize my entire worth as a wife," Jessica admitted. "I left it back in Marin County with the hot tub, the tennis court and my former spouse."

"And now that you've eschewed suburbia, you feel reborn into a modern career woman of the eighties."

"Precisely." Her tone challenged him to disagree. Something Quinn had no intention of doing.

"My car's back at the hotel," he said instead. "If you don't mind walking off some of those Szechwan prawns, we'll retrieve it and I'll drive you home."

"That's not necessary. I can take a taxi."

"Hey, I may be unfamiliar with the logistics of courting a genie, but the least you can let me do is see you home to your bottle."

"You're crazy."

He grinned down at her. "About you," he agreed.

The warmth in his deep tone and the lambent flame in his eyes caused a shiver to skim up Jessica's spine. She tried to suppress the slight sensation, which did not go unnoticed.

"You're cold. I should have noticed the fog's come in." He immediately slid out of his jacket, holding it out to her. "Put this on."

"I don't need it," she protested.

"Don't be so stubborn," he argued. "Wearing my jacket is not agreeing to a lifetime commitment." His tone was firm, but his eyes were still smiling. "Unless there's an old Irish custom I'm unaware of that states when a man lends his coat to a lovely woman, he's actually proposing marriage."

"Of course there's not." Jessica gave up, accepting the warmth of the superbly cut tuxedo jacket. "Besides, this woman definitely isn't in the market for a husband."

Quinn refrained from answering as he heard the unmistakable clanging bell. "Want to take a cable car back?"

"I'd love it," Jessica agreed, taking his hand as they ran to board the clattering, clanging national monument.

They chose an outer bench and as they made the turn at Grant and California, Jessica slid against Quinn. When she attempted to move away, his arm went around her shoulder, keeping her close. All too soon they reached the hotel.

"Want to stay on and ride for a while?" His green eyes sparked encouragement.

Jessica was feeling amazingly like Rip Van Winkle awakening after a long sleep. She couldn't remember feeling so young, so carefree. She wanted the night to go on forever. She also knew it couldn't.

"I have to get home," she said, her flat tone revealing that it wasn't her first choice.

"I thought you said your mother was with your daughters."

Jessica sighed as she jumped down from the cable car. "She is. But I don't know what she's doing there."

Quinn's arched brow invited elaboration.

"Jill said something about her leaving Dad. I haven't the foggiest idea what's going on, and to be honest, I never should have stayed out this long."

Jessica expected an argument, but Quinn surprised her. "Then we'd better get you home right away," he said, handing his parking stub to the valet. "You seem to have your hands filled with domestic spats these days."

"You know, life would probably be a great deal simpler if Congress simply passed a law abolishing matrimony."

It was impossible to miss the trace of bitterness in her tone, but Quinn was saved from answering by the arrival of his Maserati. Jessica gave him directions to her home and for a time both seemed content to allow the easy silence.

"How long have you been divorced?" he asked, knowing the answer already.

"A little over three years," Jessica said, eyeing him curiously. "Why?"

"Don't you ever consider remarrying?"

Her laugh was short and harsh. "Never."

"Never?"

"I wouldn't get married again for all the tea in China," she professed firmly. "Looking back on it now, I realize that my entire worth as a wife was as cheerleader for my husband. All Brian wanted was an avid and eager audience who'd sit spellbound while he talked about his real estate deals and recited his latest achievements."

"Didn't you have your own goals and aspirations?"

Jessica thought back on Brian's insistence that she drop

out of law school. "Of course I did," she responded curtly. "But Brian was always too busy, or too tired after a long day at work to listen to what he considered the petty events of my life."

She shook her head as if to clear it of unhappy memories. "Now, for the first time in my life, I'm doing what I want to do. Not what someone expects me to do."

It wasn't at all what he wanted to hear, but Quinn was undaunted. "What about your daughters?"

Jessica gave him a puzzled glance. "What about them?"

"Don't you want them to have a father?"

She folded her arms across her chest. "They have a father. They spend two weekends a month with Brian and Deirdre, every other Christmas and six weeks every summer. In fact, they probably see more of their father than they did when we were married. Spending time with his family was not one of my former husband's highest priorities."

"So you really did get a civilized divorce?"

"It was extremely civilized," she said dryly. "In that respect it was precisely like my marriage. Utterly predictable and devoid of any honest emotion."

What on earth had possessed her to admit that? To outsiders, the O'Neill marriage had seemed idyllic. For political reasons, Brian had wanted it to appear so, and Jessica had never seen any reason to set the record straight. That had been one of the reasons their divorce had garnered such interest. That and the fact that the handsome candidate for governor had left his wife and three children for another woman.

"Weren't you upset when he…"

Quinn's voice trailed off as he realized he'd been about to ask a highly indelicate question. Not that he wasn't curious; he just didn't know if Jessica would be willing to discuss her husband's well-publicized infidelity with him.

"Of course I was," she admitted. A slow, reluctant grin curved her lips. "I broke every dish in the house."

Quinn returned the smile. "Good for you." He reached over and squeezed her hand.

Jessica realized that aside from work, this was the first time in ages she'd been alone with another adult. Enjoying the camaraderie, she allowed her hand to remain in Quinn's larger one the rest of the way home.

"Nice house," he observed, pulling up to the curb outside her quaint Victorian town house.

"It will be. There's still tons of work to do on it, though," Jessica told him. "The first year, while I was in law school, all we could manage was a coat of paint. The next year I had the plumbing replaced. Last year I sprang for a new roof and next month we're having the entire place rewired."

"Sounds as if you've got a lifetime project going."

"I think I do." She grinned. "But it keeps me out of pool halls."

Quinn smiled at the incongruous image. Then, unable to help himself, he leaned toward her, tucking a thick russet curl behind one ear.

"Thank you."

Jessica was more than a little shaken by his suddenly solemn tone. "For what?"

"Rescuing me tonight." Quinn's hand was stroking her cheek, leaving sparks wherever he touched.

"You certainly didn't look like a man in need of rescuing. That blonde was practically eating you alive with her eyes."

Those attractive lines crinkled out from his eyes. "You noticed."

"It was hard to miss," Jessica whispered, struggling to remain indifferent to the fingers lightly spanning her throat. Quinn felt her swallow and knew Jessica was not unaffected by what was happening here.

"It was even harder to get away gracefully. I was wishing for someone—anyone—to save me. And you came. My lovely genie."

Jessica wondered if Quinn could feel the rapid rise in her pulse rate as his husky tone stirred something deep and long forgotten within her.

"You're very fanciful." She laughed unsteadily, backing away both physically and emotionally from the provocative moment.

Stifling a slight sigh, Quinn allowed her to inch toward the passenger door. "I'd better get you in before your mother decides to investigate whether we're necking out here."

His tone was far steadier than his emotions at the moment, and it was only all those years practicing trial law that allowed Quinn to pull off this nonchalant air. What he really wanted to do was pull Jessica into his arms and never let her go.

"That's a good idea," she agreed with matching casualness.

As Quinn opened his door, the dome light came on, flooding the interior of the Maserati with light. The raw desire on Jessica's face was sufficient compensation for tonight, he decided. It was enough to know that at this moment she wanted him as much as he wanted her.

"Are you free for lunch tomorrow?" he asked as he walked her to the front door.

"I've got a lunch date," Jessica stated, refraining from mentioning that it was with Vanessa Parker, the only other woman attorney employed at Bennington, Marston, White and Lowell.

"How about a drink after work?"

"Sorry."

"Another date?" he inquired grittily, not bothering to hide his irritation.

"Something like that."

Jessica knew Quinn was suspecting the worst, but what business of his was it if she wanted to date every man in San Francisco? Deciding it would do him good to discover that not every woman in the city was swooning at his feet, she didn't admit she had to pick up Sara's ballet slippers before the shoe repair shop closed at five-thirty.

"Dinner?"

She had to give him an A for tenacity. "I'm sorry, Quinn, but—"

"I know," he muttered, shoving his hands into his pockets. "You've got another date."

"Not exactly," she found herself admitting.

His expression brightened slightly. "Washing your hair?"

"No."

"Washing your mother's hair?"

She laughed at that one. "No."

"Your daughters'?"

"Close. Sara, my youngest, has a dance recital at the War Memorial Opera House. She's been practicing her pirouettes for weeks. It's like living with a human top."

Quinn laughed. "Well," he stated on an exaggerated sigh, "I suppose I'll have to settle for seeing you in court."

"Speaking of which…" Jessica suddenly realized she'd been so entranced with Quinn's company that she hadn't even insisted he make his client replace Sylvia's Mercedes.

"I know, there's still the little matter of a severed Mercedes."

"It's not a little matter," she pointed out briskly.

"Since California is a community property state, why don't we let them each take a half?"

"That isn't funny!"

"Come on, Jess," Quinn coaxed. "Can't you see the humor in the situation? By the time the two of them are finished, there won't be anything left to divide."

"You may find the entire situation humorous, but I'm not fortunate enough to be a senior partner in one of the city's most prestigious law firms," she retorted. "Your horrible client has put my job in jeopardy, and you'll have to excuse me if I can't see my way clear to laugh about it!"

From the way her voice faltered, Quinn realized Jessica was not as self-confident as she led one to believe. While that could work in his favor, he'd have to proceed cautiously.

"I'll talk to Keith," he assured her, his hands shaping her stiffened shoulders. "I promise he'll be on his best behavior from now on."

"He'd better be," Jessica grumbled. "Because Sylvia is threatening to shoot the minute she sees the whites of his eyes."

"Then the guy's safe."

"What does that mean?"

"You've heard of the three-martini lunch?"

She nodded.

"Keith Thacker is a proponent of the five-martini breakfast. On a good day the whites of his eyes look like a map of the Los Angeles freeway system." Quinn winked, earning a crooked smile from Jessica.

"You're not at all what I expected," she murmured, more to herself than to Quinn as she turned away to unlock her door. She took off his jacket, feeling oddly deprived of its woodsy, masculine scent as she returned it to him. "Thanks for dinner."

"It was my pleasure," he said, nodding his head.

Jessica had to thrust her hands behind her back to keep from reaching up and brushing back that curl that had fallen over his forehead once again.

"Well, good night," she murmured.

"Good night, Jess." He reached out, feathering a light path up her cheek with his knuckles. "Sweet dreams."

Jessica closed her eyes momentarily at the tender touch, half afraid Quinn was intending to kiss her, half terrified he might not.

Not immune to the desire he'd seen in those soft blue eyes before her lush lashes fluttered down, Quinn forced himself to back away from the sensual moment. Jessica was obviously a strong, independent woman, but when it came to relationships, the lady was as skittish as a doe. One false move and she'd take off running.

As much as he wanted to taste those lushly pink lips, he couldn't risk it. Not yet. He ruffled her hair in a friendly, almost fraternal gesture.

"See you in court, counselor," he said in a casual tone.

Jessica's eyes flew open. "In court," she echoed, watching him take the steps two at a time.

She experienced the oddest feeling of sadness as he drove away, and wondered what it was about Quinn Masterson that could make her respond so uncharacteristically. She couldn't remember the last time she'd laughed so freely. Or allowed an evening to pass without phoning home to make certain the girls were in bed on time. It was as if she had been a different person tonight. Jessica glanced up at the gleaming white moon hanging over the city, wondering if there was any truth to the notion that people behaved differently under the influence of a full moon.

The question of her uncharacteristic feelings was a complex one, and Jessica suddenly realized exactly how exhausted she was. It had been a long and tiring day, and if she knew Keith and Sylvia Thacker, tomorrow wasn't going to be one iota easier. She went into the darkened house, unerringly locating the couch, and sank down. Leaning her head back against the cushions, she shut her eyes.

"Jessica?" a voice inquired from the hallway. "Is that you?"

Jessica stifled a groan. "It's me, Mom. I'm sorry I woke you."

"I was awake." The censure in Elizabeth MacLaughlin's tone was unmistakable. "I couldn't sleep until my little girl was back home, safe and sound."

Jessica reined in the temptation to remind her mother that as the mother of three daughters, one a teenager, she was far from infancy. "I'm safe enough," she assured Elizabeth as the older woman entered the living room, tying the sash of her silk robe. "But as for sound..." Jessica's voice drifted off as she rubbed the back of her neck.

"You work too hard."

"Please, let's not get into that again. I certainly didn't plan for things to go so wrong today. Speaking of which, what on earth is going on? Jill told me you've left Dad."

Elizabeth MacLaughlin smoothly ignored Jessica's question. "What you need is a cup of tea and something to eat. I'll bet you didn't have dinner, did you?"

"I ate downtown," she hedged, not wanting her mother to know she'd gone to dinner with Quinn Masterson.

"Where?"

Jessica shrugged. "A little Chinese place. I forget the name."

"The food was probably loaded with monosodium glutamate," Elizabeth said with blatant disapproval.

"Probably," Jessica agreed. "That's what makes it taste so good."

Her mother shook her head. "Now you're teasing me. You're as bad as your father."

"Speaking of Dad…" Jessica inserted quickly, hoping her mother would explain why after forty-six years of marriage, she'd suddenly shown up on her daughter's doorstep.

"Tell me about the Thackers' latest escapade," Elizabeth said, sidestepping the issue. "Did you see his cartoon in the *Star* today? He's very talented." Elizabeth's brow furrowed. "You know, your father and I used to be very good friends with Keith's parents. It's too bad he ended up an alcoholic. However, I have to admit I'm not that surprised. Mary spoiled the boy rotten."

Jessica refrained from answering that San Francisco's most controversial political cartoonist had problems that went far deeper than an indulgent mother.

"I'd better be getting to bed," she said, rising from the couch. "I've got a hectic day tomorrow."

"What you need is a husband," Elizabeth advised, not for the first time. "Someone to take care of you and the girls for a change."

Jessica decided not to fall back into the old argument that she was quite capable of taking care of her family all by herself. She was more interested in finding out the reason behind Elizabeth MacLaughlin's recent actions.

"Speaking of husbands—"

"Good night, dear," her mother stated firmly.

Shaking her head in frustration, Jessica bent and kissed the top of her mother's head. The natural auburn hair was still as vibrant as Jessica's, without a hint of gray.

"Good night, Mom." Jessica suddenly wanted nothing more than to fall into bed and sleep around the clock.

But sleep was not that easily found, she discovered much, much later. She couldn't get Quinn Masterson out of her thoughts. It was as if his smiling green eyes and handsome face had been indelibly printed onto her mind's eye. It had been over three years since she'd had a casual evening alone with a man. In the beginning, she'd been hurting too badly to even consider the idea.

Later on, trying to juggle law school with the bringing up of three spirited children precluded anything that remotely resembled a social life. Now, while her life was going a little more smoothly, it was still a simple matter to beg off any invitations from the men she'd meet in the course of her workday. Not many men could remain undaunted by Jessica's ready-made family.

But tonight had been different. There had been such an inevitability to it. If she were a more fanciful person, Jessica might have thought her meeting with Quinn was preordained. But she prided herself on being an extremely practical woman and did not believe in kismet, fate or anything to do with stars, horoscopes or numerology. Or full moons, either, she reminded herself briskly. Those ideas she willingly left to the romantics of the world.

Yet, Jessica considered, lying in bed, her head pillowed by her arms, she'd almost felt romantic tonight. She'd forgotten how nice it was to feel a man's firm hand on her back. Or what a pleasant experience it could be to linger over dinner, sharing conversation that had nothing to do with orthodontist appointments, permission slips for seventh-grade field trips or Girl Scout cookie sales.

It was odd. She'd grown used to all the labels. Divorcée, single head of household, ex-wife, mother, attorney. Any one of those terms could accurately describe Jessica

O'Neill. But until this evening, she'd forgotten the most intriguing one of all. Woman.

For a few fleeting wonderful hours Quinn had made Jessica feel like a woman. He'd managed to transport her to a magical realm where she was alive, desirable, utterly fascinating. For that, she was grateful. She'd always remember it as a special evening with a very nice man. Of that Jessica was certain. Just as she was certain it would never happen again.

CHAPTER THREE

THE SMELL OF BURNING BACON wafted into Jessica's subconscious the following morning and she groaned, pulling the rose-hued comforter over her head. Muffled conversation drifted up the stairs, the steady drone punctuated at intervals by a raised voice or grievous shout.

"Mom! You have got to do something about Mallory and that damn camera of hers."

The insistent tone refused to be ignored and Jessica threw off the comforter, eyeing her daughter standing in the doorway. Smoke practically poured from Jill's ears.

"Don't cuss," Jessica answered automatically. "What has Mallory done now?"

"She invaded my privacy!"

Stifling a sigh, Jessica climbed out of bed, reaching for her robe. "She's been doing that all week and I haven't heard a word of complaint," she pointed out. "In fact, if I recall, you were rehearsing for a starring role last night."

"That was before I knew she was going to hide in the closet and tape my telephone conversations. Mom, she filmed me telling Lori what a hunk Tommy Drew is!"

"Sounds like the end of the world to me," Jessica agreed calmly.

"Mother! This is serious!"

Remembering her own teenage traumas, Jessica forced herself to remain patient. "I'll talk with her," she promised. "After I have a cup of coffee."

"Good." Jill nodded with a vast amount of youthful satisfaction as she left the room and headed back downstairs. "Hey, Mallory," she hollered, "are you ever in trouble now!"

Jessica shook her head, going over to her closet. A list of possible choices was posted on the back of the closet door, and she wryly decided that since Brian had forced her to join the ranks of career women, it had been nice of him to arrange her wardrobe beforehand.

It had been her inherent lack of clothes sense that had provided the impetus for the breakup of their marriage in the first place. Although after the first pain had passed, Jessica was forced to admit the writing had been on the wall for a very long time before Deirdre Hanson had entered the picture.

The entire O'Neill-for-governor campaign staff had unanimously decided that Jessica didn't project the proper image for the wife of an up-and-coming politician. Her jeans and paint-spattered sweatshirts might possess a certain cachet in the artists' communities of North Beach and Sausalito, but they were a definite liability when seeking the yuppie vote. It was the general consensus of opinion that Jessica O'Neill was decidedly lacking in style.

An interior decorator, Elizabeth MacLaughlin was as different from her daughter as night from day, and it was only natural Jessica would turn to her mother for advice. When Elizabeth suggested a visit to The Emporium-Capwell, little did Jessica realize what a difference that shopping trip would make in her life. She was introduced to the store's career dressing coordinator, a tall, striking woman in her thirties, who promised to coordinate her mismatched pieces of clothing into a workable, stylish wardrobe. Since Jessica spent most of her days in Mill Valley, it fell to Brian to stop by the fashionable department store at frequent intervals to take home the chic clothing Deirdre had accumulated.

Now Jessica's closet boasted a treasure trove of Ultrasuede suits, silk blouses, linen blazers and Italian pumps fashioned out of buttery-soft leather. And Deirdre, in turn, had Jessica's husband. Jessica had decided long ago that she'd gotten the better of the trade.

She showered and dressed quickly, then followed the billowing black cloud and the blare of the smoke detector's siren downstairs.

"Mother!" Mallory jumped up from the table. "Would you please explain the First Amendment to Jill? She's threatening to break my camera."

Jessica smiled benignly at her family, going over to pour a cup of coffee. "Good morning. Did everyone sleep well?"

"Mother, did you hear me?"

"Of course I did, dear," she murmured, pulling a pad of paper and a pen from a drawer. "But if you expect a treatise on the First Amendment before I've had my coffee, I'm afraid you're going to be disappointed."

"I told you she wouldn't back you up," Jill said, her hands clenched into tight fists at the hips of her crimson parachute pants.

"She didn't say that," Mallory retorted. "She only said we'd have to wait for a decision until after she had her coffee. So there."

"Mallory O'Neill," Elizabeth stated firmly, "don't stick your tongue out at your sister."

"She's not my sister," Mallory countered. "Gypsies stole my sister from the hospital nursery and left Jill in the bassinet in her place. By the time Mom and Dad discovered the mistake, the Gypsies were long gone and they were stuck."

Jill turned her back, going to the refrigerator to take out a pitcher of orange juice. "You're a riot, Mallory. In fact, you could probably go on the stage with that routine. It's just too bad you've got railroad tracks for teeth."

Knowing her middle daughter's sensitivity about her braces, Jessica prepared herself for the impending storm. When it didn't occur, Elizabeth and Jessica exchanged a long, curious look.

"Jill, you owe your sister an apology," Jessica said sternly.

To her further amazement, Mallory only shrugged. "That's okay," she stated blandly. Then she grinned. "I'm selling outtakes of Jill trying out Gran's mudpack. If the advance orders are any indication, they're going to go like hotcakes all over school." She picked up her camera and escaped the room, a wild-eyed Jill close behind.

Jessica shook her head. "Why did I have three children?"

"Because you didn't want four," Elizabeth offered. "Here, I thought you might enjoy a home-cooked breakfast."

Jessica stared down at the charred strips of bacon and something she vaguely recognized from her youth as scrambled eggs. "You didn't have to go to so much trouble."

Elizabeth smiled with the air of a woman who had never possessed a single insecurity. "It's the least I can do. Especially since I'll be staying here until I get settled."

"About that—"

Jessica's question was cut off as a whirling dervish spun into the room, twirling her way into a chair. "How's that, Mom?" she asked breathlessly.

Jessica grinned at her youngest across the table. "Dynamite. Dame Margot Fonteyn couldn't have done it better."

The freckled face was wreathed in a smile. "Thanks. I'm really nervous about tonight."

"Your mother used to worry, too," Elizabeth said, placing an identical plate of food in front of Sara, who looked at it with suspicion. "With good cause," she murmured under her breath.

Busy scrutinizing the morning meal, Sara missed her grandmother's qualifying statement. "Isn't this the same thing we had for dinner last night?"

"Of course not," Elizabeth scoffed.

"It looks the same."

"Well, it's not."

"It's the same color," Sara persisted with a nine-year-old's tenacity. She sniffed the air, as if noticing the smoke for the first time. "And it's burned."

"It's well done," her grandmother countered, joining them at the table.

Sara pushed the plate away. "Well, I'm not going to eat anything today, anyway. Ballerinas never eat before a performance," she stated, tossing her head regally. Then a frown furrowed her freckled forehead. "Mom, you won't forget to pick up my shoes, will you?"

"It's at the top of the list," Jessica answered, tapping her pencil on the pad.

Sara's grin blossomed. "Thanks, Mom—you're the best." She jumped up from the table.

"Sara, you have to eat something," Jessica insisted, nevertheless understanding her daughter's reluctance to sample the breakfast that had been placed in front of her.

"Don't worry, I'll stop at the deli and pick up a bagel," she promised, blowing a kiss as she executed a grand jeté out the door.

Elizabeth frowned as she watched Sara leave the house. "Your daughters have atrocious eating habits. They only picked at their food last night."

Jessica wondered how such an intelligent woman as her mother had never caught on to the fact that she was a horrendous cook. "They're all at a difficult age," she replied instead, pushing her own food unenthusiastically around the plate. "They think they need to diet."

"I still don't approve," Elizabeth said firmly. "But far be it from me to interfere with the way you rear your children. What are you doing for lunch today?"

"I'm going out," Jessica murmured, writing down her engagement with Vanessa as she answered. It wasn't that she would forget their weekly luncheon; Jessica was an incurable list maker. It always gave her a feeling of accomplishment at the end of the day when she could draw a bold, black line through the final item.

"Why?" she asked, eyeing Elizabeth suspiciously. "What's the matter now?"

"Why should anything be the matter? Can't a mother drop by to have lunch with her daughter without everyone suspecting the worst?"

Jessica sighed. "Don't play coy, Mother. What's up? Is it something to do with Dad?"

"In a way."

Jessica ground her teeth, making mental apologies to the orthodontist who'd spent years correcting her overbite. "Mother, could you simply tell me what you're up to, without making me drag it out of you, bit by agonizing bit?"

"I wanted you to come with me to look at that vacant office down the hall from yours."

"Why?"

"Why do you think? I'm thinking of leasing it."

"Why?" Jessica repeated.

"For my business, of course."

"But you've always worked out of the house," Jessica protested, having grown up surrounded by the bolts of fabric and rolls of wallpaper that were part and parcel of her mother's successful interior design business.

"I don't live there any longer, dear," Elizabeth reminded her patiently. "So, since I had to find a new location, I thought it would be nice if I leased an office close to yours. That way we could have lunch together more often. What do you think?"

Out of a deep-seated sense of parental respect, Jessica refrained from telling her mother exactly what she thought of the scheme.

"Does Dad know what you're up to?"

Elizabeth expelled a frustrated breath as she rose from the table. "Honestly, Jessica," she said stiffly. "Whose side are you on, anyway?"

"It's a little difficult to choose sides when neither of you will tell me what's going on," Jessica pointed out.

Elizabeth busied herself by scraping the uneaten breakfasts into the garbage disposal. "Since your father's retirement, he's become an entirely different man," she answered finally. "He's dictatorial, unbelievably stubborn, and believe it or not, he's behaving like the world's champion male chauvinist."

"But Dad's always been that way."

Elizabeth glanced back at Jessica over her shoulder. "Really?" Her tone displayed honest surprise.

"Really."

"I wonder why I never noticed that before," she said thoughtfully. "Isn't it odd how you can live with a man for years and never see his faults?"

Jessica thought back on her parents' marriage—one

she'd always viewed as idyllic. "Mom, don't you love him anymore?"

"Of course I do. But that has nothing to do with it. I simply can't live with the man any longer." With a slight sigh, Elizabeth changed the subject. "What would you like me to fix for dinner?"

"You don't have to cook," Jessica hurried to assure her.

"Nonsense. I want to earn my keep around here."

Jessica's mind went into overdrive as she tried to come up with a way to forestall her mother's culinary efforts. "Why don't we all go out after the recital? I'm sure Sara will be too nervous to eat beforehand. We can make it a celebration."

"All right, dear," her mother agreed cheerily. "That will give me more time to look for office space."

Jessica murmured an agreement, then, eyeing the copper clock on the wall, she jumped up, kissing her mother on the cheek.

"Gotta run," she explained. "I've got exactly two minutes to catch the bus."

With that she raced out the door, arriving at the bus stop just as the doors closed. The driver reopened them with obvious irritation, his mood not improved as Jessica dug through her purse, searching for the proper change. As she finally sank onto a seat at the back of the bus, she said a small, silent prayer that the remainder of her day would go more smoothly.

IF JESSICA NEEDED FURTHER PROOF that the gods were not on her side, the constant stream of emergencies she was forced to deal with once she arrived at her office would have convinced her once and for all. Sylvia Thacker called every ten minutes, wanting to know exactly when her husband would be behind bars.

Another client, a real estate developer suing a local television station for libel, belatedly admitted that there might be "a glimmer of truth" in the reports of several thousand dollars in kickbacks being given to members of the zoning commission, after all. Since the case had been highly publicized, Jessica knew it would be impossible to keep the firm's name out of the papers now that the man was withdrawing his suit.

When called on the carpet for not discovering the truth before filing, she couldn't resist pointing out to George Bennington that he'd been the one to file the damn suit, leaving her to figure out how to prove their case. In turn, the founder of Bennington, Marston, White and Lowell coolly reminded Jessica that she had only been invited to join the firm in the first place as a favor to her father. He, for one, had never approved of women attorneys. They were too emotional, he alleged, his steely gaze indicating that he found Jessica's irritation nothing more than feminine pique.

After that less than successful meeting, she was forced to cancel her lunch date in order to accompany a prominent neurosurgeon across town while he gave a deposition to the IRS concerning his financial interests in several Bahamian banks.

By three-thirty that afternoon, Jessica's head was aching, her stomach was growling, and she'd yet to cross a single thing off her list. When the intercom buzzed, signaling another call that undoubtedly meant more bad news, she felt like throwing the telephone across the room.

"Yes?" she bit out.

"Uh-oh. You're having a bad day." Quinn Masterson's deep voice came across the line, a welcome respite from the constant stream of petty irritations.

"I've had better," she admitted, glancing up at the mirror on the far wall, relieved that her caller couldn't see her.

Her unruly auburn hair, responding to the high humidity in the air, had sprung in a wild tangle of curls. She'd spilled a cup of coffee earlier in the day that had left a large brown splotch on her gray flannel suit. Jessica couldn't help comparing her appearance with that sleek blonde who'd seemed so fascinated with Quinn at the ball last night.

"Would you like some good news?"

"I'd love some," she answered immediately. "Please tell me that Keith Thacker delivered a new Mercedes to his wife today."

"Can't do that," he replied cheerfully. "But I'm prepared to offer a compromise."

"Let's hear it," Jessica agreed on a sigh.

"He'll give her the BMW if she returns his Nautilus exerciser and gives him custody of Maximilian."

"Maximilian?"

"The Lhasa apso," he reminded her with a deep chuckle that had her smiling in spite of herself. "Remember, the little guy that was named stud of the year by the Bay Area Kennel Society?"

"How could I forget?" Jessica answered dryly. "It sounds reasonable to me. Let me call Sylvia and get back to you."

"Fair enough," he agreed amiably. "Want to discuss it over drinks?"

"I'm sorry, but—"

"I know. You've got another date." His tone deepened. "I was hoping you'd changed your mind."

The invitation in his voice was unmistakable and Jessica glanced down at the list she'd made this morning, grateful for an honest excuse to turn him down. She was too tempted to see Quinn again, she admitted to herself. Too drawn to him.

"I can't," she murmured.

There was a slight pause before Quinn answered. "I see. Well, I'm going to be tied up in conferences the rest of the afternoon, but you can leave a message with my secretary when you get an answer from Mrs. Thacker."

"I will," she said softly, unreasonably disappointed by the fact that she'd have no further reason to talk with him today. "Oh, thanks again for dinner last night."

"I enjoyed it," he said simply. "Do you like Indian food? I know a place that serves dynamite curried lamb."

"I don't think so."

"Curry takes some getting used to," he agreed cheerfully. "How about Greek food?"

Jessica shook her head. "It's not that," she said, her tone hesitant.

Quinn wondered why he just didn't hang up and write Jessica O'Neill off as an impossible quest. He was certainly not used to courting rejection, nor was he in the habit of chasing after a woman. But then again, he reminded himself, Jessica was no ordinary woman.

"Why don't I call you later this week?"

It took every ounce of willpower Jessica possessed to refuse that enticing invitation. "I don't think so."

Quinn made an impatient sound. "May I ask a question?"

Jessica swallowed hard and nodded.

"Jessica? Are you still there?"

"I'm still here."

"Good. Are you involved with someone?"

"No," she answered honestly, preparing to tell him that was just the point.

Jessica had no plans to become romantically involved

with any man. Her independence had not come easily, and she wasn't willing to give it up for anyone. No matter how warm his green eyes or enticing his smile.

Quinn didn't give her the chance to make her carefully rehearsed speech. "Now that's the best news I've heard all day," he said on a husky chuckle that stirred her even as she fought against it.

"Quinn..." Jessica felt obliged to explain.

"Just a minute," he stated in a brusque, businesslike tone, giving Jessica the impression he was no longer alone in his office. His next words confirmed that feeling. "I've got to run. But I'll see you soon, okay?"

"It's not okay at all," she protested. "I'm trying to tell you that I'm too busy for any involvements right now. You're a nice man, and I like you, but—"

"Jessica," he interjected firmly, "I'm already late to my meeting, so we'll have to discuss this at some other time. But believe me, sweetheart, you're going to find the entire experience absolutely painless."

With that he hung up, leaving Jessica to stare at the telephone receiver. What experience? Her reverie was cut short as her intercom buzzed, announcing yet another call.

"Yes, Paula," she said on a sigh, answering her secretary's page.

"Mrs. Thacker on line two." The brisk tone displayed no sign of irritation and as Jessica pushed the button with unnecessary force, she wished she could remain as cool and composed as her efficient secretary.

"Mrs. Thacker," Jessica enthused as she greeted the woman for the hundredth time today, "do I have good news for you!"

JESSICA LEFT THE OFFICE LATE, arriving at the shoe repair store just as the elderly manager was drawing the shade on the door. His expression mirrored the one the bus driver had given her this morning, but Jessica was not about to let it deter her from accomplishing the most important thing on her list.

She smiled sweetly at the man, earning a reluctant smile from him as she complimented him effusively on the marvelous job he'd done replacing the worn sole. Jessica had warned her daughter that a new pair of ballet slippers was in order, but Sara had proven stubbornly superstitious, insisting that she absolutely *had* to have her "lucky shoes."

Fortunately, everyone was dressed and ready to go when Jessica burst in the front door. "Here, Sara," she said, tossing the shopping bag toward her youngest. "I've got to change my clothes."

"We're going to be late," Sara complained, her blue eyes appearing even wider because of her unnaturally pale complexion.

"I'll be down in five minutes," Jessica promised.

"They'll take me off the program," the youngster groaned.

"Three minutes and counting," Jessica called down, flinging pieces of her wrinkled suit onto the stairs as she ran.

She grabbed the first thing she came to, a high-necked, Victorian lace blouse paired with a softly gathered flowered cotton skirt that hit her legs at midcalf. It was one of the few outfits that Deirdre hadn't chosen, and although it had been declared far too whimsical for a candidate's wife, Jessica had fallen in love with the look at first sight.

"Laura Ashley," Elizabeth said as Jessica descended the stairs two at a time.

"Laura Ashley?" Jessica repeated blankly, struggling to pin a cameo at her throat without a mirror. With the way her luck was going today, she'd probably puncture a major artery.

Elizabeth stepped in to help. "The designer," she said on an exasperated breath. "Surely even you have heard of her."

"Afraid not," Jessica admitted. "I just liked it. I didn't know it was designed by anyone famous."

Elizabeth secured the catch, stepping back to eye her daughter judiciously. "Well, the look suits you far better than those tailored things *that woman* put you in."

Jessica stifled a smile. Elizabeth had never forgiven Deirdre for breaking up her daughter's home, despite Jessica's avowal that the divorce had been inevitable. It had put a crimp in Elizabeth's wardrobe for a time, since she'd steadfastly boycotted The Emporium-Capwell. Recently Deirdre had opened a boutique in trendy Cow Hollow, that newly restored area downtown where cash registers rang more briskly than cowbells ever had, allowing Elizabeth to return to her favorite department store.

Jessica turned to her daughters with a smile. "Ready?"

"Ready," they chorused, marching out the door single file. It was times like this, when they were sweet and cooperative, that she remembered why she had wanted a large family.

They were barely settled in the taxi when Mallory managed to destroy the peaceful mood. "It would really be neat if you'd fall into the orchestra pit or something, Sara," she declared casually. "It'd make for some really dramatic film footage."

"I think I'm going to be sick," Sara moaned, turning white as newly driven snow. Her freckles stood out even more vividly against her pallor.

While Sara had performed in recitals before, the cast had always consisted of students. This time, after months of auditions, she had gained a small part dancing with members of the San Francisco Ballet Company.

Giving Mallory a warning glare, Jessica managed an encouraging tone. "Of course you're not," she stated blithely. "Those are simply butterflies. All great performers have them."

"Really?" Sara looked doubtful.

"Really," Jessica insisted. "I read just last week that Alexander Godunov got them before every performance."

"Did they go away?"

Jessica kissed her daughter's clammy forehead. "The minute he began to dance."

"I read the very same article," Elizabeth professed firmly.

Jessica could have kissed her eldest daughter as Jill added her two cents to the fictional account. "I read it, too, Sara. Don't worry, you'll be terrific!"

Breathing a sigh of relief, Jessica decided things might go smoothly tonight, after all. She changed her mind when they took their seats in the theater and she discovered Quinn Masterson seated next to her.

"What are you doing here?"

He grinned, appearing unperturbed by her impolite tone. "Didn't you know? I'm a supporter of the arts." Before she could comment, he looked past her at the avidly interested trio of females.

Elizabeth was already sizing him up as future son-in-law material; the appraising gaze was unmistakable. Jill was staring as if Rick Springfield had suddenly appeared in their midst, and even Mallory looked as if she might consider giving Quinn a starring role in her latest epic.

"Quinn Masterson," he said, holding out his hand. "I believe we've met before, Mrs. MacLaughlin."

"Of course," she agreed with an answering smile. "Several times." Her blue gaze narrowed. "However, I had no idea you and my daughter were acquainted."

"We're very old friends," he stated, ignoring Jessica's intake of breath at his outrageous lie. His gaze slid to Jessica's daughters. "You two are every bit as lovely as your mother. I feel sorry for all the men whose hearts are going to be broken."

Jill and Mallory both appeared to melt on the spot, leaving it up to Jessica to introduce the two girls who had suddenly gone mute. A moment later the orchestra began to warm up, drawing everyone's attention to the stage.

"I remembered where we met," he murmured.

"I told you, Quinn," she insisted, "we haven't met."

"Yes, we have. Tonight brought it all back."

She shook her head, keeping her eyes directed to the stage, waiting for the performance to begin. "You're mistaken."

"I couldn't possibly be mistaken about the worst day of my life."

"Terrific," she grumbled, still refusing to believe him. "It's nice to know I made such a wonderful impression."

"It wasn't you. It was the damn dance class."

Jessica turned her head, eyeing him with renewed curiosity. "Dance class? Don't tell me that you attended Madame Sorenson's Academy of Ballroom Dancing, too?"

"Didn't everyone? At least that's what my grandmother alleged when she dragged me there."

At her questioning expression, Quinn elaborated. "My parents died when a tornado hit our farm that summer and I was sent out here to live with my grandparents."

"I'm sorry."

"It was a rough year," he confessed. "Grandmother was shocked to discover that her only living heir was a wet-behind-the-ears Missouri farm kid without what she referred to as *social graces*." Quinn winced, giving Jessica the feeling that the memories were still slightly painful, years later.

"Anyway," he continued, his tone low, his words intended for her ears only, "she talked Madame Sorenson into taking me into that class, even though I was a head taller and five years older than everyone else."

Jessica tried to recall a tall, handsome boy—a younger version of Quinn Masterson—and came up blank.

"The first class I was paired with a skinny little kid who had flaming red pigtails and a ski-jump nose sprinkled with an amazing array of freckles."

Comprehension suddenly dawned. "I remember you!" Jessica exclaimed, drawing irritated glances from the people sitting around her. She lowered her voice. "You scared me to death, Quinn Masterson. You spent the entire two hours scowling at me and cussed every time I stepped on your foot."

He gave her a lopsided grin. "I probably did," he admitted. "Although you were less than graceful, sweetheart. Next to me, you were the worst dancer in the room."

"I'm left-handed," she said defensively. "As well as left-footed. I have trouble following because everything's backward."

Quinn shrugged. "Hey, Ginger Rogers probably couldn't have followed my clumsy steps. Anyway, that was such a humiliating evening, I went back home and told my grandmother that I refused to ever go back again."

His eyes suddenly gleamed with an unmistakable desire. "However, if I'd known what a beauty that freckle-faced little kid was going to grow up to be, you couldn't have kept me away from that class."

Jessica was saved from answering as the houselights

dimmed. She was grateful for the darkness; Quinn wouldn't see the color heating her cheeks at his huskily stated words.

She kept her eyes directed toward the stage, but she was unaware of the dancers as she wondered idly if Quinn had ever learned to dance. She'd certainly seen his picture in the paper enough times, squiring a steady stream of glamorous, sophisticated women to society balls.

"We'll have to try it some night soon," he said, his lips suddenly unnervingly close to her ear.

Every instinct Jessica possessed warned her not to turn her head, but it was as if she were merely a puppet, with Quinn Masterson expertly pulling the strings.

"Try what?" she asked softly, staring at the firm lips only a whisper away from her own.

His broad white teeth flashed in a knowing grin, acknowledging that she was not alone in having these moments of odd, sensual yearning.

"Dancing. We're going to have to give it a whirl and see if either of us has improved."

"Quinn, really, this is impossible," Jessica protested, drawing a chorus of loud shushing sounds from the people seated around them.

She could feel the self-satisfaction practically oozing from him as he patted her cheek and returned his attention to the stage. Jessica didn't dare open her mouth to protest when he took her hand under the cover of darkness, his fingers linking perfectly with hers. Gradually, as the dancers whirled across the stage in the bright costumes and the music swelled, it seemed entirely natural for Quinn's thumb to softly stroke her palm.

Later, in the final scene, when Sara finally pirouetted onto the stage with a group of other young dancers, Jessica's blood ran icy cold with maternal anxiety. It was only when the lights came on again that Jessica realized how tightly she'd been gripping Quinn's hand.

"My God," she murmured, staring at the deep gouges in his skin caused by her fingernails, "why didn't you say something?"

Quinn shrugged. "It was nice to feel needed," he said simply.

Then he turned his attention to Mallory and Jill. "Does anyone else around here feel like a double bacon cheeseburger with fries?" he asked, earning an enthusiastic acceptance from Jessica's daughters, who seemed eager to avoid another evening of their grandmother's cooking.

"There's no way all of us will fit into your car," Jessica pointed out, still unwilling to encourage Quinn's company.

He gave her a slow, patient smile. "I've already thought of that," he assured her. "As we speak, a limousine is circling the block."

He certainly didn't lack self-confidence, Jessica considered, trying to think of another reason that his suggestion was impossible. Before she could come up with one, they were joined by Sara, who came running up the aisle, still dressed in the frothy pink net tutu.

"Mom, look at what someone sent me!"

Her wide eyes, exaggerated by the heavy stage makeup, appeared like two blue saucers in her flushed face. In her hand was a slender crystal bud vase, which held a pair of sweetheart roses and a spray of baby's breath.

"It's from an admirer," she stated proudly.

"An admirer?" Mallory's tone was skeptical.

Sara thrust the card toward her. "See. That's what it says." Her youthful expression grew dreamy. "I've never gotten flowers after a performance before," she said on a sigh. "I feel just like a real prima ballerina."

Jessica had a suspicion exactly who had sent the flowers,

but when she caught Quinn's eye over Sara's bright auburn head, his gaze was absolutely guileless.

"How would the prima ballerina like to go get a hamburger?" he asked with a smile Jessica was sure worked wonders on women from eight to eighty.

Sara, however, was imbued with a new importance and was not to be taken lightly. "With fries?"

"Of course."

"And onion rings?"

"Can you imagine a hamburger without onion rings?"

She pinned him with a particularly sagacious gaze. "And a double hot fudge sundae for dessert?"

"With nuts," he agreed.

"Is he with us?" Sara asked her mother.

Giving up, Jessica nodded with resignation. "It appears so."

Her youngest daughter's eyes went from Jessica to Quinn, then back again. "It's about time you brought a man home." She turned to Mallory. "I hope you got my *tour jeté* right before the finale."

Mallory nodded. "Mom wouldn't let me use the floodlight, but I think we got enough illumination from the stage lights."

"Good. It was probably my best one ever. Don't you think so, Gran?"

"It was breathtaking," Elizabeth agreed. "Now why don't you go change so your sisters can go ruin their systems with chemicals? We'll meet you out in the lobby."

She'd obviously read one of the latest pop nutrition books, Jessica decided. Her mother was given to embracing short-lived whims and she could only hope that her worries about food additives, as well as this latest decision concerning her marriage were simply the newest in a long line.

"I want to go out like this," Sara complained. "How will anyone know I'm special if I have to change?"

Jessica's stomach suddenly growled, reminding her that she hadn't eaten all day. She was in no mood to argue. "You can't run around San Francisco in that costume," she said firmly, causing Sara's expression to resemble a depressed bloodhound's.

"However," she added with a smile, "you don't have to wash all that makeup off your face until you go to bed."

Sara's smile could have brightened the entire city with its wattage. Shoving the flowers into Jessica's hands, she raced back down the aisle, disappearing through a curtain.

"A decision worthy of Solomon," Quinn murmured. "Just one more facet in the increasingly complex puzzle of Jessica O'Neill."

Jessica had been following Elizabeth, Jill and Mallory to the lobby, but at Quinn's words, she stopped to look up at him.

"I'm not all that complex."

"Of course you are," he argued lightly, reaching out to gently tug one of her curls. "You're the most aggravating, enticing, incomprehensible woman I've ever met. Just when I think I know what's going on in that gorgeous head of yours, you switch gears and leave me behind."

His green eyes gleamed as they roamed her face. "But I've always been fond of puzzles, Jessica. And you're the most fascinating one I've come across in a long time."

Jessica suddenly felt light-headed, a condition she was determined to ascribe to hunger and not the warm gaze directed her way.

"We'd better catch up with the others. That is, if you were serious about eating with us."

"I've never been more serious in my life." Quinn's tone assured Jessica that they were talking about a lot more than cheeseburgers, and her fingers unconsciously tightened about the crystal stem of the bud vase.

Her heart quickened, making her wonder if Quinn could see its wild beating under the ivory lace of her blouse. Something she recognized as desire thickened her blood, curling its way through her body, red and hot, leaving her trembling in its wake. Not even Brian, with the impetuous lovemaking she'd enjoyed in the early days of their marriage, had made her tremble. Jessica was stunned by her response to Quinn, unable to understand it, unwilling to accept it.

"You'd better let me take this," he said, prying her fingers from the slender stem before she snapped it in half. His smile was gently indulgent. "Don't worry, Jess—" his fingertips brushed a feathery path along her fragile jawline "—I won't push." Then he cupped her chin, lifting her hesitant gaze to his. "But I won't give up, either," he warned, his expression tender, but determined.

Then he winked, his grin boyishly attractive. "Come on, sweetheart," he encouraged, his hand resting lightly on her back as he directed her up the aisle. "We've got a hungry crew to feed."

CHAPTER FOUR

LATER AS THEY ALL SAT around a table at a downtown restaurant, Jessica was forced to give Quinn credit. For a lifelong bachelor, he seemed totally at ease with the disjointed conversation jumping around the table. She had grown so used to her daughters cutting one another off, addressing several varied and dissimilar topics at once, that she had come to accept it as a matter of course. Now, viewing it through Quinn's eyes, Jessica was amazed he was able to keep track of what was going on. He even appeared unperturbed by Mallory's camera whirring away, capturing the evening on videotape.

He answered Elizabeth's questions about a case he'd tried last year before Judge Terrance MacLaughlin, and Jessica was not at all surprised that her mother remembered it as a superb presentation. One did not become a partner in such a prestigious law firm as Quinn's without being an excellent attorney. She also couldn't help noticing how attractive he was, his enthusiasm for his profession brightening his tanned face.

At the same time, he fielded questions from Sara, who was vastly interested in this man who'd suddenly shown up in their midst.

"Are you married?"

"No."

Sara nodded understandingly. "Mom's divorced, too," she offered.

"I've never been married," Quinn responded, correcting Jessica's youngest daughter's mistaken comprehension.

"Why not?" she persisted.

"Sara," Jessica warned, "that's a very personal question and absolutely none of your business."

"I don't mind," Quinn replied. He leaned back in his chair, crossing his arms over his chest. "You see, Sara, when I was in college, I came up with a plan for my life."

"Mom does stuff like that," Mallory interjected. "She's the world's greatest list maker."

Quinn gave Jessica a thoughtful glance, then returned to answering Sara's initial question. "Well, it wasn't that I didn't want a wife and children," he assured his avidly interested audience. "I just didn't think I could concentrate my energies on my career and a family, so I decided that I'd go to law school, join a good firm and work to become a partner by the time I was forty. By then I figured I'd have the time to devote to my personal life."

"How old are you, Quinn?" Jill asked, ignoring the blistering warning glare from her mother.

Quinn's eyes twinkled as he slid a meaningful glance Jessica's way. "I turned forty three weeks ago."

The significance of that statement swirled about them, causing Jessica to grow extremely uncomfortable under the watchful gazes of her mother and daughters. She was distinctly relieved when Sara spoke up, continuing her cross-examination of Quinn with the tenacity of a terrier worrying a particularly succulent bone.

"So you don't have any kids, huh?"

"Not yet." He grinned unrepentently at Jessica, who began fiddling nervously with her silverware.

"Then you probably don't go to many recitals like this," Sara continued to probe.

"This was the first," Quinn agreed cheerfully. "And believe me, I thoroughly enjoyed it. You're quite talented, you know.''

Sara bobbed her bright russet head. "I know."

"Are you thinking of making it a career?"

She straightened her slim shoulders. "I *am* going to be a professional ballerina," she said firmly. "I plan on studying for five more years, then I'm going to get an apprenticeship at the San Francisco Ballet Company. Then, before I'm twenty I'll be dancing with the New York City Ballet."

"As a soloist?" he queried, a ghost of a smile hovering at the corner of his lips.

"Of course not," Sara said with youthful disdain. "You don't start out as a soloist. I probably won't get that far until I'm twenty-two or twenty-three."

The smile broke free. "You seem to have your life all planned out."

"Of course."

Elizabeth broke in. "Sara's just like Jessica in that regard. My daughter never begins a day without making a detailed list."

"There's nothing wrong with organization," Jessica snapped, annoyed by the way her mother made her sound like some boring, staid individual. Just because Elizabeth flitted her way through life like a lovely, free-spirited butterfly didn't mean everyone had to follow suit.

Her sharp tone was at odds with the carefree celebratory mood, and five heads swiveled at once to study her curiously.

"I'm going to be a cinematographer," Mallory stated into the uncomfortable lingering silence.

Quinn dragged his attention from Jessica, deciding this was no time to attempt to discern what was bothering her. "I figured as much," he said cheerfully. Then he looked across the table at Jill. "And what about you?" he asked, his gaze taking in her spiky hair and bright, neon apple-green minidress. "Are you going to be a famous rock star? Or an actress?"

Jill shook her head as she slurped the last of her cola making a loud, unmannerly sound. "No. This is just a stage I'm going through," she answered calmly. "I'm going to get married and live in a big house and have lots of children."

Jessica's expression could have been carved in granite. "I think it's time we went home," she announced, pushing her chair back from the table and standing up abruptly. "Tomorrow's a school day."

A chorus of dissent echoed around the table. "I haven't finished my sundae," Sara complained.

"Tough," Jessica retorted. "You should have spent more time eating and less time talking." Her icy gaze rose to Quinn. "Thank you very much, but we have to be going."

"Fine. I'll drive you."

"We can get a taxi."

Quinn's smile didn't waver, but his tone was firm. "I think we exhausted that suggestion last night, Jess. I don't invite people out to dinner, then send them home in a taxi."

Jessica felt as if she were being examined under a microscope as four pairs of female eyes suddenly riveted on her.

"You went out to dinner with Quinn last night?" Mallory asked incredulously.

"In that horrid old running suit?" Jill tacked on, her youthful expression displaying what she thought of her mother's casual apparel.

"That explains it," Elizabeth murmured thoughtfully.

Sara simply stared.

Jessica's eyes shot daggers at Quinn, who appeared totally unperturbed by the sudden interest in their relationship.

"Come on, girls," he said, his grin breaking free. "We'd better get you home before your mother lays down the law and grounds us all."

That earned a laugh Jessica refused to acknowledge as she marched out of the restaurant, head held high, her back as rigid as if someone had dropped a rod of steel down her lacy blouse.

If she thought she was going to get away without inviting Quinn in, Jessica was sadly mistaken. As the limousine pulled up in front of the house, she was outnumbered four to one, and her irritation rose to new heights as Quinn cheerfully complied with the majority.

Sara insisted on showing him her scrapbook, and Mallory proudly displayed the certificate won for a short animated film she'd made using space creatures fashioned from modeling clay. Jill, not to be outdone, treated him to a performance of her lipsyncing the latest rock hit.

Finally the three girls had been convinced it was well past their bedtime, and as the adults drank espresso in the living room, only the giggles drifting down the stairs revealed the level of excitement the unusual evening had created.

Jessica was annoyed, but not particularly surprised, when Elizabeth used the opportunity to do a little motherly detective work.

"My husband has always spoken very highly of you, Quinn," she said with a smile. "But I didn't realize you and my daughter were acquainted."

"We're old friends." Quinn's deep voice invested the outrageous statement with a masculine intimacy, causing Jessica to glare at him.

Elizabeth's eyes gleamed with interest, and Jessica could practically see the wheels turning inside her mother's head.

"We're simply business acquaintances," Jessica corrected firmly. "Quinn is representing Keith in the Thackers' divorce case."

Elizabeth had deftly manuevered the seating arrangements so that she had possession of the only chair in the small, intimate parlor, forcing Jessica to share the love seat with Quinn. At her prickly tone, he put his arm around her shoulder and grinned wickedly.

"Don't forget that memorable evening we spent dancing, Jessie."

Elizabeth suddenly popped up, a brilliant smile on her face. "I'm so exhausted," she claimed, her hand covering her mouth to stifle a yawn Jessica suspected was feigned. Her mother had always been a night owl. "I think I'll head up to bed now. Good night, Jessica. Quinn. It was a pleasure seeing you again."

Quinn's eyes danced with amusement at Elizabeth's less than subtle matchmaking. He rose immediately from the couch. "The pleasure was all mine, Mrs. MacLaughlin," he stated. While his words were directed at her mother, his eyes remained on Jessica.

With a throaty chuckle, Elizabeth made herself scarce, leaving Jessica and Quinn alone in the dimly lit room.

Jessica jumped up and turned on him, her hands on her hips. "Why did you do that?"

He arched a gold eyebrow. "Do what?"

"Make my mother think there's something going on between us."

"Isn't there?"

"No." Jessica held her breath, irrationally waiting for a bolt of lightning to strike her down for telling such a blatant lie. She couldn't remember either of them moving, yet a moment later she was standing in the circle of his arms.

"Jessie," he murmured, "didn't your mother ever teach you it's not nice to tell a lie?"

She couldn't think with those warm green eyes moving so slowly over her face. She stared down at the floor.

"Jess." It was only her name, but his husky voice made it a caress. And a command. She slowly lifted her eyes, shaken as she reluctantly met his desirous gaze.

He reached down, taking one of her hands in his, uncurling the fingers from the tight, nervous fist she'd made. Her fingernails had left little gouges in her palm and as he stroked her skin, Jessica could only stare, entranced by the sensual movement of his dark fingertips. When those devastating fingers curled lightly around her wrist, Jessica knew he could feel her pulse racing.

"Do you know the last time I held hands with a girl while her mother was upstairs in bed?" Quinn's tone was conversational, but his eyes were handing her an increasingly sensual message.

"No," she managed, her voice as shaky as her body.

"Neither do I," he admitted with a crooked grin. "But it's been a very long time."

He'd laced their fingers together, bringing her hand to his chest, allowing her to feel his own erratic heartbeat. His eyes were still focused on hers, and Jessica felt as if she was drowning in pools of molten emeralds. Every nerve ending in her body was alive, reaching for his touch.

"Once we settle the Thackers' problems, perhaps we should do a little matchmaking of our own," he suggested. "See if we can do anything to get your parents back together. It would be a shame to stand by and watch a marriage of that long a duration go down the drain."

"My parents are pretty stubborn," Jessica said. "I'm not

certain how they'd take to any outside interference." She hesitated. "I'm sorry she behaved that way."

Jessica could feel the rise and fall of his chest under her hand and had a sudden urge to touch his skin, to see if he was beginning to burn with the same intensity that had her body glowing with a lambent heat. She stifled a gasp as he lifted her hand to his lips, pressing a kiss against her wrist, causing her pulse to leap in response.

"That's okay—it was rather endearing. Besides, I think she had a great idea." Quinn breathed in the fragrance of her skin, needing to know if she tasted as sweet. His tongue teased the inside of her wrist.

"Idea?" Jessica's free hand moved up to his shoulder, to support herself against the desire sweeping through her.

"She's expecting me to kiss you good-night."

"I don't think that's a very good idea," she protested weakly. "Besides, you let her think we were romantically involved. 'Very old friends,' you said."

"I *have* known you since you were eight."

"Not since," she countered. "Except for those two hours, we only met yesterday."

"Isn't there an old Chinese proverb that states once you've broken a man's toes, he's yours for life?"

Jessica's heart pounded in her throat. "Not that I've heard."

"Then you obviously haven't been spending enough time in Chinatown," Quinn said with a smile. "I'm certain I heard it only last week." His eyes darkened to a deep, swirling sea, enveloping her in his gaze. "I don't think you should disregard your mother's wishes, Jessica. She has enough problems right now without worrying about a willful daughter."

Jessica watched, transfixed, as his head lowered, his lips approaching hers with sensual intent. *Too fast,* she told herself, even as her own lips parted. *This is happening too fast.*

She pressed her hands against his chest. "No," she whispered, knowing that her eyes were giving him an entirely different answer.

Quinn was unmoved by her weak protest. "Don't fight it, Jessie," he murmured, his lips altering their course, moving along her jaw. As he put his hand on her cheek, coaxing her mouth toward his, Jessica turned her head away in sudden panic.

"I said no, Quinn!" She would have moved away, to safer territory, but his hands were on her shoulders.

"Why not?" The words came out harsher than he intended. But he'd never met a woman capable of making him feel this way, and it was all he could do not to drag her by that long auburn hair to bed right now. Caveman tactics, he considered bleakly, knowing that primitive method would never work with Jessica O'Neill. But damn, how he wanted her!

His angry tone only served to fuel her irritation. Jessica felt her temper rising, but reminded herself that if she lost it, she would give Quinn even more of an advantage than he possessed at the moment.

"I don't think I owe you an explanation," she stated coolly, backing out of his arms.

Quinn bit down a frustrated response, allowing her to move away. "Perhaps you don't owe me one," he admitted. "But it would be nice to know why you suddenly changed your mind. Face it, Jess—a minute ago you wanted me as much as I wanted you."

She tossed back her head. "Even if that were the case, which it's not," she quickly added as she saw the victorious flash in his eyes, "I'm not in the market for an affair, Quinn."

''Scared?'' he taunted lightly.

Quinn knew he hadn't misread those soft gazes she kept giving him; he knew Jessica had experienced the same elemental jolt he had when they'd first seen each other last night at the Fairmont. So why did she insist on playing these ridiculous games?

She turned her back, wrapping her arms around herself, as if in self-protection. ''That's ridiculous,'' she said softly, her slight trembling giving her away.

Quinn shoved his hands into his pockets to keep from reaching out and touching her. She *was* frightened, he realized suddenly.

''Is this the same Jessica O'Neill who put her life back together all by herself and who prides herself on her independence? Is this the same woman who has gained the reputation of an *iron lady* around the municipal courthouse this past year?''

She looked back over her shoulder. ''You're making that up.''

''No, I'm not. In fact, that's one of the more charitable descriptions, if you want to know the truth. You've got a reputation for being a loner, Jess. A woman with ice water for blood and a stone-cold heart.''

She was not going to admit how that uncomplimentary description stung. ''Why is it that no one questions a man if he chooses not to marry, but if a woman values her freedom, there's something wrong with her?''

''Perhaps it's because you wear your bitterness like a chip on that lovely shoulder,'' he suggested softly, coming over to stand behind her. ''I like this blouse,'' he murmured. ''You look different tonight. Softer.'' His palms shaped her shoulders, warming her skin under the fragile ivory lace.

"I don't want to look soft," she argued. "I don't want to *be* soft."

Despite her words, Jessica didn't resist as he turned her slowly in his arms. His green eyes as they studied her thoughtfully, were gently censorious.

"I know you've been hurt, Jess," he said quietly. "But don't let your feelings ruin your daughters' chances for happiness."

Jessica knew immediately which particular daughter Quinn was referring to. "Jill," she muttered, shaking her head sadly.

"Jill," he agreed. "She's got a lot of love to give. Don't teach her to bottle it all up, just because you've found that's the safest way to deal with life."

Jessica shook her head, her distress eloquent in her blue eyes. "You don't understand," she whispered. "I was just like Jill at her age. I don't want her to be hurt."

"Of course you don't," he said, his palms rubbing lightly on her back. "But just because Jill wants a family doesn't mean she's going to be hurt. Fifty percent of marriages *don't* break up."

"And fifty percent do," she reminded him.

"Ah, sweetheart, I never would have figured you for a woman who looks at the glass and sees it half-empty," he chided.

She didn't used to be, Jessica admitted secretly. There was a time when she could have been described as an eternal optimist, always expecting the best from life. But she'd learned the hard way what happens to women who wear blinders.

When she didn't answer, Quinn heaved a deep sigh. "I'd better be going."

She slowly lifted her head, trying to remain unaffected by the lingering desire in his eyes. "Thank you for dinner," she murmured. "It was you who sent Sara the flowers, wasn't it?"

He managed a crooked grin. "Guilty as charged, counselor."

Jessica tried to smile and failed miserably. "It was a very nice thing to do. And I'm sorry if I gave you the wrong impression about..." Her voice failed her momentarily. "You know."

He shrugged. "There'll be another time."

"No, there won't."

Quinn surprised her by smiling, a slow, devastating smile. "Don't bet the farm on that, sweetheart," he warned softly, brushing his knuckles against her cheek. The dazzling smile didn't quite reach his strangely hard green eyes. "Because you'd lose." With that he was gone, leaving Jessica to stare after him.

JESSICA REFUSED TO ANSWER any questions about Quinn the next morning, her stern tone assuring everyone that she was in no mood to discuss her personal life. Even Sara remained silent, although her steady blue gaze was unnervingly knowing for a nine-year-old. Although Sara was the youngest, in some ways she was far more mature than her sisters. Jessica had often thought the child had mistakenly been born with an adult mind.

Jessica managed to reschedule her lunch with Vanessa and after a noneventful morning's work was seated in a white wicker gazebo, in a veritable arboretum, surrounded by blooming plants and live banana palms. The soothing sound of splashing fountains could be heard over the murmurs of the luncheon crowd.

"So," Vanessa said, eyeing Jessica over the rim of her glass, "I hear you and Quinn Masterson are an item."

Jessica slowly lowered her menu, staring across the table

at the other woman. They weren't particularly close, but being the only two women working in the decidedly male bastion of Bennington, Marston, White and Lowell had created a certain bond. Lunch discussions, however, seldom included personal topics.

"Where on earth did you hear that?"

"I was at a party last night and Pamela Stuart was sulking because you'd managed to spirit San Franciso's most eligible bachelor away from the Arts' Ball."

"Pamela Stuart?" Jessica's brow furrowed as she tried to place the woman.

"You know," Vanessa said, "Fletcher Stuart's wife."

Jessica knew Fletcher Stuart was one of the city's most successful real estate developers, on a par with her own former husband. She struggled for a mental image of his wife.

"Tall, willowy, blond," Vanessa added, to help out.

Jessica suddenly remembered the sleek woman whose hand had been resting so possessively on Quinn's arm. A jolt of something dangerously akin to jealousy forked through her and it was all she could do to keep a placid, inscrutable expression on her face.

"Are they still married?" she asked with far more aplomb than she was feeling at the moment.

The waiter chose that inopportune time to arrive to take their order, and Jessica was forced to wait for an answer. "Well?" she asked once they were alone again.

Vanessa was crunching on a stalk of celery from her Bloody Mary. "Well, what?"

"Are Pamela and Fletcher Stuart still married?"

Her friend's brown eyes narrowed. "So there is something going on between you two?" Her tone displayed her incredulity. "I figured it was just party gossip. Or a case of mistaken identity. I mean, let's face it, kiddo, you're not really in the same league with Quinn Masterson.''

''What exactly do you mean by that?'' Jessica asked frostily.

''Hey,'' Vanessa said quickly, ''I didn't mean to hurt your feelings, Jessica. It's just that you don't even date, and Quinn, well…''

''I know,'' Jessica muttered. ''Quinn Masterson has elevated the dating game to Olympian heights.''

''The man does have quite a reputation,'' Vanessa stated cautiously. ''I don't think he's ever shown up two nights in a row with the same woman.''

''So why was Pamela Stuart making such a big deal about it?'' Jessica asked, wondering how the idea of Quinn and all his women could hurt this way. ''And you never answered my question. Is she still married?''

''She's married, but to my knowledge that has never slowed her down. As for her relationship with Quinn, I think she has her sights set on him for husband number three. At least she was dropping plenty of hints that the golf-ball-size aquamarine ring she was sporting was an engagement gift from the man.''

Jessica suddenly realized she was tearing her paper napkin to shreds and lowered her hands to her lap. ''Look, I don't want to talk about him, okay? I did meet with him the night of the Arts' Ball, but only to insist that he control the behavior of one of his clients.''

''You're on opposite sides of a case?''

''Yes. And that's all it is.''

''Wow,'' Vanessa murmured, taking a sip of her drink. ''If there's one thing more dangerous than getting involved personally with that man, it's probably going up against him professionally.''

Her dark eyes surveyed Jessica with renewed interest.

"How on earth did you get anything that important? Usually one of the partners handle things in Masterson's league."

Jessica shrugged. "It's not that big a case. It's a divorce. I'm representing Sylvia Thacker."

At that Vanessa laughed. "Now I understand. That woman is an absolute menace and her husband's even worse. As long as her grandfather's estate represents one of Bennington, Marston, White and Lowell's major accounts, none of the guys on the top floor will touch that divorce with a ten-foot pole." She shook her head. "I don't envy you," she said cheerily, before turning her attention to the waiter who'd arrived with their lunch.

Try as she might, Jessica could not get the vision of Quinn and Pamela Stuart out of her mind. It was ridiculous to feel this jealous about a man she had no intention of getting involved with, she knew. She told herself that over and over again as the day wore on, but her heart seemed to have a mind of its own as it steadfastly refused to listen to her head.

When her secretary announced a call from her mother, Jessica stifled a sigh, hoping Elizabeth wasn't going to start in again on her incessant matchmaking.

"Hi. How's the hunt for an office going?" She hoped that starting the conversation out with her mother's life would forestall any mention of Quinn's name.

"Fine, I suppose." Her mother sounded less enthusiastic than she had yesterday. "Although I'll admit I've been having second thoughts about taking space in some impersonal office building."

Hallelujah, Jessica sang out inwardly. Elizabeth was ready to return home. "Oh?" she inquired with feigned casualness.

"I've been thinking about joining the peace corps." Elizabeth dropped her latest bombshell casually.

"Peace corps? At your age?"

She could practically see her mother's spine stiffen. "Lillian Carter was older than I am when she joined."

Deciding that her mother would definitely not appreciate her only daughter pointing out there was a vast difference in the need for nurses and the need for interior decorators in the peace corps, Jessica remained silent.

"What do you think about Alaska?" Elizabeth asked suddenly.

"I don't think the peace corps works in the United States, Mom," Jessica answered, picturing an igloo with Levolor blinds and art deco posters on the ice-block walls.

"Not for me, I was thinking about Africa.... Your father's the one talking about moving to Alaska. Can you imagine the old fool?"

"Alaska? Dad? Why?"

"He's bought a gold mine. Honestly, Jessica, can you picture your father as a prospector?"

Jessica could picture that about as well as she could her mother off in the African bush decorating huts.

"Do you want me to talk to him?" she asked.

"Don't waste your time," Elizabeth snapped. "There's no reasoning with the man lately. Well, if he thinks he's the only one who can have an adventure, he's going to find himself sadly mistaken."

That explained the peace corps notion, Jessica realized, wondering if her parents were going through some sort of delayed adolescence. They'd always been so stable—the rocks that had formed the foundation of the MacLaughlin family. She sighed. Maybe some substance had been dumped into San Francisco's water system, causing all the city's inhabitants to behave totally out of character. The way she'd been acting with Quinn certainly hadn't been normal.

That thought brought to mind Pamela Stuart and her alleged engagement ring. "Look, Mom," Jessica said swiftly, "I've got a call on the other line, but I'll be home for dinner."

"Fine, dear," Elizabeth answered cheerfully. "And don't worry about cooking. I've got everything under control."

Envisioning the mutiny the girls were going to stage if Jessica couldn't figure out some way to keep her mother out of the kitchen, she closed her eyes wearily. "I've got to hang up now," she said. "Oh, and Mom?"

"Yes, dear?"

"Please don't do anything rash until I get home and we can talk about it."

"Honestly, Jessica," Elizabeth huffed with very real indignation. "I don't know where you get these crazy ideas. Sometimes I think you must take after your father. Of course I won't do anything rash. I'm the sensible one in the family, after all."

Jessica shook her head, smiling as she hung up the phone. Her parents were driving her crazy, but she loved them both and only hoped they could work out their difficulties.

Moments later the intercom buzzed again. "Mr. Masterson on line one," Paula's disembodied voice announced.

Jessica fought down the flush of pleasure, reminding herself that to get involved with a man who in earlier times could only be described as a *rake* would be pure folly.

"Hello," she said stiffly. "What can I do for you?"

His answering chuckle was low and deep. "Ah, Jess," he teased. "You should know better than to give me a straight line like that."

His intimate tones caused a warmth to begin deep in her middle regions, spiraling outward until she could feel the tips of her fingers tingling. Her toes literally curled in her tan pumps.

"I assume you're calling to discuss Mr. Thacker," she said briskly, fighting down the unwelcome surge of desire that threatened to be her undoing.

"So it's going to be strictly business where you and I are concerned?"

Jessica tried to read an undertone of regret in Quinn's deep voice, but failed. "I've already told you that," she pointed out briskly. "Several times, in fact."

"That's right, you have," he agreed amiably. "Mr. Thacker extends his appreciation to Mrs. Thacker for having Maximilian delivered so promptly."

"I'm pleased that he's pleased," Jessica murmured, secretly admitting it had come as a surprise when Sylvia had agreed without a word of complaint to her husband's latest proposal.

"Oh, he's not exactly pleased," Quinn added casually. "In fact, I'm giving official notice that he intends to bring a civil suit against Mrs. Thacker for the destruction of private property."

"What?" Jessica's voice rose at least an octave.

As she dragged a hand wearily across her eyes, Jessica reminded herself that she was the one who'd insisted on keeping things on a professional level. Quinn's tone was silky smooth, but as dangerously sharp as a well-honed stiletto, and she suddenly understood Vanessa's comment at lunch concerning his ruthless reputation as an adversary.

"She shaved him, Jess. Right down to the skin."

"Oh, no," Jessica groaned. "She didn't?"

It was a rhetorical question and Quinn didn't bother to

answer. "As we speak, Maximilian looks more like a very fat rat than the city's most valuable stud," he informed her.

"I'm sorry."

He surprised her by chuckling, his cold attitude dissolving as quickly as it had appeared. "You probably will be," he agreed cheerfully. "I advised the guy against retaliation, but if you'll take a little professional advice, counselor, I'd warn Mrs. Thacker to take a long vacation out of town."

"I'll talk to her," Jessica said flatly.

"You do that," Quinn replied. "And Jess?"

Here it comes, she thought, a ripple of exhilaration skimming up her spine. *He's going to ask me out and I'm not going to be able to refuse.*

"Yes?" she asked, unable to keep the expectation from her tone.

"See you in court," he said, leaving her feeling slightly annoyed as he hung up.

"The least he could have done was tell me to have a nice day," she muttered as she placed a call to Sylvia Thacker, vowing that this time she wouldn't allow herself to be intimidated by the woman's veiled threats.

It was Sylvia's fault Jessica was mixed up with Quinn Masterson in the first place, and if the Thackers couldn't get their act together, Jessica was simply going to remove herself from the case. She refused to admit that her irritation had anything to do with Quinn's sudden dismissive attitude.

CHAPTER FIVE

IF JESSICA THOUGHT she'd experienced the worst her day could offer, she was in for a surprise as things went from bleak to miserable. Sylvia Thacker showed no remorse about her act of vandalism, stating briskly that a BMW was no fair trade for a Mercedes.

"Then why did you agree to accept your husband's offer in the first place?" Jessica asked wearily.

"Because, my dear, a BMW is still a far sight better than public transportation. Besides—" the woman chuckled wickedly "—I couldn't resist driving Keith's blood pressure up. I only wish I could have been there to see his face when Max was delivered."

Privately Jessica considered that Sylvia's absence from the scene was probably the only reason Keith Thacker wasn't in jail at this very minute, charged with murder.

"He has every intention of suing you," she felt obliged to point out.

"Let him." The woman's voice held a careless shrug. "And we'll sue for the Mercedes, of course."

"Of course," Jessica agreed faintly, mentally ringing up the costs of the continual charges and countercharges made by the Thackers.

While both law firms' coffers were growing the longer the couple fought their marriage out to the bitter end, she hated to consider the way she and Quinn were going to be tying up the already crowded court calendar.

"I've got to go," Sylvia said suddenly. "Keith just drove up."

"Mrs. Thacker, you wouldn't..." Jessica left the sentence unfinished, afraid to remind Sylvia Thacker of her earlier threat. Perhaps the woman didn't even own a gun, Jessica considered hopefully.

"Don't worry about a thing, Mrs. O'Neill," her client assured her. "I have everything under control."

As the dial tone echoed in her ear, Jessica could only hope so. She debated phoning the police, then decided that she was probably only borrowing trouble.

She had returned to preparing a brief for an environmental group attempting to gain funds from the EPA Superfund when her intercom buzzed again. Experiencing a fleeting wish for the good old days before telephones, Jessica answered the page.

"Yes? And if you tell me it's Sylvia Thacker, I'm going to slit my wrists."

Paula laughed. "No, it's the judge. You'd better talk to him before he explodes."

Jessica groaned. "Is he that upset?"

"The usually unflappable Judge MacLaughlin could give Mount St. Helen's a run for its money right now," she stated. "What on earth is happening in your family, Jessica? You've gotten more phone calls in the past three days than you have in the past year."

"I don't know," she said on a deep sigh, casting a quick glance at her watch. "Look, I've got a meeting with Mr. Bennington in two and a half minutes. Will you do me a favor and tell Dad that I'll get back to him as soon as possible?"

"Sure. But if you look to the north and see smoke billowing into the sky, don't say I didn't warn you."

Jessica rubbed her fingertips against her temples, gathering strength for the upcoming meeting with the head of the firm. It was her monthly review, a procedure suffered by all first-year attorneys, and though she never found it the least bit enjoyable, she was thankful she no longer broke out in hives when summoned to the executive offices.

Compared to some of the others Jessica had suffered through, this month's review was relatively painless. As she returned to her office, Paula's grave face displayed her concern. The secretary's worried expression broke into a congratulatory grin as Jessica gave her a thumbs-up sign.

"Your father called three more times," she said pointedly, single-handedly managing to burst Jessica's little bubble of pleasure.

Realizing she couldn't keep avoiding the issue, Jessica assured Paula that she'd take care of it immediately. She went into her office and dialed the MacLaughlin residence.

"That better be you, Jessie MacLaughlin O'Neill," her father said abruptly.

"It's me," she acknowledged. "What's up?"

"What's up?" Her father's deep voice vibrated with incredulity. "What's up?" he repeated. "I expected you to tell me. Do you know what fool stunt your mother has come up with now?"

"The peace corps?"

"So you do know."

He jumped on Jessica's words instantly, reminding her of Judge Terrance MacLaughlin's forceful presence on the bench. He'd been strong and tough, but fair, she conceded. She could only hope his sense of fair play extended to his own wife.

"Well, after all, Dad, you're taking off to Alaska to work that gold mine you bought. Surely you can't deny Mom a little adventure of her own."

"Leased," he corrected gruffly.

"Leased?"

"You don't *buy* a gold mine, Jessica. You lease it from the government."

"Lease, buy, what's the difference? You're heading off to Alaska, what do you expect Mom to do? Stay home and knit you some warm clothes for prospecting?"

"She could be more supportive," he grumbled.

"So could you," Jessica risked pointing out.

"You think I should endorse this peace corps thing?" Jessica could practically see her father's silvery brows climbing his wide forehead.

"Did you invite her to Alaska?"

"Why the hell should I do that? If she can't stand to live with me in that huge mausoleum of a house she's always redecorating, how long do you think we'd survive together in a prospector's shack?"

Try as she might, Jessica couldn't see either of her parents living happily in such circumstances. "Dad, why don't you at least ask her?"

"And give her the opportunity to turn me down?"

"Would that be so bad?"

"The man is supposed to be the head of the family, Jessica. It's time Elizabeth realized that."

Jessica was rapidly reaching the end of her patience. "If you don't do something soon, Dad," she told him briskly, "there won't be any family for you to be the head of."

She heard his spluttered protests as she firmly replaced the receiver.

Jessica was more than a little relieved when her excruciatingly long workday came to an end. Despite a continual dosage of aspirin all day, she had a throbbing headache and was feeling ill-tempered and out of sorts. It didn't take a Rhodes Scholar to pinpoint the cause of her discomfort. She'd been feeling rotten ever since Vanessa had told her about Quinn and Pamela Stuart at lunch. If Jessica was distressed by the idea of Quinn involved with another woman, especially a married one at that, she was aghast at how much she cared.

Deciding it would be unfair to submit her family to her bad mood, she chose to walk home, using the time to calm down and dismiss the handsome attorney from her mind once and for all.

She tried strolling through a few art galleries, pretending interest in the collections of paintings and etchings. But when Quinn Masterson's handsome features appeared to be painted on every canvas, printed on every lithograph, Jessica gave up that idea, opting instead for the peaceful respite of Golden Gate Park.

In a city renowned for its economy of space, the park was a vast oasis of open air, the once-desolate wasteland of shifting sand dunes having been transformed into a magnificent, yet seemingly natural, park. Strolling past the manicured lawns and pristine flower beds, Jessica settled down on a bench outside the Conservatory of Flowers, the park's Victorian gem. She breathed in the fresh scent of spring, the sweet perfume of the brilliant blossoms, the heady scent of newly mown grass and slowly began to relax.

With her usual careful, methodical way of tackling a problem, Jessica considered her reaction to Quinn, even conceding that she was undeniably attracted to him. What woman wouldn't be? He was handsome, successful, and although she hated to admit it, his reputation did give him a certain aura that would appeal to many women. Rhett Butler had been a rake, too, and he certainly hadn't fared too badly.

Jessica had to acknowledge that so far Quinn had been a complete gentleman. And he'd certainly managed to charm both her mother and her daughters. She shook her head, wondering at the appeal of a man who had three generations of women responding to his magnetism.

"It's nothing but a silly, schoolgirl crush," she told herself firmly as the setting sun turned the windows of the pyramid shaped Transamerica building to a gleaming bronze. "That's all."

Jessica rose, and leaving the park, headed for home. "Well, maybe it's a little bit more than that," she admitted under her breath, unaware she was talking out loud. "It's also physical. But that's all. Simply sex."

"Hey, lady," a teenage boy drawled from a nearby bench, "that ain't all bad."

Lowering her head to hide her unwilling blush, Jessica walked a little faster, inwardly damning Quinn for this latest display of atypical behavior. She never talked to herself. Certainly never in public!

As she lifted her gaze once more, Jessica's breath suddenly caught in her throat. A tall man was walking a few feet in front of her, his golden hair gleaming with sun-gilt strands in the last light of day. He had broad shoulders, lean hips and the long legs clad in gray flannel slacks were achingly familiar. She was trying to decide whether to say anything when he snapped his fingers, as if he'd just remembered something, and turned around.

Jessica's heart crashed to the sidewalk underfoot as she realized the man's eyes were hazel, not green, and his lips were fringed by a thin mustache. His features were not unattractive, but neither did they cause her pulse to race. As the stranger passed, headed back in the opposite direction, he caught a glimpse of her disappointed face and frowned slightly, as if wondering what he'd done to cause her displeasure. Then he was gone and Jessica was left with the unhappy realization that somehow, when she hadn't been looking, Quinn Masterson had laid claim to her heart.

ELIZABETH MET JESSICA at the door of her town house. "Your father called me this afternoon."

"That's nice," Jessica replied blandly.

"Nice? How can you say that, Jessica O'Neill, after the way you betrayed me. Your own mother!"

Jessica sighed, kicking off her shoes. She should have known better than to walk home wearing a pair of new pumps. She'd be lucky not to get a blister.

"I didn't betray you," she protested, hanging her spring jacket on the brass coatrack.

"Oh, no? I suppose you didn't insist that your father take me to that godforsaken wilderness with him? Honestly, Jessica, if you want me out of your house, just say so. You don't have to ship me off to Alaska like some white slaver!"

"I didn't insist, I suggested," Jessica corrected, trying not to smile at her mother's imaginative description.

"Insist, suggested, what's the difference? The fact remains that you told your father I needed someone to look out for me. So he generously offered his services. The old goat. I know exactly what services he had in mind, too!"

"Mother, you're being unreasonable," Jessica remonstrated, making her way to the back of the narrow house to the kitchen.

Elizabeth was on her heels. "*I'm* being unreasonable? What about your father? Do you know I've read they go in for wife-swapping up there? He probably just wants me along so he'll have someone to hand over to his male guests!" Elizabeth's voice trembled with righteous indignation.

Jessica opened the refrigerator, taking out a half-empty bottle of white wine. "Want some?" she offered.

"Not now," her mother said firmly. "I want to get this settled once and for all, Jessica."

Jessica shrugged, taking down a glass and filling it to within an inch of the top with the crisp white Chablis. "Look, Mother, I've had a rough day and I don't need to come home to this. Now I've told Dad, and you're going to hear it, too. If you two don't start behaving like rational adults, you're going to both end up alone. Is that what you really want?"

"Better alone than being handed over to some fur trapper for those long winter nights they have up there," Elizabeth muttered.

"You know," Jessica said suddenly, losing the last remaining vestiges of patience, "you two deserve each other!" She flung open the screen door, escaping to the small brick terrace out back.

"Bad day?" a deep voice inquired blandly.

Jessica stopped in her tracks, staring down at Quinn, who appeared perfectly at home in a white wrought-iron chair. "What are you doing here?"

"I brought Mallory a book on film editing."

"You went out and bought my daughter a book?"

"No, it was one I already owned. I took a few film classes at USC," he revealed. "In LA, it's de rigueur to graduate with at least one cinema class on your transcript."

His green eyes swept over her, from the top of her auburn head down to her stocking-clad feet. "Why don't you sit down?" he suggested amiably, as if it was his backyard and not hers.. "You look beat."

"Thanks," Jessica muttered. "It's nice to know I'm so appealing. However, I doubt if I'd ever come up to Pamela Stuart, even on the best of days."

Quinn's jaw hardened and a strange look came into his eyes as he took a long swallow of the Scotch Elizabeth had obviously served him. "Now I understand why you were so abrupt on the phone today. The gossipmongers don't waste any time, do they?''

Jessica was suddenly unbearably exhausted and sank into a chair, stretching her legs out in front of her. She sipped her wine slowly, pretending to have great interest in the ivy climbing the fence.

"Is it true?" she asked finally.

"Would it matter?"

"I don't know.... I think so," she admitted softly.

Quinn twirled the ice cubes absently in the glass, his attention directed into the dark amber depths. "If our relationship is strictly business, why would it make any difference who I'm sleeping or not sleeping with?"

"It doesn't," she retorted, rising abruptly. "Forget I even brought it up. Where are the girls?"

"I sent them out for pizza," he answered. "Sit down, Jess. Let's get this out in the open."

"There's nothing to discuss." Despite her argumentative tone, Jessica sat back down in the chair, unaware that her pale face was a study in vulnerability.

Quinn sighed heavily. "What am I going to do with you? You keep protesting that you don't want anything to do with me, but every time you look at me with those blue eyes as wide and deep as the sea, I know you're lying through your teeth. You want me, Jess. Every bit as much as I want you."

"How much does Pamela Stuart want you, Quinn?" she asked acidly.

He arched a blond brow. "Jealous?"

She shook her head vigorously. "Not at all. I just don't consider a man who gets himself engaged to a married woman to be a very good influence on my daughters."

Quinn looked inclined to say something, but refrained, instead throwing back his head and tossing off the rest of the Scotch. "You're driving me crazy," he muttered. Then he leaned forward, his elbows braced on his thighs, his hands holding the glass between his legs.

"Pam and I grew up together," he began. "It's an old pattern with her. Every time she breaks up with a guy, she fancies herself in love with me. It gives her the confidence to carry on.... Not everyone can put their lives back together all by themselves the way you managed to do, Jessica."

Jessica fought down the flush created by his openly tender and admiring gaze. "Why does she pick you?" she asked quietly.

Quinn shrugged. "Like I said, it's an old habit. When she got dumped the night before her junior prom, I agreed to fly back to the city from LA and act as her escort, though I always felt more like her big brother. She showed me off that night, pretending I was her college boyfriend from USC."

"That's sad," Jessica murmured, thinking that for all her wealth and beauty, it didn't sound as if Pamela had an overabundance of self-esteem. Jessica remembered the feeling all too well.

"I thought so at the time," Quinn agreed. "That's why I didn't complain." His somber, level gaze held hers. "And that's why I still play along with the charade every few years, hoping that this will be the time she takes my advice and seeks professional help."

Jessica didn't know what to say to that, so she only nodded, feeling as if she was being drawn into the deep green pools caressing her face.

"Am I forgiven?" he asked.

His warm gaze and slow smile were creating havoc with her senses. Jessica felt as if she was suddenly floating out of her depth, and she struggled to maintain her equilibrium.

"How can I stay angry at a man who'd rescue me from home cooking?" She managed a light, slightly ragged laugh.

"Jill assured me she'd quite literally die if forced to eat another one of your mother's meals," Quinn agreed cheerfully, sitting back in the chair.

Jessica breathed a sigh of relief as the sensual mood was effectively broken. "Jill tends to exaggerate. But your chivalry is noted and appreciated."

"Oh, I'm just getting started," he professed, reaching down with a swift movement and taking her foot in his hand.

"Quinn!"

"You're getting a blister," he observed. "Don't you think you ought to get out of these nylons and put on a Band-Aid? I want you in tip-top condition for Saturday night."

"Saturday night?"

His massaging fingers were doing wonderful things to her aching feet as he grinned at her. "How do you ever expect to rise to the exalted ranks of partner and have your name painted on the door of Bennington, Marston, White and Lowell, if you forget such important things like your boss's wedding anniversary party?"

"Oh, God," Jessica groaned. "I did forget all about it. I suppose I have to go."

"You should at least put in an appearance," he concurred.

"I hate things like that," Jessica muttered, knowing that was one more thing she and Quinn Masterson didn't have in common.

He was obviously in his element at formal society affairs. Affairs. That double entendre brought to mind Pamela Stuart, and although Jessica was willing to accept Quinn's story about the unstable heiress, she didn't believe he dated all those other women for altruistic reasons.

"I suppose you have an invitation, too."

Quinn didn't know what had caused Jessica's eyes to darken with that unwelcome pain, but he had a pretty good idea. In her own way, this strong, self-sufficient woman was as fragile as Pam, he realized. She'd been badly hurt and still carried the scars. He'd never bothered to dispute his exaggerated reputation, never caring what people thought about his personal life. Until now.

"I do," he said, standing up.

As Jessica looked up at him, the setting sun sparked her hair with a warm, fiery glow and Quinn had to restrain himself from reaching down and combing his fingers through the thick waves. He couldn't help wondering how those lush strands would feel spread over his chest after making love and the idea caused an aching yearning deep inside him.

Jessica would've had to been blind to miss the blatant desire suddenly flaming in Quinn's green eyes and she remained transfixed, stunned by an answering need. Her eyes darkened to gleaming sapphire and her blood warmed her skin, imbuing her complexion with the hue of a late summer rose.

"Come here." Quinn's voice was unusually husky as he extended his hand toward her.

As if in a trance, Jessica reached out, allowing her hand to be swallowed up by the one so much larger and stronger. Quinn brought her to her feet, into his arms, fitting her intimately against him as he gave in to impulse and buried his lips in the fragrant softness of her fiery hair. The scent reminded him of springtime—of flower-strewn meadows, fruit trees in full blossom, the rich warmth of sunshine returning after a long gray winter.

"Ah, Jess," he said on a sigh. "I promised myself I wouldn't push, but I think I'm going to go crazy if I can't kiss you."

She lifted her head, a slight, unmistakable smile teasing at her lips. "What's stopping you?" she asked softly.

"Sweetheart," he groaned, "I thought you'd never ask."

Jessica's head reeled as she breathed in a scent reminiscent of the forest after a rain—a rich, earthy aroma laced with the sharper tang of redwoods. Her arms went around his waist as she allowed herself to lean against his rugged strength.

Then he was kissing her, his lips hard and hungry, his tightly leashed control disintegrating into a mindless passion. Jessica had been expecting something gentler, something more cautious. She opened her mouth to object, but at her shuddering soft cry, his tongue slipped past the barrier of her teeth, into the velvet vault beyond, creating havoc with her senses as it swept the moist, dark interior.

Jessica's initial shock disintegrated, replaced by an emotion more vital, more electric than anything she'd ever known. Enticed by the expert sensuality of his kiss, she grew more intrepid, allowing her own tongue to venture forth, at first tentatively, then with increasing boldness, discovering the brisk taste of cinnamon mingling enticingly with a darker, stronger taste of the imported Scotch.

He was a wonderful kisser, she considered through her whirling senses. She could stay here in his arms for the rest of her life. His breath was warm and oh, so seductive as his lips scorched a path from one ravished corner of her mouth to the other. Jessica went up on her toes to run her fingers through his sun-gilt hair.

The movement fitted her feminine frame more closely to his body and as Quinn's hands roamed down her back, they caused little sparks to dance between each vertebra. She could feel the warmth emanating from his body, creating a glow that spread outward from her middle regions, flowing through her blood, warming her fingers, making her breasts ache with unaccustomed heaviness, spiraling downward to her toes.

"You feel good," he murmured, dragging his lips away to blaze a heated trail down the slender column of her neck. "So good…"

Jessica's pulse trebled its rhythm as Quinn's palms cupped her breasts, his thumbs creating an evocative pattern that brought the tight crests surging against the amber silk of her blouse.

Jessica struggled to maintain some slim vestige of sanity, telling herself that if she didn't regain control, not only her mother but her daughters, as well, would soon witness Jessica and Quinn making love on the tiny brick terrace. Even as her body clamored for release, her mind tried to make itself heard, reminding her that she and Quinn were not alone. She had no business behaving like an absolute wanton with this man.

She buried her head in his shoulder, taking deep, calming breaths of air. "Another minute of that and I would have suffocated," she complained on what she hoped was a light note. She failed miserably.

Quinn knew Jessica had been affected as intensely as he by the ardent kiss. Probably even more so. He had talked to Pamela today, seeking information about Jessica, and although his longtime friend had pouted prettily, she had assured him that as far as anyone knew, Jessica had been living the life of a nun since her divorce. She was a remarkably passionate woman; Quinn was surprised she'd been able to keep the floodgates closed for as long as she had.

Quinn felt Jessica gathering up her self-control, wrapping

it about herself like a heavy protective cloak. Deciding she had enough problems for now, he opted to match her casual attitude, but was slightly more successful.

"You're supposed to breathe through your nose. But don't worry, a little more practice and you're bound to get the knack of it."

"I don't need any more practice." Her eyes gave him a warning he chose to ignore.

"You're right," he agreed. "You're perfect just the way you are."

His dark gaze made Jessica's legs weaken, and she couldn't muster up the sharp response she knew he deserved. The slam of the front door signaled the return of her daughters, and Jessica heaved a huge sigh of relief as she extricated herself from his arms.

"The girls are back," she stated unnecessarily.

"It appears so." Quinn reached out and looped an auburn strand of hair behind her ear before tilting her chin toward him in a way that effectively captured her gaze.

"I've waited a long time for you," he said suddenly, his husky voice fracturing the silence. "I suppose I can wait until after the pizza."

"You've only known me three days, Quinn," Jessica answered dryly. "So if you think you're going to impress me with your self-restraint, you're sadly mistaken."

"That's where you're way off base," he countered in a serious tone. "I've waited my entire life for you, Jessie O'Neill. And if you think I'm going to let you walk away, now that I've found you, you're dead wrong."

He bent his head, planting a quick, hard kiss on her lips. "Let's eat." Quinn's eyes were laughing as he suddenly noticed her disheveled appearance. "You'd better tuck in your blouse," he warned, "or we'll have some heavy explaining to do to the troops."

Jessica's fingers shook as she tried to shove the amber silk back into her waistband. She finally managed the task, then, pasting a composed expression onto her face, returned to the kitchen, refusing to allow anyone to see that Quinn's statement had shaken her to her toes.

CHAPTER SIX

EXCUSING HERSELF Jessica ran upstairs to change. When she returned to the kitchen and found Elizabeth sharing the thick, gooey pizza, she was unable to resist a slight gibe.

"I see you're willing to risk a few additives, Mother."

"Quinn is very persuasive," Elizabeth replied serenely. "He assured me that pizza is actually very nutritious."

Jessica wasn't surprised; she'd already witnessed how persuasive the man could be when he put his mind to it. Which was precisely her problem, she considered ruefully. She had no intention of becoming involved with any man; at this point in her life all her energies had to be directed toward her family and building a career.

Shrugging off the problem for the moment, she went over to the refrigerator, taking out a diet cola.

"If you keep feeding me this way," she complained, "I'm going to have to roll down the hill to work in the morning."

He grinned. "I'd say you've got a few pounds to go before we have to ship you off to a fat farm."

"Mom's taken up jogging," Mallory informed him. "She says sitting around an office all day is giving her middle-aged spread."

Jessica could have cheerfully strangled her middle daughter for revealing that little bit of information, but Quinn's gaze, as he submitted her to a slow appraisal, was sparked with masculine approval.

''She hides it admirably,'' he stated, his eyes lingering on the curves displayed by the snug, well-worn jeans.

''Would you all stop talking about me as if I wasn't here?'' she protested, feeling as if she was on public display.

There was a murmured chorus of apologies as she sat down at the table, and Jessica knew she was being overly sensitive. But she didn't retract her complaint.

The conversation turned to the day's events, and Jessica was honestly surprised at how interested Quinn appeared as her daughters related their individual triumphs and small failures. Jill was particularly despondent over the grade on her latest math test, insisting that she never would understand plane geometry.

''Give me one good reason why I will ever need to know the area of an isosceles triangle,'' she grumbled.

''You've got me,'' Jessica admitted. ''I nearly failed geometry myself. I think the teacher finally felt sorry for me and gave me a passing grade just to get me out of his class.''

''I've got a makeup test tomorrow and I know I'm going to fail.''

''I can help you memorize theorems again,'' Mallory suggested, picking up a piece of pepperoni that had slid onto the table.

Despite their differences, her daughters could be very supportive of one another when the chips were down, Jessica observed with an inward smile.

''I know them all by heart,'' Jill complained. ''I just don't know what to *do* with them.'' Her expression was absolutely bleak.

''Don't look at me,'' Sara said. ''I've just figured out mixed fractions.''

The mood around the table was decidedly gloomy when

Quinn cleared his throat. "I always liked geometry," he offered almost tentatively.

"You would," Jessica muttered, wishing the man wasn't so damn perfect.

Jill's expression was that of a drowning man suddenly offered a life preserver. "Do you think you could help me study?" she asked hopefully.

Jessica broke in before Quinn had a chance to respond. "I'm sure Mr. Masterson has better things to do with his evening than spend it studying plane geometry," she stated firmly.

"No, actually I don't," he countered calmly. "If you'd like, Jill, I'd enjoy spending the evening here. With all of you."

Jill looked as if she'd just gotten her Christmas present eight months early. Elizabeth's expression reminded Jessica of a very fat cat sitting there with feathers sticking out of its mouth. Mallory and Sara exchanged a long, knowing glance, then eyed their mother, their bright eyes offering congratulations.

They'd obviously all ganged up on her and Jessica knew she'd appear like the Wicked Witch of the West if she offered a single objection. She reluctantly kept her mouth shut, wondering how she was going to keep Quinn Masterson out of her life, when she couldn't even keep him out of her house.

Lost in the problem, she allowed the conversation to continue on around her, no longer pretending an interest. The shrill demand of the phone jolted her out of her troubled musings.

"Jessica," the deep voice said as she picked up the receiver, "how are you?"

"I'm fine, Brian," she replied, drawing interested gazes from the other occupants of the room. "How are you?"

"Fine, fine. Deirdre's fine, too."

As if she cared, Jessica considered with concealed irritation.

"How are the girls?"

"They're fine, too. Do you want to talk to them?"

"I'd love to," her former husband said, "but I'm on my way out the door. I just wanted to see if you'd be willing to change weekends with me."

Jessica shrugged. "I don't see why not."

"Terrific. Thanks a lot, Jess. You're a lifesaver. I'll pick them up tomorrow after school, all right?"

"I'll have everything packed," she agreed absently, uncomfortable with Quinn's thoughtful gaze locked onto her face. She turned her back, fiddling with the telephone cord.

"Great, just great," Brian enthused. "You sound a little tired. Is everything all right? How's work?"

"Everything's fine," she murmured. "Look, Brian, we're eating dinner. The girls will see you tomorrow, okay?"

"Tomorrow," he agreed. "Will you be at the house when I pick them up?"

"I don't know," she hedged. While Jessica had done her best to maintain a friendly relationship with Brian for the girls' sake, she continued to feel uncomfortable in his presence. It brought back too many painful memories. "I may have to work late."

"Oh." He sounded vaguely disappointed. "Well, don't overdo it. You know what they say about all work and no play."

"They say it pays the bills," she countered briskly. "I've got an electrician coming next month who doesn't do charity work."

"I still don't understand why you didn't just keep the

house, Jessica. It wasn't that I didn't offer to let you have it.''

"I wanted a change," she replied. "We like living in the city.''

"I'm not so sure it's good for the girls.''

"Was there anything else you wanted?'' she asked, firmly closing the door on the argument they'd had far too many times in the past three years.

"Stubborn as always, aren't you?'' He didn't bother to hide his irritation.

"That's what I'm told,'' she agreed. "I'll see the girls are ready.''

"Yeah, you do that,'' he muttered. "Goodbye, Jessica.''

"Goodbye.'' She hung up the phone, forcing down the aggravation she knew was etched onto every taut line in her face.

"You're spending this weekend with your father,'' she announced, returning to the table.

"This weekend! I can't,'' Mallory wailed. "You'll have to call him back.''

"I won't do any such thing,'' Jessica said firmly. "Besides, he said he was on the way out the door when he called.''

"I'm not going.'' She folded her arms across her chest.

Jessica knew that of all her daughters, Mallory was the only one who still held a grudge against her father for leaving his family for another woman. She'd done her best never to say anything derogatory about him in her daughters' presence, but the relationship between Brian and his middle daughter was strained, at best. Which was especially unfortunate when she considered that Mallory had always been Brian's favorite. Although Jessica suspected Mallory was suffering her own feelings of personal rejection, she'd never gotten her daughter to discuss it openly.

"Honey," she coaxed, "you always have a good time once you get there."

A mutinous expression hardened the young face. "I had plans for this weekend."

"Plans?"

"The Charlie Chaplin film festival at the Orpheum," she reminded her mother.

She'd talked about little else all month, Jessica recalled belatedly, knowing how excited Mallory had been about the chance to view the comedian's old films.

"I forgot," she admitted. "But as it turns out, I have to work Saturday morning, anyway."

"Gran can take me," Mallory suggested, her gaze as appealing as a cocker spaniel puppy.

"I'm sorry, dear," Elizabeth said. "But I have to go down to Monterey this weekend. I'm decorating a new resort hotel and the owners are flying in from Houston to see what I've planned."

Tears welled up in Mallory's eyes, and the legs of her chair scraped on the oak floor as she pushed it away from the table.

"Terrific," she ground out harshly. "Everyone has their important plans. Why should I expect anyone to care what I want to do?"

Jessica shook her head, knowing that while Mallory was overreacting, her feelings were genuine. "I'm sorry, honey," she apologized. "I promise we'll go next time."

Mallory burst into tears, running from the room. "There won't be any next time," she wailed.

An uncomfortable silence settled over the room and Jessica sighed, pushing back her own chair. "Excuse me," she murmured, following her daughter from the kitchen.

Mallory was lying on her bed, sobs pouring forth from deep in her chest. As Jessica tried to soothe her, it crossed

her mind that her daughter's dramatic performance had undoubtedly solved the problem with Quinn. He was probably
on his way out the door about now, thankful that he hadn't
gotten involved with a middle-aged woman and her three
volatile children.

As usual, he surprised her. Jessica heard a slight sound
and looked up to see him standing in the doorway.

"May I make a suggestion?"

"It's not necessary," Jessica said quickly, guessing what
he had in mind."

Mallory looked up, rubbing at her wet cheeks with the
backs of her hands. "What suggestion?" she asked hopefully.

Oh, God, Jessica thought, *don't let her start counting on
Quinn. She's already been hurt enough.*

He entered the small bedroom, sitting down on the edge
of the bunk bed. "Why don't you and I go to the film
festival while your mother's working?"

"Mom?" Mallory's expression begged acquiescence.

"I've already promised your father you'd spend the
weekend with him," she protested weakly.

"That's no problem," Quinn assured her. "Let her go
to her father's tomorrow night and I'll pick her up and take
her into town Saturday morning, then deliver her back to
Mill Valley in the afternoon."

Mallory's wobbly smile was beatific. "That's a wonderful idea," she enthused. "Please, Mom."

Jessica shook her head. "I can't allow you to go out of
your way for us like that," she said firmly.

"Mom!"

"It's a practical solution, Jess," he argued. "Besides, I
can't think of anything I'd rather do than date two gorgeous
women in the same day."

"Two?" Mallory asked, sniffling inelegantly.

Quinn handed her a white handkerchief from his pocket. "Two," he agreed. "I'm taking your mother out dancing Saturday night."

Suddenly they were no longer alone. Jill entered the room, followed by Sara. Elizabeth remained in the doorway.

"Mom never goes dancing," Sara offered.

Quinn grinned. "That's where you're wrong, sweetheart," he argued lightly. "Your mother and I danced together once before."

"Really?" Mallory asked, sitting up cross-legged on the mattress, her curiosity getting the better of her self-pity. "After she and Dad got divorced?"

"Before they were even married," Quinn answered. "My big mistake was not grabbing on to a good thing when I saw it. I never should have let your father get first dibs."

"Wow," Jill breathed, her eyes wide. "That's the most romantic thing I've ever heard!"

"At your age, everything is the most romantic thing you've ever heard," Jessica said dryly. "And for your information, I was all of eight years old."

"That was years and years ago," Sara piped up, making Jessica feel absolutely ancient. "And you still remember?"

"Every minute," Quinn asserted, treating Jessica to a particularly warm gaze, which did not go unnoticed by their audience.

"That's because he probably still hasn't recovered," Jessica insisted, rising from the bed to get a little farther away from Quinn. "I spent the entire time crushing his toes."

"You were left-footed," Elizabeth remembered. "Madame Sorenson never could teach you to follow properly."

"See," Jessica said to Quinn, her look saying I told you so. "Why on earth would you want to subject yourself to another evening of being stepped on?"

His slow smile made her blood simmer. "I'll buy a pair of steel-toed shoes," he promised. His gaze returned to Mallory. "So is it a date?"

"Mom?"

Unable to resist Mallory's blatant pleading, Jessica merely shrugged. "Since I seem to be outvoted once again, I suppose it's all right," she agreed reluctantly.

Quinn stood up, rubbing his hands together as if he'd never expected any other outcome. "Terrific. Now, Jill, what do you say we get started on that homework?"

"All right!" she said instantly, picking up the thick text-book from the floor where she'd obviously flung it in a fit of desperation. "We can work in the den, okay?"

"Fine with me," he replied amiably, following her out the door.

A moment later, Jill was back, flinging her arms enthusiastically around Jessica's waist. "I don't know where you found him, Mom. But I'm sure glad you did."

Then she was gone, her face wreathed in a brilliant smile. "It's not what you think," Jessica insisted, uncomfortable with her two remaining daughters' and her mother's knowing smiles. "There's absolutely nothing going on between Quinn and me. So don't anyone go jumping to conclusions!"

"I wouldn't think of it, dear," Elizabeth murmured, a secretive light flickering in her blue eyes.

Jessica couldn't stand any more of the silent scrutiny. "I've got work to do," she stated briskly, marching from the room.

She spent the remainder of the evening locked in her bedroom, attempting to work on the environmental group's brief. She didn't even come out when Elizabeth knocked on the door, informing her that Jill had managed to unravel the secrets of the Pythagorean theorem and Quinn was leaving.

"I'm sure he can find his way out by now," Jessica muttered under her breath, earning an exasperated sigh from her mother as Elizabeth returned downstairs to join in the chorus of good-nights.

To JESSICA'S RELIEF, the following morning flew by, remaining blissfully uneventful. She experienced a sense of satisfaction as she crossed one item after another off her lengthy list. A few minutes before noon, she was staring down at the paper, debating whether or not to skip over the errand she'd capriciously scribbled down this morning.

The one thing Jessica had always hated most in the world, with the understandable exception of a trip to the dentist, was clothes shopping. That initial dislike had been amplified by the fiasco with Deirdre Hanson. More than three years later, Jessica was still relying solely on the clothing her husband's second wife had selected for the campaign. The last time Elizabeth had managed to coax Jessica into a department store was eighteen months ago. She'd suffered a horribly embarrassing anxiety attack and had no interest in repeating the experience.

Still, she considered, tapping her pen thoughtfully on the paper, Quinn's appreciation of her appearance the other night was etched onto her mind, making her smile whenever she remembered the sensual gleam in his green eyes. It had been a long time since a man had looked at her in that way, even longer since she'd experienced an answering response. As long as both of them understood that nothing could come of their relationship but a brief, enjoyable affair, could it be so wrong to see him from time to time on a social basis?

And, she mused, continuing along that train of thought,

if she was going to have an affair with Quinn, wasn't it only natural to want to look her best? To feel desirable?

She took a brief mental inventory of her closet, knowing that the evening dresses encased in clear plastic were expensive, chic and timeless in design. Deirdre had seen to that. But those clothes belonged to another time. Another Jessica O'Neill. If she was going to do something as uncharacteristic as have a fling with a man whose reputation made Casanova's seem tame by comparison, Jessica wanted something new. Something of her own choosing.

Telling Paula she was taking a long lunch, Jessica left her office, taking the bus to Macy's Union Square. While many cities had experienced a deterioration of their downtown area, the four-block hub surrounding Union Square housed an abundance of elegant stores and richly decorated shops. The names of many prestigious New York stores appeared over several doors, especially along Post Street.

But as the bus approached Union Square, Jessica began to experience a creeping sense of anxiety. Her breathing quickened and suddenly the half-filled bus seemed horribly claustrophobic. She reached up, pulling the cord to direct the driver to stop. Once outside on the sidewalk, she took in deep gulps of air, willing her body to relax.

She told herself that she was a strong, independent woman who should certainly be able to go shopping on her lunch hour without falling apart. But as she walked down Post Street, the street became too narrow, the sidewalks too crowded, the buildings tall and menacing as they towered over her. People jostled her as they walked by in the hurried stride demonstrative of San Franciscans. Everyone seemed to have a purpose, a destination, as they strode past, speaking in a wide variety of native tongues.

Jessica wanted desperately to return to the safety of her office, where she was able to remain in control, where she wouldn't feel as if she'd go spinning off the globe at any moment. But something kept her from turning back.

By the time Jessica reached Macy's, her scalp was beginning to burn as if she had hot coals under her hair. Dizziness, chills, shakiness—all the classic symptoms of an anxiety attack returned and she closed her eyes for a moment, leaning against a wall just inside the door. Her distressed state drew the attention of a young salesclerk.

"Are you all right, ma'am?"

The woman's voice seemed to be coming from the bottom of the sea, but Jessica forced herself to concentrate, to carefully watch the full red lips move as she attempted to decipher the words.

Embarrassment threatened to overcome anxiety as she nodded slowly, taking a deep, calming breath. "Yes," she mumbled. "I'm fine," she said a bit more firmly.

"Are you certain?" Lovely slanted dark eyes viewed Jessica with a very real concern.

"Positive," Jessica assured her, standing up a little straighter. "Could you tell me where I can find the Laura Ashley section?"

"Laura Ashley?" The woman's gaze moved over Jessica's severely tailored suit.

"That's right," Jessica said, managing a smile. "I'm in the mood for something romantic."

An hour and a half later, Jessica was watching the salesclerk ring up the results of her uncharacteristic shopping spree. Handing over her charge card, she experienced a sense of pride that could have only come with scaling Mount Everest. Without any help from the ultrachic saleswoman, she'd chosen a glorious selection of clothing that captured the romantic spirit of a bygone era. More important, she'd overcome the ridiculous anxiety that had been the final lingering result of her marriage breaking up. Instructing the store to have the purchases delivered to her home, she was practically floating on air as she returned to the office.

"It must have been one terrific lunch," Paula observed, taking in Jessica's bright eyes and flushed face. "Anyone I know?"

"I was shopping," Jessica said on a laugh.

"You must have found some real bargains."

"There wasn't a bargain in the bunch. In fact, I'm going to be in debt for the next two years. Lucky for me the girls love hot dogs."

Her secretary shrugged. "Well, whatever turns you on, that's what I always say. Your calls are on your desk."

"Anything important?"

"Sylvia Thacker called four times, your mother called once, asking if you'd be home for dinner. Your ex called, reminding you he was picking up the girls at six-thirty, and Mr. Masterson called, but didn't leave a message."

"Would you get Mr. Masterson on the phone?" Jessica asked, her color rising a little higher with her pleasure.

Paula's eyes narrowed, but she refrained from commenting. "Sure."

Jessica slipped off her shoes, tucking her feet under her as she waited for Paula to ring, announcing Quinn was on the line.

"Hi," she said on a slightly breathless tone.

"Hi. You sound in a better mood than you were last night."

"I am," she agreed. "I'm in an absolutely marvelous, wonderful mood."

"Then you probably don't want to hear my news," Quinn warned almost tentatively.

For a fleeting moment, Jessica experienced the very real fear that Quinn was canceling their date. Not that she could blame him; she'd behaved childishly last evening, displaying about as much maturity as she might have expected from Jill.

"Fire away," she said, unaware she was holding her breath.

"Keith Thacker is on the warpath again."

Jessica's relief caused a silvery laugh to bubble forth. "Is that all? What's the problem now?"

"You *are* feeling good today, aren't you?" She could hear the smile in his voice.

"I am," she said. "Not even the Thackers can burst my bubble."

"I've got an idea. Why don't we both take off and go sailing," he suggested suddenly. "Spring is in the air and you know what they say about a man's fantasies."

"I thought that was a man's fancy."

"Fantasies, fancy, what's the difference? I fancy you, Jessie O'Neill. And let me tell you, sweetheart, you definitely improve a man's fantasy life."

Jessica's body warmed to volcanic proportions. "Don't be such a chauvinist," she chided teasingly. "We women have a few fantasies of our own, you know."

Quinn's pleasure was evident. "I suppose it would be asking too much to know that I was featured in any of yours?"

Jessica realized that she was actually flirting with Quinn. Not only that, she was enjoying every minute of it. "Oh, you've got the starring role," she admitted, her tone throaty and inviting.

He groaned. "Do you have any idea what you're doing to me?"

"I can only hope."

"Let's skip the sailing. I've got a better idea."

Jessica smiled, marveling at the way she was able to

create that unmistakable desire in Quinn's tone. For the first time in her life, she suddenly felt like Jezebel, Delilah, Salome—all the sensual, alluring femmes fatales who'd known those mysterious tricks that could drive a man insane.

"Save that thought," she purred seductively.

This time Quinn's groan revealed a deep masculine pain. "I suppose that means you're not coming out to play with me today."

"I can't," she confirmed, her own voice displaying her disappointment. "But there's still tomorrow night."

"Tomorrow night," he echoed flatly, as if it was eons away. "I suppose we have to go to that damn party."

"You're the one who pointed out that my appearance is mandatory," Jessica teased. "I remember your instructing me on the politics of getting my name on the door."

"How long do we have to hang around, do you think?"

Jessica chewed thoughtfully on a fingernail, enjoying the idea of Quinn suffering as he waited for her answer. She'd never felt this sense of feminine power with Brian.

In truth, Jessica's self-confidence had been as hard to come by as her independence, but over the past three years, she'd decided she liked the woman she'd become. And apparently, Jessica considered with an inward smile, Quinn did, too.

"I'd say just long enough to put in an appearance," she finally said.

"And the girls are going to be in Mill Valley?"

"With their father," Jessica agreed.

"And your mother's going to Monterey?"

"For the entire weekend."

"So you've got the entire house all to yourself?"

"*We've* got the house all to *ourselves*," she corrected silkily.

"I'm going to die waiting for tomorrow night," he complained.

Jessica laughed lightly. "You can't. I'm counting on you to keep your word and take Mallory to that film festival she has her heart set on."

"Are you sure you can't come?" he asked hopefully. "We could neck in the back row."

"I really do have to work. Sorry."

Quinn heaved an exaggerated sigh. "Well, I guess I'll see you tomorrow night."

He started to hang up when Jessica suddenly remembered he'd called about Keith Thacker's latest complaint. "Quinn, wait a minute," she said quickly.

"Change your mind?"

"Mr. Thacker," she reminded him.

"Oh." His downcast tone indicated it was not his favorite topic of conversation, either. "He's ready to kill Sylvia for shaving that damn dog."

"He was ready to do that yesterday," Jessica said with a shrug.

"He was ready to wring her neck yesterday," Quinn corrected. "Today I think he'd receive a great deal of pleasure in cutting his spiteful wife into little pieces and feeding her to the sharks out in the bay.... It turns out the little guy is suddenly worthless as a stud."

"Why?" Jessica asked curiously. Then she sucked in her breath. "Don't tell me Sylvia had him neutered?"

"Nothing that drastic. But it seems a certain sexy lady Lhasa apso finds bald suitors less than appealing. She refused to have anything to do with him."

Jessica laughed at that, tears welling up in her eyes.

"Hey, it isn't that funny," Quinn complained. "Poor Maximilian is one frustrated male right now." His voice deepened, sounding like ebony velvet. "A state I can empathize with completely."

"He'll just have to suffer until his hair grows back, I suppose," Jessica stated blithely.

"What about me?"

"You have lovely hair, Quinn. Thick and wavy, like spun gold. It's one of those things I like best about you."

"What else do you like?"

The sensuality in Quinn's voice was so palpable that it practically reached through the telephone line to touch her. "I'll tell you tomorrow night," she whispered, suddenly shaken by what she was agreeing to. What she had, in all honesty, invited.

"I'm going to hold you to that, sweetheart," he warned huskily.

"I certainly hope so.... Oh, do you know how to get to the house to pick up Mallory?"

"She gave me directions last night," he answered absently. "So," he said on a sigh, "are you really working late tonight or hiding from your ex?"

"A little of both," Jessica admitted, not overly surprised by Quinn's accurate perception. There had been more than one occasion when he'd seemed to possess the ability to read her mind.

"I don't suppose you'd like to go out for a late supper?"

"I've got to be at the office early tomorrow morning."

"You realize, of course, you're condemning me to another night spent in a cold, lonely shower."

"I'm sorry."

"She's sorry," he muttered. "I suppose I'd better let you get back to work. Unless you want to talk dirty for a while?"

"Goodbye, Quinn," Jessica said, her smile belying her firm tone.

"Goodbye, Jess." His voice reached out to her like a caress. "I want you to know I'm going to spend the next thirty hours thinking about tomorrow night."

Jessica swallowed. "Me too," she agreed before finally breaking the connection.

Well, she'd done it. Jessica O'Neill, known for her careful, planned life-style, had just agreed to have an affair. As she spent the rest of the day attempting to concentrate on her work, Jessica wondered why, despite the undeniable sense of expectation, that idea made her feel just a little bit sad.

CHAPTER SEVEN

JESSICA GREW INCREASINGLY NERVOUS as she prepared for George Bennington's anniversary party. She told herself that at her age, it was ridiculous to be so rattled by the prospect of going out with a man. But it had been a very long time since she'd been out on a date. Fifteen years to be precise.

The term itself was ridiculous. Grown women didn't go out on "dates." There must be another word for what she was about to do. There were several, Jessica thought reluctantly, but she didn't like the sound of any of them. She knew times had changed, knew that there was nothing wrong with exploring the physical desire she'd been experiencing for Quinn Masterson. Yet some nagging little vestige of her upbringing was threatening to take the pleasure from the act.

Nice girls did not go to bed with men they weren't married to, Jessica told herself firmly. All right, she admitted as an afterthought, even in her day, that was not an unknown occurrence. She certainly hadn't been a virgin when she'd married Brian. But she'd loved him—or at least she'd thought she had—and the first time they'd made love had been the result of an unexpected flare of passion. It was certainly not as coldly planned as what she intended to do with Quinn tonight.

As she lay in the tub, surrounded by fragrant bubbles, sipping a calming glass of white wine, Jessica considered that she had spent her entire life seeking other people's approval. She'd been an obedient, studious child, eager for a word of praise or a smile from her larger-than-life father. Terrance MacLaughlin had not spent a great deal of time at home during her childhood; his career had always taken precedence. On those rare occasions that her father was willing to spend time with her, Jessica had never wanted to do anything that might possibly displease him.

She'd continued that same self-destructive behavior in her marriage, dropping out in her second year of law school when Brian insisted that he be the sole breadwinner of his family. He viewed her desire for a career of her own as a threat to his masculine self-esteem. Her place, he had instructed firmly, was home taking care of his house and his children. He'd never be able to love a woman hard-boiled enough to survive the corporate battles found in the real world.

So Jessica, eager to be loved, had acquiesced, creating a comfortable realm where Brian ruled as king, everything revolving around his wishes, his desires. If Jessica experienced resentment from time to time, she assured herself it was a small price to pay to be loved. It was only much later that she discovered what her behavior had cost her in terms of self-esteem and wasted years.

As she sipped the wine slowly, Jessica reminded herself there had been no award ceremonies for wife of the year. No plaques or trophies handed out to "nice girls." When forced out into the high-pressure world that was so different from the peaceful suburban existence she'd known in Mill Valley, she had at first felt like a foreigner in an alien land. She didn't know how to speak the language, play the games.

Jessica had had no idea how one measured accomplishments, judged the constant stream of petty mishaps. For too many years she had measured her success by sparkling windows and pristinely white shirt collars, while a sunken soufflé represented failure. The only things that had remained constant during that time of change were the girls.

Even now, each night before falling asleep, Jessica whispered a short prayer of thanksgiving that they'd avoided the pitfalls so many of her friends' children had fallen prey to. Although her daughters were certainly not the mythical darlings she'd pictured children to be in that romanticized time before motherhood, neither had they ever given her any real cause for concern. In that respect, Jessica figured, she was very lucky.

And she was fortunate to have met a man like Quinn Masterson, she decided, the wine going a little to her head in the warm, humid air of the bathroom. Every woman was entitled to one reckless fling in her life; she'd earned it. Determined to make the most of this weekend, Jessica rose from the tub, her body perfumed with the velvet cling of the bathwater.

She smoothed lotion over every pore, following up with a dusting of talcum powder that left her skin smooth and satiny. She took an unusually long time with her makeup, wanting to appear as feminine as possible, as attractive as she imagined Quinn's usual women to be.

By the time the doorbell rang, Jessica had regained her self-confidence and forced herself to walk slowly downstairs, unwilling to admit her eagerness to see him once again.

Her reward came as Quinn's eyes widened, sweeping over her from the top of her Gibson girl hairstyle, past her slender curves enhanced by the Victorian-style ivory lace gown that swirled about her calves, down to her feet, which were clad in sandals so delicate that they brought to mind Cinderella's glass slippers.

"This," he said, his voice uneven as he moved into the foyer, "was definitely worth the wait."

She smiled, twirling around in the soft glow of the antique wall light. "I'm glad you approve," she murmured, her cheeks flushed with feminine satisfaction that he found her desirable.

"I approved of you in that cute pink running suit," he countered, drawing her into his arms. "I thought you were delightful in that feminine little outfit the other night, and found you sexy as hell in those tight jeans. But this…"

He tilted his head back, gazing down at her, his eyes burning. "This is every fantasy I've ever had, come to life."

Jessica's lips curved in a teasing, provocative smile. There was a heady element of power in this situation as she realized how much Quinn wanted her. How much he needed her.

She pressed her palm against his chest, thrilled by the strong beat of his heart beneath her fingertips. "You're not so bad yourself," she murmured, her fingers stroking the front of his pleated white dress shirt.

She could feel his low chuckle. "I'm glad to know I pass inspection."

"Oh, you do," she agreed. "I've always thought men in tuxedos were very sexy."

"Men?" He arched a brow, revealing an unexpected jealous streak that Jessica found absolutely thrilling.

"Don't worry, Quinn," she said, her hands going up to curl about his neck. "Not only do you pass, you set the standard."

They were touching from their chests to their thighs, generating a heat that belied the cool evening temperature.

"You know that you're making it extremely difficult for me to think about your career advancement," he murmured, punctuating his words with light kisses against her lips.

"I know."

"Do you also know that if you keep moving against me that way we'll never get out of here?"

Her fingers were playing in the gilt strands of hair at the back of his neck, her hips moving in seductive little circles against his.

"I know that, too."

"Ah, Jess," he sighed, his breath a warm breeze against her mouth. "You sure picked one hell of a time to pull out the stops."

He kissed her then, a long, lingering kiss that seemed to go on forever. Through her dazed senses, Jessica felt his body trembling with unsatiated desire. His hands moved over her, molding her shape under the lacy dress as if she were malleable clay, and as she dissolved under his touch, Jessica realized that the soft, desperate moans were coming from her own ravaged lips.

All too soon those wonderful, seductive hands moved to her shoulders, putting her a little away from him. "We'd better go," he suggested flatly.

She nodded, her trembling fingers stroking his freshly shaven cheek. "I suppose so," she agreed without a great deal of enthusiasm.

"We won't stay long."

"Just put in an appearance."

"Offer our congratulations."

Her liquid gaze held vast feminine promises. "And then we'll come home."

"Home," he echoed, giving her a short, hard kiss on her pink lips.

"Do me one favor," he said, his voice still far from

steady as they drove toward the Benningtons' penthouse apartment.

"Anything," Jessica agreed promptly.

He looked over at her, shaking his head as he gave her a lopsided smile. "Don't look at me that way while we're at the party. Or my resultant behavior may end up getting you canned."

Jessica grinned. "I'll try," she murmured. "But you know, it just might be worth it."

Quinn reached out, taking her hand and lifting it to his lips. "I knew you were a wanton at heart," he professed happily, lowering her hand to his thigh.

Jessica felt light-headed, filled with a strange happiness she'd never known before. "Is that so bad?" she asked, batting her lashes flirtatiously, her fingers stroking the firm muscle under the black dress slacks.

"Honey, I wouldn't have you any other way.... However, if you don't behave yourself, you're going to be forced to walk into that party with a blatantly indecent escort."

"Oh?"

He moved her hand to demonstrate the effect she was having on him. "Any more questions?"

With a forwardness that at any other time would have shocked her, Jessica was in no hurry to retrieve her hand.

"Just one," she said, as he brought the Maserati to a screeching halt in the subterranean parking garage of the building.

"What's that?" he asked raggedly, closing his eyes to her intimate caress.

"Is it time to leave yet?"

Quinn chuckled and picked up her hand, placing it on her own lap. "Behave yourself, wanton," he instructed firmly. Then he leaned his head back, closing his eyes.

"Give me a little time," he muttered. "This isn't that easy a task."

Jessica studied the handsome face only inches from hers, watching his smooth brow furrow with concentration, his dark lashes resting against his cheeks, his full lips still curved in a little half smile. A warmth infused her body that went far beyond physical desire, and for a fleeting moment, she thought it might actually be love she was experiencing.

Then she forced that errant, romantic notion to the back of her mind. It was only natural that she was looking for an excuse to justify her uncharacteristic behavior. She had admittedly come a long way in the past three years, but her early socialization went deep. There was obviously still a part of her that needed to feel she was in love before going to bed with a man. That's all it was, the pragmatic side of her nature decided. So long as she recognized this odd feeling for what it was, everything would be all right.

The Benningtons' apartment took up the entire floor of the glittering glass monolith towering above the city, offering a spectacular view of sparkling lights and the darkened waters of San Francisco Bay. The party was in full swing when Jessica and Quinn arrived, and as she viewed the number of people crowding the room, Jessica knew no one would notice if she and Quinn escaped the anniversary celebration early.

"Ms O'Neill!" George Bennington greeted her enthusiastically, as if the unpleasant scene in his office earlier in the week had never occurred. "How nice you were able to attend our little party."

Jessica smiled and shook the outstretched hand of the senior partner and founder of Bennington, Marston, White and Lowell.

"Thank you for inviting me," she answered politely. "I hope my gift arrived."

"I'm sure it did," he replied absently. "Gloria takes care of that type of thing." His gaze moved to Jessica's escort, his eyes narrowing slightly. "Quinn, it's good to see you again."

"Always a pleasure to be invited," Quinn responded. "Congratulations."

"Yes, well, the party was Gloria's idea. To be perfectly honest, I've lost track of the years. It still amazes me we've managed to stay together so long."

"It's an admirable accomplishment in this day and age," Quinn agreed.

"Speaking of which," George stated, "aren't you handling Keith Thacker's divorce?"

"Unfortunately, yes."

"And you, Ms O'Neill, are representing Mrs. Thacker, if I'm not mistaken."

Jessica was not fooled by his casual tone. "That's right."

"Not that I'm questioning your integrity," he qualified his next statement, "but don't you think your, uh, relationship with Quinn might be considered a conflict of interest?"

"Relationship?" Jessica inquired blandly, not willing to help the man out.

Once again she got the distinct impression her employer was not an admirer of women attorneys. How dare he imply that she'd compromise her client because of any feelings she might have for Quinn!

"Ms O'Neill has been representing Sylvia with annoying persistence," Quinn interjected smoothly. "In fact, she's probably the finest champion the woman has found. You don't have a thing to worry about, George." His tone hardened just enough to close the door on that particular subject without being impolite.

George Bennington's smile was irritatingly unctuous and once again Jessica was reminded of Quinn's prowess as an attorney. Obviously, while not caring about her feelings, the older man was reluctant to offend Quinn.

"I'm pleased to hear that," he stated, looking past them to another couple who'd just arrived. "Why don't you two get something to drink?"

"That's a terrific idea," Quinn said, putting his hand lightly on Jessica's back and leading her in the direction of the bar, which had been set up at one end of the vast room.

"The nerve of that man," Jessica spluttered as they walked away. "To even suggest that I'd allow my personal life to interfere with my work!"

"Don't let him get to you," Quinn suggested calmly. "He's always that way with first-year attorneys."

"Women first-year attorneys," she muttered under her breath.

"*All* first-year attorneys," he corrected.

She looked up at him. "How would you know?"

"I spent my first year out of law school at Bennington, Marston and White. Lowell wasn't a partner yet."

"Oh." She was silent for a moment, considering that. "And he was that rough even way back then?"

Quinn chuckled. "You don't have to make it sound like the olden days, you know. Back before dinosaurs roamed the earth. I'm only forty, Jess."

Her irritation melted away and she grinned up at him. "That old?" she asked sweetly. "My goodness you've held your age remarkably well, Quinn." He scowled, causing Jessica to laugh lightly in return. Then her expression turned serious again. "Really, was he so frustratingly un-bending when you were there?"

"We called it hell year," he revealed. "And if anything, I think he was even rougher on me." His handsome face turned thoughtful for a moment. "No, I take that back. I know he was rougher on me."

"Why?"

Quinn shrugged. "I suppose it had something to do with bending over backward to demonstrate that family didn't receive preferential treatment."

"Family?" Jessica stared at him blankly.

Quinn arched an incredulous brow. "You didn't know?"

"Know what?"

"That George Bennington is my uncle? I didn't think there was anyone in the legal community who wasn't aware of that little fact."

His words only served to remind Jessica that while Quinn was building his career, she'd been home folding diapers. Now, although she was trying her best to catch up, she secretly wondered if Quinn wouldn't have more in common with someone like Vanessa. Or Pamela Stuart.

Quinn misread her dour expression. "Believe me, honey, it'll get better."

"I certainly hope so," she muttered. "Because to tell you the truth, I've gotten an offer from the D.A.'s office that I'm seriously considering."

"Really?" He looked down at her with renewed interest. "I wouldn't have thought that any woman who starts her day with a detailed list would enjoy the chaos oftentimes found in the D.A.'s office."

"You have to be just as thorough in your work if you want to prosecute," Jessica objected. "Otherwise there'd be no convictions."

"That's true," he agreed amiably. "However, you also have to admit that the ability to punt, when necessary, is a decided asset."

"I'm working on that," Jessica said with a slight smile. "The way I look at it, the Thackers, if nothing else, are a good proving ground."

Quinn chuckled, his eyes warm as he gazed down at her. "You are just one surprise after another, pretty lady."

Jessica's eyes met his, and there was an instant of heat. "Thank you, sir," she said lightly. Then she smiled. "I thought you'd promised me a drink."

"I'd rather ravish your delectable body."

"Your uncle would love that," Jessica said with a musical, happy laugh. As they continued to weave their way through the throng of party guests to the bar, something occurred to her. "If it gets so much better," she challenged, "why did you leave?"

Quinn laughed heartily. "Be truthful, Jess. Can you see George and me working together?"

No, she considered thoughtfully, not at all. They were both incredibly strong-willed men. "I suppose not," she decided aloud.

"You're not the only one who's experienced a need to establish a sense of independence," he stated quietly.

Jessica could read the understanding in his gaze and was trying to think of something to say that would break this silken web that was settling down around them. Then she heard a familiar voice calling her name.

"Dad," she replied with surprise, turning around to view the tall, silver-haired man forging his way through the crowd. "What are you doing here?"

"One of the disadvantages of being an august magistrate in this town is that I get invited to all these bashes," he replied with a grimace. "Hello, Quinn. It's nice to see my daughter's finally latched onto someone who's almost good enough for her."

"Spoken like a properly adoring father," Quinn answered with a broad smile. "How's retirement treating you, Mac?"

"It's the pits," Terrance MacLaughlin confided. "Don't ever retire, Quinn. If I'd known how it was going to change my life, they'd have had to drag me screaming and kicking from the bench."

"It must be quite an adjustment," he agreed sympathetically.

"That's the understatement of the year." Jessica's father took a long swallow of bourbon. "Where's your mother?" he asked suddenly.

"In Monterey."

Terrance "Mac" MacLaughlin muttered a low oath. "I figured she'd be here. That's the only reason I showed up." He ran his finger inside his starched collar. "I've always hated these monkey suits."

"Why did you think Mother would be here?" Jessica inquired curiously.

"She and Gloria Bennington are old friends."

"Perhaps she didn't feel like celebrating a wedding anniversary when you two are having problems," Jessica offered, hoping that her father would admit he'd come here to convince his wife to return home.

"She always was as stubborn as a Missouri mule," Mac grumbled. "And she's gotten a lot worse lately."

"That's the same thing she says about you."

"Sure, take your mother's side, Jessica. You women always stick together, don't you?"

Jessica sighed, putting her hand on her father's arm. "I'm not taking anyone's side," she stated firmly. "I just wish you two would get together and discuss whatever's bothering you."

"I've tried. She won't listen to reason.... Do you know she told me that I drove her crazy? The woman waited

forty-six years to let me know I was in her way. Told me
to get out of the house and leave her alone.'' His oath was
short and impatient. "Well, I figure Alaska's far enough
away that I won't be a nuisance any longer.''

"I can't believe Mother said exactly that," Jessica argued. "What were you doing?"

Her father arched a silvery brow. "Are you judging me
guilty without a fair hearing, Jessie? Your own father?"

Jessica exchanged a frustrated glance with Quinn who'd
wisely remained silent during the interchange. At her silent
request, he spoke up.

"Why don't we get you a refill, Mac," he suggested
smoothly. "It'll give us a chance to talk man to man." He
looked down at Jessica, his green eyes smiling. "You won't
mind fending for yourself for a few minutes, will you,
sweetheart?"

"Not at all," she answered gratefully. Going up on her
toes, she kissed her father's cheek. "It was nice seeing you,
Dad. We should get together more often."

"If you're ever in Alaska, look me up," he muttered,
allowing himself to be led away by Quinn, who gave Jessica a wink over his shoulder.

"Sweetheart, is it?"

Jessica's shoulders stiffened at the unveiled sarcasm in
the deep voice behind her. She slowly turned, eyeing Brian
O'Neill. This party was definitely turning into a family reunion, she thought grimly. And this was one former family
member she could go all evening without meeting.

"I didn't know you were going to be here."

"Gracious as always, I see."

Jessica refused to respond to her former husband's bait-
ing. "I thought you wanted to be with the girls this weekend. Who's taking care of them? Deirdre?" Despite her

best intentions not to show her irritation, Jessica's tone indicated the improbability of that particular scenario.

"Deirdre's in New York on another one of those blasted buying trips of hers. The girls wanted a slumber party with the Franklin kids and I didn't think they needed me around for that. Mrs. Wilson's staying at the house."

"They've missed Bonnie and Lori," Jessica agreed. "So, what are you doing here?"

"You know Bennington handles O'Neill Development's legal work," Brian reminded her. "I received an invitation at the office last week. I wasn't planning to attend until I spent last night and today hearing all about Mr. Wonderful. I decided I'd better warn you about the big mistake you're making."

"I'm not making any mistake," Jessica argued coolly. "But even if I were, Brian, you're in no position to offer advice about my life. You were the one who said I needed to become more independent." She held out her arms. "Meet Jessica O'Neill, modern career woman."

"Modern enough to sleep with a man with my daughters in the next room?" he sneered.

Jessica felt her color rise. "Not that it's any of your business, but I haven't been doing anything that could harm the girls in any way."

"You let Masterson turn their heads with his slick charm. What are they going to do when he dumps you and moves on to his next conquest?"

Jessica pressed her lips together, her blue eyes circling the room, looking for Quinn. She was definitely in need of a drink. Unfortunately he seemed to have disappeared, along with her father. She schooled her tone to appear calm, uncaring.

"I imagine they'll do the same as they did when you dumped me. Carry on."

His dark eyes narrowed. "You never used to be this strong," Brian mused aloud. "A few years ago you would have been running from the room in tears."

"A few years ago, you would have been able to hurt me," she countered.

"And now?"

She shrugged, surprised to find that although Brian admittedly irritated her, she didn't feel any lingering pain. Or any emotion of any kind, for that matter.

"I've grown up."

His gaze darkened as it moved over her, taking in her thick auburn hair, the stylish yet romantic dress, her long legs clad in sheer stockings. Jessica remained still, submitting to his lengthy study, confident that she looked uniquely attractive.

"I can see you have," he murmured. "Since it seems Masterson has deserted you, why don't you let me get you a drink and we'll talk about old times."

The invitation in his deep voice was unmistakable, and rather than being pleased by the fact that her former husband suddenly found her desirable, Jessica was stunned to discover that she felt absolutely nothing.

"This is supposed to be a party, Brian. Not a wake." Glancing around the room, she spotted Quinn headed their way. "Have a good evening," she suggested with a smile, leaving him staring after her as she went to meet Quinn.

"I see you weren't lonely." He didn't bother to hide his annoyance.

She looked up at him curiously. "Are you by any chance jealous?"

"You're damn right I am. I leave you alone for a few minutes and return to find your ex practically eating you up with those beady little eyes. How am I supposed to feel?"

She took his arm and maneuvered through the crowd of guests to the French doors leading out to the balcony. "I think I could use some fresh air."

"The fog's in; it's going to be cool out there," he warned.

Her smile was unmistakably inviting. "Then you'll just have to keep me warm."

The fog had indeed rolled in like a thick blanket, a few stars valiantly managing to make themselves seen as they sparkled in the night sky. A waning moon cast a shadowy, silver light against the top of the Golden Gate Bridge as it thrust its way above the veiled entrance to San Francisco Bay. The sounds of the party drifted away and despite the steady hum of traffic several stories below, Jessica and Quinn could have been the only two people in the world.

"I'm glad Brian was here tonight," Jessica said softly.

"You don't know what that does to my ego," Quinn muttered.

She turned, her back against the railing as she placed her palms on either side of his stern face. "You don't understand," she protested, holding his frustrated gaze with eyes as soft and blue as a tropical lagoon.

"All these years, while I've been building a life for myself, in some little corner of my mind, I've been wanting to become the kind of woman that could compete with the Deirdre Hansons of the world. The type of modern woman who could interest a man, meet him on an equal basis."

"So now you've discovered you've made it. Congratulations. You can steal your husband back from his new wife and it'll be just one happy family again."

Jessica refused to be intimidated by Quinn's icy tone. "Brian did seem honestly interested in me," she admitted. "But the surprising thing was that I didn't care." She shook her head regretfully, her voice quavering ever so slightly. "All these years I'd dreamed of that moment, imagined how I'd feel when I finally earned his approval. Not that I ever thought about going back to him," she stated firmly. "I just wanted him to realize what he'd thrown away without a backward glance."

Quinn was silent for a long time, staring past Jessica out into the billowy mist wrapping itself around the city. "I think I can understand that," he said finally. "So how did it feel?"

Jessica's laugh was rich and full-bodied. "That's the amazing thing. Nothing happened. I kept waiting to feel something—pleasure, vindication, satisfaction. But all I could think about was getting away to find you."

"Oh, Jess." One hand cupped her cheek, while the long fingers of the other splayed against her throat, causing her blood to beat against the delicate ivory cameo. "I was ready to kill that bastard when I saw the way he was looking at you. After what he did, he doesn't deserve a second chance.

"You're mine now, Jess," he professed fiercely. "I've waited too long for you to give you up now."

The possessive statement tolled a warning in the back of Jessica's mind, but she was given no time to consider Quinn's huskily stated words as his mouth fused with hers, scorching away all reason.

The night breeze was creating havoc to Jessica's carefully coiffed hair, fingers of damp fog brushed against her cheeks, but all she was aware of was the heat of Quinn's mouth, the hardness of his body pressing against hers, arousing the most primitive of womanly instincts as she molded her softness to his rigid strength. She was soaring, flying free and high, meeting Quinn's own desperate desire and surpassing it as a shock of need rocketed through her. She was beyond thought, beyond reason, crying out softly as Quinn dragged his lips away, breathing heavily as he rested his chin atop her disheveled hair.

''I think we're having an earthquake,'' he managed to gasp between gulps of air.

Jessica's own breathing was unsteady as she turned her head to press a kiss against his neck. ''I don't care,'' she whispered, her lips plucking at the warm, slightly scratchy skin. ''I want to make love with you, Quinn.''

''Here? That'd be a bit dangerous, darlin', even discounting the earthquake.''

''I feel like being reckless tonight. Let's live dangerously, Quinn.'' Her fingers were toying with the onyx studs on his shirt.

''You are living recklessly, Jess,'' he murmured, lifting her hand to his lips and eyeing her seriously over the top of their linked fingers. ''I don't think you begin to realize what you're starting here.''

Her soft smile was provocative and definitely enticing. ''Why don't we go home and put your theory to the test, counselor?''

Quinn suddenly realized how Adam must have felt when Eve waved that bright red apple under his nose. She still didn't understand. He wanted her—he wasn't about to deny that. But he wanted more than Jessica's body, as lovely and desirable as it was. He wanted her heart. And yes, dammit, he considered almost fiercely, he wanted her soul.

He understood that she'd suffered with the breakup of her marriage. He realized that she'd undergone a significant metamorphosis in order to become the self-sufficient attorney she was today. He ached for her loss, just as he was pained by her apparent inability to realize that love didn't equal weakness, marriage didn't have to mean subjugation.

Quinn wanted to spend the rest of his life with Jessica. He wanted it for himself, but he wanted it for her, as well.

And her daughters. He knew they could be a family, if she'd only let things take their natural course. If she'd only open her eyes to the love he had to offer.

If he gave in to temptation and took Jessica to bed tonight, he'd only be muddying the waters, allowing her to confuse sex with love. If he wanted to play this thing the smart way, he'd wait until she was ready to admit the feeling she had for him couldn't be anything else but love. But God, how he wanted her!

What the hell, Quinn considered with an accepting, inward shrug as he took Jessica's hand and let her lead him back into the room to the front door. He never claimed to be bucking for sainthood.

CHAPTER EIGHT

As QUINN GUIDED the Maserati through the fogbound streets, Jessica experienced a sense of anticipation like nothing she'd ever known. She was actually going to do it, she realized. She was going to have a cold-blooded, casual affair.

Not that there was anything cold-blooded about Quinn, she mused, surreptitiously studying him as he drove. He radiated a masculinity so strong, so powerful, so heated that there had been times it had threatened to overwhelm her. She trembled just thinking about the way his touch could bring her blood to flame.

"Cold?"

Those sharp green eyes didn't miss a thing, she thought. Jessica shook her head, meeting his questioning gaze. "No," she admitted on a whisper. "I think I'm burning up."

He treated her to a slow, sensual smile. "Don't feel like the Lone Ranger."

Her hand had been resting on his knee and now he covered it with his, entwining their fingers, his thumb stroking little circles against the sensitive skin of her palm. Jessica felt herself melting into the glove-soft leather seat.

"Your dad's having a hard time adjusting to retirement," he revealed, as if he found it necessary to turn the conversation to something more casual in order to survive the short drive to Jessica's town house.

"Is that what you two were talking about?"

"That. And other things. He thinks quite highly of you, by the way. I had to promise my intentions were honorable."

Jessica felt the embarrassed flush staining her cheeks and was grateful for the cover of darkness. "I hate to have you lie to him," she murmured. "But it's probably for the best."

He slanted her an appraising glance. "What makes you think I was lying?"

Jessica was horrified by the way those simple words managed to pierce her self-protective armor. No, she warned herself, she couldn't allow her desire for the man to cloud her resolve. This was a fleeting, transitory relationship. A night, a weekend, a month at the very most. Surely in thirty long days this attraction would run its course. Little habits would begin to grate on nerves, passions would cool, irritations would set in. Jessica was a realist; she knew that happily ever after was a myth originated in fairy tales, perpetuated by romantic storytellers.

"Did he say anything about the reason for Mother leaving their house?" she asked, changing the subject.

Quinn stifled the urge to shake her until those lovely teeth rattled. He'd always thought of himself as being single-minded, but Jessica's stubbornness surpassed anything he'd ever known.

"It seems that in an effort to make himself useful, he rearranged her office."

"Oh, no," Jessica groaned, recalling the cluttered chaos that Elizabeth had always worked in. Although others might wonder how she ever found anything in the muddle of wallpaper samples, paint chips and bolts of fabric, her mother had always possessed the ability to locate a desired swatch of material without a moment's hesitation.

"While she was in Houston last week, meeting with those developers, he installed shelves on all four walls and, as he so succinctly put it, 'tidied things up a bit for her.'"

"I imagine she was thrilled," Jessica said dryly.

"According to Mac, she stared at his remodeling for about ten minutes, then, telling him exactly what he could do with his handiwork, left the house without even bothering to unpack."

"I can't believe she'd throw away forty-six years of marriage just because of a few shelves. No matter how angry she was."

Quinn shrugged. "I think it was just the last straw. Apparently they've been arguing about what she calls his interference for the past six months since his retirement. Mac, of course, only sees himself as trying to help. I think he's at loose ends these days."

"Poor Dad," she murmured. "I know how it is to feel useless."

Quinn didn't comment on that, instead squeezing her fingers reassuringly. "Give them time to work it out," he advised. "If I tell you something in confidence, promise you won't warn Elizabeth?"

"I promise."

"He's on his way to Monterey."

Well, Jessica considered, that was something. "I hope he uses a little more finesse when he tries to convince her to return home," she stated thoughtfully. "I don't think Mother will respond to his usual steamroller tactics."

"Like mother, like daughter," Quinn murmured, pulling up to the curb in front of her house. He sat still for a long, silent moment, leaning his forearms on the steering wheel, staring out into the well of darkness beyond the windshield. When he finally turned to look at Jessica, his gaze was unnervingly somber.

"I don't want to push you into anything tonight, Jess," he said quietly, his green eyes locked onto her face. "If we make love, I need to know that you want me as much as I want you."

She leaned forward, brushing his lips with her own. "Let me show you exactly how much I want you, Quinn," she whispered, her warm breath fanning his face as she rained kisses over his stern features.

Muffling a groan, Quinn needed no further invitation.

Jessica was suddenly unreasonably nervous as they entered the house. "Would you like a drink?" she offered.

"Sounds nice," Quinn agreed amiably.

"I think there's some white wine in the refrigerator," she said. "But if you'd rather have Scotch, or brandy, or something else..." Her voice drifted off.

"Whatever you're having is fine."

She turned in the direction of the kitchen, then stopped. "I don't want anything to drink," she said softly.

"I don't, either," he admitted, taking her hand as they climbed the stairs.

The house was too quiet, and Jessica found herself longing for some of Jill's pulsating rock music to break the thick silence.

"I never thanked you for taking Mallory to that film festival today," she said.

"I had a good time," Quinn replied easily. "Mallory did, too, I think. Although your mother would have definitely disapproved of our behavior."

"Oh? Why?"

He grinned down at her. "Do you have any idea how much popcorn and candy an eleven-year-old can consume? Just imagine the additives."

Jessica laughed, as she was supposed to. She was grateful to Quinn for lightening the mood.

His eyes widened as he entered Jessica's bedroom, although he wondered why he was surprised by the brilliant canvases hanging on her walls.

"You painted those, didn't you?" he asked, already knowing the answer as he studied the bright, abstract swirls of color.

"When I was married," she agreed, unreasonably anxious for his opinion. "Mother cringes every time she walks into the room. She says they clash horribly with the Victorian floral wallpaper."

"It suits you," he replied, his gaze circling the decidedly feminine room, then returning to Jessica's softly flushed face. "You've got a lot of unbridled passion lurking under that enticingly delicate exterior, Jessie."

So thrilled was she by the desire burning in Quinn's dark gaze that Jessica forgot her usual assertion that she was a strong, independent woman. At this moment, she only wanted him to find her desirable.

"I'm glad it's you," she said quietly, moving into his arms.

Quinn looked down at her questioningly.

"It's been a very long time," she explained, faltering a bit as she succumbed to the lambent desire she viewed in those green eyes. "I didn't want to do this with just anybody. It seemed important that it was someone I..."

Her voice drifted off as she tried to come up with the proper word. *Not love,* she told herself firmly. Love implied commitment, demands, weakness. She couldn't allow herself to yield to its false, ethereal promises.

Quinn waited patiently, feeling Jessica's inner struggle as she tried to sort out her feelings. One part of him wanted to kill Brian O'Neill for leaving Jessica so wounded, so afraid to trust. Another part of him was thankful that the guy hadn't realized a terrific thing when he had it. If Jessica's idiot of a husband hadn't left her, she and Quinn might never had met. What a void that would have left in his life!

"Care for," she finished weakly, resting her forehead against the firm line of his shoulder.

Well, it wasn't precisely what he'd wanted to hear. But it was enough. For now.

His hands moved to her hair, pulling out the mother-of-pearl combs that held it in precarious order, his fingers sifting through the fiery waves as they tumbled down over her shoulders.

"I love your hair down," he murmured, grazing the fragrant softness with his lips. "You remind me of something from an eighteenth-century novel."

Her full lips curved in a slight smile as she tilted her head back to look up at him. "Ah," she said on a slight sigh, "we're going to play lusty aristocrat and naughty milkmaid."

His fingers toyed with the cameo at her throat, finding the catch and releasing it. "Uh-uh," he argued, opening the lacy frill at her neck to press his lips against her skin. Jessica's pulse leaped in response. "You're every inch an aristocrat, sweetheart. The kind of woman who instilled all that passion in pirates and gamekeepers."

Jessica felt her legs weakening as he slowly began to unbutton her dress, his lips grazing each new bit of freed skin, tasting her warming flesh, drinking in a sweet scent that reminded him of lilacs in April. He took his time manipulating the pearl buttons through the silk loops, like a man unwrapping the most special of gifts.

"This was a bad idea," she whispered, her fingers digging into his shoulders as she clung to him for support.

For a brief, horrible moment, Quinn thought Jessica was

about to change her mind. But as her body swayed against him, he decided he might be wrong.

"What was a bad idea?" His tongue was cutting moist swaths down the slope of her breasts, causing an ache that reached to her very core.

"This dress," she complained, flinging her head back, granting him further access to her creamy skin. "I should have found one with a zipper."

He chuckled as the dress finally fell open to her waist. "Anticipation is half the fun," he murmured, taking one pebbled bud between his lips.

Jessica's head was spinning and she was certain she'd faint at any moment. A dizzying excitement raced through her and she thrust her hands into his thick, crisp hair, pressing him against her suddenly moist skin.

The heat seeping into her body was consuming her, licking through her veins, spiraling outward until she thought she'd explode. But still Quinn took his time, moving his head to the other breast, treating it to a torture just as sweet, just as prolonged.

"Quinn, please," she begged, her fingers fumbling with the studs of his dress shirt, anxious for a feel of the hard chest hidden by the crisp white material. She'd never wanted a man like this—never needed a man as much as she needed Quinn at this moment.

He pushed the dress off her shoulders, going down on his knees as he continued to bring it over the soft swell of her hips, down her trembling thighs, to where it finally lay in a lacy puddle at her feet. As if in a trance, Jessica stepped out of the expensive dress, closing her eyes to the sensual torment as Quinn repeated the motion with her silk half-slip. His eyes seemed to burst into flame at what he found waiting for him.

Jessica had allowed her sensuality to run rampant while

shopping for this evening, and if she'd been worried that Quinn might find her purchases too contrived, too costumey, that fear dissolved as he viewed the lacy white garter belt, bikini panties and ivory silk stockings that clung to her legs.

"That outfit definitely invites ravishing," he said huskily.

"Oh, yes," she breathed, shaking like a leaf under gale-force winds.

Quinn slipped the sandals from her feet, then began kissing every inch of her long, slender leg, stopping just short of the lacy confection that framed her femininity. He forged a similar trail back down her other thigh, nibbling at the back of her knee, his tongue dampening the silk covering her ankle. A blood-red passion whipped through her and just when she knew she could no longer stand, he slowly lowered her to the bed.

"You're exquisite." His lips trailed over her soft stomach, his voice echoing against her heated flesh. "Everything I've ever imagined." He untied the ribbons at her hips, easily ridding her of the lacy bikini, his fingers forging tantalizing paths on the satin skin at the inside of her thighs.

As Jessica writhed on the bed, her hips arching into his increasingly intimate touch, she realized that she'd completely thrown away her carefully acquired restraint. But as Quinn's lips caressed her sensitive flesh, she knew that whatever she was giving away, she was receiving tenfold.

"Please," she whispered, her voice ragged. "Please make love to me."

Lifting his head, Quinn knew he had never seen anything as beautiful as Jessica's liquid blue eyes, filled with a desire that equaled his own. He held her gaze, his fingers causing havoc to her body as his hand moved up her leg, tracing beguiling patterns on her silk-covered thigh.

"I am," he said simply, lowering his head once again, his lips exploring the skin of her midriff, leaving a raging heat behind. "I knew it."

"Knew what?" she asked weakly, melting under his expert caresses. Jessica was not inexperienced—she'd been married, after all. But she had never known anything like the sweet, aching passion Quinn's hands and lips were releasing from deep within her.

"That your skin would be even silkier than that lacy confection you were wearing." His fingers drew one stocking down the long length of her leg, his lips returning up the trail his hands had blazed. "And you taste so very, very good."

"Quinn," she complained, lifting her hips invitingly off the mattress, "I don't want to wait any longer. I want to make love to you now."

Through the fog clouding her senses, Jessica was stunned to hear herself issuing such a demand. But Quinn had turned her body to flame, and she knew only he could quench the fires threatening to consume her.

"It's not that simple, sweetheart," he murmured as he slowly stripped off the other stocking. "There are certain stages one must go through before reaching the final destination."

Under normal circumstances, Jessica would have agreed. She preferred her life to run in an orderly fashion, but this was ridiculous. She sucked in her breath as he reached under her, his deft fingers manipulating the catch on the lacy garter belt.

"Can't you skip a few steps?" she suggested, quivering under his touch as the passion he'd evoked escalated to exquisite heights.

Quinn could feel Jessica's surrender as she trembled beneath him. Her body was his for the taking, but he had discovered over the past few days that he was a selfish man. He was determined to have all of Jessica O'Neill.

"That would be cheating," he stated with a breezy attitude he was far from feeling, as his lips explored every inch of satiny skin.

Quinn could feel the heat rising from her body in waves as his lips continued their erotic journey. He found himself being irrevocably drawn into his own sensual snare. His blood was pounding in his ears as he explored her welcoming warmth, and as she cried out, he vowed that she'd never forget this night.

Suddenly she was twisting in his arms, practically tearing his clothes from his body as she displayed a hunger and a power just as vital, just as desperate as his own. Her lips and hands moved over Quinn as his had moved over her, tasting, touching, creating exquisite sensations that were just this side of pain as they sought to give him pleasure.

With a vast effort, Quinn forced himself to remember one final, vital detail. "Jess," he murmured, poised over her. "Is this all right? I don't want you to think I'm the kind of guy who's always prepared, hoping to get lucky, but you did kind of imply…"

He was suddenly unreasonably uncomfortable with this entire situation. But the one thing Quinn didn't want to do was give Jessica any reason to be sorry for this in the morning.

It was at that moment, viewing the atypical uncertainty on Quinn's handsome features that Jessica fell totally, irrevocably in love with him. She reached up, running her fingers over his hair, her eyes smiling at him through a sheen of glistening moisture.

"It's all right," she assured him softly.

Knowing how the evening was going to end, she'd seen to that. As much as she wanted Quinn, one thing she didn't need was another child. Especially one born out of wedlock.

"Please, Quinn," she whispered. "Make love to me."

Quinn ceased to think and so did Jessica as they concentrated only on their feelings of shimmering, golden desire. Then he was deep inside her, moving with a fiery strength that fueled their passion until the earth seemed to tilt on its axis, spinning wildly out of control.

AN IMMEASURABLE TIME LATER, Jessica lay in Quinn's arms, content to let the slow, lingering warmth suffuse her languid body. She'd never behaved like that—flinging herself at a man, teasing him, insisting he make love to her— yet she felt not one shred of remorse. Their lovemaking had been the most beautiful thing she'd ever experienced. And although she knew nothing permanent could ever come of it, Jessica refused to allow herself a single regret.

Quinn pressed a light kiss against her temple. "Well, what do you think? Was it the earthquake? Or us?"

"I don't know," she murmured, sighing with sheer pleasure as his fingers trailed down her side. "But I'll bet it registered at least a ten on Richter scales all over the state."

"At least…God, you're beautiful."

Her eyes danced as she lifted herself up on one elbow and glanced down at his magnificent, spent body. "So are you."

She watched him laugh, enthralled by the rippling of the muscles of his abdomen. "Men aren't beautiful."

"You are," she insisted. "The most beautiful man I've ever known."

"Known a great many, have you?"

"Jealous?" She grinned down at him. "I'm not asking about the legions of women in your life," she pointed out, not willing to admit he'd only been the second man she'd ever gone to bed with. Why point out her inexperience?

"Ask away," Quinn invited, rolling over, covering her body with his. Jessica thrilled at the feel of his lightly haired legs between hers and gasped as he lowered his head, capturing an ultrasensitive nipple between his lips. "It wouldn't matter, because you're the only one who's ever counted, Jess."

His eyes met hers, and Jessica could not mistake the message she read in their emerald depths. She knew that any other woman would be in seventh heaven to be in her position right now. Figuratively and, she admitted, as his hips rubbed intimately against hers, literally. Quinn hadn't promised her forever, but it was there, gleaming in his tender gaze. Instead of thrilling her, as it once might have, Jessica found the idea of permanency unreasonably frightening.

Conflicting emotions tore at her, drawing her into a vortex of feelings so deep, so overwhelming, that she did not want to think about them any longer. Not tonight.

She nodded, moved beyond words at the love shining in Quinn's wonderful eyes and gave herself up to his tender, intoxicating kiss.

IF JESSICA EXPECTED the magic to disappear with the morning light, she was to be proved wrong. Quinn had infiltrated all the little pockets of her life, and although a part of her remained convinced that this golden-tinged pleasure would soon fade as the following days melted into weeks, Jessica found herself unable to consider a life before him.

They celebrated the Cherry Blossom Festival together, Mallory's camera never ceasing as she filmed the colorfully costumed dancers and floats winding their way through the streets to the graceful Peace Pagoda. Jessica had been attending the annual spring fete since its inception, but never had she enjoyed herself as she did this year.

A San Francisco native, Jessica could be faulted for foregoing the tourist attractions of her beloved city. But as she shared the warm, yellow sunshine of spring with Quinn, she wondered why she had never realized how romantic it could be to walk along Fisherman's Wharf, the pungent aroma of fresh crab and shrimp cooking in sidewalk caldrons mixing enticingly with the tangy sea breezes.

One mellow Sunday afternoon she bought everyone bright, fanciful kites at Ghirardelli Square, and at the end of the day whimsically released hers, watching it disappear into the ruby-and-gold sky over the bay. When Quinn came out of one of the gift shops with a delicate hand-scrolled Victorian locket, Jessica protested at the price, but he refused to listen.

"It's the perfect adornment for a lady aristocrat who possesses the heart of a naughty milkmaid," he murmured for her ears alone, fastening the sterling silver heart about her neck.

Jill decided that it was the most romantic present she'd ever seen. Sara, ever practical, pointed out that the silver was going to need regular polishing. Mallory's camera just whirred away, going in for a tight shot as Quinn's lips grazed Jessica's earlobe.

Quinn was aghast that Jessica had never taken her daughters on a bay tour, insisting they hadn't seen the city until they'd viewed the towering skyline from the water. In order to remedy that situation, he showed up one Saturday morning with tickets for the Blue and Gold cruise. Jill spent the better part of the afternoon seasick from the choppy water, Mallory and Sara argued incessantly over whose fault it was that the bag containing extra videotape cassettes fell overboard into the icy water off the shores of Alcatraz.

Jessica ended the day windblown, cold, but unreasonably happy.

Mother Nature seemed determined to bestow upon San Francisco the warmest spring on record, and one balmy day on her lunch hour, Quinn took Jessica to a ''brown bag'' opera under the branches of the gnarled olive trees in the courtyard of the Cannery. It didn't matter that she couldn't understand the Italian lyrics and was unable to follow the complex drama being played out before her. Because all her attention remained riveted on Quinn, on his every word, his every movement.

Jessica was still floating on a rosy cloud when she returned to the office, and when her intercom buzzed late in the afternoon, she answered it with a feeling of optimism. That feeling quickly disintegrated when a noncommittal Paula stated that Sylvia Thacker was waiting in the reception area.

''Send her in,'' Jessica instructed, taking a deep breath.

A moment later, a tall, expensively dressed woman marched into the room, settling regally into a chair across from Jessica's desk. Her ash-blond hair was professionally streaked, her makeup impeccable. Only the fire raging in her hazel eyes and the red spots high on her cheeks displayed her aggravation.

''He's done it this time! First, I want him fired. Then we're going to put that bastard in jail. For the rest of his natural life!''

''What did Mr. Thacker do this time?'' Jessica asked calmly.

Sylvia reached into her alligator purse, pulling out a handful of newspaper scraps that she dumped unceremoniously on Jessica's desk.

''Look at that!'' she instructed.

Jessica smoothed the pieces of newsprint with her hands,

fitting the torn scraps into what was obviously the editorial page of the *San Francisco Star*. Her attention was drawn to a skillfully crafted cartoon depicting the incarceration of a local politician for graft.

"I'm afraid I don't understand," Jessica stated, unable to see what it was about the cartoon that had Sylvia so distraught.

A perfectly manicured nail jabbed at the number printed across the politician's striped prison suit. "Does that number ring a bell?" Sylvia inquired caustically.

Jessica stared, then couldn't stop a slight laugh from breaking free. "Oh, my God, that's your phone number!"

Sylvia was on her feet, glaring down at the shredded cartoon with such fire in her eyes that Jessica was surprised it didn't burst into flames.

"Do you have any idea how many weirdos have called me today because of that cartoon? I never realized so many perverts read the editorial pages!" Sylvia wrung her hands and began to pace the floor. "The phone hasn't stopped ringing! You have to do something!" she insisted on a wail that was in direct contrast to her sleek, sophisticated appearance.

"I'll contact Mr. Masterson right away," Jessica promised. "In the meantime, I suppose you should call the telephone company and have your number changed."

"I've already done that. But do you have any idea how many notes I'm going to have to send out letting all my friends know my new number?"

"A Herculean task, at best," Jessica replied dryly.

The slight sarcasm flew right over Sylvia Thacker's head. "It'll take the entire weekend," she agreed. "I want Keith billed for my time that he's wasted," she decided. "After all, I had plans to go to Big Sur. Now I'm going to be stuck at home."

"That is a shame," Jessica said, pressing her luck a bit further. "I take it you don't want to press charges?"

Sylvia looked at Jessica as if she'd just grown an extra head. "Of course I do!"

"May I point out that it will be a bit difficult for Mr. Thacker to pay you restitution if he's locked away in a jail cell? We've already frozen all his liquid assets."

"You have a point," Sylvia agreed thoughtfully. Then her face lit up. "So we'll get him fired. Then we'll take the bastard for all his unemployment!"

Her mood lifted by that idea, Sylvia left the office, chuckling wickedly to herself.

Paula suddenly appeared in the doorway. "Ain't love grand?" she asked with a laugh.

Jessica returned her grin, shaking her head with good-humored frustration. "Would you get me Mr. Masterson?"

"He's on hold now," Paula informed her, reminding Jessica once again how fortunate she was to have such a level-headed secretary. There were times when the woman seemed to read her mind.

"Quinn, we've got a problem," Jessica said as she picked up the receiver.

"I know," he answered immediately. "After such a delightful lunch hour, I can't keep my mind on my work, either. The sun is shining, the birds are singing and I have this irresistible urge to be with my lady.... Let's go sailing," he coaxed. "Then we'll spend the rest of the afternoon and evening making love."

"Quinn," Jessica stated firmly. "This is serious."

"So are my feelings about you, Jess."

There was a suddenly solemn note in his voice that Jessica decided would be best ignored for now. "Sylvia Thacker just left my office and believe me, the woman is looking for blood."

Jessica could hear Quinn's loud sigh. "What happened now?"

"Do you have a copy of this morning's *Star*?"

"Yeah, but it was such a madhouse around here this morning I didn't get a chance to read it. Why?"

"Check out the editorial cartoon," Jessica suggested.

"Just a minute." She could hear Quinn riffling through the newspaper. His roar of laughter indicated he'd just found Keith's latest artistic effort.

"It's not that funny," Jessica insisted sternly, a rebellious chuckle slipping out despite her efforts to remain totally professional.

"No," he agreed, his voice strained as he made a valiant attempt to match her serious tone. "Keith should be ashamed of himself. I suppose she's gotten a few calls."

"The phone hasn't stopped ringing," Jessica informed him.

"I'd better talk with him," Quinn said without a great deal of enthusiasm.

"You do that," Jessica advised dryly. Then she asked a question that had been bothering her from the beginning. "I know why I was stuck with Sylvia's case," she said, remembering Vanessa's explanation. "But for the life of me, I can't figure out why you're putting up with this circus."

"Keith and I were fraternity brothers at USC," Quinn revealed. "One semester I made the mistake of taking an art history class. Since I seem to lack the ability to tell a Rembrandt from a Matisse, I was in real trouble. Then to top it all off, I got mono.

"Keith showed up at the infirmary every day, drilling me on paintings until I knew enough to get a respectable C on the makeup final."

"So you're paying him back by handling his divorce?"

"He's not such a bad guy when he's off the booze. And you can't deny the fact that he's a genius at what he does."

"If he doesn't stop drinking," Jessica suggested, "he's going to be submitting those cartoons from a jail cell."

"I'll talk to him," Quinn promised. "And, Jess?" His tone suddenly deepened.

"Yes?"

"Have a good day."

Such simple words, she considered. She heard them continually from salesclerks, bus drivers, strangers. So why did they cause her heartbeat to quicken?

"Thank you," she murmured. "You too."

"I intend to," he agreed on a thick, sensual rumble. "I'm going to spend the day thinking of you."

The smile remained on Jessica's face long after she'd hung up. What a difference Quinn had made in her life, she thought as she returned to work.

As SPRING BLOSSOMED, every day seemed unnaturally special, every moment delightfully memorable, and if Jessica ever suffered doubts about the fragile foundations of their affair, she pushed them to a far corner of her mind.

Her daughters took Quinn's presence in stride, and although they'd dropped more than one heavy hint that Jessica wasn't getting any younger, they wisely refrained from mentioning marriage. It was obvious, however, that they adored him.

Based on what Elizabeth was willing to state about Mac's impetuous trip to Monterey, Jessica determined that her father had made the mistake of demanding that his wife return with him. Now Elizabeth seemed bent on teaching him a lesson, and after forty-six years of marriage, Mac was forced to court his wife all over again. From those nights that Elizabeth didn't return home after a theater date,

Jessica could only surmise that things were looking up on the MacLaughlin home front.

They'd been together six weeks when Quinn's patience ground to a halt. Except for those times that Elizabeth was out of town, or staying with Mac, and Jessica's daughters were in Marin County with Brian O'Neill, he and Jessica would make love at his apartment, forcing him to drive her home in the cold, lonely predawn hours.

"I want to stay with you all night," he complained as the car idled outside her house. "I want to hold you in my arms when we go to sleep and wake up with you in the morning."

"We will," she promised. "This weekend."

"Dammit, Jess," he argued, banging his fist on the steering wheel, "it's not enough! I'm tired of receiving bits and pieces of you. I want to be an integral part of your life. I want to know I'm important to you."

She framed his face with her hands, pressing a soft kiss against his tight lips. "You are important to me, Quinn," she murmured.

"Then let's live together," he suggested, as if the thought had just occurred to him. In truth, he'd been waiting days for the right moment. It was now or never, he decided.

She dropped her hands, shaking her head sadly. "You know I can't do that, darling. Not with the girls. It wouldn't be a good influence."

"What if you didn't have the girls?" he pressed, believing Jessica's objections to deepening their relationship went further than she was willing to admit.

"Are you suggesting I send them to live with Brian?"

Quinn hastened to dispel her misconception. "Of course not. It was just a hypothetical question. If it were only the two of us involved, would you live with me?"

Jessica wanted to say yes, that were it not for their situation, she would open her house, her heart, her life to him unconditionally. But in all honesty, she knew that wasn't entirely true. She was happy enough with the way things were right now. Granted, her bed seemed unreasonably lonely when she crawled between the cold sheets while the world still lay shrouded in darkness. And there were times when she'd look up to say something to Quinn, only to realize he wasn't there. He was across town, in his own apartment.

But those were only minor inconveniences compared to the problems they'd have if they were living together. Separate but equal. That was the new Jessica O'Neill motto.

"That's a moot point," she said, finally answering Quinn's question. "I'm the mother of three impressionable daughters. You knew that when you entered into this affair, Quinn."

It was at that moment Quinn decided he'd better leave before he said something he'd regret.

"You're right," he agreed without a great deal of enthusiasm, getting out of the car to walk her to the door. "I'll just have to work around the barriers."

Jessica didn't know exactly what Quinn meant by that vague statement, but she didn't like the glint of determination in his green eyes or the firm thrust of his jaw as he gave her an unusually circumspect good-night kiss. His odd behavior created a sense of foreboding that stayed with her the remainder of the night, making sleep an impossibility.

CHAPTER NINE

JESSICA'S FEARS WERE REALIZED as she entered the kitchen the next morning to find Quinn seated comfortably at the breakfast table, his long fingers wrapped around a mug of steaming coffee. At any other time, the sight of him would have given her a lift, but she was still unnerved by the intensity of his demands last night. Also, the expectant expressions on the faces of her mother and daughters made Jessica immediately suspicious. She couldn't forget his softly veiled threat about working around the barriers.

"What are you doing here?"

"Good morning to you, too," he stated with a smile.

Jessica let out an annoyed breath. She was due in court in two hours, she was exhausted before the day had even begun thanks to worrying about Quinn all night, and some maniac with a jackhammer was banging away in her head. She was in no mood to be gracious.

"Dammit, I asked you a question, Quinn."

"Jessica!" Elizabeth MacLaughlin turned from the stove, staring in disbelief at her daughter's blatant rudeness.

"Don't worry about it." Quinn sent her mother a broad grin. "I've already discovered our Jessie's not a morning person."

"That's for sure," Mallory offered helpfully, her camera directed toward the action being played out before her. "Mom won't talk to anyone until she's had her coffee."

"Well, we can't expect her to be perfect," Quinn remarked casually, rising from the table to pour some coffee into a bright mug.

"Here you go, darling," he said, leaning down to give her a peck on the cheek. "Drink up." He pulled out a chair for her.

"What are you doing here?" she tried for a third time, taking the chair he offered. She turned to her middle daughter. "Mallory, I'm in no mood for your project this morning!"

"You're going to want this saved for posterity," Mallory answered, zooming in for a close-up.

"I don't like the sound of this," Jessica groaned. "What am I going to want saved?"

"We've been planning your wedding," Quinn announced blandly.

Jessica choked on her coffee at the casual way he'd just dropped his bombshell. "Wedding?" she managed to gasp finally.

Quinn handed her a paper napkin. "Wedding," he repeated.

"It's going to be the most romantic wedding ever," Jill said on a deep sigh.

"You're going to love it," Sara agreed, bobbing her bright head. "Even Gran is all for it."

Quinn nodded. "Your mother had an elaborate church wedding in mind, but knowing how you're really a romantic at heart, I thought you might prefer the Japanese Tea Gardens.... I can picture you in that ivory lace dress you wore to George and Gloria's anniversary party, cherry blossoms woven through your lush auburn waves."

He glanced disparagingly at the elaborate twist he'd made at the back of her neck. "You'll wear your hair down, of course, instead of tying it up like some old maid schoolteacher."

Elizabeth forestalled Jessica's furious response as she set a plate of scorched bacon and runny eggs before Quinn, then placed an identical breakfast in front of Jessica, her stern look indicating she expected her daughter to eat it.

Jessica ignored the food. "Exactly who am I supposed to be marrying?"

"Why, Quinn, of course." Elizabeth laughed. "We should be hurt that you didn't tell us about all this sooner, Jessica. But he explained that you'd wanted to give the girls a chance to get used to him before breaking the news."

"We think it's terrific, Mom," Mallory enthused.

"Absolutely awesome," Jill agreed.

"And about time," Sara said, adding her two cents. "It's not healthy for a woman your age to be living alone."

Jessica shot her daughters a warning glance. "If I want any remarks from the peanut gallery, I'll ask for them," she snapped. "And, Mallory, for the last time, put that camera down or you won't get any allowance for the next twenty years!"

Then, if looks could kill, the one Jessica gave Quinn would have put him six feet under. The girls shifted nervously in their seats, and Mallory reluctantly lowered her camera. Only Elizabeth remained blissfully unaware of Jessica's exacerbation.

"I have to admit, dear," she trilled merrily, "that when Quinn first brought up the subject of having the wedding at the gardens, I found it rather avant-garde. But once he started describing the flowers, your dress and the strolling minstrels, I decided it was a delightful idea."

"Thank you, Lizzie." Quinn grinned up at Elizabeth, who smiled back.

"Lizzie?" Jessica arched a tawny brow. Her mother was a stickler for formality, she couldn't imagine anyone daring to use that nickname on Elizabeth MacLaughlin.

"Quinn decided that calling Gran Elizabeth would be too stuffy, once you were married," Mallory explained.

"And I'd feel absolutely ancient having a handsome man like Quinn call me Mother," Elizabeth interjected.

"Especially since no one would ever believe you were old enough," Quinn said smoothly, directing an appreciative smile Elizabeth's way.

Jessica stared as her mother giggled like an adolescent schoolgirl. "Quinn came up with Lizzie, and after trying it out a few times, I think I like it."

"We have to talk," Jessica said sternly, glaring across the table at the irritatingly smug man.

"Uh-oh," Jill said. "I think I'm going to be late for school."

"Me too!" Mallory exclaimed, jumping up from the table.

"Wait for me!" Sara appeared as eager as her sisters to escape from the room. "Have a good day, Mom," she called back over her shoulder. "Good luck, Quinn!"

"Of course we'll discuss everything in detail, darling," Quinn agreed readily, waving goodbye to Jessica's daughters as they scurried out the door. "Have you chosen a spot for our honeymoon yet?"

"There's not going to be any honeymoon!"

"Sure there is," he corrected smoothly, eyeing her wickedly over the rim of his mug. "You don't think I'd forego that pleasure, do you? I know we both have our work, Jess, but all it'll take is a little juggling of schedules."

"I'm not juggling my schedule for you, Quinn Masterson, so get that idea out of your head. And I'm not going on a honeymoon with you, because I'm not marrying you. We had an agreement and you've no right to go changing the rules!" She was on her feet, glaring down at him, her eyes ablaze.

"If you young people are going to argue," Elizabeth murmured calmly, "I think I'll go upstairs to watch 'Wheel of Fortune' on the bedroom television." She turned in the doorway. "Speaking of bedrooms, dear, if you both decide to live here, I'd better bring home some new fabric swatches. That floral print is far too feminine for a man like Quinn."

Jessica watched her mother leave, then spun toward Quinn. "You had absolutely no right to do that!"

Quinn took his time answering, biting off a piece of black bacon. "You know, this stuff isn't so bad once you get used to it. I just realized we've been eating out so much that I never asked if you inherited your mother's culinary skills. Not that I mind continuing to eat in restaurants," he assured her with a broad smile. "Home cooking is highly overrated."

A wry glance down at his plate seconded that opinion. "Of course, there's something to be said for being greeted at the door by an adoring wife, clad in a frilly little pink apron," he mused aloud. "Have I ever told you my fantasy about—"

"Why did you do that?" she interrupted sharply.

His expression was blissfully innocent. "Do what?"

"Let my family think we're getting married. What do you suggest we do when they find out it's a lie?"

"What makes you think it's a lie?" He rose abruptly, carrying his plate to the sink where he rinsed it and placed it in the dishwasher. Then he looked back over his shoulder. "Are you going to eat that?"

"You know I don't eat breakfast."

He shook his head. "For an intelligent woman, you sure do have a lot of bad habits. You're stubborn, you steal the blankets on the rare occasion we do manage to spend an entire night together, you're a washout at plane geometry and you've got lousy nutritional habits, as well.... It's amazing that you were able to land yourself such a terrific catch.'' His grin only served to irritate Jessica further.

"It damn well *is* a lie and you know it!''

Quinn didn't answer immediately. Instead he dumped her untouched food into the disposal and finished clearing the table. Jessica's irritation rose even higher as he filled the dishwasher with detergent and turned it on, wiping the counter off with a wet sponge.

She marched over to him, grabbing his arm to turn him toward her. "Would you have the common courtesy to discuss this rationally? I love my children and I'm not going to let some louse hurt them!''

"That's a rotten thing to call your fiancé, Jessica,'' he said, shaking his head sadly.

"Knock it off, Quinn,'' she snapped. "This isn't funny.''

To her amazement, his expression was suddenly unnervingly solemn. "I never meant it to be. I've been thinking about us a lot lately, Jess, and I've come to the conclusion that I'm sick and tired of this damn affair you've got us locked into.''

"Oh.''

Jessica turned around, struggling for composure, damned if she was going to let him see her cry. Well, here it was, the goodbye she'd been waiting for. So why did she suddenly feel as if he'd knocked every bit of breath from her body?

Quinn reached out, shaping her shoulders with his hands, the gesture both soothing and possessive. "It isn't what you think,'' he murmured, his lips grazing the soft skin of her neck. "This arrangement is ridiculous. I love you. I want to marry you. This afternoon couldn't be fast enough, but I'm willing to wait until you can make whatever arrangements women make at a time like this.''

She shook her head. "I'm not marrying you, Quinn. I told you that from the beginning."

"*In* the beginning," he corrected calmly. "Before you knew how perfect I was for you. How perfect we were for each other."

"Why are you doing this?" she asked weakly, moving out of his grasp, turning to face him.

"Why do you think?"

Her mind whirled into gear, latching on to the first possible answer. Although she was inclined to disregard the outrageous idea, she couldn't forget the fact that Quinn could not be taken lightly as an adversary.

"We're not going to drop the suit against Keith for printing that cartoon," she warned. "I'm honestly sorry he was fired from the paper, but you have to admit he deserved it."

A nerve twitched along his tight jaw. "Dammit, Jessica, if you think I give two hoots in hell about that crazy couple, you're mistaken. Besides, there isn't going to be any divorce."

"What do you know that I don't?" she asked archly.

"Nothing, really. But this is the fifth time in the past four years Sylvia has sued Keith for divorce. She didn't go through with it any of the other times."

"But she seems to hate him."

"That's right," he agreed. "And at the moment, the guy isn't too fond of her, either. But what we have here is a couple of fruitcakes who can't live with each other, or without each other, either."

"This could always be the time she sticks to her guns," Jessica argued.

"Could be," he said. "But I don't want to talk about them, Jess. It's time we discussed us. We've been sidestepping this issue for weeks. Give me one good reason why we shouldn't get married.''

''I don't love you,'' she lied through her teeth.

Keep it light, Quinn tried to warn himself, realizing that he'd misjudged Jessica's aversion to marriage. The one thing he hadn't wanted to do was box her into a corner. But he'd used up his store of patience; he didn't want to continue living in this limbo she'd made of their relationship.

Jessica didn't like the way Quinn just stood there, eyeing her thoughtfully.

''What now?'' she asked finally, unable to hear the stifling silence any longer.

''Your nose,'' he murmured.

''I was wondering if it grew when you told these big whoppers.'' He paused, his gaze intent. ''I guess not,'' he said a second later. ''It's just as well. I'm particularly fond of the cute little ski-jump effect at the end.'' He ran his finger along the slightly upward tilt. ''It's downright adorable.''

Jessica scowled up at him, refusing to answer that ridiculous statement.

''You know,'' he went on, ''Lizzie's a real nice lady, and I've always respected and admired the judge, but I think your parents spoiled you. They probably should have spanked you from time to time. To keep you more manageable.''

Jessica could read the gleam in his eyes as easily as a child's primer. ''Don't even suggest it,'' she warned.

He flung his hand over his chest, looking astonished and a little hurt. ''Me? Why, Jessie, I'd never dare suggest such a thing.'' Then he grinned. ''The idea does have a few intriguing aspects, though.''

It was the smile more than anything that broke the last

fragile thread of her self-restraint. She couldn't bear the thought that Quinn considered this, the most important conversation she'd ever had in her life, nothing but a joke.

"I don't love you," she repeated firmly.

Her softly spoken words tore at Quinn and he tried to think of something, anything, to say that would change the course of events.

"You don't mean that."

It was the hardest thing Jessica had ever done, but the pain she thought she'd overcome returned from the past, reminding her that if she gave in to Quinn on this, she'd find herself right back where she'd started. Quinn was a wonderful man. But he was strong willed, as well. How long would he allow her the freedom to make her own choices? To be her own woman?

His behavior today, springing this news on her family, was proof that if she married him, she'd end up living her life under his rules. He hadn't asked her to marry him—he'd insisted as if it were a foregone conclusion.

She swallowed, having to push the words past the lump in her throat. "I do," she whispered.

Quinn flinched visibly. "Well," he said, "I guess since I don't want an affair and you don't want marriage, we've just reached an impasse."

She turned away, unable to bear the pain she viewed darkening his gentle green eyes. "I suppose so."

A stifling silence settled over them, like a morning fog that had yet to burn off.

"Then this is goodbye?"

She nodded, unable to answer.

Quinn didn't want to accept the fact that this was happening. He didn't want to believe Jessica could throw everything away, just to stick to her ridiculous principles that no longer had any bearing on who they were. Or what they had together.

"You're going to end it, aren't you? After all we've had." His ragged tone displayed his own grief and disbelief at the way things had turned out.

Tears welled up in her eyes, but she didn't dare turn around, knowing that if she looked at him, she'd recant her earlier statement. She wanted him. She wanted to be with him. Why couldn't he just leave things as they were?

His frustration finally reaching the boiling point, Quinn turned on his heel, marching out the door before he gave in to instinct and drove his fist through the sunshine yellow wall. The screen door broke off its hinges as he slammed it behind him, causing Jessica's copper gelatin molds to fall off the wall. She stared out into the slanting rain, watching him drive away. And then she cried.

THE DAYS DRAGGED BY without a word from Quinn. Ten very long days and even longer sleepless nights. Jessica attempted to keep her mind on her work, but she felt like a walking zombie as she made a series of foolish, unthinking mistakes that had her spending an uncomfortable amount of time in George Bennington's office.

She had finally made it through her first year at the firm, but Jessica knew she still was on probation. Despite his friendship with her father, the head of the law firm believed in trial by fire. Jessica decided if George Bennington told her one more time that if she couldn't stand the heat, she had better get out of the kitchen, she would save him the trouble of firing her and quit. She'd had several meetings with the District Attorney, and his offer was looking better every day.

Keith Thacker seemed to have dropped off the face of the earth, and Sylvia called several times each day, distraught that Jessica could not locate her missing husband. Continual telephone calls to Quinn's office to inquire about his errant client proved fruitless. His secretary steadfastly insisted that Quinn was out of town on business and although she dutifully accepted Jessica's messages, Quinn seemed determined to ignore her calls.

Things were no better at home. While she was in the throes of editing her project, Mallory's unusual displays of temper flared out of control at the slightest provocation. Every evening Jessica was forced to watch the latest version, her heart aching as she viewed flashbacks of those happy, seemingly carefree days she'd spent with Quinn.

Sara was unusually quiet, but had brought home a note from her teacher, stating that the straight A student was in danger of failing both English composition and math and might be held back unless her grades showed a marked improvement in the next month.

Jill, whose punk rock style had always left a great deal to be desired, came home from spending the night with a new friend, her hair dyed a brilliant fluorescent green and a trio of holes pierced in each earlobe.

Jessica knew her daughters blamed her for Quinn's disappearance from their lives, a fact she could not deny. She also suspected that their uncharacteristic behavior was a direct result of her break with him, but there was little she could do to change things, even if she wanted to. Like his client, Quinn appeared to have vanished.

The only bright spot in her life came when Elizabeth returned to the house late one afternoon, Mac in tow.

"Jessica," her father's booming voice greeted her, "I'm glad you're home. Your mother and I have some good news!"

"I could use some," Jessica muttered, looking up from the brief she was preparing. Then her glance sharpened.

Were her parents actually holding hands? "Mother's moved back home," she guessed.

"Nope. Well, that, too." Her father's blue eyes danced with merriment. "But we've even something more exciting to tell you."

"What's going on?"

"We've just put a down payment on a lovely sailboat, dear," her mother broke in.

"A sailboat?"

"A sailboat," Mac confirmed. "We're sailing around the world together. Just the two of us." He smiled down at Elizabeth, whose own gaze was brimming with affection as she grinned back.

"That's the most ridiculous idea you've come up with yet," Jessica snapped waspishly, feeling unreasonably irritated by the warm and loving looks her parents were exchanging.

She had wanted her parents to work out their problems, really she did. So why did their news make her feel even worse? There was only one answer, and Jessica hated to even consider it. She was jealous! Of her own parents.

"We used to sail every weekend, before we both got too wrapped up in our work to take the time," Elizabeth countered. "We know what we're doing."

"I don't remember sailing," Jessica muttered.

"Of course not, Jessica," her father said with the tone of consummate logic he'd used for years on the bench. "Since we gave it up before you were born, you couldn't possibly recall the fun we used to have."

"Well, I only hope you both know what you're doing," she stated on a resigned sigh.

Her parents exchanged a long look. Then Mac nodded at Elizabeth, who took a deep breath and delicately brought up the subject everyone had been tiptoeing around lately.

"We do," she agreed. "But we have to wonder if you know what you're doing, dear."

"I suppose you're talking about Quinn," she said heavily. Jessica had no desire to discuss the topic of her breakup with anyone. Even her parents. Especially her parents.

"Hell's bells, Jessie," Mac broke in. "Anyone could tell the man was head over heels in love with you. And your mother said you felt the same way about him. So what's the problem?"

"It's too complicated to explain," Jessica said, neatly sidestepping the issue, returning her attention to her work.

"You should have been firmer with Jessica when she was young, Mac," Elizabeth pointed out. "This is all your fault."

"My fault?" Mac blustered. "You were the one in charge of discipline, my dear. Besides, she certainly didn't inherit this stubborn trait from me!"

Elizabeth stiffened. "Well, don't blame me. Everyone knows the MacLaughlins have a stubborn streak a mile wide."

"And the Cunninghams don't?" he asked incredulously. "You haven't exactly been a model of compliancy all these years, yourself, Elizabeth. You're every bit as ornery as your mother!"

Elizabeth bristled. "I thought you liked my mother!"

"I never said I didn't like her," he countered brusquely. "I simply pointed out that Marion Cunningham was every bit as unbending as her daughter." His accusing glare shifted from Elizabeth to Jessica. "And her granddaughter."

"You two are going to be alone together on a boat for months and months?" Jessica questioned dryly. "It'll be interesting to see who throws who overboard first."

"Your mother and I understand each other," Mac stated firmly. "Which is more than I can say for you and Quinn."

"I don't want to talk about him," Jessica insisted.

"Just like a Cunningham," Mac muttered, raking his fingers through his silver hair.

"Just like a MacLaughlin," Elizabeth commented at the same time.

They both looked at each other and laughed.

"Look, honey," Elizabeth began again, trying reason. "It's only going to take a month to get the boat seaworthy—"

"Don't forget repainted," Mac cut in.

Elizabeth's smile was beatific. "She's named the *Sea Hawk,* right now," she explained to Jessica. "Mac's rechristening her the *Elizabeth.*"

"That's nice," Jessica admitted.

"Isn't it?" Elizabeth agreed, momentarily sidetracked.

"So you see, Jessie—" Mac picked up the conversational ball "—we're only going to be in town another month, but there's still plenty of time to have that wedding in the Japanese Tea Gardens."

"How did you know about that?"

"I told him," Elizabeth stated. "And I still think it's a lovely idea, Jessica."

"There isn't going to be any wedding," Jessica insisted firmly. "Besides, even if I changed my mind, I haven't heard a word from Quinn in almost two weeks. He's obviously lost interest."

Frustration was etched onto every line of both her parents' faces, but knowing their daughter as well as they did, both shook their heads, giving up for the time being on convincing her of her folly.

CHAPTER TEN

THREE WEEKS AFTER HER FIGHT with Quinn, Jessica was doodling idly on a yellow legal pad one morning, her mind wandering as she attempted to come up with one good reason why she should stay in her office. She was unreasonably restless. At one time, her work at Bennington, Marston, White and Lowell had been the most important thing in her life—next to her daughters, of course.

But she was slowly discovering that the world of corporate law was as dry as the legal briefs she slaved over all day. The only truly interesting case she'd had in months had been the Thackers' divorce case. While Sylvia and Keith Thacker's behavior had been admittedly frustrating, at least it offered some drama. Unfortunately, she mused, gazing absently out the window, with Keith apparently out of the city, the marital wars had settled into a period of cease-fire, so she didn't even have the battling Thackers to take her mind off Quinn.

"I hope that look isn't directed at anyone I know."

Jessica glanced up to see Vanessa standing in the doorway. "No. Just the world in general."

"Bad day?"

"Bad year."

"The only thing I know that'll put me in the dumps as low as you seem to be is man trouble."

Jessica merely shrugged, covering the paper with lopsided stars.

Vanessa came into the room, taking a chair opposite Jessica's desk. "Have you seen Quinn Masterson lately?" she asked with studied carelessness.

Jessica switched to squares. "No." At Vanessa's continuing silence, she glanced up. "Why?"

The woman's gaze circled the room as she suddenly appeared unwilling to meet Jessica's eyes. "Just wondering...Pamela Stuart just returned from Mexico."

"That's nice," Jessica murmured, her fingers tightening around the slim gold pen.

"She came back with a nice tan."

Jessica dropped the pen, placed her elbows on the desk and rested her chin on her linked fingers. "You didn't come all the way down the hall to tell me Pamela Stuart has a tan," she accused. "So, what's up?"

Vanessa fiddled nervously with her ring. "She got a divorce down there, Jessica."

"Good for her. There seems to be a lot of that going around these days," Jessica responded dryly.

"There's something else."

"I figured there would be," Jessica agreed on a slight sigh. "Here's where you tell me she was out with Quinn, right?"

"I'm afraid so." Vanessa's brown eyes were filled with consolation.

So that's where he'd been. In Mexico, holding Pamela's hand while she'd gotten her divorce. The thought caused pain to fork through Jessica.

"Not that it matters," Jessica asserted on a feigned, casual note, "but they're just old friends."

"They looked pretty friendly last night, all right," Vanessa stated, her meaning readily apparent.

"I don't want to talk about Pamela Stuart, or Quinn," Jessica said firmly.

Vanessa rose from her chair with a fluid, graceful motion. "Okay," she said companionably. "I just felt you should know. I'd hate to see you hurt, Jessica."

As she left the room, Jessica considered that Vanessa's warning had come too late. She was already hurting more than she'd ever deemed possible. If she'd thought she'd gone through hell when her marriage had broken up, Jessica was discovering she'd been sadly mistaken.

As if conjured up by some fiendish genie of her thought process, Paula announced a few minutes later that Quinn Masterson was holding on the line.

Jessica stared mutely at the blinking red button, eyeing it with the uneasiness one might view a diamondback rattlesnake, poised to strike. *This is ridiculous,* she mentally lashed out at herself, punching the button.

"Hello?" Damn. She'd planned on sounding brisk, efficient. Instead a revealing, soft note had crept into her voice.

Quinn, on the other hand, seemed to have no difficulty in maintaining a curt, professional tone.

"Jessica," he stated without preamble. "I need to know if Sylvia Thacker will agree to a meeting."

"Where on earth has Keith been? Sylvia's been driving me crazy."

"He checked into a detox center in Phoenix."

"Oh. How is he?"

"Better. He's a long way from being a recovered alcoholic, but at least he isn't at rock bottom any longer."

Jessica wished she could say the same for herself. "I'll check with Sylvia and get back to you," she agreed, struggling to match his impersonal tone. "Will you be in your office all afternoon?"

"I've got a lunch appointment that may run a little long. But you can leave a message with my secretary."

Jessica couldn't help wondering if his lunch date was with the newly divorced Pamela Stuart. "Fine," she agreed curtly. "Well, have a good day."

"If I thought you meant that," he muttered, "we just might have something to talk about."

With that inscrutable statement he hung up, leaving the dial tone buzzing in her ear. Shaking her head with frustration, Jessica dialed Sylvia Thacker's number.

"So the little worm wants to crawl back, does he?" the woman asked gleefully.

"I don't really know," Jessica answered. "Mr. Masterson called and informed me that your husband was requesting a meeting. He didn't go into details."

"Well, he's going to have a lot of apologizing to do if he thinks he's getting back in this house!"

"Mrs. Thacker," Jessica pleaded, running out of patience, "shall I set a time or not?"

"I suppose that's okay," the woman stated thoughtfully. "But don't make it right away. Let the squirt squirm for a while, that's what I always say."

"I know," Jessica murmured, wondering what kind of marriage Sylvia and Keith Thacker had that they could fight so furiously, say such terrible things about each other, then put everything aside and reconcile again. Remembering what Quinn had alleged about their past record, she had the feeling that was what was about to happen.

"By the way, what gutter did Masterson find him in this time?" Sylvia asked, as if on an afterthought.

"Your husband was in a detoxification center in Phoenix," Jessica answered briskly.

There was a long silence on the other end of the line. "Are you telling me that Keith managed to dry himself out?"

"Quinn, uh, Mr. Masterson, said he's doing better," Jessica replied noncommittally.

Again, there was a thoughtful pause. "I'll be damned," Sylvia murmured. "See if you can make that appointment for tomorrow," she instructed. "This I have to see."

Jessica agreed, then waited until late in the afternoon to return Quinn's call, unreasonably anxious for another opportunity to speak with him. But his irritatingly professional secretary informed her that Mr. Masterson was still out. However, according to his calendar, tomorrow morning at ten would be fine, the woman confirmed, promising to pass the message on to her employer.

"Burning the midnight oil?" Vanessa paused in the office doorway, regarding Jessica curiously. "Come on, kiddo. It's time to go home."

"I've got some work to finish up," Jessica stated, unwilling to admit she was hoping Quinn might call to confirm the meeting. She hadn't realized until that unsatisfactory conversation this morning how desperately she'd been needing to hear his voice.

"I thought your mother moved back home."

Jessica made a notation in the margin of a study of Marin County demographics she'd been compiling for George Bennington. "She did," she answered absently.

"So who's with the kids?"

"They don't have school tomorrow—a teachers' meeting or something—so they've gone up to Mill Valley to spend the weekend with their father. Mallory finished her movie about the family and wanted to show it to Brian."

"How did it turn out?"

"Terrific," Jessica admitted, hoping that she wasn't revealing how painful it had been to watch the final version of Mallory's ninety-minute videotape last evening. Quinn had been all too evident, and it had been incredibly distressful, watching her life played out before her eyes, a horrible flashback of her latest failure. "She's really very talented."

"You're on your own tonight?"

"I guess so," Jessica agreed glumly.

"Want to go get a drink? The Cosmic Kitten has a dynamite happy hour."

Jessica grimaced. "I've never liked singles' bars. Besides, I've heard that place is a meat market."

"Of course it is," Vanessa concurred. "But at least the meat is prime. And heterosexual, which in this town is a decided plus."

"I think I'll pass."

"You can't sit around here moping over the great Quinn Masterson forever," she advised.

"I'm not moping, I'm working."

Vanessa came into the office, perching on the corner of Jessica's desk, crossing long legs clad in a patterned navy blue hose that exactly matched her silk suit. Jessica wondered idly if other women were born with the ability for coordinating their wardrobes—possessing an extra gene, or chromosome, or something. Whatever, she decided on an audible sigh, she'd obviously been out to lunch when that particular talent was handed out.

"Jessica," Vanessa said firmly, "surviving a broken love affair is like riding a horse. Sure you fall off, but you have to get right back on again."

"I've always been allergic to horses."

"You know what I'm talking about," Vanessa snapped. "The way you've been acting, it's like you're allergic to men. Believe me, honey, it'll do you a world of good to go out and have a little fun. It wouldn't hurt your reputation any, either."

"What does that mean?" Jessica demanded.

Vanessa's perfect white teeth worried her lower lip as she appeared to be making a decision. "Look," she said, "I want you to know I never believed a single word, but people have been talking about you."

"About me?" Jessica couldn't imagine people so bored with their own lives that they'd find her an interesting topic of conversation.

"Well, until that little fling with the Casanova of San Francisco's legal world, you didn't date. Not that anyone could tell."

"I'm amazed that *anyone* bothered to notice," Jessica snapped.

"You have to admit it *is* unusual. After all, you're an attractive woman who happens to be at an age when your sexuality should be at its peak. And you're a divorcée to boot."

Jessica didn't miss the implication. She shook her head with very real irritation. "And therefore I should be hot to trot, right?"

The other woman appeared unperturbed by Jessica's prickly tone. "Well, to be perfectly honest, it's common knowledge that you've turned down dates with just about every single male in the office. And a few of the married ones, as well." Her voice dropped conspiratorially. "Some of the men don't think that's quite natural, if you get my drift."

Jessica got it all right. Loud and clear. Her blue eyes hardened. "My life is my own business, Vanessa. And I intend to keep it that way."

The woman shrugged elegantly, sliding off the desk. "Well," she murmured, "don't say I didn't try to warn you." She turned in the doorway. "Are you sure you won't change your mind about that drink?"

"I'm sure."

"Don't work too hard," she advised, her fingers fluttering goodbye as she turned and left the office.

As Jessica watched Vanessa leave, she couldn't help recalling Quinn's accusation that Jessica O'Neill was rumored to be an iron lady with ice water for blood and a stone heart. A lot they all knew. Jessica considered how lucky she'd be if that was only true. After all, stone hearts were probably incapable of breaking.

Much later, Jessica stood at her office window. Even through the thick glass she could hear the lonely whine of a siren and glanced down toward the street, where the car lights glowed like stars that had fallen to the ground.

"Excuse me?"

She turned to look at the woman who stood hesitantly in the doorway, a vacuum in one hand and a tray filled with cans of spray polish, dust rags and Windex in the other.

"Is it all right if I clean in here now?"

Jessica took one last look at the telephone, willing it to ring. Then, admitting that Quinn had no intention of calling, she gave the waiting woman an apologetic smile.

"I'm on my way out," she said, taking her purse from a bottom drawer. "I'm sorry I held you up."

"No bother. Have a nice night," the woman called after her.

"You too," she answered automatically.

As Jessica sat gazing out the window on the bus home, she decided that everyone in San Francisco was out taking Vanessa's advice. The sidewalks were crowded with throngs of happy couples, holding hands, laughing, seemingly having a wonderful time. When the bus halted at a stoplight, a couple in a convertible beside her exchanged a brief, but unmistakedly heated kiss. San Francisco might be the city for lovers, but this evening Jessica found all that romance most depressing.

When she finally arrived home, Jessica decided that she deserved a little pampering. She filled the tub to the rim with hot water, dumping in an outrageously expensive amount of bath oil. Then she dug out a novel she'd been intending to read for months and poured a glass of wine. Reconsidering, she retrieved the bottle from the refrigerator, taking it into the bathroom with her.

Although Jessica's mind wandered, as it did continually these days to Quinn, she forced her attention back to the story, letting some of the cool water out of the tub, refilling it as needed. She'd managed to make it to the third chapter when the lights flickered once. Then twice. Then went out altogether.

"Damn," she muttered, rising from the tub and grabbing for a towel in the dark. Wrapping it about herself she went into the kitchen, taking a candle from the cache she kept for just this reason.

"I'll be glad when that electrician is finished," she said under her breath, digging around in the drawer where she stored the spare fuses.

Jessica made her way by the flickering, dim candlelight to the fuse box located on the back porch. She replaced one, but nothing happened. Muttering a series of low oaths that would have drawn an arched eyebrow even from the often colorful Judge MacLaughlin, she returned to the kitchen, taking her last replacement fuse from the drawer.

"This better do the trick," Jessica grumbled. "Because I'm in no mood to spend the night reading by candlelight."

She held her breath, and was rewarded as the house once again glowed with light. "Bingo," she stated, pleased that something, at least, had worked out well for her today. Even though Jessica didn't believe in omens, a little corner of her mind latched on to this good fortune as a hopeful sign.

That slim vestige of hope began to dissolve as she awoke the next morning twenty minutes late, having forgotten to reset her clock radio after the power had gone out. Her hair dryer blew yet another fuse before she'd finished, and as she viewed her wild tangle of wet auburn hair in the mirror, Jessica considered how on the one day she wanted to look her best, she was going to show up for her meeting with Quinn looking like a drowned rat.

Her day continued its downhill slide on the way to the office. The bus driver slammed on his brakes, narrowly avoiding hitting a child who'd run into the street, chasing a baseball thrown to him by a companion. The violent motion sent coffee splashing out of the paper cup held by the passenger next to Jessica, and she watched fatalistically as the dark liquid spread all over the skirt of her blue shirtwaist dress.

"I'm sorry," the distraught commuter moaned, dabbing ineffectually at her skirt with his handkerchief.

"Don't worry about it," Jessica said on a slight sigh. "You couldn't help it."

"But your dress. Look, send me the bill and I'll pay for the cleaning, all right?"

"Really—"

"It's the least I can do," he insisted.

Jessica took the business card he offered, slipping it into her purse. She had no intention of contacting the man again. It wasn't his fault. She was rapidly coming to the conclusion that some fiendishly evil being had taken control of the universe, manipulating events so that anything that might possibly go wrong would. This individual was simply a pawn in the game being played with her life.

The Thackers were waiting for her, as was Quinn, and all heads turned expectantly to the door as she entered. Jessica's heart sank as Quinn's eyes narrowed, taking in her disheveled appearance, but she straightened her shoulders determinedly and entered the room with a false, professional smile.

"I'm sorry I'm late," she stated, taking a seat beside Sylvia Thacker at the conference table. "My alarm clock went off late. You see, I blew two fuses last night, and another this morning, and...Well, you don't care about that." She managed another brilliant smile. "Shall we get started? Who wants to go first?"

I'm babbling, Jessica groaned inwardly. *They're all going to think I'm an absolute idiot.* She risked a glance at Quinn, her heart sinking further as she viewed his incredulous gaze.

But Quinn was not listening to Jessica's breathless statement; indeed, her words were a distant hum, hardly audible over the blood roaring in his ears. She'd changed amazingly in the past few weeks. Her face was thinner, paler. A sprinkling of freckles that hadn't been visible before stood out on her cheekbones. Her eyes were bright with nervousness, but it would be impossible to miss the deep purple shadows underneath them. And while he was no authority on women's bodies, he knew Jessica's intimately. How many pounds had she lost? Five? Ten? She looked, in all honesty, as bad as he felt. But she still looked wonderful.

Jessica had been hoping that they could get right down to business, but it appeared the Thackers had their own ideas. Each proceeded to voice a litany of complaints against the other, point and counterpoint, back to the early days of their marriage.

Jessica risked a glance at Quinn, who was viewing the drama with resignation. When he caught her eye, he surprised her by winking. Realizing this was standard operating procedure for the couple, Jessica allowed her mind to wander as Sylvia began berating Keith for showing up a half hour late to their wedding.

Quinn looked tired, Jessica considered, surreptitiously eyeing his drawn expression. He was sporting a dark tan, obviously a souvenir from his trip to Mexico with Pamela Stuart, but his skin seemed more tightly drawn over his bones. His green eyes were devoid of that sparkling gleam she had often thought of during their time apart, and lines bracketed his lips. Those wonderful, seductive lips...

A sudden knock on the door captured Jessica's attention and a moment later her secretary entered, the heretofore unflappable Paula obviously distressed.

"There's a telephone call for you, Ms O'Neill."

"Please take a message, Paula," Jessica requested.

"It's an emergency," Paula stated. Her voice cracked, causing Jessica's blood to freeze in her veins. "Oh God, Jessica, I'm sorry."

The girls, Jessica thought dazedly as she made her way over to the phone in the corner of the room. Her heart was pounding in her throat and she screamed a silent prayer that they were all right. The image of that little boy this morning swam before her eyes. What if that had been Sara? Oh, dear God, she begged. Please don't let it be that!

Quinn was on his feet, staring helplessly at Jessica as he watched her face go ashen, her eyes close. "I understand," she managed to respond, her voice not much above a whisper. "I'll be right there."

But she remained frozen, her eyes staring at some unseen location out the window. Quinn was by her side in two long strides, taking the telephone receiver from her icy hands.

"Jess?" he asked, his hands cupping her shoulders as he shook her gently, dragging her attention toward him. "What is it? Not the girls?"

She could have wept at the wealth of concern in his eyes, and managed to shake her head. "No," she said on a deep, ragged breath. "Not the girls."

"Thank God!" He exhaled a deep, relieved breath of his own. "Then what?"

Her hands clasped his upper arm, her fingernails digging into the flesh covered by his gray suit. "Oh, Quinn," she said on a weak, broken sob, "it's my home. There was a fire." Tears welled up in her eyes. "Everything's gone, Quinn. Everything."

Knowing how much the house had meant to Jessica, understanding how it had symbolized her hard-won independence, Quinn drew her into his arms, holding her tight, his hands stroking her hair, her back.

"Listen to me," he said gently, putting her a little away. "It's going to be okay. Do you hear me?"

She stared at him uncomprehendingly.

"Listen to me, Jess," he repeated, his voice firmer, his tone more self-assured. "We're going to go there. Together. And I promise everything is going to turn out fine. You've got to believe me, honey."

She leaned into him, resting her forehead against his chest, taking deep breaths as she drew from his strength. When she lifted her head, her eyes glistened with tears.

"I'm so glad you're here, Quinn," she whispered.

He gave her a long, hard kiss on the lips. "Me too, babe," he murmured huskily. "Me too."

Then he led her to the door, turning back toward an avidly interested pair of onlookers.

"You two work something out," he ordered. "We've got more important things to do than watch you idiots fight."

Ignoring their shocked expressions, he left the conference room. "Ms O'Neill won't be in for a few days," he instructed Paula firmly, preparing for an argument from Jessica. Quinn was disturbed when she failed to offer the slightest protest and realized she was obviously in a state of shock. "Would you reschedule her appointments?"

"Of course," Paula answered immediately, reaching for her appointment calendar.

"Oh," Quinn added on an afterthought, "would you please call my office and tell them I won't be back today?"

"I already did."

Quinn managed to reward Paula with a weak smile, wondering why it was that everyone else saw what Jessica appeared blind to. That however loudly she wanted to protest the fact, they belonged together. Permanently.

And he was going to make her see that if it was the last thing he did.

CHAPTER ELEVEN

THE SIDEWALK WAS CROWDED with onlookers as Quinn pulled up in front of the smoldering ruins of what had once been Jessica's beloved home.

The outer walls of the Victorian house were still standing, but the windowpanes had been blown out by the intense heat. Through the gaping holes, Quinn could view the charred interior.

"What do they all want?" she asked weakly. "Why are they here?"

"I suppose it's curiosity. And a certain sense of relief that it didn't happen to them."

"Oh, Quinn," she half sobbed, "I think I just discovered that I'm a terrible person."

He took both her hands in his, his heart torn at her despairing expression. "Nonsense," he objected firmly. "What on earth gave you that idea?"

Her eyes were bleak as they turned to the crowd of gaping bystanders. "I wish it had been one of them," she whispered harshly. "I wish it had been anyone but me." She shook her head and covered her face with her hands.

Quinn drew her into his arms, stroking her back. "That's only natural, sweetheart," he assured her. "There isn't anything wrong with you." He gazed down into her stricken face. "Let me take you to my place," he suggested. "There isn't anything you can do here."

Jessica shook her head. "No. I want to see everything, Quinn."

"Are you sure? Look, honey, we can call your insurance company from my apartment. It's going to take them a while to start the claims process, anyway. You should be resting."

A thought suddenly occurred to Quinn. "We need to do something about the girls. They shouldn't be coming home to this."

At the idea of her daughters, safe with Brian in Marin County, Jessica experienced a cool wave of relief. It was only a house, she reminded herself. Boards and shingles. It could be replaced. Her children couldn't.

"They're all right," she managed through tight lips. "They didn't have school today. Mallory wanted to show Brian her movie, so they're spending the weekend with him."

"Then her tapes didn't burn?"

At the honest relief in his voice, Jessica was once again reminded of what a very nice man Quinn could be. "No, thank God. She's too young to realize that this isn't the end of the world."

"How about you? Can you realize that?"

Jessica took a deep breath. "I've been through worse," she admitted. "I can probably survive this, as well."

"I've no doubt of that," he agreed, wiping away the moisture on her cheeks with his handkerchief. "But are you sure you want to go in there right now?"

"I have to. I have to see if there's anything left."

Quinn looked over her shoulder, doubting that anything had survived the inferno that had gutted Jessica's home. *God,* he thought, his stomach clenching, *if this had happened last night, with Jessica asleep upstairs...* The idea was too unpalatable to consider further.

"Let's get it over with," he suggested grimly, opening the car door.

Jessica held tight to his hand as they walked toward the still smoldering house. As they approached, the crowd parted like the waters of the Red Sea, allowing them to pass. Jessica was numbly aware of Quinn speaking to the firemen who were cleaning up the destruction, but she didn't know what they were saying. Neither did she care.

The front door, with its lovely stained glass window, had been hacked to splinters by the firefighters' axes, Jessica noted dully. She stood in the open doorway, her eyes bleak as she viewed the devastation. It was all gone—Jill's wild clothes, Sara's scrapbook, her paintings. Everything. She moaned.

The soft sound drew Quinn's attention. "Are you sure you're all right?"

"I don't know," Jessica said, swaying slightly as her head began to swim.

Black dots appeared before her eyes and she prayed that she wouldn't disgrace herself by fainting in public. She'd never fainted before in her life. But neither had she had the misfortune to witness her life gone up in flames.

"I'm taking you home," Quinn stated brusquely, his firm tone assuring Jessica that he wasn't listening to any further objections.

"I don't have a home."

Her face was an unhealthy shade of gray, and her eyes appeared wider than usual. The shadows beneath them, which had been so evident only an hour ago were even darker and deeper.

"My home."

"Oh."

Jessica remembered little else after that. She was vaguely aware of Quinn leading her to his car, where she was able to lean her head against the back of the seat, closing her eyes against the swirling vertigo that threatened to overcome her. She offered no objection as he took her directly to his bedroom, sitting her down on the edge of the bed before proceeding to undress her.

He knelt on the lush burnt umber carpeting, slipping her pumps from her feet. His fingers made quick work of the buttons on the front of the blue silk dress, and she shrugged her shoulders, allowing him to push the material down to her waist. He laid her gently on the mattress, pulling the dress down over her hips. Her nylons followed, then her half-slip, until she was clad only in her lacy bra and panties.

When Quinn slid her under the chocolate-brown sheets, Jessica closed her eyes as her head sank into the pillow. She couldn't remember being so tired, so wrung out. Then she felt him moving away and her eyes flew open.

"Where are you going?"

"Just into the other room. I'm calling a doctor."

She shook her head. "I don't need a doctor."

"You're in shock," he said. "When it settles in, you're going to be upset. I want to get you something."

"I don't take tranquilizers," she argued weakly, finding speech a major effort. "They're habit-forming."

"One damn pill isn't going to turn you into an addict, Jess," Quinn shot back. "Dammit, for once in your life would you stop being so stubborn and let someone help you?" His concern for her made his voice gravelly, his words harsh.

"I don't need any pills," she repeated. "I need you, Quinn."

Quinn was aware that Jessica was not herself. She never would have admitted that under normal conditions. And certainly not on such a soft, pleading tone. Shaking his head, he sat down beside her, pushing her hair back from her face with unsteady fingers.

"I worry about you, babe."

Her hand reached out for him, then fell to the sheet, as if the movement required more strength than she possessed.

"I know," she whispered. "Please don't leave me, Quinn." Her blue eyes were eloquent pools of need, pulling him into their swirling depths.

Quinn suddenly felt as if he were drowning. "At least let me call the insurance company for you," he suggested, wanting to spare Jessica that initial piece of bureaucratic red tape.

"All right. I got a renewal notice yesterday," she said flatly. "It's still in my purse. I think the number's on that."

"I'll call them and be right back."

"Quinn?"

He turned in the doorway. "What is it, sweetheart?"

"Please don't be gone long."

He returned to the side of the bed, bending down to brush a light, reassuring kiss against her lips. "Don't worry," he vowed. "I won't leave you alone."

She nodded, closing her eyes, crying silently as she viewed the horrid images emblazoned on her mind. It was only a short time later that Jessica felt Quinn lie down beside her. She didn't have the strength to open her eyes, but her fingers inched across the sheet, unerringly locating his hand.

"You came back."

He linked their fingers together, bringing her hand to his lips. "Of course."

"I'm glad," she murmured drowsily. She was so tired! How could she want so badly to sleep in the middle of the day? "I don't know what I would have done if you hadn't been with me today, Quinn."

"I'll always be there for you, Jess. That's a promise."

"Ummm." Her breathing was deeper, and a soft pink color was returning gradually to her complexion.

Quinn drew her into his arms, fitting her comfortably, safely against him. Then his gaze grew thoughtful as he watched her sleep.

When Jessica awoke several hours later, the sun was just setting, filling the room with an orange glow. Momentarily disoriented, she glanced around her. Then her gaze lifted to collide with Quinn's.

"Oh, my God," she groaned, seeing the concern etched onto his harshly set features. "It wasn't a nightmare, was it?"

"No. I'm so very sorry, Jess."

"The girls," she remembered suddenly, struggling to sit up. "I have to talk to them."

"I already did. They're fine. Worried about you, of course, but I assured them that their mother is a trooper. The insurance investigator also called. It was the wiring," he stated, confirming what Jessica had already guessed.

She put her arms around him, pressing her cheek against his shirt. "I feel so empty, Quinn. I keep thinking that I should be crying my eyes out. Or screaming at the top of my lungs about the injustice of it all. But I can't feel anything."

"That's understandable. You're bound to be a little numb right now," he assured her, his long fingers combing through the strands of her tousled hair. The auburn waves smelled of smoke.

"Want a shower?" he suggested. "You'd probably feel a little better."

Jessica nodded slowly. "That might help," she agreed.

"I'll fix you something to eat."

"I don't think I could keep anything down," she protested softly.

He lowered his head, kissing her lightly on the forehead. "Just some soup and maybe a sandwich. I've got some chicken. How does that sound?"

She lifted her shoulders in a weary shrug. "You don't have to go to any trouble for me, Quinn."

"I like to do things for you," he argued. "You never let me do enough as it is. At least let me feed you." His judicious gaze skimmed her body, which appeared unusually slender under the crisp dark sheet. "Besides, you've lost weight. Obviously you need someone to take care of you."

She sighed, unable to work up the strength to argue further. "All right."

Quinn smiled down at her. Then he went into the adjoining bathroom and soon Jessica could hear the sound of running water.

"Can you make it into the bathroom yourself?" he asked with concern as he returned. "Do you need help washing your hair?"

"I'll be fine." Her voice was unsteady, but her eyes offered Quinn assurance.

"I never had a single doubt about that," he agreed. "I left my robe in the bathroom for you. It'll be too big, but your clothes smell of smoke, and you've got that stain on your dress."

Was it only this morning that her worst problem had been spilled coffee? It seemed like a lifetime ago.

"Thank you, Quinn. You're very nice."

As he left the room to fix Jessica something to eat, Quinn considered that "nice" was not how he wanted her to see him. Teddy bears were nice; television weathermen were nice; Quinn wanted to be Jessica's overwhelming passion.

He wanted her to be as obsessed with him as he was with her.

He'd gone crazy while he'd been in Phoenix with Keith. It had taken every ounce of his willpower not to pick up the phone and call Jessica, agreeing to whatever she was willing to offer. The knife blade flashed dangerously as he hacked away at the cold roast chicken with angry strokes.

Quinn's irritation disintegrated when Jessica appeared in the kitchen doorway a while later, offering him a slightly wobbly smile.

"That was a good idea. I feel better."

"You look marvelous," he said, gazing at the lovely woman wrapped in the voluminous folds of his navy robe.

Her hair fell wetly over her shoulders, and her skin, what little of it was visible, shone pinkly, as if she'd attempted to scrub away not only the smoke, but the memory of the fire, as well. She looked soft and vulnerable, and although he knew this was a hell of a time to be having such thoughts, deliciously desirable.

"Hungry?" he asked with studied casualness, turning away so Jessica couldn't view his body's reaction to her pleasantly disheveled state.

"Yes."

Her tone was soft, inviting sensual fantasies, and Quinn wondered what kind of man he was to be experiencing sexual hunger at a time like this. Jessica needed someone to take care of her right now. To comfort her.

"Good. I've made sandwiches and the soup's warming. I hope you like cream of asparagus. It's canned. But it's good."

Jessica stared at his back, wondering what to do next. She'd seen the way his eyes had darkened with unmasked desire when he'd looked at her. She knew that whatever had happened to their affair, the attraction between them was as strong and viable as ever.

"I am hungry, Quinn," she agreed, moving quietly across the room on bare feet and putting her arms around his waist. "But not for food." She pressed her cheek against his back, fitting her body intimately against his.

"Jess," Quinn warned raggedly, "do you have any idea what you're doing?"

"Yes," she answered simply.

He spun around propelling her soft curves against him with harsh, unforgiving strength. "Damn you, Jessie," he groaned, his fingers tangling painfully in the wet strands of her hair. "Damn you for making me need you like this!"

Then his mouth came down hard and demanding on hers, his tongue thrusting deeply with a greedy passion that threatened to devour her. His strong fingers splayed against the back of her head as he held her to the blazing kiss.

Her soft cry against his lips only served to fuel Quinn's spiraling passion. He scooped her up, his lips fused to hers as he carried her back into the bedroom. The soft velour robe was no obstacle as his hands moved over her breasts, his fingers kneading the flesh, creating a pleasure that was just this side of pain. In turn, Jessica's fingers tore at the buttons of his shirt, her palms pressing against the warm, moist skin of his chest.

When she dragged her mouth away from his to trail a series of stinging kisses from the base of his throat to his navel, Quinn thought he'd explode. A groan rumbled in his throat as he felt her soft breath against the wool of his pants and then he was tearing them off, Jessica helping him, her own need every bit as desperate.

Tenderness gave way to hunger, both of them giving and taking pleasure as they drove each other mad with passion. Quinn's hot moist breath burned her skin, creating an ache deep inside her as he relentlessly drove her closer and closer to the very brink of sanity. His lips and hands were everywhere, tasting, touching, creating havoc with her senses.

In turn, Jessica explored the hard lines of his body, thrilled by the way he trembled under her touch. Then his fingers dug into her waist and she gasped as he lowered her onto him, filling her with his rigid strength.

"Oh, Quinn," she cried out, leaning forward, the pebbled tips of her breasts brushing his chest. "I think I'm burning up!"

"That's right," he growled, his fingers clutching her hips, thrusting more deeply into her. "Flame for me, Jess. Let me feel your fire!"

Her body was a torch, alive with a heated passion that threatened to consume her. Jessica could only wonder what it was about Quinn that made her go so wildly, primitively out of control.

His tongue explored the moistness of her mouth, thrusting into all the warm dark corners as his movements became faster, deeper. Jessica's entire body was trembling with ecstasy. Finally, she could contain herself no longer and cried out, calling his name from the very depths of her soul.

Her unrestrained response had a shattering effect on Quinn. His mouth clamped over hers with a harsh moan and his body stiffened as he arched against her. His last coherent thought was that despite her continual assertions to the contrary, Jessica O'Neill was his woman. His and his alone.

Jessica's cheek rested on Quinn's warm chest, her hair spread in damp auburn tangles across his body. Her legs were still wrapped around his and the feel of his strong, hair-roughened thighs against hers was intensely satisfying.

His heart had slowed to a more reasonable rhythm, and as her lips pressed against his moist skin, Jessica felt his quick intake of breath.

"You are a wanton," he said, his voice rumbling from deep within his body. "I think you've killed me."

Jessica's cheeks grew pink as she considered her wild, primitive response to Quinn's lovemaking. And she understood why he'd chosen to display such passion, rather than a solicitous tenderness.

He had known exactly what was necessary to take her mind from the fire and her troubles. He'd known precisely what to do. As it seemed he always did. She breathed a sad, rippling little sigh.

"Don't," he requested softly, his fingers playing with her hair. "Don't have any regrets."

She lifted her head, her blue eyes solemn. "I don't," she murmured truthfully. "At least not about what we just did. I love making love to you, Quinn."

She gave him a faint smile. "In fact, I can't think of anything else I'd rather be doing." Her fingers toyed nervously with the dark hair covering his chest. "I think I've become a Quinn Masterson junkie."

"Is that so bad?" he inquired with what he considered amazing calmness. He certainly didn't feel that way inside.

Jessica sighed, rolling over onto her back to stare thoughtfully at the ceiling. Not knowing what he could say to forestall her probable answer, Quinn remained silent.

"When I was younger," she said finally, her gaze still directed upward, "my entire life revolved around my family. I was Elizabeth and Mac's daughter, then I was Brian's wife. We weren't married a year before I was Jill's mother, then Mallory's, then Sara's. I only viewed myself in relation to others."

When Quinn failed to comment, Jessica turned her head

on the pillow. "I know you can't possibly understand that. But after Brian left me, I realized I had absolutely no idea who Jessica O'Neill was. Who she really was."

"I think I can empathize with that," he argued.

She shook her head. "No, Quinn, you can't," she insisted quietly. "You can sympathize, but you can't empathize." Her somber blue eyes held a certain fondness. "I've the impression you sprang from the womb knowing who you were, what you wanted to do, where you were going in life."

He sat up now, the muscles in his jaw firming as he looked down at her. "You're wrong there," he pointed out brusquely. "Do you know how many times I still feel like I'm playing a role? That I'm still just some dirt poor Missouri farm kid?"

His green eyes turned hard. "Hell, yes, I can empathize with you, but I don't want to play word games, Jess! Sympathize, empathize, what difference does it make? I love you, damn it! That's all that matters."

"If it were only that simple," she said softly, gazing bleakly up at the ceiling once more.

"Do you love me?" he asked suddenly.

"Why do you insist on asking that?" she whispered. "It wouldn't really matter."

Quinn hit the sheet with his fist. "It would to me. I need to know, Jessica. Do you love me or not?"

When she slowly, regretfully turned her glistening eyes back to his, Jessica's face was a portrait of despair. She wept silently, unaware of the tears streaming down her cheeks.

"Oh, Quinn," she said on a sigh that was part moan, turning her head toward the wall, unable to view the need swirling in his stormy green eyes.

What did the man want, Jessica asked herself desperately. She'd given him her body; she'd shared her most intimate feelings, told him of doubts and fears that she'd never revealed to another living soul. She'd even let him into her daughters' lives, something she had always sworn never to do with any man she might date.

But still he wanted more. In that respect, she considered ruefully, Quinn was no different from any other man. He wanted too much. Because he wanted everything. He wanted more than she could possibly ever give.

His fingers cupped her downcast chin and turned her head back toward him. When she would have turned away again, he wouldn't permit it.

"I asked you a question, Jess," he reminded her softly. "And I'm still waiting for an answer."

"Why are you doing this?" she shouted, swiping at her tears. "Haven't I had enough grief today without you making things worse?" The last was flung at him on a wail, and Quinn closed his eyes, unable to view the misery etching ugly lines on her face.

Jessica had to press her hands together to keep from reaching up to stroke the rigid line of his jaw. If this was what love did, she thought miserably, if it could destroy two people like this, then she wished she'd never experienced its treachery.

But then, she considered honestly, she'd have never known the heights of passion and the sheer joy found in being with the man she loved. Why couldn't it have stayed that way, she agonized. Why did he have to ruin everything?

She watched Quinn's chest rise and fall as he sighed soundlessly. Then he opened his eyes and she was shocked at the raw pain she saw there.

"Oh, Jess," he groaned. "I never wanted to hurt you like this. I never wanted to hurt *us* like this."

Quinn knew Jessica was aching as badly as he was at the moment and wanted nothing more than to pull her into his arms, to bury his head between her soft breasts and drink in her sweet scent. He wanted her soothing hands to stroke his flesh, to quiet this pain.

He wanted to make love to her forever; he wanted to immerse himself in her flesh, in her love. He wanted to beg her to stay, to assure her that whatever their problems, they could work them out. But Quinn knew that although Jessica was willing to turn to him in moments of desperation and need, she wasn't ready to make a lasting commitment.

She wanted to be strong, he thought angrily. The ironic thing was that he'd never met a woman capable of turning him inside out like this. He wondered what it would take to make Jessica realize that she was far more self-sufficient than she secretly believed. Enough so that marrying him wouldn't cost her her hard-earned independence.

"The soup will have evaporated down to nothing," he said flatly, his feet hitting the floor as he turned away from her.

Jessica longed to run her hands across the hard lines of his shoulders, but resisted, knowing that it would be unfair to give Quinn contradictory messages.

"I'm not that hungry," she protested softly. "If you'll just call a cab, I'll go to a hotel."

Quinn ground his teeth, suddenly understanding those crimes of passion that were always cropping up on the six o'clock news. He rose from the bed and glared down at her.

"Don't be an idiot, you don't even have any clothes. You're staying here tonight. Tomorrow we'll have Elizabeth bring over some clothes, then we'll—excuse me—*you*," he corrected harshly, "can decide what you're going to do."

"That makes sense," she murmured in a subdued voice. "Thank you, Quinn. This is very kind of you."

He slammed his fist into his palm. One of these days, Quinn decided, after he and Jessica were married, he was going to have a long talk with Mac and find out how the man managed to live all those years with Jessica's mother. Because from what he'd been able to tell, Jessica didn't fall far from the genetic tree when it came to an extra helping of pigheaded stubbornness.

"I'm not doing this out of kindness," he roared, losing patience entirely. "And if I were you, Jess, I'd shut up before you find out exactly how low I am on that particular commodity right now.

"In fact, I'm about ready to double bolt that door and keep you in that bed while I make love to you until you can't move. That might be as effective a method of keeping you here where you belong as any others I might try!"

Jessica was not immune to the anger blazing in his eyes, but neither could she remain unaffected by the sudden flare of desire she viewed there, either. She chewed nervously at her bottom lip, inciting a muffled groan from Quinn. His fingers, as they thrust through his hair, were far from steady.

There was so much he wanted to say. So many things he needed to tell her. Beginning with how much he loved her. And ending with the fact that he always would.

"I'd better check on your dinner," he said instead. Then he left the room.

CHAPTER TWELVE

IF JESSICA HAD TO PICK one word to describe the mood the next morning, it would have been "cautious." Both she and Quinn seemed to be walking on eggs, neither anxious to renew the argument that had threatened to blaze out of control last night.

She'd called Elizabeth, who agreed to bring her something to wear; fortunately, her mother had kept her youthful figure and both women wore the same size. Then Jessica had called her daughters, relieved to find that they were amazingly unconcerned about the fire. Staying in Marin County for a few more days gave them a holiday from school, and a chance to swim in their father's new pool.

"I have to admit that surprises me," Jessica said, as she shared a Spartan breakfast of cold cereal and coffee with Quinn. She hadn't wanted to eat even that, but Quinn had insisted, and she didn't have the strength to argue this morning. "I expected them to be in tears."

"Kids are pretty resilient," he replied, slicing a banana atop the cornflakes.

"Fortunately," she agreed.

"How are you feeling?"

She shrugged. "Like I've been run over by a Mack truck," she admitted.

His gaze fell to her arm, which bore a lingering bruise from last night's lovemaking.

"I'm sorry."

Her eyes held a spark of humor, the first he'd seen since the day he'd stormed out of her house. "I'm not. I wasn't referring to that, Quinn."

"Oh."

They both fell quiet again and an uncomfortable silence settled over the room.

"Want a section of the morning paper?" Quinn asked politely.

Following his cue, Jessica nodded. "Thank you."

"Which part? Fashion? You can check out the sales."

"Business, I think," she decided. "The idea of all that clothes shopping is too depressing.... Unless you want the business section," she tacked on with consummate politeness.

"No, it's yours," he offered, handing her the pages, hating this conversation that could have been taking place between two strangers.

"Thank you," she repeated.

"You're welcome."

Jessica hoped Elizabeth would hurry. She couldn't take much more of Quinn's studiously proper manners. She eyed her coffee cup, wondering what he'd do if she suddenly dumped the cooling contents into his lap.

Quinn caught Jessica's thoughtful study of her cup. "Would you like some more coffee?"

"No, thank you."

"Would you like it warmed up?"

She smiled a stiff little smile. "Thanks, but it's fine."

"You're sure?"

"Positive."

"All right. If you want anything, just ask."

"Do you mean that?" she said suddenly.

Quinn's spoon stopped on the way to his mouth and he

slowly lowered it back to the bowl. "Of course. What can I get for you? Some toast? An omelet?"

Jessica shook her head firmly. "I don't want anything else to eat."

He arched an inquiring brow. "Then what?"

"Could you stop treating me like I'm visiting royalty? I'm starting to get very nervous, Quinn."

His level gaze met hers. "I was only trying to keep things on an even keel."

"Do you think that's honestly possible?" Jessica asked shakily.

There was a lengthy silence from across the table. "Between us?" he finally inquired.

Jessica knew it to be a rhetorical question and didn't bother to answer. As she watched warily, his eyes seemed to harden and something flickered in their depths. She flinched as he reached across the table, his fingers braceleting her wrist.

"Between us?" he repeated, turning her hand over, tracing thoughtful little circles on her palm with his index finger.

There was nothing overtly sexual in the gesture, but Jessica felt a heat building deep within her feminine core, sending little eddies of flaming current spiraling outward to warm her entire body.

Quinn's emerald eyes gleamed with beguiling satisfaction as he felt the pulse rate under his fingers increase. Jessica unconsciously licked her lips, and as he watched, her expression softened and a soft pink hue darkened her cheeks. When she dragged her gaze away from his stroking finger to meet his, her eyes were melted sapphires, dark, lustrous, shining with shared desire.

"No, Jess," he assured her in a rough voice. "Nothing between us could ever remain on an even keel. When we fight, I suppose we'll fight tooth and nail," he grated. "But when we love, Jessie—ah, there's nothing that equals the storm we make. You can't deny that, sweetheart."

Jessica tugged, retrieving her hand, lowering it to her lap where Quinn couldn't view her fingers twisting nervously together.

"No," she admitted softly. "I've never felt the way I do when I make love with you, Quinn. It's indescribable. But we can't spend the rest of our lives in bed."

"I don't know," he drawled. "The idea is rather intriguing, now that you mention it. Although we'd probably have to plan ahead and stock the freezer." His eyes gleamed with a wicked light, enticing her to give up the battle. "I wouldn't want you wasting away to nothing."

"Dammit, Quinn," Jessica snapped. "This isn't a time for you to pull out your well-honed seduction techniques!"

"Correct me if I'm mistaken," he said with a silkiness that didn't mask the gravelly note in his voice, "but you were the one doing most of the seducing last night." He allowed a wry smile. "Not that I'm complaining, you understand. I just want to get that little fact down on the record."

He was right, Jessica admitted secretly. But even then it had been an act of surrender. She'd given in to the primitive hunger he was able to instill in her with a single word, a single glance or touch. Whenever she was with Quinn, tides of emotion lapped away at her willpower, dissolving it like a sandcastle at high tide.

Quinn hated the way her face suddenly closed, denying him access to her thoughts. "Jessica?"

When she slowly, reluctantly lifted her gaze to his, her eyes were filled with self-loathing that tore at some delicate fiber deep inside him.

"I was just thinking of a line from T. S. Eliot," she murmured. "And how it seemed to fit me lately."

"Are you going to let me in on it?" he asked quietly.

Jessica braced her elbows on the table, rubbing wearily at her temples. "He wrote of the awful daring that's involved in a moment's surrender," she said tightly.

Quinn swore softly. "Why in hell do you insist on putting up these artificial barriers between us?"

"Because they're real," she retorted harshly. "What we have in there—" she tossed her head in the direction of the bedroom "—is one thing. But it isn't enough to base a lifetime relationship on."

"What do you know about lifetime relationships?" he blazed. "You went into this with the intention of having a nice, brief little affair. No strings. No commitment on either side!"

With a swift movement Jessica had been totally unprepared for, Quinn was suddenly standing over her, closing his hands over her shoulders, hauling her unceremoniously to her feet.

"You're a fine one to talk, sweetheart. All you ever wanted from me was sex. I'd say if anyone should be feeling used right about now, it's me." His green gaze raked her scornfully. "Admit it—you used me for stud service. Sexual relief for the frustrated divorcée, right?"

The sound rang out like a gunshot and Jessica stared at the hand still resting on his cheek.

"Feel better?" he drawled dangerously.

Jessica's eyes remained riveted on the red mark disfiguring his harsh features as she slowly lowered her hand to her side. Then she shrugged free, turning away. "I hate what you do to me," she whispered. "I hate the way you make me lose control."

Quinn studied the slump to her slender shoulders, telling

himself that he'd gone about that all wrong. He hadn't meant to get into an argument with her. He damn well hadn't intended to say those things. He and Jessica were like a flammable vapor meeting fire; the explosion was inevitable.

"Jess—" he tried what he hoped was a consoling tone "—I'm sorry. You made me angry and I said some things I didn't mean."

Her response was muffled, but he wasn't encouraged as she shook her head, refusing to turn around.

He moved to her, putting his arms around her. Jessica tensed at the intimate touch. "Honey, you frustrated me. You keep confusing what you feel is surrender in bed, to surrender in life."

"Isn't it?" she whispered.

He rested his chin on her auburn hair. "If it is, then we're both in the same boat because I can't keep away from you any more than you can keep away from me."

"You did a damn good job of it the past three weeks," she complained. "How was Mexico, by the way?"

"Mexico?" he asked, sounding confused. "What gave you the idea I was in Mexico?"

Perhaps he hadn't been with Pamela Stuart, after all. Although Jessica experienced a fleeting sense of relief, she reminded herself that it changed nothing. She merely shrugged.

"I was in Phoenix with Keith."

"You didn't return my calls."

"I wanted to. I must have picked up the phone a hundred times a day, but I was afraid you wouldn't want to hear anything I had to say...."

"I was going crazy from missing you, Jess." Quinn's voice held a rough, masculine plea. "Doesn't that mean anything?"

"Only that we're just like the Thackers. We can't live with each other, and we can't live without each other." She turned, lifting her distressed gaze to his. "Well, I don't know about you, but I can't go on this way. I'm not going to see you again, Quinn."

A flicker of pain flashed in his eyes, but his voice was steady. His appraising gaze surveyed her tense face.

"This conversation is all too familiar," he grated. "Be certain this is what you really want this time, Jessica," he warned softly. "Because I'm not going to keep setting myself up to be dumped like this."

Jessica stared at Quinn as his words slowly sank in. Is that what she'd done to him? Was she no better than Brian? Had she just taken what he had to offer, then turned her back and walked away, rather than offering a commitment? Oh God, she groaned inwardly, how had things gotten so confused?

Quinn watched the waves of emotion washing over Jessica's face. First confusion, then doubt, then a blinding comprehension so powerful that it caused her to tremble in his arms. He released her, allowing her to slump wearily into her chair as he waited for her to retract her incautious words.

The sound of the doorbell fractured the thick silence. Quinn's oath was brief and harsh. Refusing to leave this matter unsettled, he remained standing over Jessica, his mouth a hard, grim line. The doorbell rang again. Then, when he continued to ignore it, one more time.

"You'd better answer your door," Jessica suggested on a flat, defeated note. "I don't think whoever is out there is going to go away." The strident demand of the bell proved her correct.

He looked over his shoulder to the foyer with a withering

glance. Then his gaze returned to Jessica. "This is more important."

When the chimes pealed again, Jessica exhaled a deep sigh. "We're not going to be able to discuss anything with all that racket," she pointed out. "Go open the door, Quinn."

Muttering a particularly violent series of expletives, Quinn marched to the door, flinging it open with ill-concealed anger. He had to swallow his planned response as he viewed Elizabeth, standing in the hallway, a red suitcase in her hand.

"I was beginning to think you weren't home," she said, her smile wavering as she viewed Quinn's harshly set features. "Perhaps I'd better just give you this and leave," Elizabeth suggested, shoving the overnight case at him.

Jessica experienced a mixture of regret and relief when she heard her mother's voice. "Mom?" she called out, getting up from the chair. "You don't have to go."

"Quinn?" Elizabeth asked sympathetically.

He shrugged with feigned carelessness, taking the suitcase from her hand. "What the hell," he muttered, "we're not getting anywhere, anyway. You might as well come in."

Elizabeth embraced her daughter, her judicial gaze deciding that as bad as Jessica looked, Quinn appeared even worse, if that were possible.

"I brought your clothes," she explained needlessly. "How are you feeling?"

"I've felt better," Jessica admitted.

Elizabeth glanced around the apartment. "I talked with Brian this morning. He has to go out of town for a couple of weeks, but Deirdre said the girls could stay with her."

"No way," Jessica said firmly, crossing her arms over her chest.

Elizabeth nodded understandingly. "I told him that you'd probably want to pick them up this afternoon," she agreed. "Since it doesn't look as if Quinn has room for them here, why don't you let them stay with your father and me?"

Jessica could feel Quinn's hard green eyes impaling her as if they were shafts of cold steel. She had never seen him as angry as he had been this morning. She forced her attention back to her mother.

"Thanks, but they have to finish up these last weeks of school and you and Dad live across town. The insurance will pay for us to move into a hotel while the house is being rebuilt."

Her mother's expression remained smooth, but her voice demonstrated confusion. "But I thought you were staying here."

"I was only a convenient port in the storm," Quinn offered sarcastically. "Jessica never had any intention of staying with me." His tone made it clear that he was talking about more than living arrangements.

Elizabeth's gaze moved first from Jessica, then to Quinn, then back to her daughter. "I see," she said quietly. "Well, dear, why don't you change and I'll drive you up to Mill Valley."

"Thank you," Jessica said, eager to escape Quinn's gaze as she took the suitcase he handed her. There was a spark and an instant of heat when their fingers touched, but his eyes displayed no emotion. As Jessica left the room, she felt unreasonably like a crab scuttling away in the sand.

Ten minutes later she was standing in the doorway, trying to come up with appropriate words to say goodbye. Quinn's expression was unreadable, but she thought she could see a weary depression in his eyes. Jessica's throat tightened.

"Uh, thank you," she said softly. "For everything."

"You're welcome," he answered politely. Then an acid tone slid into his voice. "For everything."

Jessica and Quinn studied each other, each waiting the other out. Then, unable to stand the pain another moment, Jessica spun on her heel, leaving the apartment.

Elizabeth remained quiet on the drive north to Marin County, a fact for which Jessica was exceedingly grateful. She stared out at the rugged coastline, unable to forget Quinn standing there in the foyer, his hands thrust deeply into his front pockets, a raw expression of pain on his face. Jessica knew that image would remain with her for the rest of her life.

CHAPTER THIRTEEN

THE GIRLS FOUND life in a hotel an absolute lark for the first five days. Then they began to complain incessantly about the lack of privacy, the tiny portable refrigerator and the fact that their music had to be kept to a reasonable volume. Jessica was grateful that school would be out in another week. Then, since her parents were taking off to sail the high seas, she might take them up on their offer to use their home.

One advantage to living in a hotel, Jessica decided, was room service. Of course, anything would be an improvement over the meals Elizabeth had prepared during her stay in the house. She was sipping on her morning coffee when Jill approached, a tentative expression on her face.

"Mom?"

Jessica looked up and smiled. The punk look had disappeared; in its place was a lovely young girl with glossy hair and a full-skirted cotton sundress.

"Yes, dear?"

"You haven't forgotten next Wednesday, have you?"

"Forget my daughter's junior high school graduation? Don't be silly. Of course I haven't forgotten."

"Gran and Gramps are coming, too," Jill offered.

"I know," Jessica murmured. She had the distinct feeling that something was being left unsaid.

"I want to invite Quinn," Jill blurted out, confirming Jessica's suspicions.

Jessica slowly lowered her cup to its gilt rimmed saucer. "I don't think that would be a very good idea, sweetheart."

Jill's cheeks flamed scarlet. "Well, I don't think it's fair. Just because you were stupid enough to break up with him, I don't think that's any reason for us to suffer."

"Jill, my relationship with Quinn is really none of your business," Jessica stated firmly, rising from the table.

"It is, too!"

Jessica stared at her daughter. Before she could answer, Mallory entered the living room of the two-bedroom suite and offered her opinion.

"Jill's right," she argued. "Even if you don't love Quinn, we do. And we're definitely getting the short end of the stick. He hasn't been to see us for ages."

Jessica's back stiffened at the accusation in her daughter's tone. She slanted a glance at Sara, who was standing in the doorway, watching quietly.

"What's the matter?" Jessica asked dryly. "Don't you have anything to say about all this?"

Her youngest daughter's voice was soft, but firm. "We miss him, Mom."

"We miss him a lot," Mallory seconded.

"A whole bunch," Jill confirmed. "I really want him to come to my graduation, Mom. Please?"

"What makes you think he'll come?"

"He will if you ask him," Jill said, her expression brightening as she took Jessica's question to be a surrender.

"What makes you think I have any influence over him?" Jessica inquired baldly.

"He loves you," Sara said.

"And I suppose you're an expert?" Jessica couldn't resist asking. She was finding this conversation far more painful than she ever could have imagined.

"He asked you to marry him," Jill reminded her.

''That was several weeks ago,'' Jessica countered. She began gathering up the scattered breakfast dishes and putting them on the serving cart.

''So?'' Mallory wasn't going to let her get away that easily.

Jessica managed a careless shrug. ''So things change. People change.''

''Like you and Dad changed?'' Sara asked, her smooth young forehead drawn together into deep, thoughtful frown lines.

Jessica couldn't lie. She'd always tried to be honest with her daughters and she wasn't about to jeopardize their relationship now.

''No, it's different with Quinn,'' she admitted. ''I still care for him very deeply, but...'' Jessica drew in a breath. ''Things are complicated,'' she said slowly. ''Quinn and I want different things from life.''

She managed a weak smile. ''That's enough depressing conversation for one morning,'' she stated firmly. ''Now, if you don't hurry, you'll miss your bus and be late for school.''

''We're going,'' Jill said on a resigned note.

Jessica was not that surprised when Sara turned in the doorway. ''Mom?'' she whispered, her blue eyes grave.

''Yes?''

''Do you love Quinn?''

''Yes, I do,'' Jessica answered without hesitation.

Puzzlement shadowed her daughter's clear blue eyes. ''Then why don't you just tell him that? I'll bet he still wants to marry you.''

Jessica shook her head. ''It's not that simple, sweetheart,'' she replied quietly. ''Marriage is more complicated than two people simply loving each other.''

They all turned and left the suite, but Jessica couldn't

miss Mallory's heartfelt words as they made their way to the elevator.

"Boy, if that's what it's like to be an adult, I'm not ever going to grow up!"

"Don't be a dope," Jill argued. "You can't stay a kid forever."

"Peter Pan did," Sara interjected.

"Peter Pan is just a dumb story," Jill scoffed. "Boy, you two are as dopey as Mom."

While that description wasn't the least bit flattering, Jessica experienced an odd sense of relief at the fact that the girls were bickering. That, at least, was normal behavior.

They made it sound so simple, Jessica mused, as she gathered up her purse and briefcase. Two people fall in love, get married and live happily ever after. How nice it would be if that was the way it really was. However, she was living, breathing proof that not all marriages were made in heaven. Then there was always Keith and Sylvia Thacker.

Jessica had not been surprised when the Thackers reconciled, although she wondered how long they'd manage to stay together this time. She was, however, nonplussed when her former client claimed she'd been the very best attorney she'd ever hired, and promised to call her the next time the couple split.

It was at that point Jessica decided that if she needed an additional excuse to quit her job, avoiding the Thackers was probably reason enough. She had accepted the offer from the District Attorney and was honestly amazed when George Bennington not only asked her to stay with the firm, but offered a generous raise as an incentive.

While Jessica was flattered by the knowledge that despite his demanding attitude, George Bennington found her a bright, capable attorney, she remained firm in her decision.

She was looking for new frontiers in her work and the District Attorney's office was nothing if not challenging.

For the first time in ages, Jessica found herself looking forward to her future as she prepared to leave for the office. Today she'd clean out her desk, take a month off, then start her life anew. If she was lucky, she might even begin to get over Quinn Masterson, she told herself, brimming over with self-confidence this final Friday at Bennington, Marston, White and Lowell.

A newspaper was lying on her desk as she walked into her office, already open to the society page. As she sat down, Jessica's gaze was arrested by a strikingly familiar face.

"Socialite snares longtime matrimonial holdout," the headline on the gossip column screamed out at her. As Jessica stared at Pamela Stuart's elegant features, an icy fear skimmed its way up her spine. The accompanying story confirmed her worst fears. Pamela had not only announced her engagement to Quinn, they'd set the date for a week from today.

"He's making an enormous mistake," Jessica said aloud. "She's not right for him. She'll only end up hurting him."

And what do you think you did? a little voice inquired from the depths of her mind.

"I did what I had to do for both of us."

You were afraid, the little voice pressed. *You only thought about yourself.*

"I'm entitled," Jessica argued. "After all, look what happened when I spent my life thinking about everyone else *but* me."

Can you honestly compare Quinn with Brian?

"That's not the point," Jessica said heatedly, embarrassed as Vanessa suddenly appeared in the office doorway.

"Jessica?" she asked hesitantly. "Are you alone? I thought I heard you talking to someone."

"Just myself," Jessica explained with feigned cheeriness. "Which means, I suppose, that I'm getting out of here just in time. Don't they say that's the first sign of insanity?"

"Speaking of getting out, I just dropped by to wish you good luck in your new career. It should prove quite a change."

"That's what I'm hoping," Jessica agreed.

The woman's eyes moved to the paper. "I see you've read the news."

Jessica suddenly realized exactly how the newspaper had arrived on her desk. "About Pamela and Quinn?" she asked casually.

"I tried to warn you, Jessica. But you refused to listen."

Vanessa's conciliatory tone couldn't conceal the oddly victorious note, and Jessica wondered why she'd ever thought this woman was her friend. From the beginning, Vanessa had done nothing but offer damning little innuendos concerning Quinn. Professionally, personally, she'd continued to warn Jessica the man was poison.

She looked at Vanessa curiously. "How long have you worked here?"

"Ages. Sometimes it seems like forever. On a good day it only seems like half my life."

Half her life. Vanessa was slightly older than Jessica. And as far as she knew, the woman had never worked for any other firm. All of a sudden, the pieces began to fall into place.

"Did you and Quinn work together?"

Something flickered in the depths of the woman's eyes for a brief instant, so fleeting that if Jessica hadn't been watching carefully, it would have escaped her attention.

GET 2

HOW TO GET YOUR
2 FREE BOOKS AND FREE GIFT!

1. Peel off the MIRA® sticker on the front cover. Place it in the space provided at right. This automatically entitles you to receive two free books and an exciting surprise gift.

2. Send back this card and you'll get 2 "The Best of the Best™" books. These books have a combined cover price of $11.98 or more in the U.S. and $13.98 or more in Canada, but they are yours to keep absolutely FREE!

3. There's <u>no</u> catch. You're under <u>no</u> obligation to buy anything. We charge nothing – ZERO – for your first shipment. And you don't have to make any minimum number of purchases – not even one!

4. We call this line "The Best of the Best" because each month you'll receive the best books by some of today's most popular authors. These authors show up time and time again on all the major bestseller lists and their books sell out as soon as they hit the stores. You'll like the convenience of getting them delivered to your home at our special discount prices . . . and you'll love your *Heart to Heart* subscriber newsletter featuring author news, horoscopes, recipes, book reviews and much more!

SPECIAL FREE GIFT!
We'll send you a fabulous surprise gift, absolutely FREE, simply for accepting our no-risk offer!

5. We hope that after receiving your free books you'll want to remain a subscriber. But the choice is yours – to continue or cancel, anytime at all! So why not take us up on our invitation, with no risk of any kind. You'll be glad you did!

6. And remember...we'll send you a surprise gift ABSOLUTELY FREE just for giving THE BEST OF THE BEST a try.

Visit us online at
www.mirabooks.com

® and TM are registered trademarks
of Harlequin Enterprises Limited.

"Now that you mention it," Vanessa stated, brushing at some nonexistent wrinkles on her silk suit, "I believe we might have."

It still hurts, Jessica considered, hearing the bitter edge in the woman's voice. She's been carrying around all that pain for years and years, refusing to allow herself a genuine relationship with a man. Jessica couldn't help comparing Vanessa's behavior with her own and found them uncomfortably similar.

"Quinn once told me that he had planned his life very carefully," Jessica ventured.

"He was going to be a partner by age forty," Vanessa agreed bitterly. "Then and only then was he going to get married."

"Knowing Quinn, I imagine he was up front about his plans."

The woman's eyes hardened. "Oh, I'll give him credit for that," she agreed. "But we all hope that we're the one who can change a man's mind, don't we? That he'll love us more than anything else." Her laugh was short and bitter. "Quinn Masterson's first priority has always been himself."

She tossed her head toward the damning newspaper. "As you'll see, he stuck to his master plan."

He certainly had done that, Jessica thought. But he was wrong. So very wrong.

"If you don't mind, Vanessa, I've got a lot of packing to do."

Vanessa shrugged her silk-clad shoulders. "Sure. Good luck in the D.A.'s office—you're going to need it."

Her words were a distant buzz in Jessica's ear, but she managed to slowly decode them. "Thanks," she answered absently. She stared thoughtfully out the window as she considered Quinn's forthcoming marriage.

''Keep in touch,'' Vanessa stated with a cheery little wave as she left the office.

''I'll do that,'' Jessica replied automatically, knowing that if she never saw Vanessa again it would be too soon. She finished cleaning out her desk, anxious to leave.

When she returned to the hotel, Jessica tried to put Quinn from her mind, but found it to be an impossible task. The girls were spending the night with Elizabeth and Mac, leaving Jessica alone with her memories.

She went into one of the bedrooms, locating Mallory's award-winning videotape. It took a while to figure out how to hook up the portable VCR to the hotel television, but soon Jessica was sitting in the darkened room, watching selected scenes from her life flickering on the screen in front of her.

In spite of parental prompting, Mallory had not edited out the scene in which Jessica had fallen over Elizabeth's luggage in an attempt to answer the telephone. Little had she known how that single phone call from Sylvia Thacker would change her life.

Despite Mallory's goal of creating a film of the family, Quinn appeared with heartbreaking frequency. And why not, Jessica asked herself, experiencing a jolt of pain as she watched Quinn fasten the silver locket around her neck. In their short time together, he had infiltrated the household of women with amazing ease. There had been times, Jessica recalled, when his presence had seemed more natural than Brian's ever had.

Her heart stopped as she viewed the scene in the kitchen the morning Quinn had casually dropped the bombshell about their marriage. Now, eyeing him more closely, Jessica noted that although his expression was bland enough, his fingers were curved tightly around the handle of his coffee cup, his knuckles white with tension.

As she viewed her own expression, Jessica was stunned

to see not the aggravation she had thought she was feeling that morning, but pure, unadulterated fear.

Was she afraid of marriage? Of commitment? Was her demand for total autonomy simply a mask for lingering feelings of insecurity? Had she sent Quinn away because she doubted her ability to hold him? If so, she had done him an injustice. Quinn Masterson would be incapable of cheating on his wife, just as Brian O'Neill was incapable of fidelity.

The screen went blank, but Jessica didn't notice. She rose, pacing the floor as she considered her behavior over the past few months. She had been worried about Quinn's gaining the upper hand in their relationship. But the truth was, she realized belatedly, she had always been the one in control. She had insisted on setting limits, on establishing boundaries, creating obstacles to any deep involvement.

Yet somehow love had blossomed despite her machinations. Somehow she had fallen in love with Quinn, and amazingly enough, he had fallen in love with her. But what had she done to return that love? Nothing. Oh, she'd been more than willing to make love with him, Jessica admitted grimly. But on her terms. And when Quinn finally objected, when he insisted on more—on marriage—she'd sent him away.

In spite of that, the minute she had needed him, Quinn had been there for her. Opening his apartment and his heart, demanding nothing in return. And what had she done in return? Slammed the door in his face again.

"Oh, God," Jessica groaned. "Jill was right. I acted like an absolute dope."

Everything Quinn had done proved that he was not a man to force his will on anyone. Least of all someone he loved. A marriage to him would be one of equals. Two people sharing a life based on common respect. And love.

It was, Jessica realized, what she wanted more than anything else in the world. But now, thanks to her blindness, she might have lost her chance.

One thing was clear. Quinn wasn't going to set himself up to be hurt again. If she wanted to resolve things between them, she would have to make the first move.

Picking up the telephone, she dialed Quinn's apartment. She was forced to wait, her nerves screaming as she allowed the number to ring ten times. Then ten more. Finally, an additional ten. When there was still no answer, she slowly replaced the receiver to its cradle.

Jessica paced the floor long into the night, redialing Quinn's number at regular intervals. At two o'clock in the morning she was forced to admit he wasn't coming home. Where was he? With Pamela? Was he at this very moment lying in her arms on satin sheets in some luxuriously decorated penthouse bedroom? That thought was too abominable to even consider.

"It's just as well," Jessica decided aloud as she fell into her own lonely bed. "It'll be better in person, anyway. Telephones are so horribly impersonal."

Refusing to give up hope, she finally fell asleep.

JESSICA AWOKE EARLY the following morning, her resolve intact. After ordering coffee from room service, she called the MacLaughlin home.

Elizabeth answered the phone in a muffled, sleepy voice. "H'llo?"

"Mother," Jessica said, "I need your help."

Elizabeth was instantly awake. "Of course, dear. What can I do for you?"

"Would you mind keeping the girls another night?"

"You know your father and I love having them visit,"

Elizabeth replied without hesitation. Her voice took on a tone of motherly concern. "You're not ill, are you?"

"No," Jessica answered. "I'm fine. I just have something important to do and if everything works out all right, I won't be home this evening."

"You're going to Quinn."

Jessica was not surprised by Elizabeth's insight. After all, she'd undoubtedly seen that gossip item, as well.

"Yes."

A cheer rang in Jessica's ear. "All right, Mom!" Jill shouted. "It's about time!"

"Jill," Elizabeth scolded, her stern tone giving way to a low chuckle, "it's impolite to listen in on the extension."

"Sorry, Gran. But I just won five dollars in the pool."

"Pool? What pool?" Jessica asked.

"I said you'd get back with Quinn today. Sara bet last night, and Mallory had the weird idea you were going to crash his wedding, like Dustin Hoffman did to Katherine Ross in *The Graduate*."

Despite the fact that her daughter had displayed atrocious manners by eavesdropping on a private conversation, not to mention that all three girls had actually been betting on her love life, Jessica laughed.

"Tell Sara that she would have won if Quinn had been home last night," Jessica revealed.

"Jessie?" Mac's voice came on the line.

"Yes, Dad?"

"Don't worry about a thing. If Quinn doesn't take you back, we'll sue for breach of promise."

"You wouldn't!"

Her father's laugh was rich and deep. "Take your pick, daughter. It's either that or showing up at his office with my shotgun."

"You've never even owned a gun," Jessica protested.

"You know that and I know that. But Quinn Masterson doesn't. I have every intention of seeing my daughter safely married off before I go sailing into the sunset." Mac paused, as if carefully choosing his words.

"What the hell," he continued gruffly. "You may scream bloody murder, but I have to admit I'll feel a lot better knowing that you've got a good man taking care of you while I'm away."

Jessica had no intention of screaming. Because she knew that Quinn would take care of her. Just as she had every intention of taking care of him.

"I love you, Dad," she said softly before hanging up.

Jessica showered and dressed in record time. While she had no idea how Quinn would react to her interference in his life, she refused to allow her determination to falter. As she took a taxi to his office, she hoped it wasn't too late to change things.

The young woman at the desk outside Quinn's office rose as Jessica marched by. "Excuse me, ma'am, but you can't go in without an appointment!"

"D.A.'s office," Jessica announced blithely, ignoring the secretary's protest. "Official business."

Quinn's back was to the door, his gaze directed out the window as he dictated a letter to an elderly stenographer.

"In closing, I believe that Lamberson Electronics can only benefit by the proposed merger and recommend moving to file as quickly as possible. If you have any questions or comments, please don't hesitate to contact me. Sincerely yours, et cetera, et cetera. Could you please read that back to me, Mrs. Young?"

The woman was staring up at Jessica, who'd suddenly appeared beside her, and didn't answer.

"Mrs. Young?" Quinn repeated, turning around in his chair.

When he saw Jessica, an inscrutable mask settled over his features. "Thank you, Mrs. Young," he said, his eyes not leaving Jessica's. "That will be all for today. And please tell Susan to hold all my calls."

"Yes, sir." The woman rose quickly, departing from the room.

Quinn braced his elbows on the arms of his chair, making a tent with his fingers.

"Well, well," he said smoothly. "It's not often I have a visitor from the D.A.'s office. Don't tell me that there's a bench warrant out for my overdue parking tickets?"

He wasn't going to make it easy on her, Jessica thought. Then she gave a mental shrug. Why should he? Since he'd yet to offer her a chair, Jessica remained standing.

"I'm surprised you know about my move," she admitted, wondering when Quinn could have had time to keep tabs on her while courting Pamela Stuart.

"Mac told me. Congratulations, by the way."

"You've been talking to my father?"

Quinn gestured at a chair on the other side of the desk. "Sit down, Jess," he suggested patiently. "And to answer your question, Mac and I were friends long before you and I had our little affair. I'm not going to stop seeing the man just because his daughter walked out on me."

That stung. Jessica looked down at her hands, pretending a sudden interest in her fingernails.

"Jessica?"

She lifted her gaze, looking for something, anything in his smooth green eyes. Some sign that he still cared. Jessica could find nothing there, but she hadn't come here to turn tail and run at the first obstacle.

"Yes?" she asked, managing to match his casual tone.

"You still haven't told me what you're doing here," he reminded her.

Jessica gazed out at the sparkling waters of the bay. The orange expanse of Golden Gate Bridge gleamed copper in the bright sunlight of early June.

She decided to ease into it. "I called you last night, but you weren't home."

"I had a meeting in Sacramento that ran late," he answered easily. "I spent the night there."

"Oh."

The silence settled down between them again. Jessica took a deep breath. It was now or never.

"I've come to save you," she blurted out.

He arched a brow. "Save me?"

She nodded and her tone was a little firmer as she elaborated. "From making the biggest mistake of your life."

"I see." He swiveled back and forth in the chair, eyeing her impassively. "I don't suppose you'd care to explain that a little further," he prompted.

"You can't marry Pamela Stuart," she insisted, leaning forward in her own chair, her body a stiff, tense line. "I know you had this big master plan for your life. But you can't get married just because you've turned forty, Quinn! That's not a good enough reason."

"What *is* a good reason to get married, Jess?" he asked softly.

"Love," she answered without hesitation.

He picked up a gold fountain pen, toying with it absently. Every one of Jessica's nerve endings were screaming with impatience, waiting for Quinn to say something.

"What makes you think I don't love Pam?"

"Because you love me," she stated firmly, her blue eyes daring him to deny that statement.

"You know, Jess, a torch is a damned burdensome thing to carry around forever," he advised her evenly. "After a while it burns down and you end up scorching your fingers.''

"And I love you."

Quinn's expression didn't waver. Jessica thought she saw something flash in his eyes, but it was gone too quickly for her to be certain.

"I see… When did you come to that momentous conclusion?"

"I think I fell in love with you that first night we met," Jessica admitted softly. "But I knew for certain when we made love the first time."

While Jessica had not known what reaction she was going to receive by coming here today, laying her heart on the line, she'd secretly hoped Quinn would be thrilled by her confession. Instead, he flung the pen furiously onto the top of the desk and they both watched as it skidded across the wide, polished surface, finally coming to land silently on the thick carpet.

When Quinn returned his gaze to Jessica's, his eyes had hardened to stone. Jessica was forced to consider the unpleasant fact that she might be too late.

"Damn you, Jessie O'Neill," he growled on a harsh breath. "Why didn't you tell me? Why did you drive me crazy all these past weeks?"

She shook her head, feeling duly chastised. "I was afraid."

"Of me?" His tone was incredulous. "I told you from the beginning how I felt about you. How in blue blazes could you think I'd do anything to hurt you?"

"You were going to marry Pamela Stuart," Jessica felt obliged to point out, lifting her chin bravely. "You didn't think that would hurt me?"

He muttered a soft oath. "For an intelligent woman, you sure can be some dumb female." As he dragged his fingers through his hair, Jessica noticed his hands were shaking. "What in the hell am I going to do with you?"

It was now or never. Putting her feelings for Quinn before her pride, Jessica slowly rose from the chair, moving around the vast expanse of oak separating them and settled herself boldly onto his lap. Encouraged by the fact that he didn't toss her to the floor, she twined her arms around his neck.

"If you're open to suggestions," she said softly, nuzzling his ear, "I've got one or two to offer."

The muscles in his shoulders began to relax. He put his arms around her waist. "Doing a little plea bargaining, counselor?"

"Could be," she agreed with a tantalizing smile that faded as her expression turned inordinately serious. "Quinn, will you marry me?"

He paused, as if the decision were a particularly difficult one.

Her heart was beating too fast. Jessica felt as if she'd run up a steep flight of stairs. She waved her hand in front of his face.

"Quinn?"

He shook his head slightly, as if to clear it. "Sorry, Jess. It's just that I've never had a woman propose to me before."

The waiting was driving her crazy. If this was what men went through when they proposed, it was amazing that the institution of matrimony had survived all these generations.

"Well?" she asked, unwilling to wait a moment longer for Quinn's answer.

A broad grin split his face. "Sweetheart, I thought you'd never ask!"

His lips covered hers in a long, lingering kiss that neither participant was eager to end. Finally Quinn broke the intimate contact, resting his chin atop Jessica's head.

"Thank you, Pam," he murmured, unaware he'd spoken out loud until Jessica's head suddenly jerked up.

"It's not what you're thinking," Quinn said instantly, soothingly.

"How do you know what I'm thinking?"

"I can venture a guess."

"Try."

Quinn shifted Jessica on his lap, eyeing her warily. "You're thinking that I've got a helluva nerve saying some other woman's name after I've just accepted your proposal."

"I'm sure you've got a marvelous explanation," Jessica responded calmly, secure in the knowledge that it was she Quinn loved and not Pamela.

"I do want to marry you, Jessica. It's all I've wanted from that first moment I saw you standing in the doorway of the ballroom, looking as delectable as a strawberry ice-cream cone in that pink running suit."

Quinn saw Jessica's eyes soften at the memory of that night. Encouraged, he continued. "You have to understand, I was desperate. I was going crazy without you in my arms, in my bed... But most of all, I needed you in my life."

Comprehension slowly dawned, and Jessica stared at Quinn in amazement. "Pamela planted that story, didn't she? She played the same role for you that you've always played for her. It was all a hoax!"

"I'm afraid so," he admitted. "I didn't want to hurt you, Jess. I only wanted you to realize how right we were for each other. How we belonged together."

His tanned face appeared heartbreakingly vulnerable. Jessica didn't know whether to kiss him or hit him over the head with the nearest blunt object.

"How did you know I'd see the paper? I normally don't even read the society page."

"I didn't think Vanessa would miss an opportunity to show it to you. I've never been one of her favorite people."

"You were once," Jessica felt obliged to point out.

Quinn shook his head. "Vanessa made more of that than I expected. I never promised her anything, Jessica. I told her from the start about my goals. And at that point in time they never included marriage."

"I suppose I'm lucky I met you after your fortieth birthday," Jessica murmured, a sad little note creeping into her voice.

His eyes darkened with a loving gleam. "Believe me, Jess, if I'd been fortunate enough to have run into you during those days, all my good intentions would have gone flying out the window."

"Really?" she asked, tracing the hard line of his jaw.

"Really," he confirmed, turning his head to press a kiss against her fingertips. "We were made for each other, sweetheart. Timing had nothing to do with it."

Her misgivings dissolved, Jessica snuggled against him. "Quinn?"

"Mmm?"

"What would you have done if I hadn't come to your office today?"

"I was going to give you twenty-four hours, then kidnap you and keep you hostage in my bed until you agreed to marry me," he replied promptly.

"I've already agreed to marry you," she told him. "In fact, for the record, I did the proposing."

Quinn knew what an effort it had taken for Jessica to put aside her pride and come to his office today. He couldn't remember loving her more than he did at this moment.

His eyes brightened with a seductive gleam. "It's still

not such a bad idea. I especially like the part about keeping you hostage in my bed.''

''Kidnapping's a capital offense.''

''Ah, but I was hoping I could convince a certain sexy assistant D.A. not to press charges.''

''I couldn't neglect my duties, Quinn. Even for you.'' She gave him a sensual little smile. ''Of course, if you're willing to plead guilty, I could probably get you released to my custody.''

''How long a sentence are they handing out for kidnapping these days?''

''It's a very serious charge, Quinn. I'd say fifty years to life, at the very least.''

Quinn's answering grin wreathed his handsome face and lines fanned out from those brilliant emerald eyes she had not been able to put from her mind during their time apart.

''Fifty years to life,'' he agreed between kisses. ''At the very least.''

Dear Reader,

Every character I write is part of me in some way. I can relate to my hero Arch's optimism and refusal to take anything too seriously. The vanity and concern for appearances of the heroine's mother, Maude, are parts of me, too, though admittedly not ones I'm terribly proud of.

But I confess I have a special place in my heart for Amanda, whose journey of self-discovery is so close to mine. Too many women live their lives to please other people, and I was happy to teach her that asking for what she truly wants (okay, she has to figure it out first!), even if she fears hurting people she loves, is better than hurting both them and herself by living in denial.

Of course, being a romance heroine, she gets to fall in love with a funny, sexy, charm-her-pants-off guy along the way and lives happily ever after for her efforts.

Let me know how you like the story! You can e-mail me through my Web site, www.IsabelSharpe.com.

Cheers,

Isabel

WITHOUT A NET

Isabel Sharpe

To Susan Pezzack, my editor and friend

CHAPTER ONE

"*AND I want* the waist taken in. To make me look thinner."

Amanda Marcus clenched her teeth. No—scratch that—they were already clenched. Any harder and they'd fuse together. The bodice of Geneva "Genie" Straussgarten's wedding dress already looked as if it was ready to go on strike over the volume of what had been stuffed into it. Take it in any farther and Genie would probably pass out halfway down the aisle from lack of oxygen.

"Okay." Amanda wrestled with the fabric and managed to pinch an eighth of an inch of silk satin into which she stuck pins, carefully avoiding temptation as to where the sharp points should be plunged. Genie was a lovely young woman—current bridal pout notwithstanding—beautifully and generously shaped. But the strapless gown with tight bodice and huge tulle skirt was wrong, wrong, wrong for her, and it drove Amanda's dressmaking soul crazy.

She could see Genie elegant, innocent and discreetly sexy in a cream silk sheath, wide scoop neckline, off-the-shoulder half sleeves, a silk drape skirt, brought over to one side to gather at the gentle waist. Nothing tight, everything fluid.

Anything but the hefty-ballerina look.

But what could you do when your client had already spent thousands of dollars? Worse, when those thousands of dollars had been spent at Milwaukee's most exclusive shop, The Dress. Owned by the infinitely snooty proprietor

Zera Janes, arch competitor to the not-quite-as-exclusive shop Amanda had worked in for the last five years, Patterson's. Patterson's had finally succumbed to the tough economy and Zera's undercutting tricks, bringing Amanda's dreams of buying the shop when the Pattersons retired crashing down to lie face first in the mud.

So instead of being on the way to owning her own business, Amanda was reduced to altering a dress pouty little Genie never should have bought, but which was doubtless expensive enough to make it a flattering fit as far as The Dress's salesclerks were concerned.

"It should be shorter, too." The snippy voice grew snippier. "Not much. Maybe just under an inch."

Amanda stared at the filmy tulle. Yards and yards and yards. Layer upon layer upon layer. To be shortened. By less than an inch.

"Actually, the length is perfect. Look." She brushed aside a poufy fold. "Your slippers will peek out with every step down the aisle. It's lovely this way."

Genie gathered handfuls of the material and tried to find her feet. The Bridal Pout of Pique softened into a genuinely miserable one, complete with trembling lower lip. "I like it this way, too. But Mom wanted it shorter. She said if she paid that much for my shoes, people should be able to see them."

Amanda's stomach clenched, to keep her teeth company. In a sudden burst of empathy she understood Genie's tight-lipped, twenty-year-old, prewedding misery. All too clearly Amanda could remember her own mother deciding every detail of her wedding seven years ago, changing the simple picnic she and Ridge wanted into an elaborate affair, culminating in the final showdown where Amanda had summoned all her backbone and vetoed plans for a festooned horse and buggy with strolling mini-orchestra escort to take her and Ridge from the church to the reception—barely ten yards away.

"Tell you what." She winked at Genie. "I'll throw in the hemming 'for free' and then not do it. When you come back for the final fitting, just keep saying, 'Oh, you were right, Mom, this length is *so* much better.' She'll never notice. I promise."

Genie burst out laughing and, for the first time since she'd been in Amanda's apartment, looked as happy as a June bride should be. "Thank you. I swear, this whole wedding-planning thing has been horrendous. At this point, Tony and I just want to elope."

"Trust me." Amanda sent her a sympathetic smile. "I know what you mean."

Genie glanced at Amanda's left hand. Amanda sighed. Nope. No ring. Anyone could plan a wedding. But for a wedding actually to take place, the groom had to show up.

"Okay. You're set. You can take the dress off. I'll have the alterations done in two weeks."

Genie swished her fluffy way into Amanda's bedroom to change back into the cotton skirt and sweater that suited her figure perfectly. Amanda packed up her pins and tape and put them neatly away in her sewing chest. Two weeks. Right. She could make the changes to the dress tonight. But it was good for business to act as if she was so booked she needed that much leeway to do a simple seam alteration.

When Patterson's went under three weeks earlier on May first, Amanda had shoved down her pride, groveled under Zera's enormous downturned nose and been told in that high-pitched wavery voice, *Ah, non, chérie,* she couldn't possibly afford another regular employee. But from the goodness of her teeny-tiny icy Grinch heart she'd toss a few clients Amanda's way. As it turned out, a very few.

Not that Zera owed her a living, but ends weren't meeting, employers weren't biting, and it was starting to look as if Amanda might have to give up her dream and put an ad in the paper offering her services to the masses. Ugh. Goodbye exclusive dress shop, hello tedious alterations for whoever called up and wanted her.

The shaky panic threatened to take hold again and Amanda clamped down hard to shove it away. She'd be fine at least for a few more weeks. She'd find work. She was lucky in many, many ways. She'd rented the upstairs of this Lannon stone duplex in the Milwaukee suburb of Wauwatosa seven years ago for next to nothing from Mrs. Carson, the wonderful widowed lady who had lived downstairs since she'd been a bride herself over sixty years ago. For the past seven years, Mrs. Carson had also watched Amanda's daughter, Clarissa, while Amanda was at work, in return for yard work, snow clearing, occasional errands and whatever other way Amanda could find to be helpful to her.

Amanda was extremely lucky to have had that kind of arrangement as long as it lasted. Unfortunately, a week after Amanda lost her job, Mrs. Carson had announced she'd faced her last Wisconsin winter and that she was moving to a retirement community near her daughter in Orlando, Florida. Before she left, the dear lady had pushed hard to get the new owner of the duplex to keep Amanda on as a tenant at the current low rental rate, and he'd agreed. So at least she wouldn't have to move. She had small savings stashed away to see her through, though she wasn't meeting expenses with the work she'd been able to take in so far.

She let herself plunk down onto the blue-and-yellow floral sofa her mom shipped from the storage stuff that had been her grandmother's, and clasped her hands tightly in her lap. She'd be fine. Somehow. Her dream of owning her own dress shop had merely been derailed for a while. Her entire life wouldn't collapse because one thing had gone wrong. Okay, two things. Because without Mrs. Carson's help, when Amanda found a job, she'd need full-time care for Clarissa all summer, which would devour most of any salary she could pull in. But that was only two things. Lots of people had way more than two—

The pink phone rang on the end table next to her, centered on one of the million lace doilies her mom had tatted during Amanda's grade-school years, while waiting for Amanda to finish whatever lesson she'd signed her up for. Amanda narrowed her eyes. Call her superstitious, but didn't bad things always happen right when people were thinking they'd reached their limit of bad things happening?

She picked up the receiver reluctantly. "Hello?"

"Patterson's must be closed today. I called and got no answer."

"Hi, Mom." Amanda cringed. She hadn't happened to mention that she'd lost her job. "Yeah, the store's closed."

"I have news."

"Oh?" *Uh-oh.* Mom was using her something-big-is-up voice.

Genie emerged from Amanda's bedroom and held up the wedding tutu questioningly. Amanda gestured to the overly-flowery wingback chair her mother had bought her as a wedding present. "Mom, can you hang on?"

"It's *big* news."

"Okay, I'll just be a second." Amanda grimaced. Since she hadn't happened to mention to her mother that she'd lost her job, she couldn't say she had a client waiting for her. Which was about the only thing her mom would agree constituted grounds important enough for putting off any of her "big news," especially when she was calling long distance.

"It's *very* big—"

"Just a second, Mom." She put the phone against her thigh to muffle the incoming sound since she didn't trust that little mute button on the handset, and smiled at Genie. "You'll be gorgeous. I'll have it done in a couple of weeks—how about Monday, June seventh."

"Thanks." Genie rubbed her temple, nose wrinkled. "It wasn't really the dress I wanted. Mom chose it. But I guess weddings are about more than how you look."

Amanda nodded at the freckled redhead, envying her perspective at such a young age. Too many brides seemed to think the sum total of marriage was how they looked at the ceremony. Genie would do okay. She'd probably even be able to stave off her mother. "You're absolutely right. Weddings are about way more than that."

Though she herself never quite got the chance to find out.

"Thanks for your help. See you on the seventh."

Amanda saw her out, closed the door and leaned against it to brace herself for her mother's big news—no, wait, *very* big news. Could be anything from a third marriage to a new face-lift.

"Okay, I'm back."

"You ready?"

"Yes."

"You sure?"

Amanda crossed her eyes at the ceiling, the way she did as a girl right before her mom told her they'd get stuck that way and no one would want to marry her. "I'm sure."

"I've made a decision."

"And?"

"I'm moving to Milwaukee!"

Amanda stayed absolutely still except for her eyeballs, which rolled up and up into her sockets until she could picture her eyes popping right out and bouncing across her hardwood floors like ghoulish superballs. Her lungs joined in, chest inflating like a hot-air balloon. Perhaps she'd lift off the ground and go sailing around the room. The Good Airship Amanda, bound for distant lands and great adven—

"Amanda?"

"Mom, that's so…wow. It's…I mean, *wow*. I'm stunned."

"I knew you'd be thrilled. Won't it be stupendous?"

"Yes." She gestured with her left hand, fingers curved into talons. "Stupendous."

Or something.

"Now, don't worry, I won't live right next door. But I've put out feelers, and—you remember Beth Hartsfield, don't you? Thriving real-estate business, made enough to retire on already—she was in your class at Fairfield High, wasn't she?"

"No. She was older." Amanda's voice came out sounding weary. Twenty-five years ago, there were doubtless hundreds and thousands of infants who were able to roll over at an earlier age than Amanda. Doubtless every night before bed, she was told about each and every one between pages of *Goodnight Moon*.

"Well, she connected me with someone in Milwaukee, who steered me to a fabulous condo on the east side, by the lake, on Prospect Avenue. Isn't that terrific?"

"Exactly the term I would use." Only she'd mutter it sarcastically and kick something.

"I wanted to wait until it was all settled to tell you so it would be a real surprise."

"It is. It is." The skin at the back of Amanda's neck began to itch. "How settled is settled?"

"Here's the clincher. You ready?"

She curled her lip. "I'm ready."

"The condo is vacant. The movers arrive tomorrow, I'm spending a few days with friends, then I fly out there on Saturday!"

Amanda closed her eyes. The part of her that would always be this woman's daughter welcomed having Mom around when things were bad. But the rest of her—the majority adult she'd become—wanted to solve her own problems her own way in her own time. Her mother wouldn't see that as her right. Amanda's two problems had just become crowded by a third.

"Mom, it's great." She summoned genuine warmth. The woman was her mother and she did love her. It was just her timing Amanda hated. "I'm really glad you'll be around."

"Me too! We'll have so much fun. It's gotten a bit close here since George left me. You can imagine, of course. Manhattan isn't exactly a small town, like Milwaukee, but I'm always seeming to bump into him and his little girlfriend, or someone who *knows* him and his little girlfriend, at the opera, the museum, parties, restaurants, you name it. I want to make a new start."

Amanda bit her lip. She was being selfish. Her mom had loved George, as she'd loved Amanda's late father, and had tried her clueless best to be a good wife to him, but men had their own ideas about managing their own lives and after fifteen years George had ditched her for someone young, adoring and spineless, who probably couldn't even manage hers.

"Of course. It must be hell there, Mom. I—"

"Well, of course it's not *hell*. It's Manhattan! Hell is somewhere else, Detroit or Poughkeepsie or New Haven or something. It's just been a little difficult."

"Oh. Yes. That's what I meant." Amanda scrunched up

her face and rubbed her forehead. Never mind. Just never mind. "I can't wait to see you, Mom."

"I can't wait to see you either, sweet. Or that adorable girl of yours. Has she started ballet yet?"

Amanda twisted her mouth. Money hadn't been in tremendously large supply for one thing, and Clarissa hadn't exactly pirouetted at the idea. "No. Not…yet."

"Well, I'll see what I can do when I get there. I know how busy you must be, being a single mother and all. I'm sure I can be a big help to you."

Amanda's hand crept up and grabbed a lock of hair to fiddle with before she noticed and stopped. Childish habit. "Why don't you give me—"

"Let me give you my flight information."

Amanda ran across the room and copied down the airline and number onto the pad she kept by the phone. "Great. Clarissa and I will—"

"Do you think you can come pick me up? If it's not too much trouble."

"No, it's fine. I'll bring—"

"And bring my favorite little girl."

"Yes. Okay, Mom. We'll be there."

"Bye. Love you. Can't wait."

Amanda replaced the receiver and stood there staring at the pink Princess phone her mom had sent last month, "just like the one you had as a girl, dear," as if it might turn into a soul-sucking Harry Potter–type monster if she blinked.

So.

Her mother was coming to live here.

A burst of near-hysterical laughter came to her lips. She bit them and forced it back.

She could handle this. She'd be fine. Only three problems. Three. Some people lost count after a while. She was lucky.

The doorbell rang; her heart lifted. Clarissa. How had it gotten so late so early?

She ran down the flight of wooden steps to the ground floor and pulled open the door; her daughter burst through and raced upstairs, a miniature blue-eyed, blond, bobbed mini-Amanda. If Amanda wasn't so sure Ridge was biologically necessary to the process, she would swear she'd spontaneously given birth to herself.

"Hello, sweetheart." She followed her daughter upstairs and closed the apartment's door. "How was school today?"

"It stunk." Clarissa shrugged off her backpack and hung it on the front closet's cut-glass doorknob. "I sat on some jelly in the lunchroom and Ralph Edgerson teased me about it the entire afternoon. He is such a jerk."

"Aw, honey." Amanda bent and gathered the fuming little body close, then drew back to smooth her daughter's hair. "Some people need to make other people feel bad so they can feel better about themselves. I don't know why. Just ignore him."

Clarissa rolled her eyes. "Mom. How can I ignore someone yelling 'Jelly Butt Marcus' at the top of his lungs, over and over and over and—"

"He only has power over you if you give it to him."

Clarissa groaned. "Right. Whatever that means."

Amanda started to reprimand her for her rudeness, then changed her mind. Getting jelly on your rear in public would turn anyone into a grouch.

"Hey, I have some good news. Grandma is coming to live in Milwaukee."

Clarissa's eyes shot open. "No way! Awesome! When?"

"Believe it or not, next week."

"Yes!" She leaped around the apartment's living room. "Grandma's coming! Grandma's coming! Will she live with us?"

"No. She'll have her own apartment over by the lake."

"Oh, cool. I can visit her." Clarissa danced over and turned on the TV. "Almost all my friends have grandparents that live here. I'll be just like them now. Can I have a snack?"

"Sure." Amanda walked toward the kitchen. "But only a little TV. Then I want you to do something else. Go play outdoors. It's finally warming up, you should get some fresh air."

"It's no fun since Abigail moved away."

Amanda poured her daughter some cranberry-grape juice and put together a bowl of crackers and cubes of cheddar cheese. She was secretly glad Abigail and her family had moved. The eight-year-old had a strange effect on Clarissa, goading her into doing things she'd never have thought of herself in a million years. Riding her bike in the street, sneaking sweets and snacks from the kitchen cabinets, prowling along the narrow ditch dividing the properties on the west side of Sixty-seventh Street—passing yards full of strange dogs and home owners probably not thrilled at the invasion of their privacy. Not that anyone had much on these tiny lots.

Unfortunately, since her comrade had moved last month, Clarissa had become increasingly moody and dissatisfied with everything at home. But Amanda wasn't going to count that among her problems. Her daughter would adjust.

"Here you go." She took the snack out to Clarissa and settled next to her to watch *Arthur* on public TV. Her daughter snuggled close; Amanda rested her cheek on the soft blond hair, easier to reach every day it seemed. She was growing so fast. Amanda was grateful for every moment they had together, especially peaceful loving moments like this one. So things were a bit tough right now. Soon to get a bit tougher when Mom showed up. But this much she could handle. At least she had a wonderful place to live, in a nice peaceful family neighborhood, and lovely quiet moments like this to share with her—

A tremendous slamming of car doors sounded through the open windows, followed by loud hoots, raging yells, thuds and what sounded like the entire Green Bay Packers football team barreling into the apartment downstairs.

Clarissa craned her head to look up at her mother, blue eyes wide, at the same time Amanda looked down at her, blue eyes probably wider.

"What was *that?*"

"I'm not sure, sweetheart."

"Is someone moving in downstairs?"

"Um… Maybe it's the new owner of the house." Amanda put a hand to her throat and felt herself swallow hard, really, really hoping she hadn't just gotten a taste of problem number four.

CHAPTER TWO

"HEY, *hey!*" Arch Williams knelt in the entranceway of his new home and grabbed his youngest nephew, John, four years old, in one vise-grip arm, and his middle nephew, Luke, six, in another before the boys managed to remove each other's appendages. "Next person who tries to rip his brother's arms off…"

The boys quieted, hearing the grave threat in his voice.

"Next person gets…" He tightened the vises. "Do you know what he gets?"

Two heads shook warily.

"He gets…the superpowered…ultrakiller…Uncle Noogie of Death!"

The boys burst out laughing.

"Now. We are going inside this house. Once it's renovated, you will live with me in this house while your mom gets better. During that entire time, in this house, no one is allowed to maim anyone else. Is that understood?"

More nodding.

"John? Do you know what 'maim' means?"

John's nodding sped up enthusiastically.

"No he doesn't." Mark, the oldest, summoned all the scorn required by his omniscient eight-year-old status.

"Do too." John stuck out a tongue turned lollipop blue.

"Then what does it mean?"

John's face went blank. Arch whispered in his ear.

The little face brightened. "It means, 'You're not the boss of me.'"

"Excellent." Arch released the two younger boys and pushed them into the house, then gave Mark a conspiratorial wink. "You know and I know. He'll find out."

Mark tightened his lips, trying to hide his pleasure at being considered an adult accomplice, and moved forward with the others into the dim empty living room.

Silence. Long faces. Hands shoved in pockets.

Arch couldn't blame them. An old lady had lived here, Mrs. Carson. The blinds were thick, curtains bulky, carpet shag, scent sour and heavy. As far as he could make out, everything was dark beige. The boys had been argumentative and sulky most of the drive down from Green Bay this morning. Not that he could blame them. Their mom had had a nervous breakdown a week before. They were scared and upset, and now they had walked into what must feel like a nursing home after the crowded colorful apartment they'd shared with his divorced sister, Gwen.

"Okay." He strode into the room and pulled up the blinds, letting the late-afternoon sunshine into the room. "We'll have to use our imaginations here. I am open to any and all suggestions as to what this place needs."

"Air freshener."

The two younger boys giggled uneasily at Mark's comment.

"One air freshener coming up." Arch unlocked the window and gave it a firm yank. Nothing. "Must be painted shut. Let's try this one."

Nope.

He tried all the windows in the room. Apparently Mrs. Carson had not had a love affair with fresh air. After all the arguing, the boys' current silence was deafening and ominous. John let out a loud sniff and wiped his eyes.

"Okay, first job, getting the windows open. Everyone take off your shoes, it's window-whacking time."

The boys took off their shoes and had a ball whacking window frames with their thick rubber soles. Half an hour later, they had three windows open, and fresh air streaming in.

"That's better. Now." Arch rubbed his hands together with glee. "Let's start imagining. First of all, you see before you a boring living room. What does it need?"

Mark looked around in disgust. "Furniture would be nice."

"Toys." John folded his arms across his little chest and sniffed again.

"A TV." Luke stubbed the toe of his sneaker across the carpet and a puff of dust raised and swirled in the sunlight.

"No, no, no, think big."

Luke frowned. "A big TV?"

"Lots of toys?"

"How about…" Arch let the anticipation build. "An indoor movie theater."

Three mouths shot open.

"Whoa."

"Awesome."

"Yeah."

"And…" He had them now. Mark's hazel eyes, Luke's blue and John's dark brown, were all shining at him as if he was their messiah. "A kids' game room."

More exultations. He was on a roll.

"A soundproof music room with wall-to-wall CDs, a state-of-the-art kitchen and a sports den devoted to the Packers."

Hmm. Okay, not so much enthusiasm there. He wouldn't bother mentioning his plans for the bedroom. Not kid stuff anyway.

"You just have to look at things not how they are, but how they *could* be."

"I'm hungry." Luke looked around hopefully, as if a Happy Meal might have been left behind somewhere.

"Okay. We'll go out to eat."

"Subway!"

"Burger King!"

"KFC!"

Arch held up a silencing finger. Amazingly, it worked. No restaurant would be considered unless it served cold draft beer. He loved his nephews, but there were limits. "I pick the place. We eat there, go back to my condo and go to bed. Grandpa should be here in the morning and we can go to work making this place livable."

"Will you read to us from one of your books, Uncle Arch? Mom always reads to us before bed."

"Of course I will, Little John." He tousled the dark brown hair. "I will read to you from one that hasn't even been published yet. You will get to hear it months before all the rest of the boys and girls of these good United States, what do you think of that?"

"Cool!"

"You just have to promise not to tell anyone."

John nodded seriously and put his finger to his lips. "I'm good at secrets."

"Good at telling them, you mean."

Arch sent a warning glance to Mark. "Everyone has to say nice things in my house, or the crabby fairy will come and get you."

John frowned. "What's a crabby fairy?"

"A very mean creature. Once she gets hold of you, the world is an awful place. Even wonderful things you used to love become horrible. Friends become enemies." He shuddered dramatically. "Even ice cream tastes bad. We have to be very very sure she doesn't come in."

John and Luke nodded solemnly. Mark huffed. "She isn't even real."

"Think again, Mark."

"You're the crabby fairy." Luke pointed a triumphant finger at his brother. He and John started doing the Great Taunting Dance that would live generation to generation.

"Mark is the crabby fairy, Mark is the crabby fairy, Mark—"

"Enough. Come on, we have to go upstairs and meet our tenant before we eat."

"What's a tenant?"

"Someone who lives upstairs, you dummy."

"I'm not a dummy."

"Are too."

"A tenant—" Arch raised his voice "—is someone who lives in a building owned by someone else and pays them rent. We are going upstairs now to meet mine. We are going to be very quiet and very polite and impress her and her daughter with what fine young men we are."

"Whatever."

Arch laughed and grabbed Mark in for a quick hug and a playful Uncle Noogie. The crabby fairy had definitely taken up residence in this little guy. He only hoped she wouldn't stay, or the summer was going to be a long one.

He herded the boys out the back door and up the stairs; they ran on ahead and fought over the doorbell, probably pressing it about six times by the time he arrived and calmed them down. All he knew about his tenant, Amanda Marcus, was that Mrs. Carson said she was a "lovely young lady." In his experience, however, the octogenarian definition of "lovely young lady" could encompass anything from Gwyneth Paltrow to RuPaul.

A few seconds later the door swung open to reveal…

Definitely not RuPaul.

His first impression was of a mousy-looking blonde, too short for his taste, too slender for his taste, wearing tan capris not tight enough for his taste, and a loose open white shirt over a scoop-necked yellow top, not revealing enough for his taste, gripping the door, holding herself tightly as if he and the boys might be an invading force from a hostile nation. One glance at him, so brief that she couldn't possibly have seen him, then she addressed herself to the boys.

"Yes?"

Little John pointed to her. "Are you Uncle Arch's tennis?"

She smiled and glanced up at Arch again, this time long enough that he probably registered, though he detected about zero reaction.

He, however, was reacting. Her eyes were huge and blue and a little sad even when she was smiling. He got the impression either she was a fragile and depressed person, or life hadn't been good to her recently.

Then she smiled down at John, put one hand up to her face to half hide the smile and the other hand around her waist, which pushed certain things into better view and proved that her body held surprises that were exactly to his taste. On closer inspection he noticed that her mouth was full and decidedly sexy, though it needed a little more color and a lot of relaxation to show it to advantage.

"Tenant, you dummy, not tennis."

Arch put a restraining hand on Mark's shoulder. "Hello, Amanda. I'm Arch Williams. These monsters are my nephews, Mark, Luke and John."

He held out his hand and she let go of the door long enough to shake it. Her fingers were cold and bird-boned, but her grasp was firm. "Nice to meet you. I'm—well, you know who I am. This is Clarissa."

She opened the door wider and revealed a girl about Mark's age, maybe a little younger. Carbon copy of her mom, equally silent and cautious. He got the feeling the decibel level in this place generally hovered around six. Possibly ten on a really noisy day.

If that's how they liked things, they were going to hate having him and the boys living here.

"Can we come in and see your apartment?" Luke's face was uncharacteristically solemn. "Downstairs is ugly and it smells like an old lady."

Mark shot him a scornful look. "How do you know, you ever smelled one?"

"Yeah."

"Oh really? When?"

"For your information I've smelled lots of them."

"Your pants are *so* on fire."

"Are not."

"Uh, guys?" Arch grinned apologetically at the mother and daughter, whose eyes had been following the argument between Mark and Luke as if they were at a tennis match. "We should probably go to dinner."

"But we haven't seen her house yet," John whined.

Amanda gestured into the apartment and backed up against the open front door. "Come on in."

The boys tumbled into the apartment; Arch stopped in the doorway, hands in his pockets and looked down at Amanda, feeling like a giant. She raised her eyes to his and bumped her head on the wooden door behind her.

Her mouth was definitely sexy. And her eyes had a spark to them, now that he could really look. "Thanks for this. We'll only be a sec. You sure it's okay?"

She nodded rapidly, her head thudding on the door, and

gestured him in, clearly uncomfortable having him stand so close.

He considered staying, because he liked that kind of uncomfortable, but figured he'd better not start off their landlord-tenant relationship by getting her rattled, pleasurably or otherwise.

Three steps into her apartment, he was glad he hadn't lingered. The place had clearly been decorated by a committee of the Very Dainty and Extremely Uptight.

Lace. Flowers. Knickknacks. More lace. More flowers. Not a speck of dust. A *pink* phone? Not the slightest indication anyone spent any time living here, least of all a kid.

What was up with that?

A very uncharitable and very typically male thought about what Ms. Marcus needed to loosen her up sprang to mind, and he scolded himself. He knew nothing about her. Besides, some men would probably walk in here and see perfection. He just wasn't one of them. To him, her apartment looked even more like an old lady's apartment than the old lady's apartment downstairs.

Too bad. Faint chemistry in the doorway aside, it looked as if his initial instinct that she wasn't his type was the right one.

"Nice place."

"Oh." She followed him in and looked around as if she hadn't been there before, arms crossed tightly over her chest. "Well, thanks. Mom decorated most of it."

"No kidding." He put his hands on his hips and watched her. He decided she was actually rather easy on the eyes. Unfortunately the fact that he was watching her seemed to be making her uncomfortable. A hand crept up to finger a lock of hair, then as if she'd caught herself doing it, she brought the hand back down.

"She has definite ideas about decorating. Well, about pretty much everything." She laughed nervously, and stole a glance behind her, as if she'd said something she might be punished for.

"Oh yeah?" Aha. Mommy Dearest. He pictured a Sherman tank of a woman. Or an older version of Amanda, but sour-faced and made of iron. That might explain a few things about the turmoil and timidity he sensed in Ms. Marcus here. "You would have done things differently?"

She opened her mouth, then closed it, as if she wasn't sure how much to reveal. He took a couple of steps toward her, winked, put his hand to his mouth and whispered, "I won't tell."

She laughed, a white, even-teethed, beautifully musical laugh that made color flood her face and banished that anxious, tightly controlled impression she gave off, though she kept her arms wrapped around her.

He grinned. That was more like it. That was one whole hell of a lot more like it.

"Well...our taste isn't always the same," she said.

"No?"

She shook her head, then turned toward the children, obviously not wanting to share any more about her mother's taste. His nephews were behaving in typical fashion, racing from one room to another, while Amanda's daughter stood watching, half-bemused, half-eager, as if she wanted to join but wasn't quite sure how.

He had the same reaction to the daughter as he did to the mom. Okay, not *quite* the same reaction. But when he encountered that kind of tightly battened personality, he itched to set it free. Sometimes it was a lost cause. He'd bet Amanda's mother was a lost cause. But something in the daughter and something in the granddaughter made him think a little prodding in the right direction could save them yet.

"Okay, guys." He clapped his hands. "We've invaded these lovely ladies' home long enough. Time for dinner."

The boys ran toward him, each shouting out again the name of their favorite fast-food joint. He hadn't yet broken the news that he required a place with a liquor license.

Amanda moved back as the boys catapulted themselves by, her color still high, arms crossed even more tightly, but whether she was holding herself for protection or keeping herself from joining in, he'd bet even she didn't know.

"We're going out for an evening of not-tremendously-fine dining. Would you like to join us?" He bent forward to be heard over the kid-roar. Her blue eyes shot up to his and startled him with a jolt of attraction. Was it his imagination or was she getting prettier every time he looked at her?

"Oh, thanks." She released her arms from their imprisonment and gestured helplessly. "Maybe another time."

"But, Mom." Her daughter came close and tugged anxiously at her shirt. "We never go out."

"Not tonight, honey." Amanda smoothed her daughter's carbon-copy blond hair gently, but there was a warning edge to her voice.

"But I *want* to go." Clarissa's whisper came out loud enough for him to hear. "I'm *sick* of having to be careful about money. We never have any fun."

Amanda's body stiffened. Her face tightened to near tears.

Arch immediately smiled over at the boys before she could glance at him for a reaction. Was it about money? Was that the anxious tension he sensed in her? He could easily find some discreet ways to help her out.

"You guys ready to roll?"

Assorted bellowed "yeahs" answered in no uncertain terms.

He gave Mark, Luke and John a thumbs-up and turned back to Amanda and Clarissa. With any luck she'd think he hadn't heard. "Are you with us? My treat as your hospitable landlord."

"No. No, thank you," she answered stiffly, and drew her daughter close as if to reject him and his filthy money. "We're staying in tonight."

Her daughter pulled away and shot her mom a look that could probably boil water.

"Okay." He held out his hand, wanting to press her to accept but knowing it wasn't his place, at least not yet. A fun evening out would give her valuable perspective on her troubles. Staying in a silent shrinelike apartment did nothing but make them loom larger. "Nice to meet you. I'm sure we'll see you again."

"Yes." She shook his hand, not meeting his eyes. He had the feeling the second the door closed behind them, she'd lose the battle with those unshed tears.

"Change your mind?" He tightened his fingers briefly over hers. "We'd love to have you with us."

"No. Thanks." Her lips zipped tight between each word; she extracted her hand from his.

He nodded. Message received. Battle lost.

The door clicked decisively shut behind him as he hurtled down the stairs after the careening boys, already making plans to contact Mrs. Carson and do some polite snooping.

Battle lost, maybe, but the war was just beginning.

CHAPTER THREE

AMANDA SAT in her flowery armchair, stitching the hem of a silk evening gown. Tiny, precise stitches, catching the black lacy seam binding pinned in place, catching a thread or two at most of the black and rose silk of the dress. In and out, over and over, making the perfect blind hem. She reached the end of the black thread, knotted it off and unrolled an arm's length from the spool on the end table. Snip, then moisten the end, thread the needle, knot and start in again. Yards and yards, the dress was beautiful. She imagined Mrs. Gilles sweeping across a dance floor, men in tuxedos attentive to her every desire.

Well, okay, Mrs. Gilles was too dull and clumsy to sweep anywhere and men that attentive didn't exist as far as Amanda knew, in tuxes or not, but it was a wonderful fantasy.

If she had millions of dollars she'd own a closetful of dresses like this, pay men to dress in tuxes and attend to her every need, since that behavior didn't seem to occur naturally, and go dancing every night—she glanced out the rain-streaked window at the gray wet and shivered—in Barbados. Wisconsin took way too long to introduce the concept of spring.

Needle in, needle out, listening to the patter of a chilly midafternoon rain. The occasional wet swish of tires down Sixty-seventh Street.

And the sudden horrendous banging from downstairs.

Her thread tangled, she picked impatiently at the knot. There hadn't been much peace since Arch Williams had shown up four days ago with his noisy trio of nephews. Most of the lack of peace was easily explained by whatever renovating was going on, and by the exuberant boys, who apparently weren't bothering to enroll in the last three weeks of local school, not that she could blame them.

The rest of the lack of peace was harder to pin down. She hadn't slept well the past few nights, not so unusual—she often had insomnia. When better, after all, for uninterrupted quality worry time? But those hours awake in her bed hadn't so much contained worry over her future, worry over her mother's arrival, worry over how to make ends meet, or worry over how to invent one more variation of pasta with cheese before she and her daughter flung the stuff out the window and went stark raving nutso. This wasn't even worry. Not really.

She managed to unpick the knot and drew the thread smoothly once again through the black silk printed with stunning red roses.

It was more a restless feeling. A churned-up feeling. As her and Clarissa's favorite children's heroine, Eloise, would say, a *rawther* excited feeling.

And while she was lying there, restless, churned up and *rawther* excited, she noticed a recurring image in her head.

Arch Williams standing about eight inches away in her doorway, leaning forward to speak to her, close enough for her to establish the fact that he smelled manly and shaving-lotion wonderful.

This was not your garden-variety male. This was a hot-house male, lovingly tended by his DNA into something truly special and amazing.

Something about the way he looked at her—not that it had anything to do with her in particular—but the intensity of his eyes, the vibrancy of his energy, of his presence in her apartment, unnerved her. She'd only encountered potency like that once before, a long time ago, had in fact been engaged to it in the person of Ridge, for an all-too-brief time.

That energy drew her now as it had drawn her then. And still—she held up the dress to make sure the hem lay flat—even years older and purportedly wiser, her reaction to the intense attraction was to shut down and act like a shy-spinster idiot.

With Ridge that hadn't been a problem. In retrospect she thought he'd probably sought her out exactly for her shy idiocy—so she wouldn't compete with his dazzle. At the time she simply and naively thought they were drawn together by the power of True Love and Destiny.

Yeah, right.

Another loud series of thuds, then a horrific splintering that made her wince. Whoever stood down below, Paul Bunyon–like, wielding a sledgehammer, better know how to avoid support beams.

She lifted her head, stretched her neck and shoulders, cramped from sitting hunched over the material for so long, and glanced at the clock. Three-fifteen, Clarissa would be home soon. Snack, then playtime, then whatever she could scrape together for dinner, then bed. Maybe that's why she'd been so excited by their new neighbor. A break from the routine, a distraction from their plain and lately anxious lives.

If only he weren't quite so distracting.

She shrugged and picked up the next yard of hem. So, it wasn't as if he'd be coming up here all the time. After the polite visit on Monday, he hadn't so much as poked his nose around. Women like her were undoubtedly of no interest to him anyway. He probably went for tall, sensual brunette splendor. The kind of woman who walked into a room and caused male mouths to drop and female ones to purse in disapproval and envy.

Her doorbell rang, three quick dings; she frowned at her watch. Too early for Clarissa. Was the mail truck outside? She stood and draped the gown carefully over the chair, glanced out the window on her way to the front door. No truck, but she could hear feet pounding up the stairs. Male feet. Someone with a key. There was only one of those.

Her heart began copycatting the pounding feet. She redistributed her knit shirt to make sure it lay evenly under the waistband of her stretch capris and opened the door with a polite smile, feeling the damn shy-spinster reaction practically shutting down her body.

"Hi." The word barely emerged from her lips. Geez, he looked good. His dark hair was all mussed in this perfect sexy way, his brown eyes still had that intense energy that made it hard to look into them for more than a second or two. Though if she was a brunette bombshell she'd probably stare coolly and make him drop to his knees.

"Hey, Manda, how are you?"

"Fine." She nodded too rapidly and too long and had to make her head stop. *Manda?*

"We driving you crazy with all the noise?" He moved into the doorway, put an arm up on the jamb, casual, lanky, totally at ease. She wrapped her arms around herself and took a small step back.

"No, it's not bad at all." She lied. Through her teeth. Well, sort of. He wasn't quite going so far as to drive her crazy. But close.

"I was wondering." He looked back down the stairs as if he expected someone to appear, then turned those intense eyes back to her so that she had to stop herself from taking another step back. "The kids and I are barbecuing burgers tonight. Would you and Clarissa like to join us?"

"Oh, well, I..."

She unstuck one arm from across her chest long enough to make a random gesture, then stuck it back. Usually, her shyness produced an initial negative reaction to any social invitation. But it didn't seem to be operating at remotely full strength, as it had the other night when he'd surprised her with an invitation to dinner. Right after Clarissa practically shouted that they were on their way to taking up permanent residency in the poorhouse. In fact, far from reacting negatively at all, Amanda's mouth was beginning to water. Copiously. And not just because Arch Williams looked good enough to eat.

Meat. Fatty, juicy meat, cooked and settled on a bun loaded with condiments, on a plate loaded with fatty greasy side dishes.

Down, girl. She glanced at the window, trying to appear cool. "A barbecue? In this weather?"

"It'll clear." He spoke with absolute confidence, even though the radar image she'd seen that morning on weather.com indicated they should probably prepare to build arks.

"I think the weather report showed—"

He shook his head urgently, reached out a finger and put it an inch from her lips, which made them buzz and tingle even though he hadn't touched her. "It'll clear."

Then he winked. And grinned. And Amanda began a slow steady melt into her spotless off-white carpet.

"We bought way too much food and need help finishing it. You'll come?"

Amanda nodded. Just right then she'd prance naked at Mayfair Mall if he'd asked her to. "What can I bring?"

He held up a careless hand. "Not a thing. We're all set."

"You're sure?"

He drew an X on his sexy broad chest, which chest pushed out the fabric of his T-shirt in all the very rightest places. "Cross my heart."

"Okay." She made a mental list of what she could bring anyway, since she undoubtedly couldn't afford to return the invitation to him and his nephews, who equally undoubtedly ate entire sides of beef at a sitting. Maybe her killer chocolate brownies. Not a man alive who could resist—

She chopped that thought off. This wasn't about seduction. This was about accepting a friendly neighborhood invitation.

"What time would you like us?"

He glanced at his watch. "We'll fire up the barbecue in a couple of hours, let the dust settle some downstairs, around five-thirty, go from there. That sound good?"

"Yes." *Oh yes, yes, yes.*

"Terrific. We'll see you then."

She nodded before she could remember that she'd been nodding too much, and smiled instead. Then started getting very, very nervous. Because he just stood there, looking at her with this killer mischievous half smile.

She swallowed and stared at his T-shirt which said, One Day At A Time, crossed her arms tighter to grip each elbow and squeezed said elbows so hard she nearly yelped. "Looking forward to it."

"Good."

He still stood there. She darted a glance at his face and then away, at the doorjamb, at the carpet, feeling her color rising. What the hell was he still doing here? She glanced at him again, a little longer this time before she had to drop her eyes. Then summoned her courage and paid another lingering visit. It wasn't quite so bad when you just got up the nerve and looked. His eyes were really gorgeous, medium brown with dark circles around the iris, dark lashes, turned down at the corners. Not wide enough to be prettyboy, not narrow enough to look—

"You're beautiful." The words came out softly, offhand, as if he wasn't quite sure he should say them.

Amanda gasped. Which wasn't at all what a sultry brunette would do. Worse, the gasp went down the wrong way and made her cough like a tragic Act Three heroine, right before she expires of tuberculosis.

"Hey." He moved one quick step in and put a hand on her shoulder, bent down to see her face, which must be an attractively mottled beet red. "You okay?"

"Yes. I'm fine." She finished choking, patted her chest and took a deep breath. Fine, flustered and embarrassed. Had he said she was beautiful? "Sorry."

"Don't be sorry." He held up both hands. "I didn't mean to freak you out."

Oh, great. Now she was a freak. "No, you didn't. I just didn't expect you to say…that."

"Strangely, I didn't expect me to say that either." He stood there, hands on his hips, watching her recover from shy-spinster idiocy, looking huge and male in her silly frilly apartment. Completely opposite from how she must seem, she had this sudden painful urge to get extremely naked under him.

"You okay now?"

"Fine."

He winked. "I'll be sure and give you fair warning next time I compliment you."

"Oh. Okay." More nodding to go with more sparkling repartee. She might as well hire herself out for one of those little dolls in the back of people's cars. She was a mess around men like Arch. And it didn't help that she was trying to be polite and carry on a normal conversation while her subconscious imagined full speed ahead what he looked like sweaty in his birthday suit.

He backed toward the door and stopped just before the stairs without glancing behind him, as if he knew instinctively where he was at all times. ''So we'll see you soon.''

''Yes.'' She forced herself not to nod. ''Five-thirty.''

He smiled; the smile widened into a grin, and he turned and went down the stairs. Amanda wandered over to her chair, picked up her sewing and sat with it in her lap, gazing at the door she'd just shut gently behind him.

Oh no. Oh no. There it was. Same as after she'd first bumped into Ridge—literally—in the hall between classes. That dizzy weirdness. That brain-floating exhilaration.

That awful familiar certainty that she'd never be the same again.

Either she was coming down with something germ-related, or she'd just been set firmly on her way to developing a shy-spinster idiot crush on Arch Williams.

''So?''

Arch turned to his dad, Thaddeus Johnston Williams III, who everyone called Sonny. They'd finished ripping up the dirty beige carpet in the living room after a wonderful, macho, stress-relieving morning knocking down the wall between two of the bedrooms, and were now making a platter of burgers to go with the platter of sausages, the platter of hot dogs and the vats of coleslaw and potato salad and baked beans.

Man food.

''So, what?'' He swayed his body to the U2 CD warming the room with music.

''So what's your tenant like?'' His dad lifted his arm over his head and flipped a burger onto the platter with a deft hook shot.

"Fragile, prissy, attractive, currently broke." Arch circled a newly formed patty around his body, set up a jump shot and landed it onto the growing pile. "I thought it wouldn't hurt to feed them once in a while."

"Them?"

"Cute daughter, Mark's age. Lady who lived here told me that the mom lost her job a few weeks ago. Mrs. Carson used to watch the daughter. So Amanda lost day care and income."

"Ouch."

"Yeah. They both need lightening up." He backed up with a new hamburger, and looked frantically for an opening.

"Free!" His father held off imaginary defensive ends, caught the hamburger pass, ran it to the platter and did a butt-wiggling victory dance. "Touchdown!"

"Yes!" Arch lifted his arms straight up. "The greatest team the world has ever known, thanks to the magic of Arch and Sonny Williams, destined for the hall of fame before they even retire from the sport."

His father grinned and moved to the sink to wash his hands, hands that had built houses, cooked countless meals, changed countless diapers and meted out the occasional deserved punishment for Arch and his five siblings. "You going to try to take her out?"

Arch joined his father at the sink and caught the soap tossed in the air. "No, nothing like that."

"She doesn't ring your chimes?"

"Not particularly." The soap slipped through his fingers and hit the porcelain sink with a dull thud.

Oops.

"Uh-huh." His father shook his wet hands before he dried them on a kitchen towel.

"She's too serious. Sad. Bunged up. Something bad there, haven't quite figured it out."

His father shot him a look. "I take it you're planning to?"

He shrugged and rinsed his hands. "Crossed my mind."

"Any particular reason?"

"Just curious."

"Uh-huh." Sonny tossed Arch the kitchen towel. "Well, it sounds like she'll be a good neighbor."

From the living room came the unmistakable high-decibel sound of the boys not agreeing.

"Better to us than we'll be to her." Arch dried his hands, waiting to see if the boys would be able to settle the dispute themselves or if it looked likely blood would flow.

"Worried about the boys bothering her?"

"I don't think she's used to noise." He tossed the towel back.

"It's good for her. Life is full of noise. Death is silent." His dad hung the towel back on a drawer handle and wrinkled his nose the way he always did when he was thinking of Arch's mom.

The boys began yelling in earnest. Arch moved toward the living room, pausing to touch his father's shoulder on the way. "Obviously, she won't have much choice in the matter."

"You big...poopyhead." Luke's voice sounded dangerous.

"Hey! *Hey!* What's going on?" Arch lunged forward and caught Luke around the waist just before he landed a punch on his older brother's head. Apparently the *Star Wars* video he'd put on was over. Arch was beginning to understand why parents let their kids watch too much TV.

"He said...he said..." Luke sputtered and sobbed, then

took another impossible swing at Mark, who was about three feet out of range of his skinny arms.

"He said Mom was prob'ly gonna die, like your mom did." John's eyes were the size of quarters; Mark stared sullenly at the carpet, but his lower lip was shaking.

Arch let go of Luke, shrugged, and held up his hands as if he couldn't think of a single reason Mark would think such a thing. "No way."

The three boys stood looking at him with hopeful expressions that about broke his heart.

"No way. Your mom doesn't have what my mom had. It's a totally different kind of sick."

"What kind? Nanny and Gramps wouldn't tell us."

Arch gritted his teeth. His sister's ex-in-laws meant well, but obviously hadn't clued in to the fact that no matter what the truth was, kids could imagine things way, way worse if you didn't tell them straight out what was up.

"Come here." He knelt down on the floor; the kids crowded around him. "My mom died of cancer. Yours had a nervous breakdown."

"She's broken?" John's voice trembled.

"Let's put it this way." Arch tousled John's hair. "You know what happens when a car overheats?"

Silence except for a sniff from Luke.

"It…melts?"

Arch grinned at John. "Good guess, but no. The engine gets too hot and can't work anymore. So you know what you have to do?"

"Put it in the refrigerator?"

"No, stupid. Wait for it to cool down."

"Exactly." Arch threw Mark a warning glance. "But without the stupid part."

Mark looked down at his sneaker. "Sorry."

"So what does that have to do with Mom?"

"Your mom had a lot to deal with this past year. Divorcing your dad, moving, having to change her job."

"So she overheated?"

"Yup." Arch shook his head gravely. "Her face turned bright red and smoke started pouring out of her ears."

He got a giggle out of John, a small smile from Luke.

"So…" He held out his hands in appeal. "What does she need to do?"

"Cool down!" Luke and John shouted the answer.

"Yeah." Mark sneered. "Where she won't be *bothered* by us."

Arch frowned. "Is that what Nanny and Gramps told you? That you bothered her?"

"It's true, isn't it?" Mark said.

Arch took a deep breath. It would be extremely impolite and impolitic to reveal in any way how he felt about those well-meaning clueless people. "Let's put it this way. You think cars mind being driven?"

Mark kicked a carpet remnant. "No."

"Of course not. Driving is what they're made for. Cars love to drive. But when they overheat, you just got to give them a break. Even if they hate being parked and would much rather be back on the highway, that's what has to happen. You with me?"

Luke sniffed and smiled weakly. John nodded solemnly.

Arch looked at Mark, whose sullen face had lifted a little.

"I guess so."

Arch smiled at him and got a rare grin back. "Your mom adores you. She misses you like mad. And when she's better, which she *will* be, she won't be able to wait to see you guys. Maybe soon we'll even be able to visit her."

Three faces brightened.

"Okay?" He lifted his hand and got high fives all

around. "Now. Who wants to partake of a Savage and Manly Meat Fest?"

Three hands shot up. "Meeee!"

"Okay. Three manly savages are with me. But first we must wait for the lovely ladies who will be joining us."

John made a face. "Will we have to behave if they're here?"

"Tell you what." Arch winked at him. "Instead of us savages having to be civilized, maybe we can get them to be temporary savages. What do you think?"

"Cool. All right."

"Hey." Mark's eyes lit up. "Let's go out in the back-yard and find a place to burn Clarissa at the stake."

"Yeah. Awesome."

The boys raced out. Arch watched them go and got up off the floor. His father came into the room from the door-way and stood beside his son.

"You're good for those kids."

"I know what they're going through."

His father nodded, clapped Arch on the back and squeezed painfully hard, the way he always did, though now that Arch had some muscle on him, it no longer left sore spots.

"Savages, huh?" His father hitched up the pants that never managed to find a waist to ride on. "These ladies know what they're in for?"

Arch grinned and waggled his eyebrows conspiratorially. "I'm counting on the fact that they don't."

CHAPTER FOUR

AMANDA PAUSED outside Arch's door, clutching a pan of still-warm brownies, which smelled way too good to wait until after dinner to eat. Against all odds and all physical principles of meteorology, the rain had stopped maybe two minutes earlier, the clouds had lifted some, and a pleasant breeze blew. Not sunny, but fine enough for a barbecue. If it lasted. Either Arch had an in with the weather gods or he was incredibly lucky.

She raised her hand to the bell. From inside there was the usual stampede of feet and the usual assortment of loud and aggressive voices she could hear less clearly upstairs through her floor.

"Mom?" Beside her, Clarissa glanced up curiously. "Are those boys always like that?"

"Aren't the ones in your school that loud?"

"At recess, sometimes. Only not so bad. Except for Ralph."

Amanda hid a grimace. That boy had so enjoyed taunting Clarissa about having jelly on her pants, he'd found out where she'd be sitting in the lunchroom the next day and made sure her chair had jelly on it again. The day after that, he'd managed to smear jelly on her backside in the guise of a playful passing slap.

Little brat. She had a totally childish urge to wait for a moonless night, drag him to a dark alley and scare the crap out of him. Instead, she'd told Clarissa to ignore him, which

Clarissa had tried to do. But she'd come home close to tears nearly every day this week.

The little jerk couldn't get tired of the jelly thing soon enough. Unfortunately, in his underdeveloped Neanderthal mind, this was no doubt high comedy, so who knew when they could expect to have it over. These were the times she wished Clarissa had a dad around. The rest of the time she was confident she did an adequate job parenting. But Amanda had never encountered any bullying, so she felt helpless giving advice. When she was in grade school, people either liked her or ignored her, which was fine with her. And with no siblings of her own and an eternally busy father, she couldn't begin to understand the warped psyche of little boys.

Maybe she should talk to Mrs. Kessler, Clarissa's teacher, though it was best if Clarissa could solve the problem herself.

"So are you going to ring the doorbell or not?"

"Of course I'm going to." Amanda gave a nervous laugh. Okay, she admitted it. Taking refuge in a minute of thought had partly been a delay tactic. She hadn't been to a social occasion in way too long. Especially one involving an attractive, unattached male who told her she was beautiful.

She pressed the bell. A second later, she and Clarissa simultaneously took a step back. At the dingdong, true chaos took over. Yells, "I'll get it," then argument, "No, I will," then coercion, "If you don't let me, I'll break your face," then authority, "Enough, guys!" And silence.

Clarissa and Amanda turned their heads slowly toward each other.

"Geez." Clarissa's face scrunched in seven-year-old female scorn. "It's only a doorbell."

Finally, the scuffling sounds stopped and the door swung

open to Arch's grinning face and huge presence that inspired such a weird combination of lust and intimidation.

"Hey, welcome, come in, come in." He held open the screen and gestured them inside, just showered and casual-perfect in jeans and a T-shirt that read, If You Won't, I Will.

Clarissa took three steps into the house and encountered the boys, lined in a row, staring. She stopped and looked back imploringly at Amanda, who was having her own tough time squeezing past Arch, trying not to touch any part of him while discovering that he smelled even better than the brownies. Clean and male, slightly herbal.

Mmm.

"Mmm."

Amanda started and looked back. Had he heard her thoughts? Did she "Mmm" out loud? Was he referring to her?

No. The brownies.

She held up the pan. "Men never think of dessert."

"Women always do. And men are always grateful." His grin narrowed his eyes at the corners. And contrary to what she expected from a polite exchange, he kept the eye contact going. Or maybe she did. In any case, it…um…kept going.

Oh my God. She had to look away. This was nuts.

Okay, she would.

Now.

Okay, now.

Okay—

A snort from one of the boys did the trick. Had they noticed?

No. The oldest—Mark?—and the middle brother, Luke, were snickering unpleasantly at Clarissa, who'd turned to examine the apartment.

Amanda followed their pointed stares and her heart made a crash landing. Purple. On Clarissa's off-white pants. A blob that looked a bit like Texas.

The Jelly Fiend had struck again.

She moved forward to protect her daughter, put her arm around Clarissa's shoulders. "I'm afraid Ralph has been busy again, honey."

Clarissa twisted around and caught sight of Texas on her backside. Her face reddened; her eyes filled. "How long has it been there?"

Silence at her anguished whisper, since no one had any idea.

"That jerk. Mom, he did it to me again."

Her voice rose to a dangerous wail. Amanda's heart tore in half. Poor thing. In front of all her friends at school and now in front of Arch and his kids.

"Honey, I—"

"What's this?" Arch came forward, hands on his hips, the picture of protective male outrage. "Someone did this to you on purpose?"

"He's done it every day this week." Clarissa dashed a tear away with her hand, then wiped her eyes a few more times in case any more showed up.

Amanda tugged gently on her slender arm. "Honey, let's go upstairs so you can change."

"Nonsense." Arch folded his arms and looked sternly at Clarissa. "I think the jelly look is totally cool. In fact, I would like to have a purple splotch on my butt, too."

Amanda's eyes widened; she drew in a fierce breath. How dare he make fun of her daughter. Hadn't Clarissa been through—

A sound brought her up short. She gaped at Clarissa. Her daughter was giggling.

"Nephews." Arch whirled on the boys, who snapped

smartly to attention. "I have just decided that we all need jelly on our butts. No one is allowed at this party unless he or she has a purple mark on the seat of his or her pants."

A shout of laughter and enthusiasm from the boys.

"But—"

"Mark?" Arch cut her off.

"Yessir?"

"Fetch the purple marker—make sure it's the one marked Washable—from John's set."

Amanda's jaw dropped.

"Yessir." Mark ran off into another room in the apartment.

"So this guy's been bugging you, huh?" Arch squatted in front of Clarissa who eyed him warily. "What do you do?"

Clarissa shot Amanda an uneasy glance. "I ignore him."

"No, no. That's why he keeps it going. Because he wants a reaction. You have to give him one he doesn't expect."

Clarissa looked helplessly at Amanda, who stepped in to her rescue.

"I told her to ignore him. I thought it might discourage him if he couldn't get a rise out of her. And that way the trouble wouldn't escalate."

Arch nodded and rose to his feet. "Good advice. Works that way sometimes. But I think this calls for drastic measures."

Clarissa's eyes grew round; she stared at Arch, fascinated. "What do you—"

"Here it is." Mark raced back into the hallway, bearing aloft the soon-to-be-infamous purple marker.

Arch swung around. "Mark, you may commence coloring. Once all pants are decorated, you may proceed into the backyard to load up on food. We will discuss the battle plans only on appropriately full bellies."

Amanda watched with a mixture of horror and disbelief as Mark carefully sketched a replica of Clarissa's jelly stain onto Luke, John, then Arch's rear ends.

"Ms. Marcus?" Arch took the marker from his nephew and held it up questioningly. "Do you care to have Texas on your butt?"

Amanda smiled queasily, thinking laundry. Thinking schlepping pants she'd only just put on clean this morning over to the Laundromat on North Avenue and waiting hours for the machines to wash out the color.

"I don't think so."

He nodded and capped the marker. Three boys eyed her accusingly. Clarissa, too.

Amanda swallowed. Geez. The one sensible voice in the group and they were acting as if she was a stick-in-the-mud. An old stick-in-the-mud. An old, boring, humorless, miserable—

She sighed. "Well..."

Arch turned back to her.

"I mean, if it's a prerequisite for coming to the barbecue..." She shrugged. She had to wash Clarissa's pants anyway.

He barely maintained a straight face. "Absolutely."

"Okay." She smiled and he moved toward her, uncapping the marker. At that precise moment, she suddenly realized what she was letting herself in for. A man she didn't even know was going to be drawing on her...*oh no.*

She turned around stiffly, clutching the brownies like a life preserver, and closed her eyes, feeling her cheeks—the ones in her face—flame. For God's sake, what was she supposed to do, bend over?

The silence in the room became ultrasilent. She felt Arch's hand grasp her pant leg and pull to get the material taut. Then a gentle quick rubbing that made her want to sink into the floor and die. Or was that some other feeling?

"There." She felt her pants release, heard the marker cap click. "You are now officially branded as a member of this party."

Noise and movement resumed like a sigh of relief. The boys ran out of the room, shouting of course, presumably to go into the backyard. Clarissa looked questioningly at her mom until Amanda nodded, then she walked hesitantly out to join the boys.

Amanda glanced at Arch, unsure whether to follow as well. He stood where he was, in apparently comfortable silence, watching her expectantly. She forced herself not to cross her arms over the brownies, but she did turn to study the changes in Mrs. Carson's apartment, unnerved by the intimacy of being alone with him, but not quite enough to want to leave.

The dull beige wall between the dining room and the living room had been knocked down and cleared away. She had to admit she liked the result. Compared to her apartment upstairs, the openness and light were exhilarating. "Looks like serious renovation."

"Yeah, I like space. Small rooms get me antsy."

This she could believe. The man was way larger than life. "Are you going to knock down all the walls?"

"Some." He moved next to her and pointed. She tried to make her attention follow his finger, but he exerted a tremendous pull standing so close, and her attention had to be satisfied with being torn in half. "This area will be the living room, dining room, and while the kids are here, playroom. I'm going to knock down the walls between the other two rooms for the master bedroom. Then the third, largest bedroom will be the library and movie theater."

"Movie theater?" That got a good bit of her attention.

He gave her a winking sidelong glance, which got the rest of it. "Wide-screen high-definition TV and DVD player. But to the kids, it's a movie theater. I'll also have a wet bar, pullout sofa for guests and, of course, the microwave for popcorn. I'm also going to see if I can find an old vending machine for soda and snacks and a gumball machine, on eBay."

Amanda swallowed. Sounded like money was not a problem down here. Must be nice. "What do you do?"

"I write the Corporal Wedgie books." He spoke matter-of-factly, but a note of pride came through.

"Oh." *Corporal Wedgie books?* Was that some kind of S&M manual? How the heck did one respond to that? "How…interesting."

He turned to face her. "I take it you've never heard of the great and powerful adventurer, Corporal Wedgie."

"No." She was admittedly relieved to find that "Corporal" must be the rank of the "Wedgie" person, not an adjective. "Should I have?"

His eyebrows crept up and that mischievous grin just touched his lips. "Absolutely."

"Oh." She was still at a loss. Arch must be the proverbial kid who didn't want to grow up. Movie theater in his home, candy machines, books about underwear, drawing purple blotches on people's rears. He reminded her so much of Ridge. She shifted the pan of brownies to her other arm. Except Ridge had been only twenty when she'd known him, so a little boyishness was acceptable.

The brownies nearly slipped to the floor. *A little boyishness was acceptable?* The phrase could have come right out of Maude Marcus's perfectly made-up lips. Help! She was turning into her mother.

Forget it. If he wanted to live in a playground, that was his business. Who was she to judge? She lived in a shrine to femininity. He probably thought she was old before her time.

"I'll look for your books next time I'm at the mall." Though it didn't sound like the kind of reading material either she or Clarissa enjoyed.

"It's a deal." He put his hands in his pockets and leaned against the wall behind him, which he hadn't apparently tried to knock down yet. "What do you do?"

"Nothing so exciting."

He cocked his head, waiting, one eyebrow quirked.

"I'm a seamstress." She took a deep breath. "I worked for Patterson's on North Astor Street for five years. I'm—"

She was going to say, "between jobs now." But it sounded so lame and unconvincing and apologetic. For some reason, she didn't want him to know she was out of work.

He crossed his ankles, and she realized he was waiting for her to finish her sentence.

"I'm…taking some time off. Though I've kept some clients on."

"Good for you." He nodded approvingly. "The grind can get tough sometimes. Nothing like a break to refresh you."

She nodded, feeling slightly ill. She hated lying. Even misleading. Especially for no good reason except to save her ego. "Actually…the store closed and I haven't been able to find another job."

"Oh." He grimaced. "That kind of time off. I'm sorry."

She shrugged, keeping her expression unconcerned. "I'm treating it as a vacation."

"You haven't had one in a while, I bet."

His tone was gentle and concerned and a lump rose in her throat. She didn't get to hear that tone much and she was probably starved for it. "No. Not really."

"Then it's time." He gestured toward the back of the house. "Let's go outside with the kids while it's still nice."

"Sure." She followed him through the living room, stripped clean of Mrs. Carson's awful centuries-old carpet, through the kitchen, which he hadn't changed much yet, down the back steps her apartment shared with his, and out onto the driveway. She was glad she'd told him the truth—she guessed. Though how he knew she hadn't had a vacation in a while mystified her. Did she look that beaten down and exhausted? She was vain enough to hope not. Not in front of Mr. Vitality.

She stepped around the southwest corner of the house to the backyard, where Mrs. Carson had tended an elaborate English garden until the day she moved out. Roses, day lilies, hydrangea, Russian sage, clematis, iris and many plants Amanda didn't know the names of, little wandering paths between the pachysandra, dwarf Japanese maples.

She stopped short and gasped. Gone.

All but a thin border of freshly dug earth and a few seedlings next to the garage, along the back fence and along the neighbor's garage on the north side of the property. The rest was laid out in stripes of new sod.

When had he done this? Why hadn't she noticed? Had she been that burrowed in her seams and in her troubles? Maybe last week when she and Clarissa had gone to visit a friend and hadn't gotten back until after dark. Hadn't she even left the house since then?

"I got rid of the garden. Not enough room for the boys to run around. Don't have time to tend it."

"I see." She stared at the bare yard, and for a moment she was overwhelmed by sadness. She used to love looking out at the flowers, which Mrs. Carson managed to have blooming in assorted complementary heights and shapes and shades all summer long. She used to imagine the garden was hers, part of some gracious elegant summer home she'd never be able to afford.

"You liked the garden the way it was." He stated the obvious without blame or guilt.

"Yes." She shrugged, too upset to be dishonest. "I did."

"I'm sorry. I should have warned you first." He gestured over to the side of the yard where a short, stoutish man tended a domed grill. "Come meet my dad. You can put the brownies on the table there."

She followed miserably. Maybe she was being a wet blanket, but right now she didn't want any more change in her life, even losing a view.

"Dad, I'd like you to meet Amanda Marcus, my new tenant."

Mr. Williams swung around; his handsome, lined face brightened under its unruly thatch of white hair. "Hey, the lady upstairs. Welcome. I'd shake hands, but mine aren't fit for it."

He held up his large, weathered, capable-looking hands, stained gray and black with charcoal.

"Don't worry." She held out her hand and gave a phantom shake. "It's nice to meet you, Mr. Williams."

"Same here. But please, call me Sonny." He solemnly shook the air opposite. "Arch here has told me next to nothing about you."

"Ah." She glanced at Arch to find an amused smile on his face. Didn't anything disconcert him? "Well, that's probably all he knows about me."

"I'm betting he'd like to change that, eh, son?"

"Sure."

Another sidelong glance at Arch. Not a trace of embarrassment. He was rocking on and off his heels, hands in his pockets, looking casual and content. She'd eat slugs for half that much composure around him.

"Are you widowed? Divorced?"

"Dad…"

"What?" His dad held up his hands again in an incredulous shrug. "She doesn't have to tell me if she doesn't want to."

"I never married." Amanda bit her lip. She never lied about her single-mom status, but it was always hard to say. People stopped short. They were either shocked or embarrassed or tripped over themselves to reassure her they didn't judge her at all, which was almost worse.

"Ah. I see." Mr. Williams picked up a spatula and pointed it at Clarissa, apparently as unflappable as his son. "She's a cute kid. Looks just like you. Not a lot of her father there, eh?"

"No."

"He still around?"

"*Dad.*"

His father rolled his eyes. "Oh, like you don't want to know."

Arch chuckled, let his head drop and shook it in exasperation. "By the way, Amanda, you don't have to answer any of these incredibly personal questions from a total stranger if you don't want to."

"It's okay. Clarissa's father isn't around." She pressed her lips shut. That was about all she wanted to volunteer on that topic.

"Where did he—"

Arch took his father's shoulder and turned him gently back to the grill, where at least eight hamburgers sizzled, flanked by six brats, and about ten hot dogs, all doing their own share of sizzling.

Amanda's mouth started to water. "Oh, those smell so—"

Clarissa screamed. Amanda's body went rigid. She swung around to find her daughter tied to a fence post, a pile of sticks at her feet, three boys circling in bloodthirsty glee.

"What are you *doing?*" She started over toward the boys, intending to murder first and ask questions after. A strong hand grabbed her arm and hauled her back.

"Let me go." She twisted to escape.

"Relax, Amanda. They're just playing."

Clarissa screamed again. "No! No!"

"*Listen* to her." Amanda twisted again. "They're hurting her, they're scaring her."

Arch dragged her back to face him and clamped down firmly on her shoulders. She glared into his puzzled face. "Let me *go.*"

"Amanda. Turn around and look. Really look."

She turned around. Clarissa was shrieking with laughter now. Trying once in a while, unsuccessfully, to resume looking terrified, then busting out again.

Amanda relaxed in Arch's grip. Closed her eyes. Okay. Maybe she could feel a little more stupid, standing here in a garden she didn't notice had been ruined, unable to tell when her own daughter was having fun, with a big purple spot on her butt. "I'm sorry. I thought—"

"I don't blame you. She's a terrific actress." Arch dropped his hands off her shoulders. "You okay?"

Amanda nodded, suddenly exhausted, and for some idiotic reason, near tears. "Yes."

"You know what?"

She forced a smile. "What?"

"I think beer is in order."

She managed another smile. She didn't drink beer. She

was generally a white wine kind of chick and not much of that lately. But she was pretty damn sure she needed one now. "Beer sounds perfect."

He brought her a cold Leinenkugel's Northwoods Lager and twisted the top off for her. She took a long sip and smiled again, a real one this time. She was thirsty and the beer tasted damn good, cold and bubbly and perfect. She took another long sip. Maybe she'd start drinking beer when she had money again.

"Sorry about my dad." He held the bottle cap between his thumb and forefinger and with a snap of his fingers sent it neatly into the open garbage can set up for discarded picnic fare. "He's direct, but he's a terrific guy. Once he decides he likes someone he's there a thousand percent. Not too many like him."

"It's okay." She fingered the label on the bottle, envious of his open admiration for his father. "Must be nice to be close to him."

"Yeah. You have family nearby?"

"I will soon."

He lifted an eyebrow at her acerbic tone. "That doesn't sound good."

"My mom is moving to Milwaukee. Tomorrow." She took another swallow of lager, trying to avoid sounding bitter again.

"The Decorator." He emphasized the words gravely, as if she was Arnold Schwarzenegger's next big role.

Amanda snorted with laughter and nearly shot beer out her nose. He'd nailed her mom perfectly without even meeting her.

"It will be fine." She nearly snorted again, this time in disgust rather than amusement. Even she wasn't convinced by the way that sounded.

Arch gestured toward her daughter; they both watched

her slowly collapsing to the ground in the final paroxysms of her fiery death at the stake. "Do you look as much like her as Clarissa does you?"

Amanda shook her head, impressed by her daughter's theatrics now that she knew that's what they were. "I'm adopted."

"Did you ever look for your birth parents?"

She shook her head. "I didn't want to find out I was somebody's sexual mistake."

He turned from watching the kids, a half grin on his face. "I can't imagine you ever being a sexual mistake."

This time Amanda did spit beer, a thin dribble down her chin. She wiped it away, staring up at Arch. *What the—*

"Uh. That came out totally wrong." He looked around and scratched his head, finally disconcerted. "That is. What I meant was—"

She put her hand on his forearm, surprised at how hard the muscle was underneath. Geez, she hadn't touched a man in *way* too long. "Don't worry. I'm just so glad to see someone else flustered at this gathering besides me."

He put his hands in his pockets and looked down at her, smiling. "Flustered is good. It means you're in a situation challenging you. Challenges make you think about who you are and who you want to be."

"Hmm." She consulted her beer bottle, then thought said bottle would be put to better use tipped into her mouth. "Well, that's a positive spin on it."

"Everything has a positive. You just have to look."

She nodded politely. Easy for him to say when he had enough money to turn his home into an amusement park.

"Carnivore call!" His father shouted across the yard, scooping more food than they could possibly eat onto a plate, with another platter of raw meat at his elbow, waiting to take its turn on the grill.

"Hungry?"

She nodded. "Starved."

"Omigod!" Clarissa's squeal of delight carried clearly over to them. "Something that isn't pasta! Mom, check it out! There's other food in the world!"

Amanda sighed. Someday Clarissa's wit and drama might win her an Oscar. In the meantime it was a pain in the…jelly area.

Arch chuckled. "In a bit of a cooking rut?"

"I guess."

"Happens to all of us. When I'm on deadline I pretty much stick to peanut butter and ramen noodles."

She smiled, grateful for his gracious way of avoiding the real issue. "Could do worse."

"Absolutely. Come eat. Then we can get the party games in before the rain."

Amanda lowered her beer bottle before the last sip. "Party games?"

He nodded, face a little too innocent.

Her suspicion rose. She hated party games. As a kid she'd thrown up being overspun for tail-on-the-donkey after too much cake and ice cream, and earned the nickname Amanda Puker. As a teenager, Peter Tenbom had refused to kiss her during spin the bottle because he claimed she had Dorito breath, which earned her the predictable nickname…Dorito Breath. And only a few years ago, she'd been at a party where the hostess insisted the guests tell someone they didn't know their naughtiest secret, and hers had been that she threw away mayonnaise jars instead of washing them for recycling. Luckily no nickname that time. At least none she'd heard.

"What kind of games?"

"Three-legged race, balloon bust, potato relay. You know. Party games."

"Oh, for the kids." She tried not to let her relief show, but it did anyway.

"Oh no." He shook his head, grin wide. "Oh no, no, no. The only people exempt from these games are those without a purple spot on their butt. Last I checked, which was embarrassingly recently, you had one. Therefore, you play."

He walked away to the table laden with buns, rolls, condiments and side dishes. She followed, expecting to feel grumpy and cornered, but who the hell could feel grumpy and cornered with beer on an empty stomach, enough food to feed the Green Bay Packers on hand and a gorgeous guy who had just admitted to checking out her butt?

She'd eat herself sick and plead out of the games that way. She loved board games—Monopoly, Sorry!, Careers, Yahtzee, things she could play with her dignity intact. But there was a definite and distinct Amanda Marcus line drawn at three-legged races, or games involving vegetables tucked in places vegetables weren't meant to be tucked. As far as concessions to Peter Pan here, she'd already allowed the purple spot. If Arch thought he could get her to participate in that kind of foolishness at her age, he was going to find himself entirely wrong.

CHAPTER FIVE

ARCH LIFTED his third beer to his lips and found himself grinning too hard to drink. There was nothing right now that could give him more pleasure than the sight of Amanda's purple-splotched butt high in the air as she crawled across the exercise mats he'd put over the wet grass, pushing a potato with her nose, trying to beat Mark to the finish line, to the cheers and jeers of the other kids.

It had taken another Leinie's lager, subtle persuasion from him and outright cajoling from the children before she'd consent to play. She started awkwardly, half-sullen, half-nervous, then gradually got caught up in the fun and proved herself to be a fearsome and enthusiastic competitor.

He lifted the bottle, tried to drink again, and again failed, chuckling, not wanting to miss a second of the race. She was too fun to watch, bumping the potato with her nose, patiently keeping it in line when it tried to wobble in all directions—a stray sheep escaping the sheepdog. She reached the end of the mat, seconds ahead of Mark and stood, flushed, triumphant and only slightly self-conscious.

The combination was deadly. Desire hit him so hard he gave up smiling, gave up trying to drink the beer, and stared.

Against the heightened color in her cheeks, her eyes were brilliant blue and full of life; her hair had been mussed by the potato trip and by her valiant efforts during balloon burst to stomp on balloons tied around her opponents' ankles, including his. He'd never dreamed the game could be so sexy. When he'd managed to pop her balloon, she'd given him a look of I'll-get-you-next-time mischief that had practically made him hard.

She was breathing slightly fast now, and when she turned and caught the dark look on Mark's face, she went over and shook his hand, said something, laughed and patted him on the back, making him blush and grin in spite of his these-days-sour self.

She was magnificent. Nothing like the controlled hesitant waif he'd first encountered upstairs in her flowery apartment. This woman was incredible. This woman was alive and real. This woman would probably read Corporal Wedgie books and get them.

She turned to him, still smiling, and he lifted his beer to salute her victory. Eyes level with his, confident, secure, she walked straight over to where he leaned against the table. As she approached, he found himself swallowing, nervous, awkward, like in seventh grade at a school dance when Mary Jane Lanken marched up to him out of the blue, just like this, and kissed him on the mouth—his first kiss.

Amanda handed him the potato and rubbed the bridge of her nose. "That's hard work."

He nodded, struck dumb by the image of Mary Jane's kiss and by how much he wanted to grab Amanda right here and plant a serious one on her. To congratulate her on the awesome victory in potato rolling. And to satisfy his curiosity as to how much passion simmered, hidden, in that petite body...

A strong male hand thumped him on the back and nearly made him drop his beer. "Arch. Come back. Picnic's over, it's going to rain again."

He glanced at the darkening sky and forced himself back

to planet Earth, though planet Amanda had offered a lot more amusement than cleaning up a picnic.

"You with us now?" His dad winked at Amanda and jerked his head toward Arch as if to say, "Get a load of this sap."

"I'm here, I'm here." He rolled his eyes at Amanda as if to say, "Get a load of this old fart."

Amanda shook her head at the two of them and laughed, a musical portrait of delight that nearly sent him into another Amanda-induced stupor.

"I thought you were going to stare at this woman the rest of the week." His father pointedly dumped a pot of potato salad on the table next to Arch.

He put down his beer and picked up the pot. "Can you think of anything more worthwhile to do?"

His father grinned, reached across the table and playfully nudged Amanda's shoulder. "No, by God. Glad to have you around, Amanda."

She looked startled, then pleased, shot a look at Arch he couldn't read, then a warm smile at his father. "Thank you, Sonny. It's been a great evening."

"Not over yet." He hefted a Crock-Pot of Arch's mom's favorite baked-bean recipe. "Kids," he shouted. "Come help your ancient grandpa clear up."

After a few grumbles, the kids joined in and helped clear the picnic, brought the mountains of leftover food inside, and the equipment they'd used for games, scoured the yard for bottle tops and scraps of popped balloon.

The second they got the last table loaded back inside, the skies opened up.

"Now, was that timing or was that timing?" Arch closed the door and grinned at the crowd in the kitchen.

"Timing." Luke eyed the pan of brownies. "When do we eat those?"

"Now sound good?"

The boys shouted out long and deafening versions of "Yes."

"Let's take them into the living room. We still need to hold a conference on what to do about the Evil Jelly Boy."

Amanda looked at her watch, her high color faded, a more serious look returning. "We should go, it's Clarissa's bedtime."

"Hmm." Arch calculated his next attack. No way was he letting her leave now. Not when he'd gotten this far. He wanted to get the kids settled in with a movie, pour her a finger of brandy and see if he could get her talking. "Tomorrow's Saturday. In fact, we'll even impose a silence curfew down here so Clarissa has some hope of sleeping in."

"Please, Mom?" Amanda's daughter turned those beseeching eyes kids were so damn good at on her mother. "Can we stay? I need to know what to do about Ralph."

Arch grinned at the indecision on Amanda's face. Clarissa had jumped in right on cue. Supported his efforts to put Mom in the hot seat.

Amanda flicked a glance at Arch that told him clearly she knew what he was doing, and that while she might forgive him eventually, right now was not that time.

"I'm sorry, Clarissa, but we need to go. It's nearly nine."

"Mo-o-om." Clarissa stamped her foot.

"Clarissa." Amanda said the word in that quiet tone only women with children could produce, a tone that could bring grown men to their knees.

Clarissa's face darkened; she stomped out of the room.

"Thank you for the picnic. We had a very nice time." Amanda held out her hand to Arch, who shook it grimly. He no longer wanted to kiss her. He wanted to drag her into a room and ask her where the hell the woman she'd let out had gone and why the hell would she ever want to send her away in favor of this creature?

"You're welcome. We enjoyed having you." He mimicked her formal tone and was rewarded with a flicker of recognition in those now-dulled blue eyes.

She stood for a moment, hand still in his, forehead creased, looking indecisive. *Come on, Amanda.*

"Do you really think you could help with the bully? The jelly boy?"

He grinned and squeezed her hand. "Yes, ma'am."

"Then...it would be great if you could talk to Clarissa."

Ha! He grinned wider. Victory was so damn sweet. "I'd love to—"

"In the morning." She withdrew her hand primly and he had to resist the urge to growl at her.

"Glad to. Glad to." He stroked his chin, considering intently. Archibald Williams didn't give up easily. "Of course...it would only take a second. And it might cheer her up now..."

The boys watched the standoff with silent interest. Amanda glanced at them, then back at Arch. He gave her a mischievous "gotcha" grin and was rewarded with a reluctant smile.

"Okay."

"Over coffee?" He was pushing it, but curious how far she'd rethaw.

"No. Thanks."

Apparently not that far.

"Okay, gang." He clapped his hands and rubbed them together. "Let's plan our strategy to defeat the Evil Jelly Warlord."

The kids exploded into cheers and began the screaming frenetic dance of the Extremely Overstimulated.

He caught Amanda's expression and managed to get them quiet before they went in search of Clarissa, who they found at the front door peeking hopefully back over her shoulder to see if anyone would come after her.

"Now, Rissa." Arch gestured at his nephews. "We are going to help you with your problem."

Clarissa's eyes brightened. "Awesome."

He held out his hands to the boys. "I'm entertaining suggestions from the floor."

Silence.

John wrinkled his little face. "The floor?"

Right. Rephrase. "Anyone have any ideas?"

Luke raised his hand. "Put peanut butter in his shoes."

"No, no." John jumped up and down. "Dog food in his shoes."

Mark snickered. "No, dog *poop* in—"

"Okay, I think this is one for Uncle Arch to handle."

He walked forward, bent over, hands above his knees, and looked very seriously at Clarissa. "This kid has got you just where he wants you, ashamed, embarrassed, not fighting back."

Clarissa nodded and threw a you-are-*so*-lame look at her mom. Arch cringed. Bad start.

"Your mom's suggestion was excellent. Most bullies respond to that weapon. But what you have here is a prime grade-A super-nasty bully, and those need to be dealt with appropriately."

Clarissa's eyes grew round. "How?"

He beckoned Clarissa closer. The boys crowded behind him to hear. Arch grinned. He loved kids. He loved how excited they were, how open to new ideas, new experiences, how fascinated they were by everything they hadn't yet encountered. Ms. Amanda could take some lessons there.

"Tell me what this Ralph guy does."

"He puts jelly on my chair, then he and his stupid friends call me Jelly Butt Marcus all day long."

"Hmm. Okay." Arch nodded and tapped his cheek thoughtfully. "What's the name of your school?"

"Roosevelt Elementary."

"Okay..." More cheek-tapping. He let the suspense build. Behind him the boys were jostling for position. Clarissa bit her lip and clasped her hands together. Even Amanda took a step closer for a better view.

"Aha!" He held up the finger he'd been using to tap his cheek. "I've got it. Here's what you do. First, hold your head up high and make sure you are talking loud enough that everyone around you can hear. Then say, 'Yes, Ralph, I have the most fine and tremendous jelly butt in all of Roosevelt Elementary.'"

"Then do the jelly-butt dance like this." He put one hand to his stomach, the other lifted next to his head, and strutted around the hallway. "Jelly Butt Marc-us, walking in the park-us, scaring all the bad guys after dark-us. Keeping the world safe from wussy bully bad guys like you."

The boys went nuts, laughing at the top of their lungs, imitating his dance, attempting the lyrics; Clarissa giggled madly, bent over forward, hand over her mouth; Amanda— he sighed at the sight of her half-bewildered, half-skeptical face. Well, Amanda would come around. Seeing her unbend tonight had been all the permission he needed for what he planned to do for her. He had a feeling she'd need him more than ever after her mom showed up tomorrow.

Things happened for a reason. Something had drawn him to this house. At first he thought it might be the neighborhood. He could afford Shorewood, Glendale or Whitefish Bay, but something hadn't felt right about living in any of those places. Then this little Lannon stone duplex in the modest Wauwatosa neighborhood had called to him when he'd been planning on something bigger. He'd thought maybe it was the chance to bring youth and light into the old lady's dark downstairs space. Now he was thinking he might have been brought here for another reason. A tiny, blond, anxious-looking soul named Amanda Marcus, who needed liberating from whatever oppressed her.

And after some of the powerful wonderful feelings he'd felt tonight, he was more than merely willing to help her in any way he could.

Unlocking Amanda had become an obsession.

MAUDE MARCUS SMILED her extra-charming smile at the handsome gentleman who'd just lifted down her suitcase, which another gentleman had stowed in the overhead luggage compartment for her when they boarded. An extra-charming smile was necessary not only because he was handsome, though too young for her purposes, but also because he had no idea what he was getting into when he went to lift her case down, and extra-charming smiles could go a long way toward preventing hernia lawsuits.

Not that he'd gotten one, of course, but his eyes had rather bugged out and he'd collapsed forward with an *oof* while her suitcase practically shook the cabin when it landed on the floor.

Maude Marcus was a champion packer. She didn't know a soul alive who could stuff more into a suitcase than she could. Thank God they made luggage with wheels nowadays.

"Thank you very much."

"You're welcome." He pulled down his own carry-on items, muttering something she was quite sure she was glad not to be able to hear.

She waited, outwardly calm and smiling, while the flight

attendant took forever to unlock the damn door, and people in the rows ahead of her took forever to get out of their seats and leave. She wanted off. Flying was dismal, but driving would have been unthinkable on her own. Too many miles, Manhattan to Milwaukee. And Midwest Airlines, with its all-business-class cabin and chocolate chip cookies baked on board, was a damn sight better than the usual cattle car.

Perhaps Milwaukee might have one or two advantages, though giving up Manhattan was like losing a major limb. The city was the very center of the universe, of that she was certain.

The family in the row in front of her took about three hours unloading and strapping on their various gear. Ridiculous all the fussy safety equipment they traveled with. Like a little plastic seat was going to keep their toddler alive in an airplane smashing into the earth at six hundred miles per hour.

The child's mother hoisted the last bag to her shoulder and smiled apologetically at Maude, hair a mess, zero makeup, face pink from being so harassed. "Sorry."

"Quite all right." Maude beamed as if she had all day to stand there. "Traveling with children is always an adventure."

She got no disagreement from the mother whose toddler had started screaming.

Maude smiled graciously at the little monster, thinking it deserved a good spanking, not an indulgent hug. Parents let their kids go wild nowadays. Amanda had caused a public scene only once. You had to show them who was boss and Maude had done so immediately and in no uncertain terms. Amanda had figured it out quickly. But then she'd always been of above-average intelligence. Not that she'd done a whole lot with it as of yet. But Maude hadn't given up hope. Not by any means.

She finally made it off the plane, pausing to thank the flight attendant and the pilot, who looked exactly like every other pilot she'd ever seen, as if they required them to match. Perhaps she'd find a retired pilot for her special friend. Didn't they get to fly free for life? Jetting off to the Caribbean during the long Wisconsin winter would be lovely.

She hauled her suitcase up the boarding ramp, wishing the businessman hurrying by had offered to help as any gentleman in her day would have done. But these fem libbers, though they had a lot of good points that she supported thoroughly, had definitely ruined a lot of the pampering women used to enjoy.

Out into the gate area at General Mitchell International, she looked around, her smile slipping. Why wasn't Amanda here? She'd said she'd come. Maude had taught her always to be punctual. Had something happened?

Another look around and it struck her no one was waiting to meet the flight. And no one from the flight was waiting here either. Oh God, yes. Those terrorists. The airport people weren't letting anyone past security without a ticket. Which meant hauling her suitcase the length of what looked like an endless carpeted hallway.

By the time she made it to the end of the endless carpeted hallway, turned a corner and found herself facing another endless carpeted hallway, the smile she kept on at all times to identify herself as a pleasant, happy, attractive person, began to feel forced. Her breath was coming too heavily and her face had probably turned as pink as that of the woman with the toddler.

A nearby rest room beckoned and she ducked into it so she wouldn't meet her child and grandchild looking old and out of shape. A check in the mirror confirmed that she looked neither and her smile came back easily.

Moving here was the right thing to do, she felt it in her bones. Escape the shame of Manhattan and start her new life with a new man. Being a widow once and a divorcée the second time was tough. She couldn't bear the thought of having to introduce someone as her third husband. Made her sound like one of those women who went through husbands on a regular basis, collecting alimony like some people collect postage stamps.

What she wanted, what she'd come here to Milwaukee to find, away from the memories and closer to those she loved best, was a romance. An old-fashioned romance. She was too old for passion, too weary of the sloppy, groaning mess of sex. She was after a distinguished elderly gentleman who'd take her to the opera, to plays, out to dinner. Who'd kiss her at the doorway and bid her good-night.

But *not* expect her to take care of him. Men always expected her to take care of them, then the myopic fools resented her when she did what they wanted. From now on she would be in charge of her own destiny and her own life. Period.

But a romance would be nice. As soon as she settled, she'd find out where to meet the top-drawer eligible men so she could get started. She knew she was still attractive, cultured, at a good weight, unlike so many of her friends who had let themselves go. But even she couldn't compete with the gold-digging, forty-something bimbo who'd wormed her way into Maude's marriage and carted off her husband of fifteen years.

She lifted her chin. So? In twenty years that forty-something, gold-digging bimbo would be sixty-something, just like Maude. Age happened. You camouflaged as much as you could and carried the rest graciously and with dignity.

Her purse snapped shut, and with lipstick and breath restored, she wheeled her case back out into the second endless carpeted hallway, down its length, past two young handsome armed soldiers, who gave her the heebie-jeebies. As if she lived in some third world country and not the United States of America.

"Grandma!" A young girl detached from the crowd at the mouth of the security gate and came running.

Maude dropped the handle of her suitcase and flung her arms wide.

"Clarissa!" She clasped the young body to her, then pushed her granddaughter to arm's distance and laughed, tears of joy making a brief appearance, but thank goodness not spilling over. "Look how big you've gotten! In second grade already! Look at you!"

She clasped the child to her again, laughing more, remembering how she used to hate it when relatives told her how much she'd grown. But it was so amazing every time, to see her beautiful grandchild, so like her mother at that age, blossoming toward young womanhood.

"Hi, Mom."

She stood and embraced her daughter, feeling guilty for the pang of disappointment that always mixed with deep love for her child. In her imagination Clarissa stayed as she'd last seen her, while Amanda was always transformed into a taller, more stylish, more self-assertive woman. Every time Maude saw her, there was that stab of recognition and realization that her only child was tiny, mousy, dressed as if she didn't care, and gave off the aura of someone life was going to crush at any moment.

More than anything, Maude had wanted a daughter she could teach about how to be a woman. Maybe her expectations were unrealistic, maybe her desire had been a silly self-centered dream. But it was hard when one's dreams didn't come true. Even silly self-centered ones.

They started across the main room of the airport, Maude pleased when Amanda took her suitcase, and even more pleased when she seemed to have trouble pulling it. Nothing to do with being old. The suitcase was heavy.

"Did you check any baggage, Mom?"

"Heavens no, I don't take chances with them losing my things, you know that."

"Okay." Amanda ducked her head as if she'd been punished. Maude pressed her lips together in frustration. "So you'll take me to my new place?"

Amanda glanced at Clarissa, as if she needed her daughter's permission to speak. "Clarissa and I thought you might like to come to our place for dinner first. Maybe spend the night if you don't feel up to being on your own."

"I've been on my own for quite some time now." She didn't mean to sound bitter, but she couldn't help it.

"Oh, I know. I just thought it would be fun."

"Like a sleepover." Clarissa's eyes sparkled with excitement.

Maude smiled at her and bent to give her a hug. "A sleepover sounds wonderful. Thank you." She glanced up to include her daughter in the thanks and Amanda grinned.

"You should smile more often." Maude caught her chin and gave it a gentle squeeze. "You have a dazzling smile."

"Thanks, Mom."

"Men would notice you more if you smiled." A trio of them, in fact, very nicely dressed, had just passed by and not given Amanda a glance. If she'd just get herself dolled up a bit, and keep that smile on, she'd knock 'em all dead, Maude was sure. But then she'd never been able to figure her daughter out.

Amanda's dazzling smile faded. "I'm not really interested in whether men notice me."

This was so bizarre, Maude had no idea how to respond, so she got on the elevator for the parking garage without comment. Sometimes she wondered how they could be from the same gender. If it wasn't for Ridge, she'd think her daughter was a lesbian.

"Arch notices you."

Maude looked keenly at Clarissa, who was watching warily for her mother's reaction after she spoke. "Who's Arch?"

"He bought the duplex from Mrs. Carson." Amanda spoke much too casually. "He seems nice."

"How nice?"

"Nice." The doors opened on the third level and they started on the enclosed walkway to the garage, but not before Maude caught the blush on Amanda's cheek.

Eureka. Maude's move to Milwaukee had suddenly taken on newfound importance. If this Arch character was at all suitable, then Maude was *just* the right person to keep Amanda from screwing up her second shot at love.

CHAPTER SIX

AMANDA LET HERSELF into her apartment and breathed a momentary sigh of relief. Momentary. Her mom was not far behind. She'd spent another gloomy, gray, oppressively humid day catering to her mother's whims helping her get set up in her new place. It was a beautiful apartment facing Lake Michigan, newly renovated, fabulous facilities in the complex, but nothing was good enough for Maude Marcus.

Amanda sighed and sank into one of her flowery chairs. Saturday, the first night home from the airport, hadn't been too bad. The initial excitement at seeing each other had gone a long way toward making Mom's first-night "sleepover" pleasant. They'd changed into pajamas and the three of them had made popcorn and stayed up way past Clarissa's bedtime talking. Clarissa's enthusiasm had carried them over the few rough spots—notably when Amanda had tried to parry questions about her employment while not revealing she didn't have any. But today, the old painful patterns had reasserted themselves. If her mother thought Milwaukee was such a dinky undersupplied town, why the hell had she moved here? Every sentence was preceded by, "Well, in New *York...*" and then a long list of the wonderful stores and services available in the Big Apple. It got a bit much after a while.

She flipped on a light to combat the gloom and glanced at her answering machine. One message.

"This is Catherine Loring, attorney with Grammick,

Schenckel and Fortz. I have important business to discuss with Amanda Marcus. I'll be busy today and out for the rest of the week but will try back or you can call me.'' She left a number with an area code Amanda didn't recognize and hung up. The machine's robot voice announced the time the message had come in—that morning, shortly after Amanda had left for her mom's apartment, ostensibly taking a day off work to help.

Amanda frowned. What would an out-of-state lawyer have to talk to her about? The Pattersons and Zera of The Dress both had local representation, so it couldn't have anything to do with the store. Nor could she be in any kind of legal trouble.

She shrugged and deleted the message. Probably some scam involving a deal on real estate in a Florida swamp. If it really was important, Ms. Loring would call back.

The bell rang; she sighed and went down to open the door. Her mom swept past her, carrying a bakery box and went up the stairs.

"You know, it would be a lot easier if you just gave me a key. Save you having to run downstairs every time I come over."

Amanda bit her lip and trudged up the stairs after her mother. How the hell was she going to handle this one? The idea made her bones turn to ice. "I'll get a copy made at the hardware store."

If she managed to remember. Ahem.

"Terrific, dear. Where's Clarissa?"

"The Saunders should be dropping her off soon after school."

"Good. What a day." Her mom sank onto the couch and let her head loll back. "I'm exhausted. Were you thinking of offering me a cup of tea?"

Amanda gritted her teeth. She never managed to think

of these things before her mother did. Afternoon tea was one of her mom's rigid habits. One of her many rigid habits. "Of course. I'll put the kettle on."

"And I meant to say when I was here last time, if you ever need help cleaning this place, I'm happy to give you a hand."

"Thanks for the offer." Amanda would have gritted her teeth, but her teeth were already gritted. So she stalked to the kitchen and filled the kettle instead. What made her think Amanda needed help cleaning? Wasn't it clean enough in here? Not like Amanda had a whole lot else to do all day; the place was spotless.

The doorbell rang. She put the kettle on the stove and fled downstairs to answer it.

"Mom, it was *awesome!*" Clarissa burst in through the door. "You should have seen it!"

Amanda followed her daughter up the stairs, heart sinking at the sight of yet another purple splotch on Clarissa's jeans. Maybe she should just call the boy's parents.

"Wait till you hear this! Hi, Grandma. I did just what Arch said, Mom. I yelled out how my butt was the best jelly butt at Roosevelt, I did the song and the dance, told him he was a wussy bully, and it was totally, totally amazing. All the kids started laughing, just like Arch said they would, but Mom, they weren't laughing at me, they were laughing at Ralph! They all did! Then they started doing the dance, too, and some of them even put jelly on their own butts and we all did the Jelly Butt Marcus dance all over the lunchroom until the teachers made us stop and it was *so…cool!*"

She stopped, breathing hard, eyes flashing, grinning triumphantly into the deathlike silence.

The kettle started to whistle, a tiny tinny whimper that built up gradually into a full-boil screaming head of steam.

Amanda's mother slowly turned her head toward Amanda, wearing her I-demand-an-explanation-for-this-appalling-behavior face. Clarissa turned her head to her mom wearing her what?-what-did-I-say? face. Amanda responded with her I'm-going-to-get-the-kettle-so-leave-me-the-heck-alone face and beat it to the kitchen.

Families were such a joy.

She turned off the kettle and opened the cabinet to the left of the sink, groaning when she realized she had no loose tea for a proper potful and would have to make do with the abomination of tea bags and mugs. Her mom might forgive her for that transgression, but she'd probably never understand about Arch's solution to the jelly problem. Amanda wasn't sure she understood it herself, except that Clarissa was happy and felt, at least for now, that she'd scored some kind of victory over this Ralph person. As long as he didn't take his humiliation as a challenge to do something worse...

The doorbell rang, three times, quick. Clarissa shouted that she'd get it and thudded down the stairs while Amanda spent too much time arranging the cookies her mom brought onto a plate, adding snipped bunches of grapes and slices of Wisconsin cheddar. Call her chicken, but she was too spent to go back in there and face her mother alone, to have to listen to a lecture on the horrors of having a daughter whose child bragged in public about her rear end.

Arch's deep voice rumbled in the stairwell and up into her apartment, punctuated by Clarissa's excited babble. Amanda felt a silly upwelling of happiness, as if the cavalry had ridden in when all looked to be lost. Three quick rings—she should have recognized his signal.

She walked back into the living room, carrying the plate, and without her instructing them to, her eyes locked on Arch, who was carrying two paper grocery bags. His eyes seemed to lock as irresistibly on hers and a big grin split his face, which made her upwelling of happiness turn into a geyser.

"Hi, Amanda, I could use your help with the leftover food from the party, hope you don't mind if I brought some up."

"Oh. No. That's very nice." She knew her voice sounded insincere, but she also knew why he was bringing food up, and she couldn't decide if the gesture was thoughtful or patronizing. She did know, however, exactly what Maude Marcus would think about someone offering his leftovers as a gift.

"I'll put them away." He strode through the living room and disappeared into the kitchen as if he owned the place—which, actually, he did. Bag-rustling and refrigerator-door-opening sounds emerged from the open door.

Amanda's mother's eyes narrowed. In her world, walking uninvited into someone's kitchen meant Sex Had Happened. Also in her world, once Sex Had Happened, you'd better be On the Way to Being Engaged.

Amanda turned toward the kitchen, then back toward her mother, frozen in place, holding the plate of food. "That's Arch."

One eyebrow crept halfway up her mother's lined forehead. "I gathered."

Arch came back into the living room, and straight over to Amanda's mother. "Now that I have my hands free, hello and nice to meet you."

"This is my mother, Mau... Mrs. Marcus. Mom, this is Arch Williams."

Her mother held out her hand like the Queen Ourself and attempted to look pleasant. Arch leaned down to shake. "Nice to meet you, Mrs. Marcus."

"Arch. What is that short for?"

"Believe it or not, Archibald."

"Hmm."

Amanda's mother could make "hmm" sound like anything from you-are-lying-and-I-want-the-truth-*now* to that-is-the-most-repulsive-thing-I-ever-heard. This "hmm" lay somewhere in between.

"What do you do, Archibald?"

"It's just Arch, Mrs. Marcus." He smiled, but something in his words and in that smile made Amanda's eyes slide immediately to her mother to see how she'd take it.

"I see." Mrs. Marcus arranged her uncrossed ankles even more correctly against the side of the sofa. "And what do you do…Arch?"

"I write children's books."

"Oh!" Maude practically sang the word; her condemning look softened into a glowing smile and she clasped her hands in delight. "How *interesting*. What are some of your titles?"

Amanda clenched everything in her body as tightly as she could, but nothing could smother her snort of laughter.

"Let's see." Arch put one hand to his hip, and scratched his head with the other, clearly about to enjoy himself. "Among others, there's *Corporal Wedgie and the Gas Attack, Corporal Wedgie and the Atomic Mutant Mammals,* and my latest, *Corporal Wedgie's Trip Through Your Guts.*"

Amanda's mother kept the smile on. She blinked once. The plate in Amanda's hands started to shake.

"Arch, I just made some tea, would you like a cup?" Amanda only just managed to get the sentence out. Because the idea of anyone as energetic and masculine as Arch sitting in her frilly apartment having tea and cookies with her mother after what he'd just told her about killed her.

Ridge had managed the tea ritual only once; she still had

the picture of his lanky body on her mother's flowered apricot sofa, the cup and saucer looking like a doll's set in his big hands, fidgeting until her mother had told him to stop or she'd ask him to leave. And *he* hadn't said anything about taking a trip through her guts. Funny how Amanda hadn't really thought about Ridge, except fleetingly, in years. Not until she met Arch.

"No, thanks." He swung his arms forward and clapped his hands, swung them in back and clapped again, grinning at Amanda. "I was going to ask if you and Clarissa wanted to go to the park with us. And of course your mother can come too if she likes."

"Oh! Yes! Mom, can we?"

"I...don't know." Amanda looked at the plate in her hands, feeling as if the air had just been sucked out of her apartment. She wanted to go. She wanted to be out there in the great outdoors with Arch more than anything in the universe, even if it did look as if it was about to pour. She didn't want to sit here with her mother. But that would be horribly rude, to leave her mom alone. She'd have to let Clarissa go and dutifully stay here to be verbally bludgeoned.

"Why don't you go ahead with Arch. I'll stay and have tea with Grandma." She tried to sound enthusiastic, but the words came out more along the lines of "Don't mind me, I'll stay and eat worms with the Evil Empress."

Her mom made an impatient gesture. "For heaven's sake, Amanda, go if you want to. I don't need baby-sitting."

Amanda glanced at her mother. Was this a test? If Amanda went, would she forever after be reminded of the time she left her mom all by herself to drink tea-bag tea out of a mug?

Arch moved forward, took the plate out of her hands and

put it on the coffee table in front of her mother. "Sounds like a plan. Let's go."

"Awesome!" Clarissa grabbed two cookies and some grapes off the plate. "I'm ready. Mom?"

"I...I..." She took a deep breath. Why the hell not? Her mom had said she'd be okay. She had her hallowed tea for company. And it wasn't as though they'd be gone for hours. "It's not going to rain?"

"Nope." Arch shook his head vigorously. "Not a drop until we get back."

"Okay." She grinned up at his handsome face, feeling absurdly free and slightly giddy. "Then I'm ready too."

MAUDE FINISHED her cup of tea and stretched luxuriously on the couch she'd shipped to Amanda from her mother's furniture in storage. Maybe it needed re-covering, though the blue-and-yellow floral print was still respectable. Maude had grown up on this couch; her own mother had read her stories on it; taught her how to hold a teacup properly; her father had sometimes napped here, until Mother caught him and scolded him into an upright position.

She moved her hand over the soft fabric, trying not to notice how clawlike and old and undecorated her hand looked without its diamond. The sofa fit just right into this apartment. The whole place looked lovely, soft and tastefully feminine. Just right for Amanda. Maude's place wasn't quite there yet. Didn't feel like home just yet.

She straightened briskly and got up from the sofa to leave the sinking feeling behind, and peered out the window at the gray day. Funny to look out and see cream-colored stone and shingle and brick houses. Not what she was used to in Manhattan. But nice to see lawns and gardens.

This house had a spectacular garden. Maybe she'd chase

away this restless sadness she'd been accumulating of late by taking a turn around it.

She went into Amanda's bedroom, nodding approvingly at the neatly made bed, the white comforter with tiny pink roses that she'd given her daughter for Christmas the year before. Amanda must work so hard to keep the place looking so perfect. Funny how she hadn't accepted Maude's offer of help. Now that ''Mom'' lived here, she might as well try to make life easier for her only child.

Behind the bedroom door was a full-length mirror. She gave herself a quick check, skirt on straight, blouse firmly tucked, lipstick reapplied.

''Maude Marcus, you look good for an old dame.'' She nodded and tried to smile her most gracious smile, but she ended up looking as if she was trying hard to be brave.

Enough of that. She marched firmly out of the apartment, down the stairs, outside and around back where she stopped, gasped and covered her mouth with her hands. The garden had been utterly ruined. Sod lay in artificial-looking stripes where Mrs. Carson's lovely plantings had been. What a horrible, horrible thing.

''Can I help you, ma'am?''

She whirled around, hands still clasped to her mouth. A short barrel-chested fellow was approaching down the driveway, white hair looking as if he'd slept on it and not bothered combing. ''Who are you?''

''Sonny Williams, ma'am.'' He extended a grubby hand, which she was tempted to but couldn't bring herself to ignore. ''Arch's father.''

''I see.'' She shook his hand, surprised by his warm, firm grasp. For some reason she'd expected sweaty and limp. ''Is that your real name? Sonny?''

''No. My real name is Thaddeus, so I go by Sonny.'' He

stood watching her, hands on his hips, pants riding low on his belly in an absurd workman's cliché. "And you are?"

"I'm sorry." Where were her manners? His unexpected intrusion into her chase-the-blues-away stroll coupled with the shock of discovering the ruined garden had flustered her. "I'm Amanda's mother."

He scratched his head, drawing his smudged thumb back and forth across his hairline. "You have a name?"

"Maude. Maude Marcus."

"Welcome to Milwaukee, Maude Marcus." He grinned; his teeth were straight and unstained, eyes dark and full of character, eyebrows bushy and still salt and pepper, unlike his hair, which had gone totally white.

"Thank you." She drew herself up, not quite sure where to put her hands. She didn't generally socialize with workmen, and while that sounded snobbier than she was, it was the truth. Worse, she was more on his turf than he on hers. "I was out for a look at the garden, only it turns out there isn't one anymore."

He came closer to stand beside her; she expected a smell of sour male sweat and was surprised at the clean subtle scent of aftershave. "Arch and I got rid of it. Flowers and little boys don't mix."

She started to bristle, then realized he was right. The garden would have been trampled within minutes. "Well, it's a shame. It was a lovely garden."

"Sure was. You have gardens at your place?"

"The building has some that look promising. Your spring comes later than ours in New York. My apartment has a balcony and I intend to put pots out there, too."

"You need anything, let me know, I have a friend who owns a nursery out on Capitol Drive."

She blinked. People in Manhattan were not as rude as legend had it, but they weren't known for volunteering to go out of their way for complete strangers. "Well, thank you."

"Well, you're welcome. So are you widowed or divorced?"

Maude gave a short laugh, part amusement, part disbelief. "What kind of question is that?"

He shrugged and folded his arms, resting his hands in his armpits, which made her wince at the thought she'd just shaken that hand. At the same time, she couldn't help noticing the way the muscles in his arms and chest bulged under his dirt-streaked T-shirt.

"It's a perfectly natural question. You're not wearing a ring. I'm guessing divorced because you seem the type to keep a ring on if your husband died."

"What…how do you…what makes you…" She couldn't believe this person had reduced her, Maude Marcus, Queen of Grace, to spluttering sentence fragments. Outrageous for a perfect stranger to be asking her such personal questions.

At the same time, he was eerily correct. She had worn Bruce's ring for two years after he died, until she met George.

"I'm a widower myself. I lost my wife twenty years ago to cancer. Took her two years to die, but we cared for her at home up until the end. Raised six children by myself. Still miss her every day."

Her mouth, which had been open to cut him off with "I am sorry to say my personal life is none of your business," snapped shut. She knew what that felt like, to lose a spouse. Bruce had dropped dead of a heart attack on the way home from the office, where he spent ninety percent of his time. Twenty-seven years of marriage, and all the time they thought they'd spend together later, in their retirement years, never happened.

"Actually—" she cleared her throat "—I'm widowed, too. My first husband died. I'm…divorced this time."

God she hated the word *divorced*. Such a shameful word. A word of failure and stain.

"He left you, huh?"

She drew in a sharp breath. How could he know? "Has Amanda been gossiping?"

"'Course not. I just figured a woman like you would never leave a marriage."

"Why do you keep saying 'a woman like you'? What could you possibly know about a woman like me? You've only just met me."

He shrugged, apparently not at all put off by her tirade. "I have a good feel for people."

"Well, you don't have a feel for me."

"So I'm wrong? You left this guy?"

Maude drew in another breath and held this one, counting to ten, as she'd tried to teach herself to do when Amanda was small. "I don't care to discuss it."

He turned and gave her a look that made her words reverberate into her own ears the way they must have sounded to him. Snooty. Prissy. Ridiculously defensive.

She let out the breath. "He left me. For a younger woman."

"Idiot." Sonny snorted and shook his head. "What the hell is a young woman going to understand about what he's going through at his age?"

She turned and met his eyes, nearly level with her own, dark and intelligent eyes. "Exactly."

"Guys like that are just scared of their own mortality. End of story. You're well rid of a coward like that." He removed a hand from his armpit to make a dismissive gesture then tucked it back in. "So are things going okay with Amanda? You guys get along well?"

Maude simply gaped. ''I think this has gone far enough.''

He shrugged again. ''We all have issues with our kids. Arch, for example, needs to stop playing and settle down. His sister needs to relax and get her head on straight. My four other sons have their various issues, too. That's life.''

''Amanda and I have no...'issues.''''

''Right. You're divorced, she's unemployed and you have no issues.''

Maude felt as if someone had just socked her. Amanda didn't have a job? And didn't tell her own mother? What happened with Patterson's? How long had this been going on? She opened her mouth to ask, then realized she'd be admitting outright that Amanda didn't confide in her. ''None that I care to discuss.''

''Okay,'' he agreed cheerfully. Didn't anything get to him? ''Let's discuss something else. You pick.''

She was tempted to stalk away, but she really didn't want to face the empty apartment, and being outraged was a hell of a lot better than feeling lonely and having to try to understand why Amanda had kept something so important from her own mother.

''Let's discuss...'' She grinned triumphantly. Get some of her own back. ''Opera.''

He nodded and hitched up his pants, which fell right back down where they didn't belong. ''A-okay.''

She barely suppressed a snort. ''I saw the new production of *Dialogue of the Carmelites* at the Met last season.''

''Oh, Poulenc. I caught the Saturday-matinee radio broadcast. They use a paper cutter near a microphone at the end of the opera to make the sound of the guillotine, did you know that?''

No.

Maude didn't.

"Yeah. Pretty creepy sound. Gives me the shivers. I cry like a baby at the end of that opera. Every time."

She swallowed.

She did too.

"Oh, and I got a question read on the Texaco Opera Quiz a couple of years back, maybe you heard it. About the significance of sleep in Wagner's operas. Won a ton for it. Books, recordings, great stuff."

Maude turned to him. Okay. He got her. She admitted it.

He turned back to meet her stare, his really very handsome face brimming with mischief, and did the very last thing she'd ever expect.

He winked.

In response to that wink, Maude Marcus, sixty-three years old and way past any foolish romantic notions about her own faded appeal, did the very next to last thing she'd ever expect.

She blushed.

CHAPTER SEVEN

ARCH DROPPED onto the bench Amanda was sitting on at Center Street Park, rested his arms along the back and grinned. The approaching storm had turned the light strangely pinkish; lines and colors seemed sharper, more defined under the low, gray ceiling of clouds. And Amanda simply glowed. There was no other word for it. Except for those huge eyes, which looked troubled and sad as they too often did. The look that at the same time made him want to protect her forever and goose her mercilessly into a more spirited mood.

"Whew. I thought John was going to want to be pushed on the swing the entire week." He gestured to where his youngest nephew was climbing on the play structure with his brothers and Clarissa. "Those kids wear me out."

"I don't think anything could wear you out."

She said the words innocently, but the second the remark left her lips, he was treated to the image of Amanda in his bed, flushed, perspiring, hard at work to prove she was one thing in the world that could.

Oh man.

He turned, not bothering to hide what he was thinking. See how she reacted, see how far he could push her into revealing what he suspected of her inner nature.

She gave a nervous laugh, looked down at her hands then back. Something changed in her eyes, responding to him. "Whatever you're thinking, stop."

"Why?"

She sat up ramrod straight, deliberately prudish, trying to control her laughter, eyes shining. "Because I have a feeling it's extremely naughty."

"And your point would be...?"

Laughter burst out; she wrestled it back, face flushed, breath high. "Naughty leads to no good, young man."

"Hmm." He lifted his eyebrows and reached out to touch her cheek. "That's highly debatable."

She swallowed; her playfulness ebbed. "You shouldn't touch me like that."

"No?"

"Not here." She met his eyes, the message clear, though he wasn't sure if she knew she was sending it. *Somewhere else.*

He leaned closer, but made sure his tone stayed light. "Then where, Amanda?"

"In the... You should..." Her mouth snapped shut.

"Okay." He held up his hands and moved away, watching with satisfaction as disappointment flickered over her features. He'd pushed too far but the desire had been there, the flirtation, the excitement, before she slammed the vault shut. As he suspected, she liked the edge much more than she let on. "Didn't mean to bother you."

"It's okay. I just...didn't want the kids to read more into it than you meant."

"How much did I mean?" He wasn't really sure himself. Just that he'd been wanting to touch her for days and now that he had, he wanted to again.

She rolled her eyes good-naturedly. "I didn't want them to think we're involved when we aren't."

"Well, maybe we should be." He still spoke playfully, but his whole being seemed to go on alert waiting for her answer. "What do you think?"

Bad move. She collapsed in on herself; her hair swung forward, covering her face. "I don't know."

He put a hand out to move her hair, then stopped. He didn't know either. He didn't even know how this conversation had gotten where it had gotten, except that now that the situation was put so bluntly, he realized that yeah, he did want to get involved. Physically for sure. Emotionally, who knew. But something about this woman piqued his interest where others merely attracted him or didn't.

"Look." He nudged her shoulder gently and pointed to where Clarissa and the boys had set up a game of leapfrog on the grass next to the playground area. She needed a break from the intensity of the conversation. He probably did too. "The kids are having a blast together."

"Yes." She laughed, but he still sensed her tension. "I haven't ever seen Clarissa this active. Thanks, by the way for the jelly solution. Knock wood, but it seems to have worked. Short-term anyway."

"Sometimes the least obvious solutions work the best. In this case, being as bold and childish as little Ralphie."

"You've had experience with this kind of situation, I take it? In your childhood?"

"No." He lifted his arms and dropped them back on the bench railing. "But I would have loved the foresight to do something like that when I was younger."

She frowned, still watching the kids. "You mean you weren't always—*Clarissa, be careful, honey.*"

Arch followed her worried stare and caught sight of Clarissa who had finished leapfrogging and was on top of a colored metal climber, waving her arms and whooping. "She's fine."

Amanda shot him a sheepish look. "I know. I can't help it."

"You are an only child." He settled his hands behind

his head. "In my family there weren't enough eyes to keep track of every child, so we all sort of bumped and scraped and bruised our way to adulthood."

"And survived intact."

He turned his head in the circle of his palms and grinned at her. "Exactly."

Her gaze went from his face to his leg and she plunked her hand firmly on his thigh, just above his jiggling knee. "Don't you ever stop moving?"

"I guess not." He relaxed, enjoying the warm feel of her hand. "You want to take a walk or something?"

Her eyes narrowed teasingly. "What's the matter, you can't just sit here and talk?"

"Of course I can." He sat up straight and folded his hands in his lap, minus jiggling leg. "There. Let's talk."

She crossed her arms with an I'd-like-to-see-this grin. "Okay. Let's see how long you last."

"No problem." He shifted away from where the bench was hitting his back in an awkward place. "Go."

"So what kind of kid were you if you didn't sing songs about jelly butts?"

"Serious, studious, cautious, tim—"

"Come on, I'm serious."

"So am I."

She stared, jaw dropping in a caricature of astonishment. "You?"

"Yup."

"How on earth did that happen?"

He shrugged. "I was the oldest of six kids. My mom died of a lengthy illness when I was twelve. Your basic oldest-son-shouldering-burdens-beyond-his-age type of story."

"And you're making up for it now."

"I hope so." He saw her glance pointedly at his tapping foot and stilled it. "What kind of kid were you?"

She sighed and slumped back against the back of the bench. "Same kind of adult I am now."

"Oh, Ms. Manda, we need to work on that."

"We do?"

He turned and smiled at her. "You game?"

"What, you want to turn me into *you?*"

He sent her a look like it was the biggest no-brainer he could think of, and stretched his arms wide. "Can you think of anything better, anything in the entire universe, than being me?"

"Don't tempt me."

"Okay, okay." He hooked his arms over the back of the bench. "So tell me something else."

"What?"

"I don't know, something revealing about yourself. What are you afraid of?"

Her eyebrows shot up in surprise. "Why do you ask me that?"

"Because, Cautious Amanda, I want to know."

"Okay." She rubbed her arms as if she was cold, though he couldn't imagine she was in this humidity. "I'm scared of mice, thunder, spiders if they're close to my bed, and—"

"Your mother."

She gave him a strange look. "My mother?"

"Yeah." He half stood, changed positions and sat again. "How come?"

"I'm not scared of my mother."

"Come on, even *I'm* scared of your mother."

She gave him a scornful look. "She doesn't scare me."

"Then how come you don't stand up for what you want?" He put his fists up into a boxer's stance and took a couple of jabs into the air.

"How come you never sit still?"

"I am sitting still." He rose from his seat, dancing in the ring, ducked a hook, took another jab. "You got to stand up to that woman. Show her you grew up already."

She got up from the bench and grabbed his arms, eyes brimming with mischief. "At least I *did* grow up. *And* I can sit still."

He opened his mouth to clown some more, protest his innocence to her charges. But she was still holding his arms, laughing up at him, a tiny elfin woman, blond hair hanging sweetly down to her chin, eyes warm and trusting.

Something inside him went a little nuts.

"Amanda."

She caught his tone; her eyes went serious, laughter died.

His throat thickened; his words were going to come out husky and strange. "I really want to kiss you."

She dropped his arms as if he'd suddenly caught fire; took a step back, looked frantically around them. "Not here."

He laughed. "And there, in a nutshell, is the difference between you and me."

She rolled her eyes and became interested in the wood chips scattered at her feet.

"Let's take a walk."

"Leave the kids?"

"We won't be out of sight."

She met his eyes, just briefly, a shy little sexy look that made him want to roar in a testosterone rush and carry her off to his cave.

"Okay."

They fell into step, shoulders bumping occasionally, hands bumping occasionally.

"Tell me a fantasy of yours."

She started to splutter; their hands bumped again and he

took hers and held it. ''Not that kind. I mean some way in which you think your life would be ideal.''

''Well...'' Her hand fit perfectly into his; he swung their arms back and forth. ''I'd like to get a job in a dress shop again, one I could own eventually. I'd like to have enough money to be able to travel, to New York, to Rome, to Paris, once in a while, to check out the fashion scene. I'd like to be able to buy my own house. I guess that's it.''

''That's *it?*''

She gave him a wounded look. ''Something wrong with that?''

''Yes!'' He turned and picked her up under the arms, swung in a half circle and put her down so her back was against a tree and they were out of sight of the park and the kids, clamped his hands on her shoulders and leaned down into her breathless, laughing face.

''I want you to want the entire world wrapped in a box and handed to you. I want you to want the moon, the planets, the sun, all at your command. I want you to want the most amazing guy in the world to prostrate himself at your feet and worship your beauty for the remainder of time.''

''Oh. Gosh.'' Her laughter slowed. ''Well, that would be something.''

He dropped his head in mock despair. ''I'm talking about owning the entire universe and she says, 'That would be something.'''

A giggle sounded just above his head. ''How about this.''

''Oh—here it comes, you're going wild. Let me guess. You also want a new toothbrush.''

''No.'' She took a quick breath, in and out. ''I...want you to kiss me.''

Chemical lightning zagged through his system. He lifted his head and met her eyes. ''Here?''

Her smile turned cautious and uncertain. "Maybe we shouldn't."

"Oh no. We definitely should." He traced her hairline down her cheek, along her jaw, her chin, then up to touch her lips, loving the softness of her skin, the gleam of anticipation in her eyes.

He leaned in and kissed her, one sweet lingering kiss, not too long or too deep so she wouldn't back off. And so he'd be able to stop...barely. Painfully.

"That was very nice, Ms. Manda," he heard himself whispering, his voice thick with emotion that had hit unexpectedly.

"Yes."

"I'd like to do that again sometime more thoroughly, would that be okay?"

"Oh...yes. That would be very okay."

"In fact, I think from now on I'm going to kiss you whenever I feel like it no matter who is watching."

Her eyebrow crept up. "Let's not push it."

He grinned. She tasted perfect. Felt perfect. His entire system was buzzing and on fire. Definitely on fire. He'd been so into his work, so into his new house, so into worry over his sister and her kids, over his career, and his future, he hadn't taken the time for this kind of fun in quite a while.

He kissed her again, longer this time. This kind of fun was one of his very, very favorites.

"I suppose you'll think I'm uptight if I say we should go back to the kids now." Her voice was about as thick and whispery as his, she was breathing hard, backed against the tree.

"Yes. I will. So instead, I want you to take your clothes off and lie down right over there."

She looked where he was pointing; her dreamy expression changed into surprise, then laughter. "Near the garbage can where the person dumped their picnic and let it rot for several days?"

"I want only the best for you."

"You're so romantic."

He kissed her once more and took a step back, fixed her with a grin and held out his hand. "Back to the kids?"

"Yes."

She took his hand and walked at his side, a bounce in her step, color in her cheeks. He would have felt smug except he had a pretty good idea he looked the same way. "So…"

She gave him a wary look. "More questions?"

"They bother you?"

"Not really. You're a lot like your dad that way."

"How else do you find out about people you want to find out about?"

She twisted her lip and frowned. "Oh, I don't know, maybe find someone that knows them and gossips a lot, like my mom does?"

"Ah, the Maude Marcus method?"

"Yeah."

Her voice held too much sadness for his taste. "Okay, next topic. Something fun. What's the worst thing that ever happened to you?"

She gave him an incredulous stare. "That's fun?"

"It can be."

"How so?"

"Because the worst thing that ever happened to you generally turns out to spawn the best. If you look at it the right way."

"I…don't see how you think so."

"Tell me your story and I'll prove it."

"You first."

"Okay." He took a few more steps, pondering. The impulse to be honest was strong, not that he ever lied, but he didn't generally talk about the bad stuff in his life, especially his mom's illness. Still, Amanda should hear so she would understand his point.

"I told you about my mom. Every night I'd go into her room and she'd do my homework with me. I was the oldest, so I got to stay up later than the other kids, even though I wasn't that much older. That was our special time together. Eventually she got too sick to help. I think that part was harder than when she actually died."

Amanda squeezed his hand tightly. He squeezed it back, three times fast, to show he was okay, before it hit him that was his mom's signal for I Love You. Funny how she was coming back to him just through talking.

"After that I hated my homework. For a while I even stopped doing it, until my dad found out. I told him it wasn't fun anymore. He gave me this killer look and instead of saying, 'Homework isn't supposed to be fun' like any other parent would, he said, 'So make it fun.' So I started thinking of characters and people who could help me with my homework, teach it to me. And that's what my books are about."

She stopped walking and turned to him in astonishment. "Corporal Wedgie is educational?"

"Hey, go figure, I've got depth."

She snorted, clamped a hand over her mouth, then split her fingers so she could speak. "I'm sorry to laugh. That's an amazing story, Arch."

"It is what it is. Your turn now."

She started walking again. "Well, mine's easy to pick. And no happy ending. I was supposed to get married and the groom never showed up at the church."

"Hmm." Ouch. Hard to find fun in that one. "You could say that has its own happy ending, right there."

"How do you figure?"

"Because if he had shown up at the church and married you without really wanting to, he'd have made you miserable."

"That's true." She frowned thoughtfully. "I guess. I hadn't thought about it that way."

"And what would have been worse, far, *far* worse…"

They reached the bench near the playground where they'd been sitting before and stopped. Amanda looked up at him expectantly.

"…is that I wouldn't have been able to kiss you today."

Her face drifted into a smile, which slowly widened into a grin and nearly made him kiss her again. "That's very true."

"So you see now how your groom showing up would have been an unmitigated disaster?"

"Point made."

She kept grinning at him, chuckling a little as if the grin couldn't be satisfied just on its own. He loved making her smile. Serious Amanda needed to smile a whole hell of a lot more.

"So what was this guy like?" His voice came out gruff and a little sulky, as if he was feeling a tad jealous. Which might possibly have been because he was feeling a tad jealous. Irrational, but then humans were. Often.

"He was flashy, confident, full of energy, a very magnetic person." She gave him a surreptitious glance. "Handsome, witty, full of fun…"

"Hmm." He puffed himself up. "Why is this sounding *so* familiar?"

She snorted. "The kind of man I now avoid like the plague."

"Really?" He felt absurdly deflated.

"Let's just say I have my guard up."

"Because we handsome, witty, full-of-fun men are all the same."

She made a helpless gesture. "He broke my heart. It's natural to be cautious."

"I've never made a promise I couldn't keep. Especially anything as important as marriage."

"So you've never been that serious about anyone?" She said it as if it was his death sentence as far as any relationship with her was concerned.

"Uh…" No. He hadn't. He liked women, thought they were terrific, enjoyed them like hell, then after a few months something clanged down in his heart and he just turned off. He didn't understand it; in fact, it scared the hell out of him. Which is why he preferred not to think about it.

"Not really serious. No." He cleared his throat and pretended to be fascinated with the sky. "Think it's going to rain soon."

She nudged him gently. "You witty, fun, confident, full-of-energy, handsome men *are* all the same."

"Fascinated by you?" He winked at her, suddenly desperate to get back on an easy flirtatious footing.

She laughed. "For now."

"Now is fun. What's wrong with now? You take a whole lot of 'nows' and line them up, eventually you could even get to forever."

She shook her head, smiling. "Did I mention he had a glib line for everything?"

"Who?"

"Ridge. My ex-fiancé. Short for Ridgeway."

"Wow. Archibald and Ridgeway, you know how to pick 'em."

She tipped her head, considering him solemnly. "Have I picked you?"

"If you haven't, I damn well think you should."

She shook her head again, smile fading. He felt a strange burst of uncertainty and turned her to him, gazing earnestly into her wary face, willing her to take him seriously this time. "All I know, Manda Marcus, is that we didn't do nearly enough kissing."

Her eyes got wider, darker, he loved the way she changed, from prissy to sensual, shy to bold, troubled to laughing.

"No."

It was all she said, or whispered, really, but whatever had tightened inside him loosened into relief. A gust of wind swept over them; a raindrop plopped onto his head, then another, and one onto the end of her nose. The sky had turned gray-black and a soft rumble of thunder promised more fun on the way.

He whirled and clapped his hands. "Mark, Luke, John, Clarissa, up and at 'em. It's going to rain."

They herded the kids back down to the sidewalk and jogged along Center Street back to Sixty-seventh, laughing and trying to dodge raindrops. At their duplex, Arch took out his keys and looked questioningly at Amanda. "You guys want to come in? We're staying here tonight, having a sleepover."

"I think we'll go up and get ready for dinner. Thanks."

"Your mom still up there?"

"No. Her car's gone, guess she's on her own tonight."

He nodded, and felt the protective surge of annoyance at the relief in her voice. No doubt if her mom had still been here, Amanda would have resigned herself to playing hostess for the evening rather than kick her out. Granted, he'd only had a few impressions of the seemingly formidable

Maude Marcus, and he imagined crossing her would not be easy, but if Mom was going to live in Milwaukee, Amanda needed to start standing up for herself.

"Okay then." He sent her a smile that let her know he was thinking about certain intimate moments during their afternoon together. "Thanks for coming to the park."

"I had fun." She blushed and smiled shyly back. "Thanks, Arch."

"You're welcome, Ms. Manda. We should—"

A clap of thunder interrupted him.

"Open the door!" John squealed in terror.

"It's coming closer."

"What are you waiting for?"

He sighed, shrugged, and opened the door for the stampeding buffalo herd behind him. The house was dark and strangely deserted. His dad must have packed up and left, probably to drive home to West Allis before the storm hit.

He moved forward, looking around. He'd loaded a big pile of sleeping bags, air mattresses and supplies for their campout tonight in the middle of the living room; that was still there. But something didn't seem right. Too empty. Odd.

The boys grouped around him, tugging his clothes, demanding snacks, dinner, TV. He got them settled with a bag of pretzels and SpongeBob SquarePants—of *course* he had called the cable company first thing to start service and brought his little TV over for the campout.

He went into the kitchen to heat up hot dogs and beans for their dinner, the nagging feeling still with him. Lightning lit the windows; thunder rumbled a good thirty seconds later, the storm was still far away.

Amanda had said she was scared of thunder; he wondered what she'd do tonight if the storm was as severe as predicted. Maybe he'd have to go up there and...ahem...

comfort her while Clarissa slept. He bet she wore some lace-trimmed flowery cotton nightgown that matched her sheets. Something her mom got for her. He wanted to see her in something bright, red, silk and skimpy that would look scandalous in that prissy apartment.

The rain came down in earnest now, a steady shower that should have made the warm dry kitchen feel cozy. All he could think about was Amanda, how she'd come so alive today after he'd managed to pry her away from her mom, how her soft lips had tasted, how he wanted to run upstairs right now and talk to her more, kiss her, make love to her.

She was what was missing from the house, what felt wrong. Something about her had gotten inside him and wouldn't go away even when she wasn't with him.

He'd known her one week and he was a goner.

Typical Arch. He fell hard and fast. Threw himself in and consequences be damned. Maybe that's why nothing seemed to last. Maybe he needed lessons from Cautious Amanda as much as she needed them from him.

The hot dogs plopped into the pan of water; he set the gas on low and put the baked beans into the microwave.

So what now? Rethink his basic philosophy? He'd decided years ago that caution and timidity got you nothing but frustration, the paralysis of indecision and the pain of loss. But he didn't want to do this the wrong way, didn't want to run the risk of hurting Amanda by getting bored. How did you ever know what would last and what wouldn't? All his relationships seemed so promising at the start. This felt different, yes, but what did he know?

The microwave beeped; he stirred the beans and set it to heat more.

The problem was, he knew what staying away from her would do. Staying away would only make her more desirable, more attractive, make him more obsessive. He'd tried that, though he couldn't remember being this fascinated by any other woman he'd dated. She was such a mixture, such a combination of innocence and sensuality, of humor and sadness, of timidity and strength.

So wasn't the alternative jumping in with both feet? His usual style. Not to shy away from what life had to offer. Not to waste a second of it worrying or compromising or giving in, because you never knew when it could be taken away.

Another lightning flash. The thunder grumbled, nearly died out, then grumbled again. Bottom line—he was an incurable optimist who had great respect for the power of positive thinking. Maybe Amanda would be "It" for him, the way his mom had been "It" for his father. As far as he knew, Dad hadn't looked at another woman since she died. Arch couldn't sit by and allow the chemistry and camaraderie with Amanda to go unexplored, and possibly wasted.

He turned off the gas under the hot dogs and nodded firmly. Tonight, after the kids were asleep, he'd go upstairs to check on her. If Clarissa was asleep and Amanda was willing, he'd make sure he got to kiss her again.

After that he had a feeling what to do would become perfectly clear.

CHAPTER EIGHT

AMANDA LAY RIGIDLY in bed, eyes open as far as they could go, listening to the wind howling outside. She hated thunderstorms, always had. The rage of nature made her feel small, helpless, out of control. And Wisconsin storms were nothing like the relatively gentle thunderboomers of her childhood in Connecticut. Storms here could go on and on all night, produce lightning so constant it looked like a strobe, not to mention hail, tornadoes and other goodies. Not fun.

This one was nasty. To keep from panicking, she had to lie here, tense as a board, and reassure herself that the house had stood solidly since 1941, it wasn't going to go to Oz anytime soon.

Said reassurance was barely working.

A fiercely bright flash of lightning lit the window; she winced and closed her eyes, adrenaline pumping, waiting for the crash.

Crack. Boom.

As if the earth had split in half. She held her breath, listening for Clarissa's call. Nothing. The child could sleep through an atomic blast. Thank goodness. Amanda would rise to the occasion as best she could, but in her current state, she'd probably terrify her daughter more than the storm.

The wind intensified, the pounding of rain on the roof

changed to a deafening metallic roar. Hail. Her heart pounded almost as hard.

Oh God, if the tornado sirens went off how the hell would she hear them? Should she waken Clarissa and take her down into the basement now? Wait it out? What?

She threw off the covers, sat up, pressed her hands to her face. *Calm down, Amanda.* Tornadoes had to be louder than this. Right? Unmistakable. Right? And why bother waking Clarissa so she could be terrified, too? No point. Right?

A gust of wind shook the house; stone houses didn't shake easily. The windows rattled, more lightning, another crash of thunder.

Help.

Moments like these she wished to hell she didn't live alone. Moments like these she even wanted her mother.

How would she know if a tornado was coming? What could be louder than this? How could she tell? She got out of bed, unable to stay helpless a second longer, went into the living room and turned on a lamp for comfort. Her foot encountered cold and wet where there should only be warm and dry.

"Oh no!" Leaks. Drips everywhere. Lightning lit the room and she reached out to touch the sofa. Wet. The floor. Wet. The chair. Wet. Had the roof blown off?

A drip hit her head; she whirled to get pots from the kitchen—whirled back—no, she had to get Clarissa to the basement—tripped and landed in a heap on the floor as thunder smashed down again. The wind was stronger than ever, pounding on her—

She lifted her head. Door?

"Arch?" She ran to her front door and yanked it open. Arch.

Okay. She was a wimp. Certifiable. In fact, just elect her

Queen of Wimps and be done with it. But damned if seeing him striding into her apartment, big and solid and reassuring, wasn't the most fabulous sight she'd ever seen.

"You okay up here?"

"Yes. Fine." She nearly laughed at the lie. Except, really, she was okay if you didn't count pee-in-your-pants petrified. She could probably fool him, too, if he didn't look close enough to see her shaking. She pointed a wobbly finger at her soggy furniture. "The roof is leaking. I was just going for pots."

"Oh sh—" Thunder drowned out the word, but she had a pretty good idea what it had been and had considered using it herself. Right now she just had to get through the storm. Later she'd let herself think about what it would cost to re-cover or replace her furniture.

He followed her into the kitchen, took the pots and bowls she handed him back into the living room and helped her place them under the leaks.

"I'd say we lost part of the roof." He moved her armchair out of drip's way and put a Dutch oven under the stream.

"I'd say." She got onto her knees to mop up splashed water with a sponge, loving the "we" part of "we lost part of the roof," even though it was his house.

"Were you nervous?"

She glanced up at him. "Nervous? No. Not at all. I bypassed nervous and went straight to terrified."

He grinned and threw a couple of damp cushions wet side up onto a dry spot on the rug. "I hated to think of you up here alone, so I snuck up to check on you."

"I'm glad you did." She smiled at him, then forced her eyes away when they wouldn't leave by themselves. They lifted the damp rug and put a pot under it to allow air to circulate. Then he joined her on his knees to mop up the wet.

Lightning flickered, thunder crashed, she barely winced. Being busy helped, but the storm had been downgraded in severity the second she had Arch to share it with.

"It helps having you here."

He gave her a warm smile. Another crash of thunder, not quite so loud this time; the wind a little less ferocious, the hail changing back to rain. The storm outside was receding. But with that warm smile directed at her, another one was starting to brew inside her. This man did things to her she hadn't felt since Ridge.

The sponge she was holding began dripping water back onto the floor and she bent to finish the job.

They mopped up the worst of the mess and pronounced it dry as it would get tonight. Amanda tossed the sponges in a nearby pot and turned back to Arch, who was checking the ceilings.

"Looks like it's slowing." He pushed tentatively at a crack in the plaster. "I don't think we'll have more trouble unless the storm starts up again in earnest. Any leaks in any of the other rooms?"

"I don't think so. I'll check Clarissa's room."

She turned and took a step; he grabbed her hand, pulled her back against him and kissed her, twice, hard. Then let go, leaving her blinking stupidly in surprise.

"Okay, now you can check."

She turned loopily and lurched into her daughter's room, padded quietly about on the carpet, among the stuffed animals and dollhouses Clarissa rarely played with. Everything seemed dry; her daughter slept serenely, unperturbed by the storm.

About as far from Amanda's mood as anyone could get. Even before the chaos hit, she'd been lying awake in bed, thinking about Arch. About the way she felt when she was around him, about the physical feelings he stirred in her, ones she hadn't felt to that degree for so long she'd forgotten she was capable. All of which didn't even take into account the emotion he brought out in her. Having Sir Galahad here at night when she'd been so vulnerable only underscored the dilemma. Her crush was in danger of becoming something deeper. And she wasn't sure if that was good or not.

She went back into the light of the living room, realizing with a flutter in her stomach that with everything under control, he was no longer Sir Galahad but a very real, very magnetic man in her apartment, late at night.

"Clarissa's room seems fine." Her voice came out froggy and she cleared her throat. "My room was dry, kitchen's fine."

"Good." He watched her in that quiet contented way he had, which she expected to make her extremely nervous, but which only made her moderately nervous tonight, and in a good way. She even tried watching him back, and found that it wasn't hard at all.

Except that the longer she returned his stare, the less "quiet and contented" described his gaze. His eyes were starting to look heated and hungry, and chemical sparks were showering all over her body.

Not to mention, all she was wearing was a cotton nightie her mom had bought to complement her bed set. And panties. Tiny red ones with lace, which she'd bought herself at Victoria's Secret, just for fun.

And across from her stood Arch, large and male and powerful, *GQ*-perfect in nothing but sweats and a T-shirt that said, Just Do It. His body was incredible. Ridge had been tall, but slender. Arch was much broader, more muscular, a real man's body.

Mmm.

There was only one problem. No, two. The first problem was that there was a noisy thunderstorm and Clarissa was sleeping in the next room, and could realistically wake up at any moment. Two, his nephews were downstairs alone and shouldn't be left—

"Amanda." He spoke softly, moved forward with a purposeful look in those heated, hungry eyes, until he was about six inches away, which was suddenly about six inches too many.

"Yes?" Her brain shut down while her whole body responded to his nearness. Her voice came out weak and strange; her torso seemed to want to lean toward him, her hands itched to touch him. Don't even ask about what her mouth wanted to do.

"What are we going to do about what's going on between us?"

She swallowed. She knew what she wanted to answer. She knew what he wanted her to answer. But she had just realized that there weren't two problems—Clarissa and his nephews. There were three.

She was on her way to being crazy about him, and if she slept with him, she'd get crazier about him, and he'd never been serious about a woman in his life. Those were bad odds.

"I don't know." She cringed at her whisper. *Damn it, Amanda, for once take a positive step.* "Wait."

He lifted his eyebrows expectantly. "Yes?"

"I do know."

"You do?"

"Yes." There. She did it.

He waited a few seconds, then frowned slightly. "Were you going to let me in on what you think? Seeing as I'm involved?"

She swallowed and flicked a glance away from his steady gaze. *Okay, Amanda. If you announce that you have taken a stand, it is generally advisable to actually have taken one.* Unfortunately, the options were still battling it out in her brain. Get involved. Stay away. Sleep with him. Send him downstairs. Rip her clothes off. Throw him—

A huge clap of thunder crashed over the house; she jumped and clamped her hand over her mouth so she wouldn't mortify herself by screaming. The lights flickered and went out. Eerily, the rain stopped abruptly, as if someone had turned off a faucet.

Total silence, except for the random ploinking of drops into various metal bowls and pans. Then a swishing sound from Clarissa's room and a soft grunt as she turned over. More silence, then a soft snore.

Child still asleep. No more storm. End of problem one.

Arch put his hands to her waist. Drew her forward against him, his features barely visible in the soft white-orange light of the street lamp outside her window. She lifted her face slightly, breathing his scent, more familiar than it should have been for the short time she'd known him. He bent forward, rubbed his lips against hers, lightly, then kissed her, a gentle teasing pressure that made her entire body turn into longing.

Problems—she tried to get her brain to function fully— there were still problems. "What…about your nephews?"

"Dad came back after dinner to join the campout."

End of problem two.

He covered her right hand with his left, drew it smoothly out to the side and led her in a slow dance, humming a melody she didn't recognize, turning, leading her in a slow spin, dancing some more. He turned them again, stopped humming, kept dancing. His leg came between hers, she let herself press her sex against the hard muscle of his thighs while he swayed. *Oh*. Total turn-on.

"Amanda?"

"Mmm?"

He pressed his forehead to hers. "May I stay for a while?"

She knew what he was asking. Knew how she wanted to respond. But problem three wasn't going to be resolved as easily as the other two had been.

"I don't think it's a good idea."

"No?" He kissed her forehead, her cheeks, each corner of her mouth. "What do you think is a good idea?"

"You going back downstairs and me…going back to bed?"

"Um…no." He swung her around in a slow tight turn. "That's not even close to a good idea."

She nearly laughed; she couldn't help it. Almost every part of her loved that nothing was sacred to him. Except the part which realized that included her.

Why was she only attracted to men who wouldn't take life seriously? The few earnest solid men she'd made herself date in a vain attempt to correct her mistake with Ridge had bored her to death. Arch would never bore her to death. Neither would Ridge have.

And yet…Arch had showed how her entire life bored her to death the second he came into it.

So which was better? Painless boredom? Or excitement with the invariably painful letdown?

"I'm hearing silence from you, Ms. Manda."

"I'm sorry."

"Don't be. It's your right." He dropped her hand, gathered her closer, waltzed her back and then forward. "Are you really going to send me away?"

She clamped her teeth shut behind closed lips. Oh God,

she didn't want to send him away. She didn't want to send him away at all. She wanted to drag him into her bedroom and force him to make love to her until she died of an overdose of ecstasy.

But...

"I'll go if you want me to, but I'd rather be here with you. I'd be happy just talking to you and touching you only this much." He kissed her neck, moved up and took her earlobe in his teeth for a brief painless bite. "I don't know when I've met anyone I wanted as much as you, where only that much would satisfy me."

She leaned back to see his face. "Honest? That would be enough? Just talking?"

He grimaced and moved her against his shoulder again, turning his head to murmur into her hair. "Well, okay, it might kill me. But I'll take the chance. And I'm not just saying this and planning to put the moves on you later. Which, to be honest, makes me think there's something the matter with me."

She laughed into his chest, burying her face against the soft cotton of his T-shirt. "Sounds serious."

"Maybe I should see a doctor."

"You should."

"A thorough examination."

"Definitely."

"Can I stay, Amanda? Just for a while."

She stopped dancing. A car swished by in the street. The tuneful drips into the pots and pans in her living room slowed. His heart beat strong and solid under her cheek; his arms around her were comforting, not trapping. He waited, patient and calm.

And it suddenly seemed silly to send him away.

"Yes."

"Yes, I can stay?"

"Yes."

"To talk."

"Yes."

"There's one problem."

She knew. But his problem was undoubtedly different from hers. "What's that?"

"Your couch is wet."

She looked up into his face, his mischief visible even in the dull light from the street. "Why do I have the feeling you're about to say that my bed is dry?"

"Isn't it?"

A thrill shot through her. This was a dangerous, fabulous game. "You want to go into my bedroom with me, sit on my bed and just talk."

"No."

Another thrill. At least he wasn't pretending to—

"I want to go into your bedroom with you, *lie* on your bed and just talk."

"Lie on my bed. And just talk."

"Yes, Amanda, I am capable of just talk. Even on a bed."

"Okay." She moved away from him and he followed her into her dark bedroom. She felt her way to the bed and climbed on, brimming with excitement. There was no way he was going to lie here and just talk. And no way she was going to be able to resist him. Someday soon she'd get her head examined. But not right now. This felt too good.

She lay down and scooched over to make room for him. "Let's see you do it."

"You're on."

His weight lowered the mattress next to her, his arm came around and pulled her close, nestled her into his side where she fit as if she was born for the spot.

If he was going to lie here and just talk, she was her

own grandmother. And by the way her body lit up at the feel of his along its length, if she wanted him to lie here and just talk, she was her own grand*father*.

She pulled the covers over them and rested her hand on his chest. "So talk."

"Okay. Tell me…"

"Ye-e-es?"

"When you were with Ridge, how did you know it was forever?"

She snorted. "It was forever because I got pregnant and my parents threw a fit until he proposed."

Silence. Amanda raised her head. "I shocked you."

"Yes."

She drew in a breath, helpless to know how to fix it. "I'm sorry. It was stupid, we were young, we were careless, I—"

"No." He squeezed her shoulder, then caressed her arm gently up and down. "I was shocked that you'd marry someone for that reason."

"Oh. Well, I mean, I loved him. Or thought I did. I don't know. I really thought I did." Her voice thickened; she felt him stiffen slightly, though his hand kept up its reassuring stroking. "As I said, we were young. I was eighteen, Ridge was twenty, my dad hit the roof, my mom wasn't far behind him. Not that I blame them."

"And since then have you been in love?"

"Not even close."

"How about now?"

"Now? I barely *know* you, what do you—" She heard his chuckle in the darkness and nestled back against him with a groan. "You're going to push me over the edge."

"I'm thinking likewise for you." He moved his stroking from her arm to her hair. She relaxed into the sensation, waiting for his movements to become more seductive; already her response was rising even higher. She knew her libido would betray her better sense, as it had with Ridge, as it invariably did.

His hand went from her hair to her cheek, down across her lips; she had to hold herself still to keep from taking his finger into her mouth.

"So tell me."

"Yes?" Her voice came out breathless, excited. Could he tell how near she was to surrender after so short a battle?

"What do you think of what I'm doing to the apartment downstairs?"

Amanda blinked. "I...think it sounds fun. The kids will love it."

"Yeah. Kid heaven."

"Mmm-hmm."

"Oh, and I talked to my agent today. Did I tell you that?"

His hand kept stroking, back to her hair, down her neck, down her shoulder. Her breath was growing shorter, body heating up like crazy; she wanted him to touch her everywhere.

She moved her arm up his chest so he could brush carelessly along the side of her breast. "No, you didn't tell me."

"The next Corporal Wedgie book was approved with no revisions."

"Oh, that's terrific!" Her enthusiasm was genuine. So was her impatience. His hand went back to her hair briefly, then he let it fall back next to him on the bed. No careless breast-brushing. Not a one.

"My sister is feeling much better. I think we'll be able to visit her soon. The kids miss her."

"That's wonderful." She tried to be happy for his sister and her kids, but she missed his hand on her face and body.

And it was slowly and rather horrifyingly dawning on her that he really truly intended to lie here in her bed and talk to her.

And it was dawning on her even faster that this was not what she had in mind at all and that it might be up to her to do something about it.

He cleared his throat. "So tell me."

"Yes?" She bit her lip to keep from growling.

"Are we really going to lie in bed like this and talk?"

"No." The word exploded out of her.

"No?" He turned toward her.

"No." She wished she could see his face. Her breath was coming higher, faster; she was about to do something, she had to do something, but she hadn't a clue what.

"Then what, Amanda?" His soft low whisper undid her. "You tell me."

Okay, she had a clue what. But could she really? She couldn't forget problem number one, still sleeping now, but who knew. And then there was problem number three, which wasn't going to—

She gave a silent groan of frustration. Damn it, was she always going to second-guess herself? Always lie here and wait for everyone else to decide her life for her? Wait for everyone else to take all the action she could and should take herself?

Probably.

"Amanda?"

He was waiting. He was willing. He was so sexy. The courage hit her again and just as quickly as it hit, she felt herself wanting to back away from it.

No. No backing away this time.

"Arch."

"Yes?"

"If you don't kiss me right now I'm going to go crazy."

He rolled on his side, cupped her head and leaned over her, a big male shadow in the darkness, his face inches from hers. "That sounds bad."

"Yes." She moved restlessly closer, drew her hands along his muscled arms to reach his neck. "It's horrible."

He leaned down and kissed her, gently. Too gently. She put her hands to the back of his head, pulled him closer to turn the kisses hot and wild, the way she felt—the way he was making her feel.

Arch went right along with her, thank God more than ready himself, gathering her close along the length of his body. She lifted frantically to pull her nightie up and out of the way, opened her legs and tugged him to move on top of her, wanting to feel his erection where it belonged, even through two layers of material.

He rolled over her, lifted his torso, supporting himself on his forearms and lowered his hips between her eager legs. The contact made her writhe and moan, thrash her head; he was hard and warm and she wanted him inside her so badly she could barely stand it.

He whispered her name, pushed the bulge of his erection against her sex, using his hips like a weapon, circling, pushing, so warm through his sweatpants, making her wild.

"Arch." She panted out his name. "This isn't enough."

"I know," he whispered. "But it's all we get tonight, Manda."

"Why? What?" She wrapped her legs around his back to increase the pressure, lifted and pressed against his hard heat. "Why not?"

"Unless you have condoms lying around…"

She made an animal sound of frustration and clutched her hands into her hair.

He chuckled. "I thought not."

"How can you take this so calmly?"

"Trust me. I am anything but calm. I am so close to saying to hell with it, tearing off your clothes and burying myself in you as far as I can, that it's just easier to stay calm because otherwise I'm going to cry like a baby."

She burst out laughing and reached to take hold of his face in the darkness. "You amaze me."

"Why?"

"Because you can make me laugh no matter how upset or angry or intensely sexually frustrated I am."

"Not as much as you amazed me just now."

"What do you mean?"

He let himself drop fully on top of her so his lips were right next to her ear. "You're a wild thing, Amanda. A totally unexpected wild thing. I want to make love to you so badly I can barely stand it. I want to make you scream, I want to make you completely off-the-wall crazy. But I want to be alone when we do it, and I want us to be protected. Okay?"

She opened her mouth, but no sound came out. She had never ever been this aroused in her entire life.

He rolled off her and pulled her to him. "So right now we are going to take a nice platonic breather."

Her breath came out in a resigned whoosh. She lay next to him, still slightly shell-shocked, turned on out of her mind, trying to resist the urge to push him onto his back and sexually assault him.

A distant rumble of thunder sounded. The apartment creaked and settled.

"Okay, that's enough of a breather." He lunged over her again and kissed her—or tried to, because she was convulsed with laughter.

This man made her feel so good, so alive, so strong and able to handle whatever happened. Ridge had made her feel the same way once upon a time, which was why she had adored him in the beginning. But Arch was one in a million.

"What am I going to do about you, Manda?"

"Buy condoms?"

"First thing in the morning. I promise. Osco Drug, Sixtieth and Center, aisle 8."

She felt the giddy excitement wilt. He knew the aisle number.

Of course, what did she expect? But wow. Instead of one *in* a million, it made her feel more like one *of* a million.

She had the sinking feeling that this would all be different tomorrow morning. That her foray into wild sexuality would fade. Daylight, no thunder, they'd be back to being two fully dressed people with kids to take care of, responsibilities, worries. Two people who had known each other a week and who would have to live in close proximity for who knew how long, even after the fling inevitably died.

"Did I tell you?" He nuzzled her cheek. "About my plans for the master bedroom downstairs?"

She shook her head.

"King-size bed, TV, whirlpool tub, dark-glass mirror on the ceiling, VCR…" He let out a groan of longing. "I can't wait to get you in there."

Rrrrrip. Amanda's reaction split in half. Her sexual side wanted nothing more than to visit his pleasure palace and be the one to initiate every piece of equipment many, many times.

Her rational, proper half didn't like the idea at all. It only underscored their differences, their views on sex, relationships, the whole world.

Was this smart? One thing to be swept away by passion and the darkness and her brush with fear and her raging hormones. Another to invite him expressly to finish what they started, knowing that to him this was another chance to play, while she was dangerously close to offering him her heart.

"Okay, out with it."

She tried to make out his features in the dark and failed. "What?"

"Whatever just made you tense up on me."

"I don't…I mean…" She closed her eyes, impatient with her own stuttering. One big difference between Ridge and Arch. Ridge had been interested primarily in his own feelings, not hers. Though granted, he was barely out of his teens when she knew him. But she wasn't in the habit of talking things out. Not with anyone, now that she thought about it.

"Is it that we're happening too fast?"

She breathed a sigh of relief, mixed with unexpected regret. He'd hit it exactly. "Yes."

Arch sat up and touched her arm in the darkness, trailing his finger from shoulder to elbow and back. "I don't generally do slow. I guess you probably could have guessed that about me."

"Somehow, yeah."

"But I'm willing to take it slow with you." He leaned forward and kissed her nose in the dark, though who knew what he'd been aiming for. "Don't ask me why. Maybe you'll change me."

"Oh, I hope not." The plea came out fervent and sudden and hung between them while he sat there, a big warm wonderful presence in her bed and in her life.

He chuckled. "We'll see. Now, however, if I don't get downstairs and take care of some business, I'm going to be very, very unhappy."

She blinked, startled, then giggled. At least he didn't try to pretend men took cold showers. "I'll do the same."

"Think about me?"

"Oh, yes."

He leaned forward again, found her mouth on the second try and kissed her, a slow and lingering kiss that made her cooled-down reactions boil to the surface again.

"Sleep well," he whispered. "I'll see myself out."

"Good night. And…thanks, Arch."

"You're welcome, Ms. Manda."

He left the room; she snuggled down under the covers, grinning like a goof. She didn't need a mirror to know exactly what she looked like right now. Her eyes were shooting sparks, color high. She was nuts about him already. He was everything she responded to in a man. Confident, secure, good-natured, funny, hung like a horse…

Mmm. She reached down, felt her own moisture, remembered the heat of his erection, and started a stroking rhythm. Stroking…stroking. *Oh yes.*

Her breathing grew faster, louder; she moaned, whispered his name, stroked harder. The wave built, she moaned again, spoke to her fantasy of him, told him what to do to her, what she wanted, how much she wanted it. Then the peak hit; she gasped, cried out softly, panting, *oh, oh, oh,* and slowly came down, flushed, hot and breathless…

To hear a soft male sigh, footsteps crossing her living room, and the final closing of her front door.

CHAPTER NINE

ARCH QUIETLY OPENED the door to his apartment and tip-toed inside. *Oh man.* The sooner he got himself to a private spot to ease the ache Amanda had started, the better. He'd been a total pervert listening to her finish her own bliss, but if he had to be a pervert, he couldn't think of a more worthwhile way.

Except staying hadn't felt kinky or weird; it had felt right, and strangely intimate. He'd emerged hard enough to cut diamond, yes, but also tender and protective, humbled to have been there for the stolen, unguarded moment.

He'd suspected—maybe he'd only fantasized—about that kind of uninhibited erotic energy breaking free from the bonds of Amanda's everyday personality, but listening to her words, the swishing sound of her body thrashing against the sheets, never mind when she'd been under him, pressing against him as if nothing in the world mattered but what he had going between his legs…

Okay. Move. The situation was getting desperate. He took two steps forward and heard a sound, saw a light on in the kitchen. His erection drooped. Damn. Was one of the boys up? His dad?

Maybe he could still sneak—

"Hey, Arch, that you?" His father's voice emerged from the kitchen. Arch sighed and went in, to find him clutching a bratwurst smothered in leftover fried onions. Sonny Williams was the only person in the world who could eat a sausage sandwich at 2:00 a.m. and sleep like a baby afterward. "Where have you been—oh, with her."

Arch nodded, not even trying to deny it or question how his dad knew. Sonny Williams could see through any and every deception his children had ever tried to pull. Arch started learning that at age nine when he'd tried to cover for his brother Ted, who'd flushed the house and car keys down the toilet. Continued at age twelve when he'd tried to cover for brother Cliff, who'd sold comic books at vastly inflated prices to his friends. And with his sister, Gwen, high on glue, and so on, and so on. By now all six children knew better than to try.

"I checked on her during the storm to make sure she was okay."

"Uh-huh." One bushy eyebrow lifted.

Arch turned away from the knowing grin to open the fridge. "What's up with you? Couldn't sleep?"

"Nope. Love begets insomnia…. Hmm. Don't think Shakespeare said that but he should have."

Arch winced, gazing into the refrigerator without registering its contents. His father's devotion to his mom was beyond anything he himself had ever felt or might ever be capable of feeling. To carry that depth of emotion for so long… "Sorry, Dad."

"Yeah. I haven't felt like this since I met your mother."

Arch reached for the milk jug, then stopped, turned and stared at his father. "Felt like what? What do you mean?"

His father scratched his head with his thumb, seeming deep in contemplation. "Have you met Amanda's mother?"

"Yeah." He grabbed the milk jug, rolling his eyes, understanding that Dad needed to change the subject but would get back to it in his own time. "Piece of work, huh?"

"She sure is."

Arch narrowed his eyes, clutching the cold plastic. Something in his father's voice hadn't quite sounded like ridicule. Or scorn. Or disgust. Something in his father's voice had sounded more like reverence. "Amanda's mother?"

His father took a bite of bratwurst and nodded, chewing solemnly.

Arch put the milk on the counter with a thud. "You have a thing for Amanda's mother?"

"Mmm-hmm." His father chewed his way down a strand of onion that had refused to sever on his next bite.

"You mean you're attracted to her? To Amanda's *mother?*"

His father gave him a look that made Arch realize he was sounding like the village idiot.

He couldn't help it. *"Maude Marcus?"*

This time it was his father's turn to roll his eyes. He washed down the latest enormous bite with a half glass of beer. "She's The One."

"Wait." Arch's brain was trying very hard to wrap itself around this concept. This was more than attraction? Attraction was hard enough to fathom. "I thought Mom was the one."

"She's dead, son. Has been for twenty years."

"But I thought you were…" He gestured helplessly.

"What, keeping myself pure in her memory?"

Arch's mouth shut with a snap. He wanted to protest having thought anything so ridiculous, but unfortunately, that's exactly what he'd thought. In fact he'd clung to the ideal, childishly as it turned out. He owed it to his father to take this calmly, not show his unjustified flash of anger, the feeling that his father was betraying his mom. Not make it plain he was on his way to an acid stomach at the thought of having to deal with Maude Marcus in any capacity but an upstairs neighbor's unfortunate relation.

"I loved your mother. I miss her. I did have trouble letting go, I admit. But when the right one comes along, you don't mess around. I knew when I met your mother and I knew when I met Amanda's. I'm just lucky it happened to me twice. A lot of people don't even get it once."

"But she's so…" Arch made a circular motion with his hands, encouraging the words to come out of his mouth, though he couldn't even begin to think of any adjectives to describe her that wouldn't be insulting.

"Repressed? Negative? Unhappy? Insecure?" His dad rolled the words out as if he'd been chanting them to himself all day.

"Don't forget controlling."

His father waved him off. "She needs the love of a good man. The sooner the better, while she's off balance on new territory here."

Arch managed to get down a glass and pour milk into it. "Has she…I mean does she know this?"

"Not yet."

"What makes you think she'll…return your feelings?" He picked up the glass of milk and held it under his mouth as if he was about to drink it, but for some reason the action was beyond him. He could not conceive of Maude Marcus unbending or unsnobbing or un-anything enough to be remotely receptive to his father. And he hated her already for the pain she'd cause Sonny once he realized.

"The second I saw her I knew. She just needs work. Same as her daughter." He gave Arch a significant look over the top of his sandwich.

Arch bristled. "But Amanda's not anything like—"

"Repressed? Negative? Unhappy? Insecure?"

Arch clutched the glass of milk harder.

"Didn't you decide it was your mission to help her see the light?"

Arch nodded, feeling about twelve years old, sure of himself one minute and twisted into a mass of confusion by his father's sure, confident logic the next.

"I can do the same for Mom. And *my* long-term intentions are honorable."

"What…whoa, wait a second." Arch put the damn milk down and held up both hands. "You're getting way ahead of—"

"No, I'm not." His father drank more beer and cleared his throat. "You want to help her like a friend, that's one thing. That's what you told me you were doing the day of the barbecue, though I knew you were attracted to her. But sneaking up for nooky in the middle of the night is different. You better be willing to take the consequences. You just want to play some more? Go find someone who can take it. This one can't."

Arch clenched his teeth. And fists. And stomach. His impulse was to run away like a child, hide in his bed and block out what his dad had told him. But he wasn't a child. He needed to listen, needed to slow down and think and reason this out. He'd been so carried away by the joy of being with Amanda, so taken with her, so tuned in to her moods and passions, and yeah, shoot him, so damn horny. Being around her messed up his brain, made him want nothing more than to find out everything about her, make her his in the worst caveman way.

But his dad was right. This couldn't be just about relieving sperm buildup. If he wanted to make love to Amanda, he had to have his reasons and intentions straight. What kind of partner/lover/boyfriend would he make for her? He had to think beyond tomorrow, had to think what was best in the bigger picture. In the meantime, he was going to have to deal with the fact that his dad had the ridiculous notion that Maude Marcus would even look at him twice.

"What are you going to do, Dad?"

The bushy eyebrows lifted. "I was going to ask you the same thing."

Arch shrugged, feeling hollow and down. Not his usual style at all. "I guess I'm going to take some time to think it over. You?"

His father grinned broadly and smacked Arch's shoulder. "I'm going for it, son. Leaping off the platform and high-flying without a net."

SEAMSTRESS AVAILABLE, experienced, reasonable rates, big jobs or small. 555–5738.

Amanda threw her pen down on the end table with the pink Princess phone, feeling once again as if life was going to swallow her whole. Monday, that incredible twenty-four hours with Arch when she'd felt so free, so powerful—the walk in the park, the crazy passion in her dark bedroom, the emotional charge of sharing something so private when he'd stayed to listen to her pleasure—had receded like the dream it was.

The next morning, reality had come crashing down and stayed ever since. She had no job. No prospects. Dwindling money. Her furniture had huge brown water stains, making her apartment look shabby. She could make slipcovers, but the material was expensive, they wouldn't look as nice, and she needed to use her time for paying jobs. Plus, the continued humidity had made the rug dry too slowly; it was starting to smell and would need cleaning. All this cost more money than she could afford to spend.

Maybe it was just as well. A little dose of reality. She'd been in denial too long about what she could accomplish without a steady income. All those fantasies about dancing in Barbados with tuxedoed males, jetting off to Paris and Rome, buying her own house. Foolish. She should be thinking income and groceries.

It's just that as soon as she made the call to place this ad, she'd be kissing her dream of working on fabulous jobs for exclusive clients goodbye, at least in the near future. Soon she'd be hemming jeans, letting out skirt waistbands and shortening sleeves ad nauseam. People she didn't know would have her number, and unless she wanted to drive all over town to pick up the work, her address.

She felt as if she were going out among swarming bees naked and relying on dumb luck she wouldn't get stung.

Then there was Arch. She'd seen him a few times in the last two days; he and his father had come up to talk about work on the roof the day after the storm, and she heard plenty of banging above her head while they replaced the shingles that had blown off. But something was different. She couldn't tell if the change came from her or from him. Maybe both. Maybe they'd both realized the impossibility of finishing what they'd started. Or if not the impossibility, the inadvisability. He'd been friendly, charming as usual— a couple of times they'd exchanged intimate glances, but they'd both held themselves aloof. And now he'd taken the boys up north indefinitely to Green Bay to visit his sister.

Part of her was relieved. But the part of her he had awakened was definitely and painfully disappointed. While she could well believe *she'd* come to her senses, a secret part of her had hoped he wouldn't come to his. She couldn't quite believe he was the type to start something and not try to finish it, without even talking about why he couldn't, not that she'd brought it up either. But then he'd been busy... And men were totally confusing creatures anyway.

Look at Ridge, who hadn't even shown up for his own wedding and hadn't been in touch since. One day it was,

marrying-you-is-the-best-thing-that-ever-happened-to-me;
the next it was, sorry-I-can't-go-through-with-it-love-Ridge
on a note she found under her door when she got back from
what was supposed to be the ceremony, stunned and exhausted. A rather blatant example of a male not finishing
something he started.

She picked up the phone to call the *Milwaukee Journal-
Sentinel* Classified section, her stomach churning. This was
it. End of denial. Close relatively happy chapter of life.
Open seemingly dismal new—

The doorbell rang; she slammed the phone down and
sighed with relief. Even dealing with missionaries would
be a welcome postponement.

She glanced out the window and immediately ducked to
a crouch. Her mother, peering over at the driveway, craning
her neck as if she was looking into Arch's apartment.

What was Mom doing here if she thought her daughter
was at work? Amanda hadn't quite gotten around to having
that extra key made, ahem, so it wasn't as though her mom
could come over and let herself in.

She lifted slowly until she could just see over the edge
of the sill. Her mom rang the bell again, unusually impatient.

Amanda gritted her teeth and straightened. This was ridiculous. She wasn't going to hide from her own mother.

The bell rang again, then Maude's voice came in through
the screen along with more humid air, "Open up, dear, I
know you're in there."

Amanda let out a short sigh and went downstairs, feeling
a complete fool. Her mom must know already that she'd
lost her job. Maybe she'd tried to call Patterson's. Amanda
should have told her right away. She couldn't even quite
remember why it had been so important to hide. It seemed
silly now to have been ashamed, or even to have thought

she wouldn't be able to handle Maude's reaction, no matter how smothering.

She opened the door. Her mother turned from staring at Arch's doorway, cheeks pink, resplendent in an emerald linen suit that as usual made Amanda feel frumpy in her cotton pants and top. "Oh, hello, dear. I came by to say good morning. Lovely day."

Amanda glanced briefly at the overcast sky. "Come in, Mom."

She led the way up the stairs. Maude swept into the apartment behind her and stopped, nose wrinkled. "Gracious. What happened here?"

"The storm on Monday night. My roof leaked."

Her mother turned to face her. "Why didn't you tell me? I could have helped."

The words were exactly what Amanda had expected to hear. But the tone was something completely new. Her mother sounded...hurt. Not sulky-whiny-pouting-injured, but truly hurt.

"I'm sorry, Mom."

"You lost your job. You didn't tell me that either."

Amanda swallowed. "No."

Incredibly, her mom seemed at a loss for words. She blinked rapidly and Amanda was horrified to think she might be about to cry. Maude Marcus crying in front of someone? Amanda had never even seen a tear when Dad died, though she didn't doubt plenty were shed in private.

"Well, Amanda." Her mom sighed heavily, her you-are-such-a-disappointment voice back on full power. "I understand that your life is your own business and I respect that. But I'd hoped that by my living here, we could become...closer. That you could rely on me and confide in me."

Guilt. Massive guilt. Amanda curled her hands into fists.

How could she explain that "closer" to her mother meant doing everything her way? "Sorry, Mom."

Her mother put her hand to her forehead and closed her eyes. "Will you stop apologizing for everything? Have some backbone, for God's sake."

Amanda's jaw dropped, too shocked to be hurt, though she was dimly aware that would come later. Her mom had nearly cried and barely a minute later lost her temper? What was up with that? Had something happened? Or was she just having trouble adjusting to her new surroundings? She'd been through a lot this past year.

Amanda opened her mouth to offer tea, get them back on familiar, impersonal footing, when something stopped her. The memories of Arch reaching out to her, wanting to know and understand her feelings. The realization that Amanda had never had anyone to talk them over with.

She looked at her mother. What the hell. Worst she could do was think Amanda was an idiot, which she already did anyway.

"Anything the matter, Mom?"

Her mother looked startled. Amanda moved forward, feeling totally disoriented, took her mother's elbow and steered her awkwardly to an unstained portion of the couch. "Want to talk about it?"

Her mother blinked. Amanda waited. It was the most uncomfortable moment of her entire life.

The phone rang.

"Better get that."

Amanda lunged. "Hello?"

"Amanda Marcus?"

"Yes."

"This is Catherine Loring, attorney with Grammick, Schenckel and Fortz. We specialize in adoption law. I called and left a message the other day."

"Oh, yes." Amanda turned away from her mom who was still looking at her as if she'd been replaced by an alien clone.

"I have some important information for you. I know this will be something of a surprise."

"Oh." She sank onto her stained wingback. What was this? Adoption law? Had she broken one?

"First of all, I'm assuming you are aware that you were adopted at birth by Maude and Bruce Marcus of Fairfield, Connecticut."

"Yes." She clutched the phone hard, a strong foreboding in her stomach. Something big. This was going to be something big.

"Did you ever make any attempt to find your birth parents, Ms. Marcus?"

"No." She closed her eyes. Oh God, don't let this be another parent trying to barge into her life. She'd considered and rejected the idea of finding her birth parents years ago. Her life was complicated enough right now.

"I'm sorry to say that your birth mother died a few weeks ago, your birth father many years before that."

"Oh. That's…awful." A small shock and less relief than she might have expected. Maybe she'd be genuinely sorry later, when she could process all this properly. Maybe she'd grieve after all, for a mother she didn't get the chance to know.

"I'm calling about the terms of her will."

"Her will." Amanda's brain went blank, then started spinning furiously.

"Provided that we could find you and that you turned out, in her words, to be a good citizen, she left her entire estate to you."

"To me." Her words came out in a bewildered whisper. The shock was much bigger this time and the emotion. Her birth mother had left all her money to a daughter she never knew—but hadn't forgotten. Had maybe even mourned.

"There is another daughter, Natalie, who would be your half sister. She and her mother were estranged, I don't know if she'll try to cause trouble or not."

"I see."

"I know it's a lot to take in right now." The professional voice turned more human. "I'll give you my number and mail you the details, okay?"

"Yes. Okay."

"One more thing."

"Yes?"

"I think you might like to know that your birth mother was Jennifer Canter of Canter furniture. You've heard of it I imagine."

Amanda's jaw dropped. Yes. And she'd heard of Skippy peanut butter and Oreo cookies and Kleenex tissues.

The attorney chuckled softly. "I'm pleased to inform you that you've inherited close to two billion dollars."

MAUDE MARCUS looked up from her book to the gold and crystal clock on her mantle, chiming the hour. Five o'clock. She slammed the book shut, headed into her dining room, straight for the carved-wood liquor cabinet that had been her mother's and poured herself a healthy dose of Jameson Irish Whiskey. More than she needed. Much more than was smart to drink in her current mood.

Who cared.

She went into her kitchen, about half the size of the ones she'd always had, damn it, and opened the freezer. No automatic ice maker. Cubes in those little trays. She pried one out and dropped it into her drink. She should probably put in more than one to make the drink last longer, but it was a crime to dilute good whiskey.

The refrigerator door made a sucking squeak noise when it closed. She hated that. In Manhattan she'd had a built-in refrigerator, ice dispenser in the door…and George.

Who was probably humping his sweet dumb thing right now.

She took a healthy swallow of Jameson's. George was boring in bed. She'd come close to hurling that particular fact in his face last time she saw him, but couldn't quite descend to that depth. Hell had no fury, and so on—he'd know she was trying to inflict pain to ease her own humiliation. No one should ever see her own humiliation. It was hers and it was private.

Though fat lot of good it did to pretend it wasn't there. Here she stood in a tiny apartment on a Friday night, drinking by herself the fourth evening in a row, an old woman with an adopted daughter who'd inherited two billion dollars from her *real* mother, not coincidentally four days ago. Might as well have had the satisfaction of telling George about the faked orgasms, for all the difference it made.

Another gulp of whiskey before the loneliness could hit her, and the despair. Alcohol was about the worst thing she could put into her body. Bruce, her first husband, the doctor, had told her alcohol might give an initial high, but it was actually a depressant.

So, bring it on.

Being good and depressed for one night might help. Like an emotional enema. She snorted, spraying a mist of whiskey through her lips. Uncharacteristically vulgar thought. So, maybe she'd make a whole evening of uncharacteristic. Skip dinner and settle in for a party, with bad TV, the whiskey bottle and her self-pity for guests. Change out of her Ann Taylor pants and sweater set and into old sweatpants and a ratty T-shirt. Except she didn't own either one.

The apartment buzzer rang. She narrowed her eyes at the

intercom. Who the hell was that? There wasn't a human being in the whole country she wanted to see right now.

"Yes?" She released the talk button and listened.

"Maude?" A gruff male voice, unfamiliar. Who did she know well enough to call her by her first name? "It's Sonny."

Sonny. A shot of adrenaline, part excitement, part annoyance. Mostly annoyance. What the hell was he doing here?

"Thaddeus. Arch's father."

He mistook her silence. Thought she didn't know who he was. "What are you doing here?"

"I've come to call."

She swallowed abruptly, took another gulp of whiskey to unclench her throat. "I see."

She heard him chuckle, a low male sound. "Let me up. I want to see you."

Oh God, the man wasn't going to turn into a nuisance, was he? She bit her lip, then jabbed her thumb on the buzzer to unlock the building's front door. What choice did she have? It would be rude to turn him away. Maybe he just wanted to talk to her about Amanda. Or Amanda and his son. Or Amanda's money, which was all anyone wanted to talk about. The story had even made the local news.

She hovered near the door, then impulsively dashed to her room, ditching the whiskey on her kitchen counter on the way. Thirty seconds and she'd changed her white sweater set for a rose-colored silk one and added lipstick. Just because he wasn't much of a gentleman didn't mean she could be caught looking frumpy.

Her doorbell rang, then a gentle knocking. She hurriedly put down the bottle of Fleurs de Rocaille which she'd picked up without really thinking. The perfume had been

George's favorite. Thank goodness the bell brought her to her senses. Why waste the stuff?

She hurried to the front entranceway, then stopped, took a deep breath, adjusted her skirt, smoothed her hair—what was *wrong* with her?

She opened the door and made herself smile coolly. "Hello, Thaddeus."

"Hey, Maude." He made no move to come in, just stood there, staring unabashedly, as if he was reacquainting himself with the sight of her. Then with a flourish worthy of a bullfighter, he produced a bouquet of stunning pink roses from behind his back. "For you."

"Oh." She accepted them, hating the heat and no doubt the color that sprang to her cheek. "Thank you. They're lovely, Thaddeus."

"You're welcome. And it's Sonny." He stepped inside and looked around. "Nice place."

"I've barely started on it, really." She brought the roses up to her face, for politeness, since most floral-shop roses had little or no scent, and to give herself a minute to compose herself. She hadn't gotten flowers from a man in years and was more pleased than she should be.

The fragrance was so unexpectedly exquisite that she kept her face buried in the blooms, inhaling deeply. The scent reminded her of the garden she and Bruce had had in Connecticut—well, *she* had really. Bruce had had no time for much of anything besides his work. "They smell wonderful."

He nodded in satisfaction. "A friend of mine has a shop. He gets beautiful things in."

"I'll put them in water right away. Would you like some Irish whiskey?" She went into the kitchen, laid the bouquet on the counter. "I'm just having some."

"Sure, love some." He glanced at her glass next to the flowers, then, rather questioningly, at her.

"I don't usually drink this much. In fact I probably won't be able to finish it. I just wasn't paying attention when I was pour—"

"Sometimes it's what you need when the pain gets bad. Or what you think you need."

She turned away from his gentle voice and busied herself filling a vase with water and arranging the flowers. How did he know she was in pain? She could hide her emotions from anyone. Years of practice with busy important husbands who didn't need unnecessary distraction.

"It rarely works."

She turned back, holding the vase. He was taller than she remembered, though still way too short for her. Also more attractive. There was something else about him, something she couldn't quite identify that set him apart from the men she knew. "I'm sorry, what rarely works?"

"Alcohol. Doesn't really help the pain, just numbs it for a while. Then you're back where you started, sometimes worse."

"Ah. I see." She grabbed her glass, pushed past him into the living room and put the flowers on her mantel. One step back, looking them over critically. The blooms on the left should be higher. One bud on the right stuck out too haphazardly. She moved forward to rearrange them, when she felt a hand on her wrist.

"They're beautiful like that. Not quite perfect. Makes the place look homier."

She took in a sharp breath and smiled to mask her annoyance. "You don't think my place is homey?"

"Nope." His expression stayed cheerful. "Looks like my mom's parlor. No one allowed in there except on Sundays or when someone kicked the bucket."

She tightened her lips. Not a single person she knew, not one, would ever say anything that appallingly rude. "I'm sorry you think so."

"Don't see why." He shrugged. "We can disagree, can't we?"

"I'll get your drink." She fled to the dining-room liquor cabinet and extracted another cut-crystal tumbler from the set Bruce had bought her for Christmas shortly after they were married. "How do you take your whiskey?"

"Straight up."

She nodded, keeping her back to him. Her hand holding the bottle was trembling. Her throat constricted. What on earth was the matter with her? First, four fateful days ago she'd nearly broken down in front of her own daughter, now tears threatened in front of this strange little blue-collar person who came over uninvited, insulted her home and set her on edge with practically every sentence. Gentlemen of her own kind she knew how to deal with. How to flirt, how to chatter, what subjects to bring up. Instinctively she knew those rules weren't at work here and she hated feeling so out of her element. Especially on her own turf.

"Here you go." She poured him a half tumbler full— not wanting to give him less than she'd given herself—and turned to hand it to him, startled to find him practically at her elbow. For a man with a few pounds on him, he moved very quietly, which unnerved her further.

He thanked her and lifted his drink. "Here's to no more pain."

She gave him a tight smile and motioned gracefully to the living room. "Shall we move to the other room to chat? We'll be more comfortable there."

"Why certainly, Madame Marcus, I'd be delighted." He shot her a grinning glance and she realized with a shock that he was teasing her for her formality.

Her temper spiked; she tried to make her eyes go cold, but then he winked, and she couldn't quite manage it. "Okay, how's this. 'Ya wanna siddown?'"

He threw back his head and laughed, a loud long laugh that would have mortified her if they'd been in public.

"Luv ta, tanks." He crossed the room, sat on the sofa, stretched his legs out and leaned back, sipped his drink.

She followed slowly, all at once realizing what was different about him. He was entirely comfortable. In his own skin, in her apartment, sitting on her furniture, drinking her liquor. No reserve, no pretension, no feeling that he didn't belong here—what had they called it during her entirely unsuccessful attempt to master a computer? *What you see is what you get.*

"So your daughter's a billionaire now, huh?"

Maude suppressed a stab of irritation in another rather large sip of whiskey and sank onto a burgundy and gold–flowered chair next to the sofa. "Yes."

"How does that feel?"

How did it *feel?* What kind of question was that? "I'm very happy for her. She was struggling."

She kept her eyes on her drink, aware he was watching her. Damn it. For being such an easygoing informal man, there was an intensity about him that surprised her every time she looked into his eyes. Right now she didn't want to see it and didn't want to know why. *Change the subject.*

"I went to your city's art museum yesterday. Small collection, but fine things. The new Calatrava addition to the building is superb. A real coup for a city Milwaukee's size."

Her words hung in the room, and for some reason she wanted to cringe. In any other social situation, the introduction of the topic would have been appropriate. With

Sonny Williams in the room, it sounded forced and pretentious.

"I agree." He sent her an amused look that made her want to hurl her drink in his face. "It's like being inside a futuristic boat. Or a *Star Trek* spaceship."

"Yes." She opened her mouth to make an intelligent and perceptive comment about the exhibit and realized it would only make her want to cringe again, so she drank more whiskey instead. To tell the truth, she didn't give a fig about art tonight. Or anything else for that matter.

But he was making her very uneasy, sitting there, grinning at her, apparently not bothered by the agonizing silence between them.

"Do you like to read, Sonny?"

He sent her another sharp amused glance. "Just finished *The Bean Trees*, Barbara Kingsolver. Before that *The Poisonwood Bible*."

"I love her work. So evocative." She gritted her teeth. The words sounded so silly, so vain hearing them through his ears. But this was the only way she knew how to behave. The only way she knew to strike up an acquaintance. Everyone in her world did the same. "The characters stay in your head for days."

"Yes. They do. So…" He took another sip of whiskey. "Do I pass your little culture test?"

"My—" Maude's mouth dropped. Her cheeks started burning.

"Can we talk about something real?"

She put her whiskey glass on her grandmother's butler coffee table, resisting the urge to slam it down and risk shattering it or damaging the table. *How dare he.* "I'm not going to sit here and be insulted. I think you should leave."

His eyes grabbed hers and held on, all easygoing Sonny gone. "I don't want to talk about stuff that doesn't matter.

I'm here because I'm worried about you. You look tired, you look miserable, and I want to help.''

She gasped. No one had ever, ever spoken to her that way. The men she knew…both husbands…no one ever.

Maude Marcus was infinitely capable. Men leaned on *her,* spilled their troubles. She took them in, soothed them, and set them about their life again, healed, mended, satisfied in her power and purpose. That was her role.

He put down his drink, scooted closer on the couch until they were nearly knee to knee, reached out and took her hands. ''Talk to me.''

She looked down at her old-lady hands clasped in the warmth of his. Her emotions rose, a seething jumbled incomprehensible mess. He was prying places he had no right to pry. He had no right to try to break her down this way.

''It's okay.'' He squeezed her fingers. ''Just say whatever comes out. We'll take it from there.''

His hands were rough and strong, not like the fine, tanned hands of George, or the long, white fingers of her surgeon husband, Bruce. These hands had done life's work by themselves. Her pain rose further, to the back of her throat, threatening to spill. The desire to confide in this compelling stranger was fighting to get through. The desire to lean on someone else. Find some relief from all this confusion. Since when had she been like this? Why now, with *him* in the room?

''You're safe with me.''

She should have laughed at the soap-opera line. Instead she found herself desperately wanting it to be true.

She'd had too much to drink, that was all. The urge to connect would leave as soon as—

''Maude…''

At his gruff whisper, her mouth opened, without her

brain having any idea what it was going to say, but the urge to speak overwhelmed her.

"I…wanted to pay for Clarissa to have ballet lessons."

The words hung in the silence, absurd, meaningless, whiny. She closed her eyes, tears threatening again. He must think she was a complete loon.

"Go on."

Her eyes opened, looked again into his. Calm, waiting. He wanted to hear more. Something lifted in her heart. "I think she should take ballet. I…wanted to do that for her."

"And?"

She grimaced. "I'm not making any sense."

"Keep talking."

"Why do you want to hear this?" She pulled her hands free. "What does it matter?"

"It matters to you. Therefore it matters to me."

The declaration was so simple, said so casually that its meaning nearly escaped her. "Why should the things I care about matter to you?"

"Because I love you."

She froze. He watched her with a curious unreadable expression. Then, thank God, he winked.

A giggle escaped her. Then another. Then laughter burst out; she bent forward, clutching her stomach, fighting for control. "I'm…sorry. It's just so…funny."

She struggled through another few seconds, clamped down hard to get the best of the hysteria and lifted back to a sitting position.

"Oh my word." She wiped her eyes carefully so as not to smudge her makeup.

He recaptured her hands. "Better?"

"Yes." A stray giggle erupted. She forced it back, took a deep shuddering breath and nodded, worn out but strangely at peace. "What on earth made you say such a thing?"

A slow grin lit up his face in a way that was becoming pleasantly familiar. "Just for kicks. To see what you'd do."

She smiled gratefully back, noticing that his lashes were very dark and long without looking remotely feminine. "Thank you, Sonny."

He leaned toward her, no longer smiling, and her heart skipped a beat. "Money isn't going to replace you."

Her body stiffened. "What? Of course not. What do you think I—"

"Shh." He held up a hand. "You can still pay for lessons."

"She doesn't need me to."

"Who cares? It's a gift, not a matter of necessity. If you want to do it, go ahead and do it." He held up a warning finger. "But I'd ask Clarissa if that's what she wants. I'm guessing she'd rather take soccer or softball."

"Sports?" She bristled. "You don't know my granddaughter. Her mother loved ballet at Clarissa's age. And so did I."

His salt-and-pepper eyebrow lifted, the message clear. *What does that have to do with Clarissa?*

She ducked her head, confused, grateful he'd said nothing out loud, ashamed of how her words had sounded. Was that true? Did Clarissa not want to take ballet? But then why hadn't Amanda ever *said* anything? At the very least to spare Maude having to face a stranger who seemed to know more about her granddaughter than she did.

She looked back down at their nested hands, wanting to show her annoyance by taking hers away, but not wanting to leave the comfort of his warmth.

"Maude."

She looked up reluctantly. His gaze was deep and wise

somehow, not what she'd expect from such a man. Bruce's gaze had always betrayed that his brilliant mind was occupied elsewhere. George's had been sexy, masculine, but shallow. Shifting. These eyes were focused exclusively on her, warm and gentle and compassionate.

"They still need you."

She stiffened against a bolt of fear. "Of course they do. What a foolish—"

He moved so fast she couldn't think of stopping him. Cupped her head in those big warm hands, and kissed her, sweetly lingering, as if he had exclusive rights to her mouth.

She moved clumsily to push his hand away and ended up hanging on to his wrist for dear life, kissing him back like a woman half her age with sex on her mind.

She'd never ever, ever been kissed like that.

He pulled back, eyes no longer warm and wise but very dark and very male. She could barely breathe.

"Maude Marcus, you are one hot mama."

She burst out laughing again, real hearty laughter she didn't care if anyone in the building heard and found too raucous. She couldn't remember the last time she'd laughed so much. She must be going slightly mad or she'd slap him for saying such a thing.

He drew her close again, rested his forehead on hers. "They still need you, Amanda and Clarissa. And I've got news for you."

"What?" Her voice came out dreamy and breathless, like a woman in her twenties discovering love for the first time.

He kissed her again, another wonderful kiss that left her hungry for about a million more. "So do I."

CHAPTER TEN

ARCH GRITTED HIS TEETH at the dump truck doing a leisurely sixty miles an hour in the left lane of Route 43 South, Milwaukee-bound. The sky was a gorgeous blue overhead, but brown fog clouded the horizon, and every now and then grit and tiny pebbles hurled themselves out of the back of the damn truck to click and clatter against his windshield, like a reminder that nothing was perfect.

He'd spent the last five days with his sister and the boys. The visit had been fun, really good to see his sister, still pale and tired, but—thanks to a combination of antidepressants, counseling and rest—with her determination and energy on their way back. Also really nice to see the kids reassured that Mom was okay, especially Mark, who'd been much more his old fairly cheerful self. All in all a resounding success, except for the nearly constant ache of missing Amanda, not less and less as the week went on, but more. And more.

Three days into the trip, his father had called and said simply, "Turn on the TV." He'd gone into his sister's family room, stepping over piles of Yu-Gi-Oh cards and Rescue Hero action figures and turned on the set. His heart had leaped into triple time. The very last thing he'd expected to see—Amanda's face, gracious and smiling for cameras she mostly likely didn't care to have shoved into her face. The ache of missing her had intensified to stabbing pain, even before he registered what the fuss was all about.

Ouch.

After the initial jaw-dropping excitement, half of him went on celebrating for her—for her secure future, for the easing of her worry load. The rest of him wasn't so sure. Cinderella, they'd called her. Rags to riches. Overnight. Anyone would be thrilled. Anyone would celebrate. Her troubles were over, right? Money changes everything.

Just not always for the better. Not that he'd lived it really, not to the extent she would. What he earned for his books, successful as they might be, could hardly be called a fortune. But plenty, sure. And a big change from the constant not-enough of his childhood. He enjoyed buying his toys, indulging whims he'd always denied himself, no longer having to worry about what was to come.

But fame had also made him public property to a certain extent, begged for interviews and public-speaking engagements, turned to for advice from people who seemed to think anyone with a name out there had a better grip on life than they did. When in reality everybody thrashed around together in this mysterious puddle of existence.

But success and wealth hadn't changed his life the way this bizarre, out-of-the blue inheritance would change Amanda's. For one thing, he had a good seven years on her; he was surer of who he was and what he wanted. And he'd been deliberately working his butt off for years to get exactly where he'd gotten.

The truck finally pulled ahead of the minivan it had been straining to pass. Arch turned on his wipers to dispel the last dirt shower and put his gas pedal down hard. Aside from the money issue, he'd done a lot of thinking about Amanda, as he promised his father he would. And though he hadn't gotten a handle on the entire situation, he did know a few things.

One, he and Amanda needed to have a talk about what

was going to happen between them, or at least what they wanted to happen. That night of passion between them needed some kind of follow-up, some clarification of what the rules would be going forward. Not his usual style, he was happy letting things fall where they might, but Amanda would want that.

Second, he knew as well as he knew himself that right now she needed him. Amanda was still a work in progress. The gains she'd made in confidence and spark since he'd known her could easily be erased by a change of this magnitude hitting her so unexpectedly. The shock could send her clinging back to old habits for the security she seemed to crave.

That fact had made him anxious to bail out on his sister and her kids, which, for someone who'd put his family first for the last twenty years, should be telling him something about how important she was becoming—had already become.

Third, as much as he wanted her, he shouldn't be the one to push the physical part of their relationship. His father had been right; for all her hidden sensuality, Amanda wasn't one to enter into a sexual relationship lightly. Especially now, with all the recent changes in her life, she'd be particularly vulnerable and most likely wouldn't want to complicate their friendship by becoming lovers.

So he'd leave that step up to her, though he'd stooped to carrying condoms just in case. He'd be there for her emotionally while this crazy adjustment was made, but keep the passion aloof, be a good friend.

And ignore the voice screaming at him 24/7 how badly he wanted to be a whole lot more.

"YOU LOOK LOVELY, Geneva." Mrs. Straussgarten boomed out approval over the sight of her daughter standing in

Amanda's living room, modeling the secretly unhemmed tutu wedding dress. "That length is perfect, I was right to insist on it being shortened."

Amanda, crouching by the hem in front, dared a wink up at freckle-faced Genie, who first glanced back to make sure her mother was absorbed in fussing over her train, and then winked back. "It's beautiful, Mom. Amanda did a great job."

"She certainly did." Mrs. Straussgarten straightened and beamed at Amanda. "Our little Cinderella is very talented."

Amanda's polite smile froze on her face. Was there anyone, *anyone* in the city who hadn't heard of her inheritance and/or the stupid nickname? In the entire country? Since the news had leaked, she'd been subjected to a steady barrage of mail and phone calls. Every charity on the planet wanted a piece of her. *People* magazine wanted a rags-to-riches tale for their next issue. Local and national news and human-interest TV shows wanted interviews. Endless reporters from endless newspapers hounded her, wanting to know who she was, what she'd done with her life, how she'd lived, her politics, her passions, her toothpaste brand... And over and over, how did this all *feel?* How did it *feel* to be struggling one minute, a gazillionaire the next? When they found out she'd inherited money after she'd lost her job, one smart-aleck reporter came up with Cinderella and the nickname stuck.

Puke.

It had all happened so fast, so furiously. Everyone seemed to feel entitled to her. She'd said no so many times to so many people she felt like a toddler. With the media camped in the yard those first days, she was just glad Arch was in Green Bay, for fear they'd plaster him across the nation as her Prince Charming and freak them both out.

The worst of it was that because of the media circus, she'd barely been able to take in the fact that her troubles were over. Hadn't had a second to relax and simply enjoy the fact that she could do whatever she wanted now. That she was done hemming unflattering dresses. That she would never have to put that odious ad in the paper. She had the power now to make every single one of her dreams come true.

The idea was too mind-boggling to grasp.

She rose to her feet from where she'd been arranging the fluffy tulle layers of Genie's dress and practically ran to get her bill, the last one for alterations to someone else's design she'd ever have to write.

"Here you are, Mrs. Straussgarten." She handed the bill to Genie's mom with a hand that shook. Stress and Amanda had become terrific friends.

Mrs. Straussgarten frowned at the modest charge.

Amanda smiled patiently, feeling anything but. She wanted these people out of her apartment. Now that the fuss had died down somewhat, she wanted to take a breather and plan her future, a future that looked way, way different than she'd ever imagined it could.

Genie went to change out of the dress while Mrs. Straussgarten wrote a check, big lips pressed in a disapproving line, probably thinking that Amanda should be donating her services to people who were only minorly disgustingly wealthy.

"Thank you." Amanda accepted the check and when the bride-to-be was dressed, showed mother and daughter out, touched when Genie turned and gave her a quick hug of gratitude. The wedding would be lovely. Genie would glow. Mom would be proud. The groom would probably even show up.

Good luck to all of them.

Between the endless phone calls, she'd done a lot more thinking while Arch was in Green Bay taking care of his family. Given how cool he'd been—they'd both been—before he left, after that one night of carried-away passion, she had little reason to think he wanted their affair, or whatever it was, to continue. That was okay. She was at a crossroads right now. Her life would be very different moving forward. Better that she remained disentangled until she could get herself settled in this new persona, until she could figure out which end of her was up.

By then, she'd be in a better position to choose someone. A position of total strength. Not relying on anyone else for who she should or shouldn't be. Not letting anyone else decide what she wanted or how her life should go.

The door closed behind the Straussgartens. Amanda turned to face her apartment, the smile on her face sagging into uncertainty.

Now what?

Clarissa was in her last week of school. After that, the summer stretched before them, endless and empty.

She crossed her arms firmly over her chest. What was she thinking? They could do anything. Go anywhere. See Europe. Stay in sumptuous hotels, eat at the finest restaurants. Hire a sailboat and sail the seven seas. Hire a rocket and explore outer space.

She *could* take off for Barbados and dance with those tuxy guys. She *could* jet to the fashion capitals of the world. She could own her own house, hell she could own five. Open dress shops wherever she chose, featuring her own designs. Consult with brides-to-be, steer them away from mother-inspired bad choices. She was Someone now. People would listen to her.

It was just a question of choosing from the vast and slightly terrifying list of possibilities. Of figuring out exactly what she wanted, now that she could have everything. She laughed too loudly and flung her arms wide, trying not to panic. Everything!

The doorbell rang, three quick dings. Her heart skipped and she pulled her arms in over her chest. Was Arch back from Green Bay earlier than he'd planned to be?

Deep breath. Go easy. Stay calm. She was someone to be reckoned with now. No longer panting after whoever showed interest. A woman who could afford to be highly discriminating. Who could make sure the man she chose was the best choice for her.

Right?

She straightened her capris, pushed back her hair, started downstairs and was treated to the sight of the front door opening and Arch on his way up.

"Amanda." His voice rang with the warmth she saw in his face, warmth and concern. "Are you okay?"

"Yes. I'm fine."

Her words didn't come out with nearly enough confidence or conviction. One glimpse and she was simply meltingly, achingly glad to see him. So much had happened, so much had changed in such a short time, he suddenly seemed like a lifeline to her previous sane, predictable existence and routine.

Hang on, Amanda. Stay cool. Remember what you decided, who you are now, what you…um…what you…

He trudged up the stairs toward her, gorgeous and reassuringly familiar in jeans and a T-shirt that said, Live It Up. Her breath rose in her throat; her cheeks flushed.

Wait a second.

Hadn't she just decided he was a lifeline she needed to cut if she wanted to move forward?

Another step closer. She could see the shadow of stubble on his face, the creases at the corners of his eyes. Smell the faint whiff of outside air above the enticing smell of his aftershave and...

"Arch."

God, was that her voice, that hungry gasp? What was she doing?

"Amanda." His voice sounded the same as hers. Hoarse, needy, tinged with passion.

Oh no.

He reached the step below hers and without her brain's permission, her arms flung themselves around his neck and she was kissing him like a madwoman.

"God, I missed you."

"Me, too."

He bent and lifted her; she gave a little jump and wrapped her legs around his back, holding tight so he could carry her up the stairs, still kissing her madly, and into her apartment. Over to the couch, where he tried to lay her down, but she refused to unwrap, so he ended up lying there with her, nestled between her legs.

Oh yes.

Except he pulled up and away from her. "Amanda, are you sure you want this?"

She nodded breathlessly. "Oh yes. Don't you?"

"God, yes, but—"

"I do, Arch. Please."

She drew his head down again, felt his caution melt until anything in her mind that remotely resembled reasonable, rational judgment was lost to the power of his kisses, the power of his body. She felt swallowed up in him, overcome by his passion, his size and strength, and she welcomed it all. In a stunning flash, the last few days were revealed for the desperately lonely trial they'd been.

She stroked the strong, broad muscles in his back, lifted his shirt to feel the masculine smooth skin, the firm wide sweep of his upper body. His warm hands came up under her shirt, to stroke her sides, higher, higher, until his thumbs swept over the curve of her breasts, brushed across her nipples again and again. She moaned into his kiss, lifted her hips in a frantic rhythm, urgent, needy, yearning. Forget the money, forget the strain, forget the world; she wanted only to lose herself in this man and this moment.

He moved her shirt higher; she lifted her arms to let it slide over her head. The cool air moved deliciously over her skin, the flowery couch felt soft and smooth at her back.

He would feel even better.

She tugged at his T-shirt, got it up and over and off, and *ohh,* was the sight of that chest wonderful. Dark hair, distributed perfectly—he looked such a *man.* She felt small and fragile under him and loved the sensation shamelessly.

"Amanda." He lifted off her, unfastened her pants with slow precise movements, looking into her eyes. She answered his silent question with a calm direct gaze, ignoring the tiny voice sending a warning, closing her mind to everything but the pleasure in her body and the feeling in her heart.

She wanted this, she wanted him; she'd been lonely, vulnerable without even realizing it, and he was the only person in the world right now who could make it all better.

His hand stroked over her stomach, warm and possessive, then slid under the waistband of her panties, farther, farther, into her curling hair…farther, where she most wanted his fingers and his warmth.

Yes, there.

His hand cupped her sex as if he owned her; his thumb found her clitoris and began a circular rhythm that was going to set her off way before she wanted to be set off.

Not yet.

She worked frantically at his fly, unsnapped, unzipped,

thrust her hand inside to grasp the thick hard column of heat she wanted so desperately. Her reward was a male groan and the sudden fumbling of the fingers that seconds before had been so skillful between her legs. They were so good. So good. She wasn't going to think beyond this second, beyond these incredible minutes they had together now.

His penis hardened further under her stroking; he kissed her with savage, hard kisses, his breathing fast and ragged. Then he suddenly shifted his weight forward, shed his pants, his briefs, rooted briefly for the condom in his pocket, then knelt back to remove the rest of her clothes. Her bra, unhooked, slid tenderly off. Her jeans, tugged down and tossed. Then slowly, reverently, her panties, not the red lace but it didn't seem he'd care if they were made of burlap.

She lay open to him, no shame, no apology for the imperfections in her body. Naked under his deliberate gaze, which wandered over her, his hand following, from her breasts, to her stomach, down between her legs once more. His fingers found their previous rhythm, touching, stroking, rubbing again to bring her where he wanted her.

And oh, she was exactly where he wanted her, hot, ready in seconds. She took the condom, tore it open, unrolled it onto him, then let her fingers linger, tight and moving on his erection, until he caught her hand away.

He lay over her, supported on his forearms and held himself still. Amanda closed her eyes in anticipation, legs eagerly open, waiting impatiently for the intimate, breath-stealing moment when he entered her for the first time.

"Amanda."

She opened her eyes.

"Look at me," he whispered. "I want to see your face when I go inside you."

She stared up into his dark gaze, waiting, wondering what he wanted to see.

He pushed in. Her eyes widened at the feel of the first glorious inch of him, sliding slowly inside her, then the second, then more and more, until she suddenly couldn't bear the intensity of their eye contact and closed her eyes, clasped him to her, blindsided by emotion more powerful than anything she'd ever felt.

He slid the rest of the way in, lighting brighter, even hotter fireworks. Then he began to move, slowly, leisurely, as if he had all day to make love to her, kissing her throat, her cheeks, her mouth.

Amanda lay back, tried to relax into his rhythm, but it was suddenly too much, all too much. She was out of her depth, disoriented, way too vulnerable.

She loved him. Had recognized that on some level, and despite all her noble protests and firm resolves, she'd responded to him on sight, passionately and instinctively. With every cell of her being, with every atom of her heart, she loved him.

Too much.

She gave in, shut off her mind, allowed her body all the greedy ideas it had on its own. Her hips pushed to speed his thrusting. Her hands urged his movements on. He reacted instantly to her silent message, pumped harder, faster. His breath accelerated in her ear; his muscles flexed, contracted under her fingers.

"Oh." She broke out in a sweat. He was driving her wild. She was getting so close. "Oh!"

Close. *Close.* She grabbed his shoulders, ground against him, aware he'd lifted to watch her, aware that nothing would stop her now. *"Oh!"*

The orgasm rocked her; the powerful wave swept her to a consciousness that included only feeling. On and on, surge after surge, she went with it, rode it, indulged it, reduced only to the pleasure in her body and the intensity of their sharing, of their intimacy.

She cried out his name; he tensed; his rhythm quickened, then he crushed her to him, groaning as his own climax hit.

They lay together panting, foreheads touching, still occasionally convulsing in delicious aftershocks, as if their bodies couldn't quite let the moment go, not just yet.

Not just yet.

Because as reality intruded further and further, a feeling of dread oozed in to pollute Amanda's bliss, and she didn't want to face it, didn't want to acknowledge its source.

"Am I squashing you?" he whispered.

"No." Yes. He was, even holding some of his weight off her, but she didn't care. He could have been so heavy that her breathing stopped and her heart stopped and her brain activity stopped, and she still wouldn't want him to move. She'd wanted to connect with him, lose herself in him, let him wipe away the panic and fear of the last few days. And in the process she'd gotten herself into trouble she should have seen coming a mile away. She loved him— and was guaranteed nothing in return.

He slid out of her, slowly, and rolled to the side, grabbed a tissue over his head from the, yes, *flowery* box on her end table and disposed of the condom before he settled back next to her and held her to him again.

"Amanda, this is not what I intended to happen when I showed up here today."

She raised her head to see his face, flushed and so handsome that her heart ached with it. "Me neither."

He pushed the hair back off his forehead and left his hand there, eyes warm but cautious. "I was going to *talk* to you. About us. About where we wanted this to go."

"I guess we answered that."

"Yes." He grinned and let his arm drop back over his head. "Temporarily anyway."

She tried not to let her expression falter, tried not to let her body stiffen. Here it came. The dread could have its day.

"Temporarily?"

She sounded as heartbroken as she felt.

"We still need to talk about the future." His voice was light and even; he stroked her cheek with the tip of his finger. "I won't make long-term promises to you, Amanda, that wouldn't be fair. I love that I'm with you today. That might be true for every day from now until forever. But tomorrow has a tendency to booby-trap me. I can't lie about that."

"Okay."

Ka-boom. Mushroom cloud. For one glorious impetuous moment, she'd fooled herself into thinking she could solve all her problems with sex. Okay, fabulous sex. But sex all the same. One glimpse of him and she'd buckled, gone right back to being Doormat Amanda, spreading her legs so fast they'd probably been a blur, making up reasons why she should take the path of least resistance once again.

For what? He'd been nothing but honest from the beginning, never offered anything but who he was. Mr. Temporarily. The never-grow-up guy with the sex-palace bedroom, ready to receive the female du jour. She'd known that, and she'd simply chosen to ignore it. Now she got to pay.

"Hey." He lifted her chin. "Don't look sad. What we've found together is amazing. Focus on what we have, not on what might go wrong."

She managed a wan smile. Don't worry, be happy and everything will be fine.

Whee.

In a moment of typical weakness, she'd turned to him as the one stable adult she could depend on in a world gone mad. A self-deluding mistake. Just calling him "her life-line" didn't make it so. The person she needed to learn to depend on was herself.

"Amanda." He lifted his head and kissed her. "I'm crazy about you. That's not going to change tomorrow."

"No." She laid her head back on his shoulder. Not tomorrow. But what about the next day? Or the day after that?

He stroked her hair, down onto her bare shoulder, tracing her arm. "So how are you doing with all this…insanity?"

"It was tough for a while." Her voice came out flat, and she hoped he'd attribute it to the fact that her mouth was buried in his neck. "But I did fine."

He grimaced up at the ceiling. "I wanted to be here to help. I know you must have needed support."

She frowned. Didn't he hear her? "I was fine. I did fine."

"I have to go to Green Bay in a few days to bring the boys back. Gwen's much better, but needs a little more time. That's only one day away, though, so I can be here for you while this is all still settling."

She lifted her head so he'd look directly at her. "I'm doing fine, Arch."

He brushed her hair back. "The strain has got to be hell."

Her temper rose. Yeah, okay, the strain *had* been hell. She'd been on such robotic autopilot that she hadn't even realized until she saw him how hard it had been. But she didn't want him or anyone to think of her as helpless. More to the point, she didn't want to *be* helpless, not anymore. "I can handle it."

His hand stopped moving in her hair; he lifted his eyebrows. "It's not a question of whether you're able to. People manage to die of horrible illnesses all by themselves just fine, but it's a hell of a lot nicer if someone's there to help."

She swallowed, remembering his mom. "Right. Okay."

He raised up to kiss her. "No worries, Ms. Manda. Be happy. We'll take it one day at a time."

She drew her fingers through her hair, resisting the urge to play with a strand for comfort. One day at a time. Was that what she wanted? Or would it be better to make a clean break and spare herself hanging on, wondering when and if he'd tire of her. She didn't know. The last week had been so frustrating; she'd struggled so hard to make sense of what was right, to understand what she really wanted, and hadn't come up with any answers.

One day at a time.

Cutting Arch out of her life would be the most painful decision she'd ever made. But then she hadn't made that many tough decisions—life just seemed to happen to her, and that was part of her problem. Avoiding pain wasn't enough reason to stay. Especially when she'd be facing pain much worse down the road if and when he got restless and wanted to move on.

One day at a time.

He cupped her head and brought it back down on his chest where his heart beat under her car and his scent was warm and strong and wonderful. While his arms were around her and he was holding her as if she was the most amazing woman he'd ever known, anything seemed possible.

One day at a time. She could do that. She guessed.

She just wasn't sure for how long.

"GOOD NIGHT, honey." Amanda kissed Clarissa's cheek and turned out her Pooh-bear lamp.

"Mom?" Clarissa lifted up onto her elbow, the rosebud bedspread falling off her thin shoulder. "I miss the boys. Are they coming back soon?"

"I think so, sweetheart." Amanda sat on her daughter's bed. "Arch said he'd be going to get them in a few days."

Clarissa's face lit up. "That'll be great! When school is out I can play with them all day long!"

Amanda grinned. A few weeks ago, her initial thought would have been that loud, aggressive boys were not ideal playmates for her daughter. But the boys were harmless... okay, as long as they were supervised. When she was Clarissa's age, she'd had no one to play with in her neighborhood at all. She should be glad Clarissa had company so close by. At least for the summer, until the boys went back to Green Bay.

Looked like those Williams men would be great company for both of them. Temporarily.

"Mom?"

"Yes, honey." She smiled down at her daughter, stroked the soft blond hair so like her own.

"You know Ralph, the jelly guy?"

"Mmm?"

"Ever since the day I sang that song and proved I wasn't scared anymore? Well, he still teases me, but nicely now." Clarissa beamed shyly. "I think he likes me."

"That's wonderful."

"Yeah." She nodded vigorously. "Arch is a smart guy. He taught me how to stand up for myself."

Amanda suppressed a smile at her words, which sounded suspiciously like a repetition of some adult interpretation of the event. True nonetheless. And a lesson Amanda was starting to think she needed to learn better for herself.

"Mom?"

Amanda laughed. "Ye-e-e-es?"

"Can I take baseball this summer? The Tosa Baseball League? Mark is going to. He seems kind of grouchy, but I think I can cheer him up. He laughs at stuff I tell him. And he's pretty fun."

Amanda pressed her lips together. "Your grandma wanted you to take ballet this summer."

"Ugh." Clarissa held her nose. "I'm not like you and Grandma. I hate prissy stuff."

Amanda tried to hide her wince. "You think I'm prissy?"

"Well, not all the time. Like when we were at Arch's party and you were playing the games, that was cool. But you took ballet, right?"

"Yes." She rolled her eyes.

"You didn't like it?"

"Not much."

"Why?" Clarissa sat upright and hugged her knees.

Amanda frowned. "Parts of it I liked. But I counted beats like a musician, I didn't *feel* the music like a dancer. And once we got *en pointe*, I was hopeless. I couldn't stay up there to save my life."

She chuckled, remembering the tall gazellelike girls, deftly pointy-pointying around on their little toes, and short Amanda feeling like a tottering buffalo.

"So you quit?"

"Yes. But I took it for six years."

Clarissa wrinkled her nose in horror. "Grandma made you take it for six years?"

Amanda laughed nervously. "She didn't *make* me."

"Well, if you didn't like it, why did you take it?"

"I guess because she wanted me to. It made her happy."

Clarissa frowned. "You didn't stick up for yourself."

"No." Amanda leaned forward and kissed Clarissa's forehead, feeling a little off balance. Clarissa might have gotten her looks from Mom, but the self-assurance was all Ridge. "I guess I didn't."

"So can I take baseball?"

"We'll talk about it later."

Clarissa groaned. "I hate when grown-ups say that. It always means no."

"It means we'll talk about it later. Good night, honey."

"Good night, Mom."

She blew Clarissa another kiss and walked out into the living room, smiling wistfully at the unaccustomed soreness between her legs. At the leaded-glass front window, she stopped and watched the sun setting behind the houses across the street.

Welcome to Make Amanda Feel Like a Wimp Day.

First, she gave in to the mere sight of Arch seconds after she'd resolved not to, even knowing that she could get carried away by exactly the wave of emotion that carried her away, and dropped her bang on her head when it receded.

Then her daughter pointed out, albeit innocently, that Amanda had been a doormat her entire life. A dutiful, obedient child. Doing what was expected of her, trying to please others.

She'd already decided she was tired of being a wimp. Tired of going through life worrying and cautious and letting people walk all over her. She just had to put her decision to change into practice.

Her mistake, brought on by the euphoria of her inheritance, had been thinking she could just decide to be different and it would happen. Money might be power, but it wasn't going to change who she was. Only she could do that. She'd have to work hard, take baby steps toward where she wanted to be. One change at a time.

Starting by facing something she hadn't wanted to face.

She took a deep breath and leaned her forehead against the diamond-paned glass, absently watching a Toyota just like hers, only a funny shade of green, pull up in front of her house. If she took charge of her life. If she called the shots and lived it the way she wanted to…then her uneasy decision to take things one day at a time with Arch, essentially letting him control the relationship, being in love with him, but knowing if he got bored, as was his pattern, he could end it at any time…that decision was uneasy for a reason.

It was the wrong one.

She was worth more than that. She wanted more than that. Commitment and eventually marriage. She had financial security; she wanted emotional security, too. When she gave her heart, it stayed given, didn't boomerang back. And Arch wasn't prepared to give that security to her, not now, and most likely not ever. He'd made that clear today.

Grow up, Amanda. Face the facts. Don't just drift along, pulled by what other people want or what feels good at the moment. Do what's right. For you. Choose a path and walk it.

A man got out of the car, his figure blurred by the sudden tears in her eyes. He was tall and familiar, wearing a dark suit. He came toward the house and looked up, saw her at the window and broke into a heart-stopping grin she knew as well as she knew herself.

Ridge.

CHAPTER ELEVEN

AMANDA WENT cautiously downstairs to let Ridge in, feeling as if she was starring in the wide-awake version of a very bizarre dream. After so many years of fantasizing this exact moment, first with joy, then anger, then dread, and finally relative indifference, it was just too strange to be living it.

She opened the door. He was older—of course, so was she—but still terrifically handsome, tall and elegant in his suit. She didn't think she'd ever seen him wear one. Certainly not at their wedding.

"Hey, Amanda Panda."

She grinned at the familiar nickname, which she'd actually always hated, but loved him enough not to care. Now with so many years passed, with all the pain and humiliation that had come out of their young love, the nickname seemed like a homage to the parts of one's life that never change.

She still hated it.

"Come in." She turned and led the way up the stairs, starting to think this *was* a dream. Everything around her existed in a strange combination of hyperdistinct and fuzzy. Details sprung out at her—dust on the stairs, a tiny gouge in the wooden railing. And yet her brain was having a lovely uninvolved freefall through space, unable to settle on any one thought or reaction or feeling.

Ridge was back.

She ushered him into the apartment, praying Clarissa had gone off to sleep instantly as she usually did, closed the door behind him and stared. He looked damn good. He hadn't put on weight, his dark nearly black hair was still thick and lustrous, his suit fit to perfection on his tall frame. More than that, he seemed more mature, more solid, more centered. His eyes didn't dart around the same way they used to; his hands hung still at his sides, no tapping foot. He didn't give off nearly the same amount of restless energy or spark.

Of course, he could just be terrified...

"You look incredible, Amanda."

"Thank you."

He did too, but if she told him so the atmosphere would get a little thick in here and it was plenty thick enough already. She crossed her arms over her chest, feeling eighteen again, young and uncertain next to him, remembering how desperately she'd loved him, how desperately he'd hurt her. "What are you doing here?"

He chuckled without humor, started to take off his suit jacket, then paused. "May I?"

She nodded, amazed he would ask, then even more amazed when he took it off, folded it carefully and laid it over the arm of one of her stained chairs. The old Ridge would have flung it to lie wherever it hit.

"Have a seat." She gestured to the armchairs and plonked down in one, unable to handle the weird symbolism of sitting with her old fiancé on the couch where she and Arch had been rolling in unbridled passion only hours ago.

Ridge loosened his tie, unbuttoned the top button of his shirt. "I'm not really sure how to do this. Do we chat impersonally for a while or just dive right into what we're both really thinking?"

Amanda shrugged, shoulders so tight they didn't want to go back down afterward. "I guess…just dive in."

"Why did I leave, why **h**aven't I been in touch and why am I back now?"

She looked down at her hands, which were gripping each other as if their only hope of survival was to hang together. "That would be about the size of it."

He leaned forward, arms on his thighs, training that intense, dark gaze on her that always turned her insides to mush. God, it was so eerie being with someone so familiar, yet someone who was really a stranger now. And her insides *still* reacted, damn them, though mush would be pushing it.

"I left because I panicked. We were too young to get married. It would have been a disaster. You know that, right?"

She nodded. "I know that."

"Okay." He let out a breath. Relief. "I wasn't old enough or mature enough to handle the consequences. I wanted to get back in touch with you, but every time I did, every time I picked up the phone, something stopped me."

He dropped his head to examine his tented fingers. Amanda waited, then realized she was supposed to ask what.

"What?"

He trained that magnetic gaze on her again. "I still had nothing to offer you. I vowed that I would work my ass off, become someone, and then find you and our daughter. So I could be a father she'd be proud of. And so you…so we could maybe…well, I knew I was taking a risk there, but I deserved the failure if it didn't work out."

Amanda blinked. This was Ridge? The guy who thought drinking an entire beer without stopping for breath was real achievement? "Wow. I'm…I'm…"

She stopped. Frankly, she hadn't a clue what she was.

"I finished college, transferred from UConn to Yale as a sophomore, put myself through law school at Boston University. I stayed in Boston, passed the bar on my first try and just took a job as an associate with Brennington, Blyer and Schultz, one of the top firms in the city.

"I know I must have put you through hell, but I went through hell, too, knowing you were here, that our daughter was here, and that I had promised not to come back until I was worthy, until I had a decent life to offer you. I got this job last week. That same day, I was in the bar celebrating and I saw you on TV. It was like a sign, Amanda. I knew I had to see you. And I had to see…"

"Clarissa."

"Clarissa." He cleared his throat, wiped apparent moisture from his eyes. "Is she here?"

Amanda's heart pulled back short of melting over his story and jolted into protectiveness for her daughter. She'd been honest with Clarissa about what happened to her father—or rather what her father had made happen to them. Clarissa didn't talk about him, rarely asked. For the past seven years, he essentially hadn't existed. How was this going to affect her?

"She's sleeping."

"May I…see her?"

Amanda went stiff. Then nodded. What was wrong with that? He wanted to see his daughter. Not as though he was suing for custody. This was one time when Arch's philosophy would be helpful. One day at a time. No, one hour at a…okay, minute. One minute at a time. She could handle each one as it came.

She led the way into Clarissa's night-light-lit room, trying not to feel as if she were leading a wild carnivore to a feast. Ridiculous. She had come to terms with Ridge's abandonment. He just wanted to look and he was entitled. Sort of. She guessed.

Ridge stood next to her, and side by side like real parents, they gazed down at their child, sleeping like a blond angel on her rosebud-strewn pillowcase.

Was there *any* air in this room?

"She's beautiful." His deep voice resonated all the way through her. The stiffness in Amanda's body grew more stiff.

"She was beautiful when she was a baby, too." Her voice came out low and harsh.

"I'm sorry, Amanda Panda." He sounded miserable; she glanced at him. Except for his fascinated gaze still fixed on his child, he looked miserable, too. "I can't change what's happened. I'm doing the only thing I can now, which is try to make it right."

She took a deep breath, held it. Then blew it out, waiting for control to set in. When it didn't, she realized she better say something anyway, because who knew when it would show up. "It's okay. I'm not angry."

She *was* angry. Livid. How could he leave her to raise a child by herself? Walk away from moral and ethical and physical and emotional and financial and God-knew-what-all responsibility? He had no clue what that took, what she sacrificed, how she'd had to live.

"I wouldn't blame you if you were furious."

She was, she *was*. Damn it. Why couldn't she tell him off? Why couldn't she tell anyone off? Not Ridge, not her mother, not the lady in front of her in the express lane with more than fifteen items. No one. "It's been hard, Ridge. That's all."

"I know." He put his arm around her waist, drew her against his side. "It was hard on me, too. I made poor choices and didn't own up to them. Until now."

She made a superheroic effort and brought her rage back under control. The man was already groveling. What point in blasting him? He'd screwed up big-time, he knew it, admitted it, and he'd paid a price, too. He didn't have to be here. She'd never tried to contact him, never insisted he come back. She should give the guy some credit.

He turned her toward him, took her shoulders gently. "I've missed you, Amanda. I haven't found anyone I've loved as much as I loved you. I was just…too young to know what I had."

Uh-oh.

His hands tightened, he pulled her close; she leaned stiffly against him, trying not to compare the sensation to the feel of Arch's body, the strength, the sense of security. She closed her eyes wearily. False security. Mr. Temporarily.

"Ridge…"

He slid to his knees, clasped her around the waist and looked up with the one thing she could never have imagined seeing on Ridge Nelson's face: humility. Utter vulnerable humility. "Can you forgive me?"

For one surreal second she expected an upwelling of string music in the quiet room. Ridge on his knees? Begging her forgiveness? How could someone like him change that much?

The next instant she chided herself. She was trying to change herself, too, and who knew whether she'd have as much success as he had. Besides, he'd have no reason to come all the way back here just to lie to her.

She should forgive him. She should. For Clarissa's sake. For his sake. And someday she'd probably figure out why for her sake, too.

"I forgive you, Ridge. It's all in the past. We were different people then."

He swallowed so hard it made a little squawking noise in the silent room; then he bowed his head, leaned it against her stomach. "Thank you."

She looked down at his thick dark hair and gave in to the impulse to touch it, remembering how it felt under her fingers when they were making love.

She frowned. Except his hair was coarser now, felt as if it had some gel in it or something.

"Amanda." He rose to his feet, clasped her close, pressed his cheek passionately to hers. Then drew back barely an inch, so they were face-to-face, nearly mouth to mouth. "Oh, Amanda."

She stood there, still bemused by this vulnerable earnest side of him she'd never seen, knowing he was going to kiss her, waiting curiously to see what it would be like, the way you waited at the beginning of a favorite childhood movie to see if it could still carry you away.

His lips were gentle, felt so familiar, tasted so familiar. So much of her past came back. Groping make-out sessions in the back of his father's Honda. Groping make-out sessions in the back of her mother's VW. Groping make-out sessions that eventually became teenage humping sessions, which led, not surprisingly, to the birth of her daugh—*their* daughter. Nice memories. Most of them. But as for the kiss, her heart had clearly become an uninvolved bystander.

She pulled away. "Ridge, I don't—"

"I'm sorry." He took a step back. "I don't know what I was thinking. But seeing you, seeing Alyssa…"

"Clarissa."

"Right." He grimaced, looking so embarrassed she felt sorry for him. "There's a girl in the apartment downstairs from me named Alyssa…"

"It's okay."

"Amanda."

What? She forced herself to smile politely. Okay, she was a little taut. "Yes, Ridge?"

"I've got some time before my job starts. I'd like to hang around for a few weeks. Get to know my daughter. And get to know you all over again."

His voice dropped into the last words. Husky, filled with promise.

She took a deep breath. *Whoa.* This was too much, too soon. Too soon after he arrived, too soon after she'd been with Arch. Yes, she'd just decided that she and Arch had to end whatever they'd barely started, but bouncing right into the arms of her ex wasn't exactly taking charge of her life.

However.

Clarissa should know her father. Not that Amanda would announce at tomorrow's breakfast table that hey, ho, Daddy was back and Clarissa should love him immediately. But if she got to know him, to like him first, then maybe...

Well, she should know her father. It wasn't up to Amanda to keep them apart.

"Clarissa should meet you. I'd like her to know you. But not as her father yet, Ridge. No offense, but I need some time to be sure you're not going to run out of here again and hurt her."

Breath blew out of Ridge in a huge gust, as if he'd been holding it and quietly turning blue in the darkness. "I understand. Thank you for the chance to prove myself. You won't regret letting me back into your life this time, Amanda. I promise you that."

She shifted beside him, edging away. He might want to give their relationship another try, but she couldn't pretend Arch didn't exist. Not when he was still such a huge part of her.

"You should know I...am just ending a relationship."

His gaze sharpened. "Was it serious?"

Amanda closed her eyes wearily, feeling the familiar pain of grief wash over her. "No."

"Oh, Amanda." His hand touched her shoulder. "It was for you. I can see that and I'm sorry."

Her eyes jumped open. Huh? The old Ridge would have said, "No kidding. Are we out of chips?" God, she'd been slavish. She'd thought that man was so perfect.

"I don't…think he's right for me."

"Then I'll stay."

She frowned up at his handsome face, lit gently by the night-light into eerie shadows. "Wouldn't you stay for Clarissa anyway?"

His face fell; he looked down, reached out his foot and touched it to hers. "Yes. I would. But if you and someone else were serious. I don't know. For one thing, I'd kind of hoped…you and I…I don't know. It wouldn't quite be the same."

She moved to him and gave him a long hug, feeling more like an older sister than a long-ago lover with sparks waiting to be rekindled. But maybe she had to start somewhere.

"Nothing's the same, Ridge. I'm not. You're not. So we either accept that and be defeated, or start over with what we have now."

"You're wonderful, Amanda. If our positions were reversed, I'm not sure I could have forgiven you this easily."

She buried her face into his thin-in-comparison chest, angry at the voice in her head shouting, "That's because you're not a wimp like I am."

Think positive, Amanda. Think new beginnings. Look on the bright side.

She wanted to roll her eyes. Listen to her. As if Arch were dictating into her ear.

Just when she'd decided she needed someone who could

offer stability and commitment, Ridge had come back into her life talking about wanting to get back together, talking about being a father to Clarissa. She wasn't sure she believed in the hand of fate. But at least Ridge had gotten to the point of committing until death did them part once, which was more than Arch had ever done. And yes, Ridge had run out on her, but he was right, they'd been too young, marrying for the wrong reasons. It seemed as if he'd done a lot of growing up. More than Arch ever had.

"I want to try for forever again, Amanda." He whispered the words into her hair and she shivered with the eerie feeling that he could read her mind. "It feels so right. When I saw you on TV, right then I knew it felt so, so right."

He kissed her again, but she pulled away when he started getting into it, trying not to let herself think of other kisses she couldn't help thinking of.

Who the hell ever would have thought that Ridgeway Nelson would represent maturity and stability? If miracles on that grand a scale could happen, a scale that would include the proverbial pigs flying and hell freezing over...

Then it was almost conceivable she might someday be able to remove Arch Williams from her heart.

ARCH LOOKED AROUND his apartment in satisfaction. He'd wanted the place at least mostly done before the boys got back and he'd made it. The home-movie theater was finished, complete with big-screen TV, pullout sofa, snack machine, gumball machine, soda machine. Paradise. He couldn't wait to show it to the kids.

A couple of rooms still needed paint. His bedroom needed new furniture. He did still have the set his father bought him for a college-graduation present. The movers could always bring that over from his condo. Nice pieces.

Decent quality. But his original plans for the room included a king-size bed, dark mirror on the ceiling, VCR and TV, mini-refrigerator, whirlpool tub...

Party central.

Except he couldn't bring himself to get the stuff. He'd made the plans with tremendous enthusiasm, done the research halfheartedly and stalled out completely when it came time to make the purchases.

Truth was, the playboy palace didn't appeal anymore. And he didn't have to look any further than upstairs to figure it out. He just couldn't see Amanda in there with him, though he wasn't exactly sure why. Not as if she was lacking in sexuality. Not as if he worried the room would put her off. It just seemed...

Arch scratched his head and grimaced.

Silly.

He sighed and slid down the wall to squat. And another thing. For a nice change, he needed to use his brain around Amanda instead of his manly parts. The second he got back from Green Bay, he'd done exactly what he told himself he wouldn't. Made love to her, not even bothering to take her to a comfortable bed, not even taking time to get to know her body's every last detail. Let alone make absolutely sure she was in a place where she could handle it.

But he didn't expect the rush of seeing her to be so intense that it blocked out all logic. And he certainly didn't expect that when he was inside her, he'd have to concentrate so damn hard to keep from telling her he loved her.

Danger. He had to pull away, let this all settle. Not jump in as he had too many times before, letting his feelings, his passion and his enthusiasm take him farther than he was meant to go. He couldn't tell her how he felt, couldn't tell her he loved her, when for all he knew, three weeks down the road he'd suddenly realize he didn't.

She'd already had one man let her down; he was desperate not to be the second, though his track record was pretty dismal. He and Amanda had talked some, but they needed to talk more, get their expectations on the mat, make sure she understood that he wasn't balking because he didn't want to commit to anything, but because history showed he couldn't honor that commitment. He wasn't going to screw this up. Amanda was way too important to him to take any risks.

The doorbell rang. He shoved himself back up the wall to standing and went to open the door.

Amanda. Flushed, eyes wide, lips full. His brain, which had been working just fine, thanks, shut down immediately and handed the controls to his lower half. He knew what those breasts looked like under her soft shirt, and what she hid under those clingy capris. He drew her against him, kissed her gorgeous mouth.

"Mmm. Hi. Is Clarissa in school?"

"Yes, but—"

"Good." He pulled her into his hallway and kissed her for real. He was pretty sure he could never ever get enough of kissing Amanda Marcus. And now that he'd been kissing her, his body was suggesting a whole lot of other things he'd probably never get enough of doing to Aman—

"I need to talk to you."

He stopped with his lips pressed against the smooth soft skin under her ear, drew back and studied her face. Something was bothering her. If he hadn't been under penis control he would have noticed. "Come in and—"

He was going to say, "sit," but the movers weren't due until the next day, and options were limited to the floor. "Your place?"

"No."

He studied her harder. Something big was bothering her. "Okay, not your place."

"Let's go somewhere."

"Children's Museum? The Domes? The zoo? The park?"

"No." She looked at him in exasperation and he started to get distinctly uneasy. Something was different about her. Some confidence, some determination. And while he would ordinarily celebrate that, since he'd been trying to unearth it for the last three weeks, for some reason this time he felt it like a brick wall keeping her away from him.

"I don't want to play, Arch. I want to talk to you."

He opened his mouth to point out there was no law keeping them from talking at the zoo, but in her current mood, that would be entirely the wrong thing to say.

"Right. Okay. I'll get my keys."

He pulled them off the counter in the kitchen where he'd chucked them earlier. He had a bad feeling about this. Bad. And he didn't do bad feelings.

The keys caught on his back pocket; he swore under his breath, shoved them in and made himself saunter back to the hall. *Chill, Arch.* No point trying to figure it out now or worry. She'd tell him. Then he could fix whatever it was. He hoped. "I'm ready."

They drove to a coffee shop on North Avenue in silence. Not companionable silence. Strained, jittery silence, which unnerved him further. He was tensing up, becoming anxious and irritable. He didn't like this feeling at all. The feeling that someone else could have so much power over his moods and his life. He'd left this tense, anxious, irritable person behind after his mother died, after he'd been able to get over his grief, live to be older than she'd been, and see that life held more than sadness and giving in to an inevitable decline. That you could fight and win, choose to make your life what you wanted it to be.

Who would choose *this?* This feeling of miserable vulnerability. Maybe this was why he avoided permanence in his relationships. The initial high of falling in love inevitably led to conflict, aggravation, dissatisfaction, pain. Who needed all that when life was so damn wonderful and full of joy without it?

He found a parking place and yanked up his brake, aware the cynicism functioned as armor, a protective defense against what he didn't dare acknowledge might be coming. Bad karma all around.

They got out of the car and filed into the café without looking or touching. By the time they got coffee, and sat opposite each other at a tiny square table next to the window, the tension was so thick it would take more than a knife to cut it.

Chain-saw tension.

And all she'd said so far was, "I want to talk to you." The most evil phrase on the planet.

"So what's up, Ms. Manda?" He tried to sound light and jovial but by now he was just dying to get this out on the table so he could deal with something concrete.

She swallowed a sip of coffee as if it were a ball of cotton. "Ridge showed up last night."

Wham. He held his cup and stared at her over the top of it. "*Ridge* Ridge?"

She nodded.

"As in 'For better or for—oops, see ya later'?"

She frowned and nodded again.

For one ridiculous second, he was madly jealous. Then relief flowed through him and he managed to get the coffee to his lips for a sip. No wonder she looked so upset. Must have been hell seeing him after all this time. "Why didn't you call me?"

She looked startled; her eyebrows crept up. "I didn't think you would have enjoyed meeting him."

He chuckled, then wondered why he was the only one who found that funny. "You didn't need help."

"No. I *didn't* need *help*."

Okay. Offering help was the wrong thing. He stared at her, trying to gauge her mood and she lowered her gaze to the table, a blush creeping up her cheek. His relief found itself staring at the end of a very short life. The plastic of his cup threatened to buckle under his grip. "He's still there. He spent the night with you. That's why you didn't want to talk to me upstairs."

Her anguished gaze lifted straight to his. "Oh no, Arch. I didn't...I mean, he stayed at my place, but only because we stayed up so late talking."

"Talking."

She nodded.

"Did he kiss you?" The question tore out of him and he nearly kicked himself. God, he sounded like a raging caveman.

She said nothing.

Jealousy blinded him, seized his body and brain so he wanted nothing more than to find this guy and beat the crap out of him.

Okay. Now he *was* a raging caveman.

"God, Amanda, we made love yesterday."

"No...*he* kissed *me*. I didn't...I felt nothing."

He took in a breath, fighting for control. Okay, he could see that. Affectionate kiss between old lovers. He could handle that. Maybe.

"What does he want?"

She bit her lip; he could see the wheels turning in her

head, see her choosing the words carefully. And if he thought the pain couldn't get any worse, he would have been wrong. "He wants you back."

"He wants to try."

"What do you want?"

"I...don't know."

He took another deep breath. Then another. She didn't know. "Is he staying with you?"

"No. I couldn't do that. He slept on the couch and left before Clarissa got up."

"Clarissa." He swore savagely. "He's her damn father."

"Yes." She was whispering, tears rising into her eyes. "He's coming back this afternoon to meet her."

Run. *Run.* The urge was so strong it was all he could do to stay in that café and in his damn chair. He wanted out. He was suffocating. He wanted out into the cool impartial infinity of space; he wanted to run until his muscles wouldn't run anymore, the way he'd run when his mom died, out the door of their house, methodically through the streets Forrest Gump–like until he simply had to stop or risk collapsing on the concrete.

"So what does this all mean, Amanda?" He was out of his mind. Furious, at himself, at her, at this jerk who showed up just when things were going so well.

"I don't know."

"You don't." He let out a burst of sick laughter. "Damn it, Amanda. How could you not?"

"Because there isn't a manual that goes with my life."

"But for God's sake, after yesterday..."

"What, after we had sex?"

He couldn't believe she'd say it that way. Like it was sex with anyone. Like it was physical relief and nothing more. Who was this woman? "I'd say it was a little more than just getting off on each other."

Her face turned red with anger. She was working up to something and he managed to emerge far enough from his own rage to want her to let it out.

"Say it, Amanda."

She lifted her eyes, and if he weren't so crippled by fear, he'd have cheered madly for the light and strength in them. "Okay, Mr. Temporarily. So I'm supposed to call it making love, is that it? Fine for you to hold back, but I'm supposed to act as if screwing you is something sacred that binds me to you for all eternity."

He glared at her incredulously. "Who is talking about eternity? We're talking about you making love—sorry, *screwing* me one afternoon and ditching me the same night for some louse ex-fiancé who happens to show up the minute you inherit billions of dollars."

"I'm not ditching you for *him.*"

"You're telling me there's nothing going on with this guy, no potential, nothing."

She bit her lip, withdrew. "I...don't know."

He rolled his eyes. "You don't know. When *will* you know?"

Shrug.

Arch swore and shifted in the seat so hard it gave an ominous cracking sound. "So I'm supposed to sit around and wait until you decide whether you want me or not?"

Her eyes flashed triumph. "Isn't that exactly where I was yesterday afternoon with you?"

Boom.

She had him.

KO'd in the first round.

Damn.

He put down his coffee, put his elbows on the table,

leaned his head onto them. Damn again. He wanted things simple. Neat. Manageable. This was unbearably complicated.

"Okay." He sat back in his chair, gripped the sides of the table. "I see your point."

"And?"

"And nothing. I can't control what you do with this guy, because I have nothing better to offer than right now. I don't believe in promising forever, Amanda. Anyone can open his mouth and say, 'I promise.' It's doing it that counts. Nothing is forever, for sure. Not life, not love, not anything. All I can give you is the certainty of right now, which may or may not last forever. And what I hear from you is that isn't enough."

"No." She lifted her head proudly, but he could see the pain in her eyes. "It's not."

"And you think this guy might be able to give you what you need."

"I...don't know."

"Do you *want* him to be able to give it to you?"

She hunched her shoulders; her hand crept up to fiddle with a lock of her hair.

"I see." He lifted his hand, let it slam down on the table so their coffee cups jumped. "He's Clarissa's father. It would be so perfect. Right? One joyful, happy-freaking-ever-after family reunion."

She clenched her jaw. "I think you're getting a little ahead of things, Arch."

"Really."

"I haven't decided if I want to pursue a relationship with Ridge."

"Pursue a relationship?" He laughed rudely before he could stop himself. "Now *that's* passionate. You sound like your mother."

"Leave my mother alone." Her voice rang out to the point where people in the shop started glancing curiously at them. Her eyes held his, not flinching, not looking away.

Damn it, she was glorious. But when she let the real Amanda out, she wasn't supposed to unleash her against *him.*

"Okay. That was low. I'm sorry."

He leaned back, stared at the ceiling, felt her hand clamp down on his jiggling leg. He gave her a painful half smile, which she answered in kind, looking so strong and beautiful that it hurt.

"My feelings for you haven't changed, Arch. But I can't just think of today. I have to think of Clarissa, of her future, and of mine."

"With the guy who ran away from you without a backward glance and stayed away seven years."

"He's back now. And he's changed, Arch. He's different. Older. More solid. More sincere. He's grown up."

Arch ignored the slight emphasis on "he" and shook his head. Even in the middle of this agony, he wanted to protect her. "People don't change that much."

"You did. You told me you were a serious kid."

"My mother was dying for two years. That'll take the giggles out of anyone."

She winced, closed her eyes briefly. "Well, he seems to have really changed. And he said he wanted to try again."

Arch nearly exploded in frustration. "But what do *you* want, Amanda? Ideally?"

"Ideally?" Her confident gaze turned miserable, hunted. "I'd want...*you* to be what I want."

"I can be." His voiced softened, threatened to shake. He leaned forward and willed her to listen to his words with her heart. "All you have to do is change the terms a little."

"No." Her gaze hardened. "I'm going to live life on my terms now."

His shoulders wanted to slump; he refused to let them. "Then I'm sorry. I am what I am. I can't change that."

"Yes, you can." She put a hand to her chest. "I'm changing. Ridge changed."

"You're not changing. You're finally finding out who you are." He grabbed her hands, felt the spark neither of them could control flare when they touched. "But come on, Amanda. This Ridge guy changed into what you wanted him to be right after you inherited two billion dollars. You don't want me, what I have to offer isn't enough? Okay. But be careful. Please, look before you jump."

"Like you do."

He dropped his head. Touché. Again. "Okay. Never mind."

"You don't know him at all, Arch."

"No. But my spidey sense is telling me there's something seriously fishy about his timing."

She inhaled, straightening her spine. Her chin lifted. She swallowed, withdrew her hands from his and folded them primly in her lap. Stared at him as if he were the rain on her child's outdoor birthday party. And shook her head.

And in that brief agonizing second, that one little shake of her gorgeous newly stubborn confident head, he knew that unless he took drastic measures, unless he managed to figure out where he'd gone wrong even as he'd tried so hard to do this right, unless he could win her back, convince her he loved her, show this gold-digging bastard up for what Arch suspected he was...

He was going to lose her.

CHAPTER TWELVE

HA! Amanda took the pink princess phone off her end table, unplugged it from the wall and dumped it into a box she'd bought from a mailing store. Someone would be glad to have it. Maybe some adolescent girl getting her first phone in her room. Not Amanda.

She took the crocheted doily that had been underneath it and dropped that into the box, too, watched it flop down forlornly over the phone. Double ha! Frilly crap! She was done with it. Forget even the pang of guilt thinking of her mother patiently tatting lace in her station wagon, waiting for Amanda to get out of ballet lessons. As of right now Amanda was a new person. Done with taking orders from anyone. Done with living her life the way anyone else wanted her to.

From now on it was her way or the highway.

Next! She stalked around the living room on a search-and-eliminate mission. Ceramic bride and groom supposed to go on her wedding cake, outta here! Pink flowered keepsake box with the words Things Most Precious. Garbage! Figurine of little girl lacing up toe shoes. History!

"And let's not stop with the small stuff, shall we?"

Into her bedroom. Rosy, cute bedspread, out! Matching sheets, so long! Rug with the picture of the terriers playing fetch, *good*bye!

Trip to the bed-accessory store coming up. Solids con-

trasted with decorative pillows. Or stripes! Or a bold geo-
metric design. Not a flower in sight. Not one!

And if she didn't like it? Toss it out and start over. She
was Amazon Amanda now. Money had given her power,
and she'd been holding back, overwhelmed, afraid to use
it.

Not anymore. The New Her was here to stay.

That fight with Arch yesterday had started it. She'd actually been able to get angry at him. To his face! What's
more, she'd scored points, stood her ground, made him see
her side, hadn't just gotten off one meek blast and then
cowered into apology for the next twenty-four hours.

Ha! She'd come back and told Ridge to find a hotel if
he wanted to stay here in town and get to know her. Told
him to come back after she'd had time to tell Clarissa a
friend was coming for an extended visit. And he had! Not
given her more than a look of mild surprise. Which she
couldn't blame him for. He thought she was still Old Wussy
Amanda.

Then when Clarissa had come home from school,
Amanda hadn't fretted forever, worrying about how she'd
sound when she tried to pretend Ridge wasn't Clarissa's
father. Nope! She'd sat down calmly and told Clarissa that
an old friend was visiting and they'd probably be seeing a
lot of him for the next month.

Clarissa hadn't blinked, of course. Though she and Ridge
hadn't exactly hit it off, at least at first. Ridge was charming
and funny—though he didn't have Arch's touch with
kids—but for some reason Clarissa resisted him.

Amanda shrugged and placed a pink-and-yellow angel
figurine into the box. She shouldn't put pressure on either
Ridge, Clarissa or herself. Clarissa would get to like him
in time. They had a month until Ridge's new big lawyer
job started in Boston. After that, they'd just have to see.

When it came time to worry, she'd worry. Now just wasn't going to be that time.

She paused at a painting of an English country house with massive garden her mom had gotten at someone's yard sale. As for Arch… He'd have to accept her terms now. She was going to see what happened with Ridge. Their relationship was comfortable and familiar. She felt on even ground with him, no longer the adoring eighteen-year-old intimidated by his dazzle. Though truth to tell, he hadn't much dazzle left. Especially compared to—

That thought she chopped right off. No point.

If nothing did happen with Ridge, if they never managed to recapture what they'd had, she'd be fine on her own. But no more playing victim. No more panting and whining on the sidelines until someone remembered to throw her a crust.

The painting went into the box. Next on her list after the apartment renovation was a trip to Europe with Clarissa. Paris, London, Rome… A mother-and-daughter adventure. No grandmas or ex-fiancés allowed. Though the idea of negotiating foreign countries on her own was a little daunting, she'd admit. But nothing ventured, nothing gained. If she stayed home, she'd never learn to cope.

Back in Milwaukee, she'd work on a business plan, bring out her cache of dress designs, find a location for her new shop. Contact the Pattersons and see if they'd like to come out of early retirement and work for *her!*

She lifted a lamp with an elaborate bouquet of roses and lilies painted on the frosted glass. "Amanda Liberty! Free from oppression! No longer a huddled mass yearning to breathe—"

The doorbell cut her off. She put the lamp in the box, caught herself creeping to the window to peek, marched firmly downstairs and opened the door.

Her mother. Who'd left two messages since yesterday and Amanda hadn't called back. Not even to let her know that Ridge had shown up. Oops.

"Hello, Amanda."

"Hi." She stood at the door, waiting for her mother to brush past her and start telling her what to do.

"I…brought over some upholstery samples." Her mom held up a wad of fabric swatches and Amanda didn't need to look far to see flowers, flowers, flowers, and then for a change, more flowers. "I thought we could look them over together."

Deep breath in. Deep breath out. *Okay, Lady Liberty, let's see if this is just talk, or if you can really do it.*

"Come on up, Mom." She marched upstairs ahead of her mother. "Sorry I didn't call you back, but with Ridge Nelson here…"

She waited for the gasp and the cry of "Ridge?"

"Yes, I heard he'd come back."

Amanda stopped and turned on the stairs. "You did?"

Her mother nodded, still looking strangely hesitant. "Sonny told me."

A blush rose up Maude's cheek. Amanda's eyes bugged out. "Sonny? As in Arch's father?"

"Yes…I…he came over to…do some work on the apartment."

"Oh." Amanda laughed. "For a second I thought—" She broke off. Absurd.

"What did you think?" Her mom was still using that strange flat tone and it was making Amanda very uneasy.

"Nothing."

"That I was involved with him?"

Amanda shrugged. No way was she touching that one.

"He's…not what he seems to be. In fact, I'm…starting to think I'm not either." Maude gave a high embarrassed laugh that didn't sound like anything Amanda had ever heard coming out of her.

Amanda's mouth dropped. What the hell was she hearing? This was too entirely bizarre.

"Well." Maude started climbing the stairs as if she'd just returned from her foray into Not-Herself-Land. "I hope you'll send that idiot Ridge Nelson packing. I think he's caused you quite enough—"

A gasp at the sight of Amanda's pillaged apartment. "What are you doing?"

"Redecorating." Amanda drew herself up, arms crossed defiantly over her chest, telling the nagging fear and guilt in her body to get the hell away from her. She was twenty-five. Time to stop living in fear of her mother's reaction to her every move.

She stepped forward firmly and ran her hand over the back of the ruined sofa. "I'd like to redo the couch in multicolor stripes. Or maybe just black with colorful pillows. And I want new art, maybe some modern stuff. I want the place to reflect who I am."

She put a slight emphasis on "I." Not enough to be in-your-face rude, but so her mom would get the message.

Her mother's face took on a pained expression; she walked over to the end table, clutching her upholstery samples, and trailed her fingers over the empty space where the doily used to be. "Well. Good for you. Where have you put everything?"

Amanda gestured to the overflowing discard box. Her mother approached it as if she'd just discovered a family member's body bludgeoned to death, and pointed to the flowery lamp Amanda Liberty had used to receive the tempest-tossed.

"That was my mother's."

Amanda swallowed. "I wasn't going to throw anything

away without asking, Mom. If you want it back, you're welcome to it.''

Her mom picked up the lamp, traced the roses and lilies lovingly.

"It was her favorite. She used to sit in that chair.'' She pointed to the water-stained floral armchair. "She'd turn on this lamp and put on her glasses and darn socks, or read the Bible.''

Amanda suppressed a growl. *Just lay on the guilt a little thicker, why don't you?* "I'm sure your mom would like knowing you love it so much. I think you should have it.''

Her mother nodded, cradling the lamp like a baby she'd found abandoned in a landfill. Her eyes swept the apartment, the walls bare of the art she'd sent, the box with the bedspread and sheets she'd given Amanda clearly visible in the doorway to the bedroom.

Amanda's stomach churned. *Guilt!*

No! She shoved it away. Ruthlessly. She didn't want a little-girl flowery bedspread. She wanted the room to look like her. Not her mother's version of who she was. She was doing the right thing.

"Well.'' Maude put on a strained smile. "I guess you don't need me, then.''

Ouch. The woman was a champ. "I'm doing fine, Mom. Thanks for wanting to help.''

"You're welcome.'' She looked around again, aimlessly this time, as if she was lost and had given up hope of being found. "Maybe I could take you and Clarissa out to dinner this weekend?''

"You don't need to do that, Mom. I can treat. I've got all—''

"Then what *will* I do?'' Her mother's voice rose to a near wail.

Amanda nearly recoiled. Nearly receded into mute horror

the way she always did on those rare occasions when her mom got emotional. Nearly.

Instead, she managed to face her mother calmly. "Live your life, Mom."

Tiny emphasis on "your."

Her mother stifled a gasp. For one fraction of a second, it looked as if her face would crumple. Then she swept it blank and drew herself up. "Yes. Good idea. I've been in the way too long, I can see that."

"Mom…" Amanda's head started throbbing.

"No!" Maude lifted a perfectly manicured hand. "You're right. I won't bother you anymore."

She swept out of the room and down the stairs. Closed Amanda's front door a little too hard, and practically burned rubber driving off.

Amanda stood in her half-torn-apart living room, eyes closed, the scent of her mother's French perfume lingering. Her stomach churned up more acid; her head traded throbbing for pounding. Was the stunning victory of total self-actualization supposed to feel this terrible?

Maybe she just wasn't used to it. Maybe she needed a little more time…

The phone rang.

She steeled herself the way she'd had to do all week long when it rang, chanting in her mind, "It's not Arch, so don't think it is," to keep her traitorous hopes from rising.

It was probably her mother calling on her cell. Either playing it haughty and accusatory, or limp and lifeless. Either way it would be some manipulative ploy to make Amanda look like the bad guy.

Okay, she'd come this far, she had to stay tough now.

She braced herself, trying very, very hard not to let the tension ratchet her back down to her usual wimpy Amanda self, and picked up the phone.

"Is this Amanda Marcus?" The deep, throaty female voice was unfamiliar.

"Yes." She rolled her eyes, not very secretly relieved it wasn't her mother. Which paper or magazine or local TV show this time?

"This is Natalie Canter, your half sister."

Amanda blinked. *Uh-oh.* The half sister. As in the legitimate daughter of Jennifer Canter. The one who didn't get the two billion dollars. Her lawyer had mentioned this might be trouble. "I—"

"Jennifer Canter was my mother." Under the friendly politeness, her voice was faintly hostile and defensive. Not that Amanda could blame her. Quite a shock after your mother died to find out she had another child who'd now get all her—

"I'm coming to Milwaukee next week. I'd like to come see you."

Amanda froze. How should an Amazon handle this one? Slam the door in her face? Declare her too late? Tell her to contact Amanda's lawyer and that Amanda had nothing to say to her? After all, it wasn't Amanda's fault Natalie hadn't been able to get along with their mother. Not Amanda's fault Jennifer Canter had left her billions to an illegitimate daughter Natalie didn't even know existed. Not Amanda's fault Natalie had been cheated out of her inheritance, betrayed unknowingly by the woman who'd raised her, her own flesh and blood....

"I...um..."

"I know you must be busy. I'm sure it's been quite an adjustment."

Natalie's voice made it clear it was an adjustment Natalie herself would like to be making.

Amanda put her hand to her head, got a fistful of hair

and squeezed until her arm started trembling. "Thanks. I'm managing so far."

"Good for you." Natalie's voice was softer, gentle, slightly husky. "You know, it's funny talking to you. I actually always wanted a sister."

Amanda sighed and sank onto her soon-to-be-not-floral armchair. The woman was her sister. She must have been through hell. What was the point of being hostile to her? Of telling her to get lost when she had a right to be in touch? Amanda didn't quite have this Amazon stuff down. When to use it, when not to. She was still figuring it out. Still trying. Still groping her way.

She sighed again and let go of all but one lock of hair, which she let herself start twirling between her fingers.

"I always wanted a sister, too."

MAUDE MARCUS LEANED closer to the mirror in her room, carefully applying another layer of under-eye concealer. She had a date that night with a gentleman she'd met in her building. A Mr. Sherman. He seemed very nice, a promising candidate for the top-drawer gentleman romance she wanted, and was taking her to a Milwaukee Symphony concert, which she deemed an auspicious beginning.

The fact that she didn't seem to be looking forward to it wouldn't stop her. Because when things got rough, if you let anything stop you, you might as well give it up entirely. That was how she operated. The tougher it got, the harder she smiled, the more she was admired and the easier it got. Sit home brooding, or worrying about who you were and what you wanted, and you might as well enroll yourself in therapy for the rest of time.

Just. Keep. Going.

Amanda had never really rebelled in high school, if you didn't count getting herself knocked up by that ass Ridgeway Nelson. Who, even if he seemed to have gotten his life back in gear, seemed ready to take responsibility for things he should have taken responsibility for seven years ago, she would bet was still an ass. She had a pretty good idea what he was after, appearing right after Amanda inherited. He wasn't any more right for her now than he'd ever been before—but that wasn't up to Maude. Apparently nothing was up to Maude anymore. Apparently Amanda's adolescent rebellion was going on now, at an age when mothers and daughters were finally supposed to get close.

Maybe this Mr. Sherman…what was his first name? He'd introduced himself as Hank. Maybe Henry Sherman had an unmarried son Amanda's age. Of course, Arch was already in love with Amanda. Maude had come to like Arch. Maybe Amanda would have the sense to pick the right man this time.

She finished with the under-eye concealer and straightened to check the results. Her eyes stared back, tense and hard, but now they had big light circles under them instead of dark ones.

So, she wasn't at her best. They played orchestra music in dim light. And one of her and her second husband George's favorites was on the program, Samuel Barber's *Adagio for Strings*.

She went into the living room to get her good jewelry, which she hid in the gas fireplace under the fake logs in case burglars got in. The roses Sonny had brought were drying, drooping in their vase on the mantel, ready to throw away, but she couldn't quite bear to. She missed him in a strange way. He'd been horribly busy scrambling to finish the renovations of Arch's apartment on time, before the boys got back. But he called fairly frequently. She'd gotten to like the sound of his voice.

Except he'd stopped calling after she told him about the

date with Mr. Sherman. Not that she blamed him, really. Except…well, she missed him. That was that.

Maude pulled out the tiny flat tin box she kept her best things in, a box that once contained imported French truffles, and pulled out a diamond necklace Bruce had given her for their twentieth anniversary. So thoughtful, Bruce had been. Not big on spending time together, but he'd made up for it with gifts and cards on every occasion. Never missed a one.

The buzzer rang. She put the necklace on hastily, buzzed Mr. Sherman in and did one last quick check in the mirror. She hated days when she looked her age. Today was one of them.

A loud authoritative knock; she opened the door with a smile to the sight of her escort's handsome face and impeccable dress and felt nothing but disappointment.

Mr. Sherman was going to bore her to death.

Three hours later, sitting at the concert in Uihlein Hall, she was unhappy to say that her initial judgment had been correct. They'd chatted up the usual topics over dinner at Eagan's before the concert. The food was excellent; he was an intelligent, lively and charming companion. The Milwaukee Symphony was superb, the program intelligently planned. But she couldn't help feeling she'd done this all before, too many times. She couldn't help feeling as if she needed someone to talk to about what had happened today with Amanda.

And she couldn't help feeling as if there was only one person in the world who would really understand.

The Barber piece came on. Strings only, a melody of such quiet, grave and heartbreaking beauty that she was horrified to feel tears pricking at the back of her eyes.

Just. Keep. Going.

The music swelled, rose and fell, lifted again and built

to a gentle climax that tore her heart. The tears spilled over. A sob burst from her throat. Then another. Then a steady stream of them, threatening to choke her.

Mr. Sherman glanced at her uneasily, and her tears very nearly turned to hysterical laughter. Ladies were not supposed to burst out sobbing on a first date. No doubt the poor man was horrified.

"'Scuse me." She grabbed for her jacket, her purse. "I'm g-going home."

He made to rise and she put her hand on his elbow and shook her head. "N-no."

She fled the hall, ignoring the annoyed or concerned looks of patrons whose knees she had to climb over while the piece was still going on. There was only one thought in her head: to get to Sonny.

In the lobby she threw herself on the mercy of a box-office employee for a phone book, which she scanned for Sonny's address with a shaky finger. Then stabbed triumphantly—there.

Taxi next, took forever to find one, for God's sake, what kind of city was this? And then the long ride to West Allis during which she needed to cry more but couldn't bear to let it out in front of the driver.

They pulled up in front of a modest bungalow. She got out, flung too much money into the front seat, hurried up to the door clutching her purse and leaned on the bell.

He came to the door. She knew he would. A man like Sonny would never let her down. He'd always be there when she needed him. A man like Sonny would never let her run away crying from a symphony concert without following her to make sure she was okay.

"Maude." The look of concern in his eyes nearly broke her heart. He drew her inside, closed the door behind her and took her into his arms, enveloping her so she felt nearly absorbed into him. She lost it then, comfortably and safely, wetting his T-shirt, streaming silly makeup onto its cotton softness. She cried until it was time to stop, that strange indefinable moment when her body simply told her, "Enough."

He pulled a strong clean handkerchief out of his pocket and tenderly wiped her tears, let her blow her nose, and didn't flinch taking it back, full of her grief.

"Tell me."

"Amanda's…redecorating." She let out a rogue sob, feeling old and absurd and utterly superfluous.

All he did was wince and nod, but she realized to the core of her being that he understood what she meant without her having to say another word. And that thought brought her such unutterably lovely peace that she could barely stay standing.

"Sonny."

"Yes, sweetheart." He pushed back her ruined hair, tenderly, lovingly. As if she was something so rare and precious he didn't dare touch her any other way for fear of damaging her.

"I…seem to be in love with you."

He grinned, that slow, wonderful toothy grin. "Yeah?"

She laughed, tearing up again. "Yeah."

"I've loved you since the second I laid eyes on you. In the driveway at Arch's place."

"Oh, Sonny." She nearly felt teenage again, falling in love with Bruce. Or in her prime, falling in love with George. Except this was so much deeper, stronger, so much more sure, she wasn't certain now that she'd really been in love either of those times.

He drew her close again and kissed her, a long hot hard kiss that would have made her cry again from the power of it, except that instead, a furnace started inside her, one that hadn't been stoked in a long, long time.

Then this small man with powerful shoulders lifted her up into his arms as if she was a young girl, and without asking her permission or uttering a word, walked up the stairs.

And Maude Marcus, age sixty-three and madly in love for the very first time, wound her arms around his strong thick neck and simply let him.

CHAPTER THIRTEEN

"SO, CLARISSA." Ridge got up from Amanda's sofa where they'd been sitting, chatting and making Amanda restless, and crossed to the dining-room table where Clarissa was drawing. He slapped her gently on the back, grinning. "Would you like to go down by the lake and fly kites again today?"

"No, thanks." She capped a purple marker and selected a blue one without even glancing at him. "We couldn't get them off the ground."

"Well." He chuckled nervously. "It's windier today. If at first you don't succeed and all that."

"I don't think so. I'm drawing."

"Oh, what is that a picture of?" He pointed to her work, then raised his hands. "No, wait. Don't tell me. I know."

Clarissa lifted her eyes from her paper and looked at him as if it was his last chance to prove he wasn't a total loser. "What?"

"It's a...princess. Here." He jabbed his finger on the paper. "And this is her beautiful daughter. And this is the prince, who has just rescued them and is going to marry the princess and live in her castle. Right?"

He winked at Amanda, who managed a smile back while her stomach lurched. Married? *Her* castle?

Clarissa sent him a look of seven-year-old contempt, which Amanda knew, could be a withering experience. "*So* wrong."

Ridge withered. "Okay. What, then?"

"She's a princess *warrior* and that's her teenage super-hero daughter and that isn't a prince, it's a mutant soldier of death and the mother and daughter just killed him with stun power and laser-heat vision. See the blood?" She gestured emphatically to a giant pool of red.

"Oh." Ridge cringed. "I thought that was his noble, princely cape."

Clarissa rolled her eyes and went back to her drawing.

Ridge glanced at Amanda, who tried to smile encouragingly while she wanted to say, *"Pack it in, Ridge."*

He gave her a thumbs-up. "So, Clarissa."

She didn't lift her head. "What."

"Why did the turkey cross the road?"

"How should I know?"

"Clarissa…" Amanda sounded the mom-warning.

"I'm sorry." Clarissa looked disgusted rather than contrite. "Why did the turkey cross the road, Ridge?"

Ridge clapped his hands and spread them apart. "To show he wasn't chicken!"

Clarissa put down her marker. "Yeah, I heard that one. It's funny."

Ridge's face fell. Amanda winced. He was trying way, way too hard; it was even irritating her. "Would you like some tea, Ridge?"

"Sure. I'll help you." He left Clarissa with obvious relief and joined Amanda in the kitchen where she was filling the kettle. "Tough crowd."

"She's just a little shy." Which was true, sort of. Except with people she liked. "Give her time."

"Yeah. Okay. I'm just kind of impatient, I guess. I dreamed so many times of having my family back…"

Amanda smiled at him, though a tiny little nasty part of her couldn't help hearing Arch's voice. If she and Clarissa were such dreams come true, why had it taken seven years for him to make his appearance? Why not let her and her daughter share in his troubles for that time, the way families were supposed to? Bad times and good. And okay, yeah, why *did* he show up right after she inherited?

She sighed. Unfair. The male ego insisted he not return until he was able to provide for them. Come back having slain the dragon or not at all. Not that she and Clarissa needed supporting now. Except emotionally.

It was just the strain. She was feeling the effects of all the changes—calls from the press were still rolling in, now she had this Natalie woman to deal with, her lawyer was telling her to hang tough, Ridge was telling her to marry him, her mother wasn't speaking to her—and Arch…she hadn't seen him for almost a week, even though the renovations were done and he was officially living downstairs. It was killing her.

She got down the Darjeeling tea bags and two mugs. She really should get a teapot. She'd even fallen in love with one at Mayfair Mall when she'd been there trying—unsuccessfully—to find new things for the house. Funky cats in teal and purple and orange. She'd been in a strange mood, nothing appealed and everything appealed, she'd settled on nothing, and gotten so grumpy she hadn't even felt like buying the teapot. Not even a thirty-dollar teapot she could throw out if she decided she didn't like it. She'd have to work on this. Go out and buy a yacht or something.

"So are you going to buy a new house?"

Amanda blinked. "Eventually."

"Remember that cottage in Maine? Where we were going to have our honeymoon?" He lowered his voice, put his arm around her waist. "With the skylight in the bedroom? Remember how we were planning to stargaze, after…"

She nodded, willing the memory to seem warm and fuzzy, picturing the bed they'd been so excited about in the brochure. But the memory didn't get warm and fuzzy until in her imagination the body next to her wasn't Ridge.

"You could *buy* that place now. Or one like it. Or one even better."

The kettle whimpered, crescendoed and screamed. She lifted it off the stove and poured water into the mugs, wishing Ridge wouldn't spend quite so much time talking about how she could spend her money. She really, really didn't want Arch to be right about Ridge. She wanted something that seemed honest and real and right to turn out that way.

Unfortunately, as the days dragged by in Ridge's company, it seemed more and more likely that this lovely dream of reuniting with her first love, of giving Clarissa a father in blood as well as name, was not going to work.

She sighed. It was a nice dream, though. And all was not lost, not completely. A few times when she'd been looking into Ridge's eyes she thought the chemistry was still there, struggling up through all the years of hurt and betrayal. She should give it a little more time before she—

Her doorbell rang; three quick buzzes. Feet pounding up the stairs.

Her heart jumped up from the nap it had been taking all week and started to boogie.

"Hey, Mom, it's Arch!" The sound of a dining chair being shoved back and Clarissa's feet running to the front door. "Hey, Arch!"

"Hey, Rissa."

Clarissa let out a squeal; Amanda imagined him swinging her around. She set the timer for five minutes for the tea and put the tea bags away, resisting the impulse to run out and greet him. They hadn't exactly parted on lovely terms after their last meeting. Though her heart didn't seem to be able to hold a grudge.

"That's him, I gather. The guy you were seeing."

Amanda glanced nervously at Ridge, shocked by the dark expression on his face. Wow. So he hadn't turned into a total kitten. "Yes. How did you know?"

He shook his head grimly. "Never mind."

"Okay." She pushed past him into the living room, half realizing it was rude to walk out on him like that, and then fully realizing she didn't care, she just wanted...

Arch.

At the sight of him, she stopped, unsure of her reception.

He stood in her doorway, hand on his hips in his larger-than-life way, wearing his signature jeans and a T-shirt that said, He Who Dies With the Most Toys Wins, eyes wary but unmistakably warm. "Hey, Ms. Manda."

"Hi, Arch." Her voice came out a throaty croak, same as his. Oh, Lord! She adored the guy. It would take all her energy to remind herself that adoring him didn't make it the right relationship for her. "Did you have a good trip?"

"Yup. Boys had a great visit with their mom, but they're okay back here, enjoying the new digs downstairs."

"I bet. I'd love to see the place." She bit her lip, mind racing, realizing what she was offering, then stopped caring about that when he grinned and her mouth decided to grin back, and their eyes caused all those wonderful sparks to happen, even standing on opposite sides of the room and *why* had she thought being with him was a bad idea?

Ridge stepped out from the kitchen to stand beside her, and Arch's wonderful grin instantly went stale.

"You must be Ridge." He crossed the length of the room in his energetic strides and shook hands.

Next to him, Ridge looked thin and lifeless, ill at ease

both in his fancy fashionable clothes and in his own body. "Hello."

"Ridge and I were just going to have a cup of tea." She winced at the image. Tea at four o'clock. Her mother and father. Her mother and George. Ridge and Amanda. *What was she doing?* "Would you like some?"

"Actually, Dad and I are taking the boys to the zoo. Wanted to see if Clarissa would like to come."

"Oh, cool! Mom, can I? Can I?"

"Well...sure." She turned to Ridge, feeling panicked and desperate. "The zoo sounds fun. Would you like to go, too?"

"To the *zoo?*" He appeared to catch himself and sent her an intimate smile. "I'd—rather stay here. With you."

Amanda sent a nervous glance to Arch and was treated to a view of what he looked like when he wanted to maim someone.

It was so pleasant being a guppy in a shark tank.

She caught her own thought and censored it. Wait a second. She wasn't a guppy anymore. Right? She was Amazon Amanda and she knew what she wanted and how to get it. Right? And what she wanted was not to be at Arch's beck and call, not to be seduced into falling back into his arms, into the false security of right now with no thought of tomorrow.

Right?

Her head started to pound. No. What she wanted was to go to the zoo with Arch and Clarissa and have a wonderful time, not sit here drinking tea with someone she'd never fall back in love with in a million years.

Aw, hell.

"You go ahead, Clarissa. Ridge and I will have our tea and then I need to go shopping." She emphasized the word *need.* If she couldn't get herself to decide on something for her apartment soon she was going to "need" an apartment with padding.

"Excellent!" Clarissa jumped up and down. "Thanks, Mom!"

"I can go shopping with you." Ridge opened his arms wide. "I'm at your service."

"No, thanks." Amanda smiled tightly. "I'm going by myself."

Ridge's eyebrows drew together in that pouty expression he always put on when he didn't get his way. "Okay, Amanda Panda."

She gritted her teeth. This panda stuff had to stop. "And Ridge?"

He cocked his head and sent her an affectionate smile. "Yes?"

"Don't... Don't..." Her head pounded harder.

"Don't what?"

The phone rang. She squeezed her eyes shut, took a deep breath and answered it.

"Hello, Amanda, dear, it's Mom."

"Mom?" Her mother sounded nothing like herself. She sounded...giddy. And there was yelling in the background. Was she drunk? Had Amanda driven her to it? *Guilt.* "Are you okay?"

"Of course, dear, never better. Sonny and I picked up the boys, we're all crammed in the van waiting down here for Arch and things are getting ugly. Maybe it's better he rides with you?"

"I'm not going. You're with Sonny?"

Her mom giggled. Amanda couldn't quite grasp it. Giggled? Her mother? "Sonny and I are an item, can you believe it? Why aren't you coming today?"

"Sonny? And you?" She looked over at Arch, who was

grinning broadly until Ridge's hand came to rest on her back and his grin changed to a scowl.

Ridge started massaging her shoulders. "Are you okay?"

She shrugged him off, still holding Arch's gaze.

"I'm in love, Amanda, dear. Madly. He's the most amazing man I've ever met. And a tiger in the bed—"

"Sonny Williams?"

Her mother made a sound of impatience. "Get a brain, dear. I'm not saying it again. Now, why aren't you coming?"

"Is that your mom?" Ridge murmured into her ear.

Amanda nodded impatiently. Arch glowered at Ridge. Her mom giggled again. The boys yelled in the background.

"Mom, Ridge and I are staying here for a cup of—"

"Oh, God, that little weasel isn't still around, is he? Lose him, he's not right for you."

"Can I say hi?" Ridge whispered.

Amanda shook her head. "Mom, I—"

"In fact, let me tell you what I've always thought of him—"

Ridge took the phone out of her hands and put it to his ear. He got out the "h" sound of "hi" and stopped, listening, a look of horror growing on his face.

Amanda closed her eyes. Put her hands to her jackhammering temples.

Warm hands closed over her upper arms. "You okay?"

She opened her eyes to Arch's concerned face. She was vaguely aware of Clarissa urging Arch to come downstairs, vaguely aware that an animated discussion was ensuing between Ridge and her mother, and acutely aware that her headache was diminishing and warmth enveloped her body as if a down comforter had been spread over her.

"Come to the zoo with us."

"I can't."

"Why?"

She hunched her shoulders; the headache gave a throb. "I don't want to."

His eyes went cold. He glanced at Ridge; dropped her arms. "I see."

She stood in silent misery. Why did doing the right thing have to hurt so much? She wanted to yell to him that it wasn't Ridge. Not anymore, probably never had been. It was just her, and this need to be sure, to be strong, to be right about something she chose to do.

He turned abruptly. "Come on, Clarissa, let's roll."

Clarissa danced ahead of him down the stairs; the door shut behind them; Ridge hung up the phone.

"Your mom is a real spitfire."

"Yeah." A spitfire who had sounded happier than Amanda had ever heard her sound. Happier and freer. Which was about as opposite to what Amanda felt right now as you could get.

"So." Ridge rubbed his hands together, watching her nervously. "How about that tea?"

She went to the kitchen to get the damn tea so she could sit there in her living room with a man she didn't love and think about one she did. She'd made all the right moves. The right choices. She was on her way to becoming a stronger person. Strength was freeing, right? Power? Knowing herself?

So why, when she'd done the right thing not allowing Arch to waylay her carefully planned afternoon with one of his of-the-moment play dates, when she'd hung tough and chosen her own path—why did she feel nothing but miserable and trapped?

"UNCLE ARCH?"

"Yeah?" Arch turned his head from the latest episode of SpongeBob SquarePants and stuffed a potato chip into his mouth. Then an M&M. Then another potato chip. Beside him, Mark ate M&M's exclusively and Luke chips. Only John shared his enthusiasm for alternating salt and sweet.

Except enthusiasm seemed to be missing. For anything.

"Can we go to the park?" John laid his warm little hand on Arch's forearm.

Arch shook his head. "Not today."

"Why?"

"It's going to rain."

Luke scowled. "It always rains around here."

Arch shrugged and tousled his hair. "Weather's not up to me, my man."

"Shh." Mark held up his hand. "I want to hear this."

All heads turned back to the giant screen. Another potato chip. Another M&M. The apartment was finished. Everything was unpacked. Arch had sent back the line edits for *Corporal Wedgie's Trip Through Your Guts.* Hadn't been motivated to start anything new. Hadn't been motivated to do much of anything since Lawyer Boy showed up and Amanda suddenly decided she was so strong she didn't need him anymore.

She had something much better. The father of her child. A mature and solid and forever kind of guy. Miraculously cured of his phobic tendencies. The ones Arch at least was honest about.

Gold-digging phony. Showed up out of nowhere after seven years the second Amanda inherited a fortune, and she treated him like the Prodigal Son, letting Clarissa "know her father."

Know her con man more like it. Just looking at the

sleazeball made Arch want to alter the appearance of the man's perfect white teeth. Leopards couldn't change their spots. He'd walked out on her seven years ago, walked out on his promise, hadn't even bothered to find out how his daughter turned out, and now he was suddenly mature?

Sorry. People didn't change that much.

He got so upset, he ate two M&M's in a row. Now what? Two chips? Or go back immediately to alternating and live with the imbalance?

He drew his hands over his face and lodged them in his hair, greasy chip crumbs and not-in-your-hands melt be damned. Nuts. He was jealous as hell. This man had once promised Amanda permanence. Showed every sign of gearing up to promise it again. Granted, he hadn't delivered seven years ago, but he was sure as hell making every effort to do it now. Never missing an opportunity to touch her. Making pointed references to their shared past. The creep had been here a week and Arch had seen Amanda all of once.

Okay, so maybe he'd been down here sulking a lot. Throwing himself into his renovations and the move to avoid the whole situation. But he wasn't going to enter some duel for Amanda's favors. If she wanted him, she could have him. Hell, maybe the guy *was* on the level, though Arch sincerely doubted it.

But what did Arch have to offer to compete? He wasn't Clarissa's father. He wasn't dangling memories or planning a lifetime together; he didn't have a conservative grown-up job. He wrote toilet humor and turned his apartment into Playworld. Though Amanda would probably like what he did with the bedroom.

Maybe she *should* marry Ridge. Money could be a pretty powerful attraction, could make the marriage last, even if what was between them wasn't so much anymore.

That much he was sure of. She looked at Ridge with affection, but she lit up when she looked at Arch. And he was pretty damn sure he did the same.

From the front of the house came the plop of mail hitting

the tile in his hall, followed by the metal clank of the mail slot dropping back into place. Time for action.

Well, some semblance of action. Standing up, leaving the room and the three glazed-over boy faces, and walking into the front hall to pick up his mail. That was about all the action he could take right now.

He sorted through the bills, junk mail and circulars, and pulled out a large envelope from his publisher. Tore it open and peeked in. A pile of letters from readers—maybe that's what he needed to cheer him up.

He took the envelope into his favorite room, the Music and Green Bay Packers Worship Center, and spread the letters out on his glass-topped coffee table, which housed underneath a football signed by Brett Favre, ticket stubs, mugs and a green-and-gold jersey.

Two piles, the way he usually sorted his letters. One for grown-up handwriting or typewritten labels, and one for those written by kids. His favorites. That done, he tore open the top envelope from the kid pile and extracted a piece of blue-lined notebook paper.

Dear Mr. Williams,

My name is Amber Placa. I am nine years old. I read your book *Corporal Wedgie and the Gas Attack.* It was really, really funny. But it also helped me. I learned a lot about gases, but also, I am very shy. And the way Ryan, the boy in the book, used his imagination to help him think of good things happening when he had a problem helped me, too.

Thanks. I can't wait to buy the next one.

Amber

Arch stared at the letter a long time, then picked up the next.

Hi Wedgie Man!

I'm Brian. I think your books are so cool! My mom says they are funny and my mom doesn't usually get

things that I think are funny. But your books are
funny. Also I learn stuff: And one day when I wanted
to get a Power Action Buddy but my mom said no, I
thought of what Ryan would do, and I didn't give up
or sit there and think how bad it was not getting what
I want. I made an adventure of my own that was better
than the toy! I'm serious about that.

Thanks a lot.
Brian

Arch put the letters aside. Put his head in his hands and
did some serious thinking.

When his mom died, he'd been furious at her. From his
childish perspective, the whole time she was sick, she did
nothing about it. Just lay there and got weak and weaker
and weakest and then died.

He'd wanted to scream at her to fight. To sit up and laugh
and sing and make it all better. Just pretend, at least for a
while. Anything but lie there focusing on death, waiting for
it, giving up the small amount of time she had left when
she could have tried, just *tried*, to find some kind of happiness in still being alive.

Other people found nobility and strength in her resignation. It just pissed him right off.

His father had fought. He still fought. Grief got the better
of Sonny Williams only a few times, but he always bounced
back, ready to take everything on. The man had even managed to land the formidable Maude Marcus, who had, even
more incredibly, turned out to be a salvageable person just
as he said she was.

Giving up was as good as being dead.

"Uncle Arch?"

He looked up at John, who'd come in, mouth grimy with
chip crumbs and chocolate, face serious.

"Yeah, John, what's up?"

"Did the crabby fairy get you? You're not fun anymore."

Arch grinned, then chuckled. Out of the mouths of babes. "I think she did, John, somewhere along the way. Okay if we kick her out now?"

"Yeah." He bobbed his dark head enthusiastically. "Let's kick her all the way to another planet."

"You're on." He stood up, moved to a clear place in the rug with John beside him, cocked his right leg back and balanced. "Ready? One, two, three, *kick!*"

They both kicked hard and high and pretended to watch the crabby fairy's long fateful journey out of their solar system.

When the pretend speck had faded, Arch beamed and high-fived John, feeling energy and purpose putting the positive spin back on his life.

No good sitting here concentrating on the bad stuff. No good letting the crabby fairy get him. He'd done nothing but focus on how things with Amanda might not work out. How he might have a change of heart—though the way he felt about her, it didn't seem possible.

Staying away because of something bad that might happen went against everything he believed in, and he hadn't even noticed he was doing it. Worse, he'd been willing to lose to Ridge without lifting a finger. All in the name of doing the right thing. Even when holding back from Amanda felt totally wrong.

Okay.

Now he was ready for some action.

He strode to the wall phone and dialed his father to see if he and Maude would come and watch the boys for the afternoon. Time to stop agonizing, be himself, do what came naturally. Follow his instincts instead of some twisted logic, his heart instead of his head.

As his dad had said that night in the kitchen, on a bellyful of sausage and onions, it was time to leap off the platform and go high-flying.

This time without a net.

CHAPTER FOURTEEN

"OF COURSE, Paris is *lovely* at this time of year." Natalie, Amanda's disgustingly stunning brunette half sister sighed wistfully from Amanda's still-stained couch. "My ex-husband and I used to stay at a wonderful little hotel on the Champs Élyseés, a block from the Arc de Triomphe. Those were the days."

She sighed again, uncrossed her roughly eight-foot-long legs, which poked not at all discreetly out from under a roughly two-inch-long skirt and crossed them again. Then in case anyone in the room had lost sight of how stunning she was, she tossed her mane of perfectly tousled dark locks. Next to her on the couch, Ridge appeared to be having trouble breathing.

Fine. Just fine. Amanda fished an ice cube out of her iced tea and crunched it noisily. She'd about had it. Her stomach hurt, had been hurting for days. And her head. Any second now, Natalie was going to glance her way and say something about how she couldn't afford to go to Paris now.

Natalie glanced her way. "Of course—that was when we could afford to go to places like that."

Ridge made a commiserating noise, apparently, from the direction of his gaze, feeling deep sympathy and kinship with her thighs.

Amanda stared back down at her iced tea, wanting to growl and gnash her molars. Something would have to give soon. But what was she supposed to do? Amazon Amanda, of course, would throw the beggar out. At the same time, if their positions were reversed, if Amanda had grown up in the lap of luxury and had her entire comfortable future yanked out from under her and given to some love child half sister she'd never met, she…she…

She frowned. She hadn't a clue what. Probably just accept that her mother had wanted her estate settled that way. But then, wouldn't that just be wimpy Amanda all over again? Shouldn't she admire Natalie? Take lessons from what she was doing? Going after what was rightfully hers? And yet…

Quite frankly, Amanda didn't *want* to be a grasping bitch.

Natalie droned on, Ridge entirely too attentive. His lapdog act bothered Amanda on two levels. No, three.

She curled her lip. To hell with levels. She was just annoyed. Sick and tired and confused and annoyed, with a stomachache. Her apartment still looked like hell. She'd made this big leap toward wanting to redecorate but she still hadn't a clue what to buy.

Nothing made sense. The money was supposed to help set her free, give her strength and purpose, and for a while she thought it did, but right now she was pretty sure it had just made her miserable.

The word *Clarissa* jumped at her from the mumble of conversation in the room. She rewound her subconscious memory and realized Natalie had asked where Clarissa was.

"She's with her grandmother today."

"Ah." Natalie kicked the perfect fashionable shoes off her slender perfect feet and curled her legs under her on the couch, which about sent Ridge to heaven. "My daughter will be five next week. Must be so nice to be able to provide real security for your child."

"Yes. It is." Amanda nodded, feeling as if she was going to explode, wanting to tell Natalie to go away. Tell Ridge to go away. Tell everyone to go away and leave her the hell alone.

Why couldn't she? She'd done so well getting angry at Arch. Told him everything she'd been thinking. The high had been incredible. She was strong! She was invincible! She was *woman!*

And it had all gone downhill from there. Why? She didn't even care about these people. But where was her famous strength now? Why was she reduced to cowering here, crunching ice to let out her frustration?

"That kind of money means security." Ridge put on his most authoritative manner, still scarfing Natalie down with his eyes. "Security and independence. It's real power. No more catering to other people, doing their dirty work, having to lie and be polite to people you can't stand. You can be whoever you want and everyone will let you."

Natalie agreed. She agreed so heartily she even lifted her leg in the guise of adjusting it on the couch so he could peek under it and imagine himself into a frenzy.

Amanda popped another cube into her mouth and positioned it between her teeth. Security. Independence. Power. Catering to no one. Being whoever she wanted. She was rich and she felt none of those things.

Except when...

Amanda's eyes grew wide. She crunched down on the ice so hard that Natalie and Ridge both turned and looked at her.

Except when she was with Arch.

She put down her glass, shot to her feet, Natalie and Ridge watching her warily.

"Amanda? Are you okay?" Ridge adopted his "I care" tone, which was really getting on her nerves. Whatever had happened to change him, she'd liked him better the old way. With spark, dazzle, flair, confidence.

Kind of like Arch.

"I'm fine." She had to talk to Arch. Had to get this straight. Had to be with him and figure this whole thing out. "You know what?"

"What?" Both Natalie and Ridge were eyeing her strangely. As if she looked as peculiar as she felt.

Recklessness built in her. She could feel it growing. A roaring tidal wave of impulsiveness she was helpless to resist.

"I'm not so into this money as I thought."

The four eyes staring at her strangely, blinked.

"Natalie." She pointed giddily to the alarmed-looking woman playing leg games with her ex-fiancé. "Why don't you take it. I just want enough to live comfortably. You can have the rest. How does that—"

"Amanda!" Ridge got to his feet, scowling. "Stop fooling around."

"What's the matter, Ridge?" She used her own "I care" voice and most gosh-darn earnest expression. "It won't matter to you if I'm not wealthy, will it? You waited until you could support us to come back, right?"

"I...I...you're not thinking clearly, Amanda. You can't be serious." His handsome face turned red. That little blue vein in his forehead made its appearance. The one that always stuck out when he was upset or having an orgasm. "Throwing away our—your security like this."

"I don't want it." She threw her arms out, laughed like a crazy person. "I don't! How's that!"

"Are...are you...do you mean it?" Natalie's face was transformed by hope and greed. Amanda was sure her half sister had never looked lovelier.

"I'll call the lawyer in the morning. She'll be in touch with you soon, I'm sure."

"Amanda, for God's sake, think what you're doing!" Ridge could barely get the words out. A little fleck of spit flew out of his mouth and landed on Amanda's nose and she wiped it off, not even worrying whether calling attention to it would embarrass him.

"Ridge." She walked to him and put her hands on his shoulders. "If I give this money away, will you still stay here with me and be a father to Clarissa? Even if I don't have a dime?"

"Of...course." He did his best to smile. He really did. She had to hand it to him. For a minute, it actually hurt. He hadn't wanted her back, not really. And now Clarissa never would know her father. But then Amanda hadn't wanted him back either, not with how she felt about Arch. And maybe it was just as well Clarissa never knew her father, since the glimpse she'd gotten hadn't impressed her that much. Maybe someday Amanda would tell her. Maybe not.

She gave him a hug. Poor Ridge. He'd be gone by the end of the week. Or sooner. Maybe she'd even kick him out. Right now she had to get downstairs and—

The doorbell rang. Three quick rings. Feet on the stairs, two at a time it sounded like. Amanda practically dragged the door off its hinges opening it.

"Hey." Arch stopped in the doorway, looking down at her the way he had the very first time she met him, confident, male, handsome, eyes dark and flashing with the joy of being alive. And the room, which had felt like a sensory-deprivation chamber, exploded into life.

His eyes clung to hers, she felt her cheeks bloom into color, her heart—

"Who is *this?*"

Her heart pulled back. Natalie. God, even the woman's voice was sexy. And from the sound of her words, she thought Arch was about as amazing as…he was.

"Arch Williams." She gestured to the couch, feeling her joy tinged by something a little nervous. If Arch started in on the lapdog thing, Amanda would slug him. "This is Natalie. My half sister."

Arch's eyes narrowed. "Half sister?"

"Mmm." The half sister uncurled her legs from the couch so Arch could get the full-length view, sent him a smile that would have Ridge's eyes popping from their sockets. "Yes. Same mother, different fathers."

Arch's eyes narrowed further. Not a trace of popping. The warmth resumed blooming in Amanda. Apparently *some* men didn't go instantly into caveman-drool mode at the sight of a stunning female. Had she really thought staying away from Arch was the right thing to do? They had to work this out, talk this out. Find some way to be together.

"You're here for a *visit?*" Arch spat the word out at Natalie as if he thought it was dirty.

"Yes." Natalie looked taken aback by his lack of interest and glanced at Ridge, who all but panted his lack of lack of interest. "I wanted to get to know my sister."

"Right." Arch put his hands on his hips and turned back to Amanda, his expression grim. "You ready to go?"

She blinked. "Where?"

"To the park."

"The—" She gaped at him. They'd broken up after a fight, hadn't seen each other for a week, had issues of burning importance to discuss and he still wanted to play?

"Park." He winked. "P-A-R-K. They have swings there."

Her gape turned slowly into a grin. She gazed up into

his dark, lively eyes, eating up the fact that said dark, lively eyes were gazing down at her. Maybe he never would stop playing. Did she really care? Or was playing her way through the rest of her life sounding better all the time?

"Excuse me, are we interrupting something?"

He didn't even glance at Ridge. "Yes."

"But it's going to rain." Natalie leaned forward and pointed to the window, an exaggerated gesture that displayed her cleavage perfectly.

"It's not going to rain." Arch didn't spare a glance for the female-produce section either. "You ready, Amanda?"

She lifted her chin. Amazon Amanda didn't take orders. Didn't allow herself to be manipulated. She did what she wanted.

"I'd love to."

He blinked. Apparently he'd been expecting resistance. "You would?"

She nodded, still grinning the grin that his eyes made unavoidable. Just being around him made her happy. Her stomach and head were settled and clearing. This had to be right. They had to find a way to make it work.

Because she wasn't spending the rest of her life in a Maalox moment.

"Let's go, Manda." He said the words in a low intimate tone that made her shiver.

"You're leaving? With him?" Ridge had risen off the couch, though how he'd managed to tear himself away from leg duty she hadn't a clue.

"I'll be back in a while." Amanda took the arm Arch offered her. "In the meantime I think you should show Natalie to her car. I have this funny feeling you and she suddenly have a whole lot in common."

Arch glanced at her curiously; she winked and started them toward the door. "I'm ready, Arch."

They walked down the stairs and out into the cool gray late-June day, down the front steps and onto the sidewalk heading for Center Street. Amanda took deep breaths of the outside air, thick and damp as it was, feeling free and refreshed, finally away from that room and those two...turkey buzzards. Out here with Arch.

Their hands bumped and she made a grab and held on to his, smiling when he squeezed it three times fast.

"So this Natalie half-sister person of yours seems like one scary female."

"You don't think she's totally hot?"

"Are you kidding? Wearing all that fake-up?" He sent her an oh-please expression that made her smile. "She here to fight for a piece of the billion-dollar pie?"

"Mmm-hmm."

"Could see that a mile away." He swung their hands back and forth. "She getting any?"

"Maybe from Ridge."

He looked surprised, then caught her meaning and laughed. "Well, good luck to him. She's not my type at all. Too tall, too dark, too obvious. And her biggest flaw? The one that makes her most unattractive? Besides that she reeks of greed and manipulation?"

"Yes?" Amanda was all ears.

He shot her his devilish Arch look. "She's not you."

"Oh, come on." Amanda shoved down her delight. "She'd make a rock horny."

"You think I'm just flattering you?"

"You think I was born yesterday?"

He stopped suddenly and used her forward momentum to swing her back around to face him, eyes dark and intense. "Would you like me to show you, in front of all the good people of Sixty-Seventh street, Amanda, how unbelievably, incredibly, mind-bogglingly hot I think you are?"

"No!" She put her hands over her mouth, covering her laughter. "Someone would call the cops."

He pulled her hands down, kept them in his. "Don't hide laughter. Don't hide anything. Let it all hang out, I want to see all of it. The good, the bad and the truly hideous. Okay?"

She rolled her eyes, pretending annoyance, but his words rang in her head. He wanted all of her. Not just the money. Not just the dutiful daughter. Her. In all her flawed glory. All she needed to hear now was that he wanted her for longer than it was fun. For longer than just when he felt like having her around. "Okay, Mr. Karma."

He chuckled and pulled her to resume walking, turning onto Center Street toward Sixty-fourth.

"Are you okay about Ridge?" His voice got cautious, wary. "Did you fall for him again?"

"No." She gestured with her free hand, trying to put into words what she'd only sensed about Ridge. "I thought I would. I really thought he'd changed. Grown up. Gotten more serious, more committed. He seemed to want things to work between us. And I thought maybe I could find the feelings I used to have for him…"

"But?" He sounded so hopeful she couldn't help smiling at him.

"But then I realized he seemed sort of…suppressed. I mean he used to be so full of life and now…his spark is just…gone. Or maybe it never existed, maybe I romanticized him."

"You know what this means, don't you?"

She shoved at his shoulder with hers. "I know what *you* think it means."

"I said nothing."

She smiled up at him. "He wasn't you."

"Exactly, Ms. Manda." He smiled back, but something

about his smile came across as deadly serious. "There's a message in all this. You getting it?"

She ducked her head, nodding. She loved this man. There was no question in her mind. Clue one, she could get angry at him, stand up to him, without wanting to apologize for what she thought was right. Clue two, for all his childlike, impulsive qualities, he'd been there for her every time she needed him, even when she insisted she didn't. Clue three, he made her whole world happy. Clue four, the sight of him made her juices flow like Niagara Falls.

They just had the commitment issue to work out. Yeah, he'd always been there for her, but did he want to stay there? Maybe they could reach a compromise. Maybe he could see his way clear to committing for a week at a time, first. Then a month. Then maybe an entire year…

She grinned at her own ludicrous thoughts. She wasn't out to chain him. Or freak him out. But she couldn't stay with someone who pointedly reserved the right to disappear at any moment.

They came to the park; Arch steered them past the bench they'd shared a month ago, which felt like several centuries at least, over toward the tree where he'd first kissed her. "Did I ever tell you about *Corporal Wedgie's Trip Through Your Guts?*"

Amanda grimaced. "Uh, no."

"Ryan is the little-boy hero of my books. He's kind of shy, kind of out of the ordinary. Kids don't like him much. Whenever he gets into a tight spot, Corporal Wedgie appears in his imagination—an ordinary guy with extraordinary powers."

"Like you?"

He laughed, clear and honest and unaffected. "Exactly. In this book Ryan has to study for a science test on the digestive system. But instead of using his textbook, he has

Corporal Wedgie go after a thumbtack a little boy ate by mistake. Has to make sure it gets through without hurting him.''

''Is this a story with deep meaning for me?''

''Going to be.''

''You think I should swallow a thumbtack?''

He squeezed her hand again. Three times. Like the doorbell ring she loved. ''There's a subplot. He's having trouble at home. With five older brothers, he gets pushed around a lot. So he has to learn to ask for what he wants.''

''Let me guess. First he has to figure out what he wants.''

''You're way ahead of me.''

She took in a deep breath. ''I thought I knew what I wanted. The money made me feel so powerful, so strong. I loved that. But then when I'd go to spend it, I realized I hadn't any idea what to do with it. I couldn't even decorate. I wanted the apartment to reflect *me,* but how the hell do you find your essence in a table lamp?''

He chuckled. ''At the risk of sounding like Mr. Karma, maybe you have to find it in you first.''

''I'm trying. And I do think it's coming. A little. At one store I saw a teapot I liked. But then I thought, well, I like that one pretty well. But is it *really* me? And then teapots are so Maude Marcus, really, and so am I—''

Arch made a strangled sound of frustration, grabbed her and swung her around so her back was to their first-kiss tree. Then he leaned in close as if he was about to kiss her again and her body went on delicious alert.

''Stop thinking so much,'' he whispered. ''Just feel.''

''Oh, Arch.'' She echoed his frustration sound. ''That's the big difference between us. I believe in doing the right thing for the right reasons. You believe in doing what you want when it feels good.''

He put a finger on her lips. ''If you have your head on

straight and listen to your heart, most of the time they're the same thing.''

''But if you—''

''For example...'' He leaned closer, until their mouths were only a fraction of an inch apart, making hers buzz with anticipation. ''Here's something I want. And it's definitely right.''

His lips touched hers, a kiss that started sweet and slow, his mouth barely moving on hers, but warm and oh God, so exhilarating. Then the kiss deepened, turned hot and passionate, involving her body and emotions in a nearly overwhelming combination.

''Amanda.'' He broke the kiss and leaned back with a groan. ''Do you have any idea what you do to me? How powerful this thing is between us?''

''Yes.'' She could only whisper, scared to death she'd cry from the desperate intensity of the feeling.

''And doesn't that tell you something?''

She managed a playful smile. ''That there's a powerful thing between us?''

He chuckled but his eyes stayed serious. ''Since when do you have the line for everything? You're getting to be like me.''

Despair settled into her stomach. ''I can't be like you. People don't change. I thought I was changing, then it turned out I wasn't, I thought Ridge had, but he—''

Plonk. A baseball smacked the side of the tree near their heads and dropped onto the ground. They peered into the playing field next to the park, at the batter coming toward them to retrieve her ball. Amanda's eyes shot wide. ''What the—''

''Whoa!'' The batter reached them, breathless and laughing. ''How's that for a home run in entirely the wrong direction?''

Amanda's jaw dropped. *Mom?* Her mother was wearing sweatpants. And a T-shirt that said, One Hot Grandma. Her cheeks were pink; her eyes sparkled. She looked casual, relaxed, gorgeous. And happier than Amanda had ever seen her. In fact, now that she thought about it, she didn't recall ever seeing her mother look happy. Not like this.

"Come play with us." Her mom pointed over to the baseball field. "Sonny and the boys are teaching Clarissa and I how to bat. I'm going to enroll her in the Tosa league with Mark."

"But." Amanda was having a very hard time wrapping her brain around this. "That's not ballet."

Her mom looked at her pityingly. "No, dear, it isn't. It's baseball. And it's fabulous."

"What…happened to you? You look amazing."

Her mom smiled a secret smile. "I'm in love, dear. Love makes you play baseball and go bowling and do all kinds of fun things. You should try it."

"Love made you go bowling?"

"Twice." She smiled proudly.

"But…but…" Amanda gestured helplessly. "That's so…not you."

"It is though, Amanda. It's me and Sonny. I've never been happier or felt more like I *could* be me." Her voice caught; she straightened briskly and wiped her eye. "You coming? We brought extra mitts in case you showed up. Though if it rains we're packing it in and taking the kids to Robert's Custard."

"Maybe later." Arch must have made some signal to her mother, because Maude's eyes lit with understanding.

"Very good. Have fun." She jogged back to the field, holding the ball aloft to the cheers of the outfield.

Amanda managed to close her mouth and turn to Arch. "Was that my mother?"

"Uh-huh." He moved in front of her and pressed her gently back against the tree. "What were you saying about people not changing?"

She shook her head. "That wasn't my mother."

"Looked like her to me."

"It did, didn't it." She stared at him. "So if I go bowling, I can find myself?"

"Absolutely." He leaned in for another kiss. "As long as it's with me."

She smiled, couldn't help it, her arms wrapped themselves around his neck and she kissed him thoroughly until her brain interrupted with a thought.

"Remember when we were here before? When I said all I wanted was to own my own shop and go to Europe and you teased me because it wasn't enough?"

"Yes." He stepped back, grabbed her hand, put his other at her waist and started swaying with her, dancing, the way they had the night of the storm. "I shouldn't have told you your dreams weren't big enough, Amanda. They're your dreams, they should fit you."

"Well, you were partly right. They're not quite big enough. But I'm only going to keep enough money to make them come true and give the rest to Natalie."

"Wow." His eyebrows shot up. He stopped dancing for a second, then turned her in a slow spin. "I'm impressed."

"You are?" She finished the spin, came back to him. "Ridge nearly had an apoplectic fit."

He chuckled. "Is that why you said he and Natalie suddenly had a lot in common? Because she's got the billions now?"

"Mmm-hmm." She buried her face in his chest, inhaling his scent and comfort, swaying to the silent music.

"So now you've got everything you need."

She shook her head, her face rubbing the soft cotton of

his T-shirt that said, Love Is All You Need. "No. As I said, my dreams weren't quite big enough. You were right that I also need the most amazing guy in the world to worship me for the remainder of time."

His body tensed; he missed a step, then pulled her along to find their rhythm again. "Where are you going to find this guy?"

Her eyes shot to his, panic ready and waiting. "I didn't already?"

He stopped dancing, cupped her face, closed his eyes and pressed their foreheads together. "I'm not the most amazing guy in the world, Amanda. But I love you. And if you decide I'm what you want, I will try my best to make you happy."

Her heart missed several beats. *He loved her.*

But...

"Always?"

"Uh...yes." He looked wary. "Why, did you want to be miserable some of the time?"

"You mean forever?"

He chuckled. "I want to show you my bedroom."

"Your...bedroom?"

"Remember? The new bedroom. The one I was planning with the king-size bed, etcetera, etcetera."

"Oh. Yes." Her heart sank. The porno palace. The bachelor get-laid pad. Maybe she was making a mistake. A raindrop hit her nose. Then another hit her cheek.

"It's finished. I want you to see it."

Her heart threatened to split. He was dodging her question. Dancing in the park—all around The Issue That Wouldn't Go Away.

"Come on." He took her hand and pulled her, running most of the way back through the rain, which had started coming down in earnest.

He pulled her up the stairs to his front door, fumbled with his keys, breathing hard. She leaned over to catch her own breath, and couldn't help peeking and noticing Natalie's and Ridge's cars were gone. If Ridge had his way, they were halfway to Vegas, eloping.

"Come on in." Arch gestured impatiently through the open door.

She stepped inside, not at all sure she wanted to see this sex palace. Not that she objected to sex palaces, but it was hard to accept the concept of committing to someone whose bedroom looked as if he were planning to entertain every female of his species, one at a time. Maybe two.

She followed him down the hall. He put his hand on the door. "Ready?"

She nodded, trying to be brave. Even if it was sleazy, it didn't mean hope was gone. Did it? She didn't know.

Grrrrrrr. She was so *sick* of not knowing!

All right then! She *did* know. She was just going to relax. Take a cue from her mom and from Arch and dive in. Do what *felt* right, because nothing she'd ever done in her entire life felt as good as being with Arch. He'd brought her alive, drawn her out, made it safe to be her at her most unguarded.

"Arch." She stopped his hand. "Remember what you said about taking a whole lot of 'nows' and lining them up until you get to forever?"

He nodded, grinning a slightly secretive grin.

"I want you to know that I love you. And I want to be with you. As many todays as we can have. One at a time. No matter…" She was going to say, "what your bedroom looks like," but that would sound weird. And anyway, he was grinning again, but no longer secretively. Now with so much love in his eyes that her words died away.

He pushed open the door.

She inhaled sharply and let the air out on a surprised "Oh!"

The room was stunning. Deep burgundy bedspread, with gold, teal and burgundy–striped pillows. A dark antique-looking bureau. A handsome chair in upholstery that caught colors from the bed. A bookcase. A white marble bedside table with a striking iron lamp.

Not a VCR, hot tub or mirror in sight. Except one thing was odd... All the furniture was on one side of the room.

"It's beautiful, Arch. Really lovely." She pointed to the two blank ivory-colored walls. "Is there more stuff coming?"

He put his arms around her. "I hope so."

"Did some things get lost?" She tipped her head back to look at him, puzzled.

"Nope. Some of it's upstairs. Some of it you haven't bought yet."

Her mouth dropped. She could swear her chin was hanging one inch above the floor. "You want me to move in with you?"

"I thought we could share the house, turn it into a single-family. Not right away, give us all time to get used to the idea, maybe wait until the boys go home, make sure Clarissa is okay with everything. Keep some spaces separate, share others."

"You mean I'd be here not only today but also—"

"Tomorrow, yeah, can you believe it?" He pressed her against him, kissed her forehead, her cheeks, the corners of her mouth. "I want you in all my tomorrows, Ms. Manda. Every single one. What do you think?"

"Oh my gosh." She was having trouble thinking at all. So much joy was bouncing around her brain that it couldn't get a handle on anything else. "It sounds...perfect."

He kissed her mouth, over and over, walking her slowly

backward to the burgundy bed. And her brain didn't have to have a handle on anything else but Arch.

They made love, slow, tender, beautifully sensual, accompanied by the cozy patter of rain and certainty. Amanda snuggled next to him, body and heart utterly satisfied, arms wrapped tightly around his magnificent chest as if she couldn't bear to let go of this brand-new idea that she suddenly had everything she wanted. That she was on her way to being everything she'd ever dreamed of being. With Arch.

"So, Ms. Manda." He pushed away hair that had fallen across her cheek. "When would you like to do all this shopping for your essence?"

She grinned. As much as she hated to move from this spot, she had the instinctive feeling that today she'd know what to get. Something that would fit her, but also that would fit into this room, with the things Arch had selected.

As for having to get out of bed now—she smiled to herself—there was always tomorrow.

"Let's go."

"You want to leave now?" He jerked his head at the window, streaming with the rain outside. "In this weather?"

"Hey!" She laughed and kissed him. "Don't worry. Be happy. It's going to clear up and be wonderful forever."

Forrester Square
LEGACIES . LIES . LOVE .

*Award-winning author Day Leclaire
brings a highly emotional and
exciting reunion romance story to
Forrester Square in December...*

KEEPING FAITH
by
Day Leclaire

Faith Marshall's dream of a "white-picket" life with
Ethan Dunn disappeared—along with her husband—
when she discovered that he was really a dangerous
mercenary. With Ethan missing in action, Faith found
herself alone, pregnant and struggling to survive.
Now, years later, Ethan turns up alive. Will a family
reunion be possible after so much deception?

*Forrester Square...
Legacies. Lies. Love.*

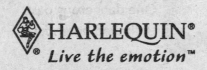

HARLEQUIN®
Live the emotion™

**From Silhouette Books comes
an exciting NEW spin-off to *The Coltons!***

PROTECTING
PEGGY

by award-winning author
Maggie Price

When FBI forensic scientist
Rory Sinclair checks into
Peggy Honeywell's inn late
one night, the sexy bachelor
finds himself smitten with the
single mother. While Rory works
undercover to solve the mystery
at a nearby children's ranch, his
feelings for Peggy grow...but
will his deception shake the
fragile foundation of their
newfound love?

Coming in December 2003.

THE COLTONS
FAMILY. PRIVILEGE. POWER.

Where love comes alive™

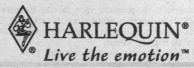

If you enjoyed what you just read,
then we've got an offer you can't resist!

Take 2
bestselling novels FREE!
Plus get a FREE surprise gift!

Clip this page and mail it to The Best of the Best™

IN U.S.A.
3010 Walden Ave.
P.O. Box 1867
Buffalo, N.Y. 14240-1867

IN CANADA
P.O. Box 609
Fort Erie, Ontario
L2A 5X3

YES! Please send me 2 free Best of the Best™ novels and my free surprise gift. After receiving them, if I don't wish to receive anymore, I can return the shipping statement marked cancel. If I don't cancel, I will receive 4 brand-new novels every month, before they're available in stores! In the U.S.A., bill me at the bargain price of $4.74 plus 25¢ shipping and handling per book and applicable sales tax, if any*. In Canada, bill me at the bargain price of $5.24 plus 25¢ shipping and handling per book and applicable taxes**. That's the complete price and a savings of over 20% off the cover prices—what a great deal! I understand that accepting the 2 free books and gift places me under no obligation ever to buy any books. I can always return a shipment and cancel at any time. Even if I never buy another The Best of the Best™ book, the 2 free books and gift are mine to keep forever.

185 MDN DNWF
385 MDN DNWG

Name	(PLEASE PRINT)	
Address	Apt.#	
City	State/Prov.	Zip/Postal Code

* Terms and prices subject to change without notice. Sales tax applicable in N.Y.
** Canadian residents will be charged applicable provincial taxes and GST.
All orders subject to approval. Offer limited to one per household and not valid to current The Best of the Best™ subscribers.
® are registered trademarks of Harlequin Enterprises Limited.

-R   ©1998 Harlequin Enterprises Limited

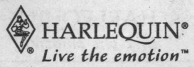

SNOW ANGELS

BRENDA NOVAK
B.J. DANIELS

As winter storms rage, passions collide…

Cut off from the outside world, strangers become lovers—
and perhaps parents?—in these two full-length stories.

*Make your winter sizzle with SNOW ANGELS—
coming in March 2004.*

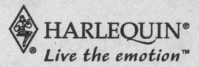

HARLEQUIN®
Live the emotion™